## *Blind Spot*

She downed her fifth drink and watched him continue to drink straight shots. Abruptly he stood up, removed his jacket and shed his holstered gun without a glance at her. He strode over to the chair where she sat, reached down and pulled her up to him. The kiss was hard and fast and she wondered if it was the only prelude she'd get to whatever was coming next. The room he led her into was neater, a small lamp in the corner the only refuge from the shadows. There were some pictures on the walls, indistinguishable, but a large bed dominated the room. Through the haze of alcohol, a voice in her head yelled *Leave, leave now,* but the specter of her apartment rose up in front of her and she ignored the voice. She needed this night, an escape from the desert of loss that threatened to suffocate her.

*What They Are Saying About*

## *Blind Spot*

Hold onto your seat for a fast paced novel that will keep you reading page after page. Ms. Romaine weaves her story with great realism, allowing the reader to experience the highs and lows of her characters. The storyline is moving and awakens the fear of every parent. Just when you think you know the outcome, you'll be caught up in the complexity which follows. An excellent read.

—Carol McPhee
http://www.geocities.com/carolmcphee2003

What do you have when you mix an edge of your seat thriller with a hot and sexy romance? You get *Blind Spot* by Lynn Romaine, a definite page-turner and hard to put down. Fans of romantic thrillers will not be disappointed!

*Blind Spot* is a very good read. I loved trying to solve the mystery, I loved the romance and I especially loved how well they were both intertwined in the story. I would recommend reading it!

—Julie Kornhausl
Romance Readers At Heart

*Blind Spot* is a romantic thriller with a twisty, turning plot. Jack and Sofie must backtrack and try to build a relationship around their daughter, and deal with their attraction for each other at the same time. Just when you think you've got it all solved, *Lynn Romaine* tosses in another plot turn and spins the story in another direction. This is also a story about family, and belonging, and it was fascinating to see the solitary Sofie fit into Jack's big Italian family. Taut, suspenseful and chock full of realism, *Blind Spot* is an entertaining read.

—Michelle
Fallen Angel Reviews

### Other Works From The Pen Of

## Lynn Romaine

**Leave No Trace**

What began as an investigation of ecoterrorism turns into murder and DNR agent Nick Seek is running for her life.

*Wings*

# Blind Spot

by

Lynn Romaine

**A Wings ePress, Inc.**

**Romantic Suspense Novel**

# Wings ePress, Inc.

Edited by: Lorraine Stephens
Copy Edited by: Karen Babcock
Senior Editor: Lorraiine Stephens
Executive Editor: Lorraine Stephens
Cover Artist: mpmann

*All rights reserved*

Names, characters and incidents depicted in this book are products of the author's imagination or are used fictitiously. Any resemblance to actual events, locales, organizations, or persons, living or dead, is entirely coincidental and beyond the intent of the author or the publisher.

No part of this book may be reproduced or transmitted in any form or by any means, electronic or mechanical, including photocopying, recording, or by any information storage and retrieval system, without permission in writing from the publisher.

Wings ePress Books
http://www.wings-press.com

Copyright © 2006 by Judi Romaine
ISBN 1-59705-983-8

Published In the United States Of America

July 2006

Wings ePress Inc.
403 Wallace Court
Richmond, KY 40475

## *Dedication*

To the City of Detroit Bomb Squad

and my sister, Debbi Wilkes,

who provided the background information

and contacts for this book

and who always supports me in whatever I do in life.

## *Prologue*

*Four Years Ago*

It was warm, one of those rare October evenings that made you forget it was Detroit. Claire picked the spot and Sofie agreed to meet her, a throwaway night of fun. That was the first lie; for Sofie this wasn't about fun.

She pushed her way into the smoky room and was overtaken by a burst of despair so intense it caught at her throat and choked her. Her mother had been dead two weeks and she fought to keep her head above the tidal wave of grief that threatened to swamp her life. The sense of aloneness was overpowering, and unexpected, in spite of knowing that it was coming.

Claire was no more than an acquaintance but when she suggested going out dancing, what Claire really had in mind was men. With no clear outcome in mind, Sofie threw herself into the occasion, careless and irrational as it was, but only one night.

So here she was. It had come to this, a small, noisy bar, a room full of strangers and desperation.

Claire was late and Sofie scanned the room, refusing to think beyond the moment. Anything else would cause panic. She'd tried to prepare herself for being alone, but she'd never considered it would involve so much pain. All she'd ever known had been women—her mother, her grandmother, her great-grandmother before her, each with a daughter, raised alone. This matriarchy, this family of women, was the world she knew and she'd never been alone—until now.

By the time she finished her second drink, she knew Claire wasn't coming and she pushed down a sense of alarm. She'd counted on Claire to set the pace for the evening, hoping to be swept along in the wake of her innate confidence.

Now what? Should she leave? The image of her empty apartment swam before her like a gray fog, and all she saw was an unbearable future. She allowed her hand to move only to raise the drink to her mouth, swallowing mechanically. If she sat perfectly still and kept drinking, she could will away the terror.

Sofie spotted him at the bar. He stood out, towering over the men around him. He was dark, his hair a little too long, curling over the collar of his bomber jacket. From a distance she could see he had strong features, perhaps Slavic or Italian. And there was something about him that said he was someone sure of his place in the world. He was what she was most afraid of in men and just what she wanted tonight, a contradiction to her life and someone she would never see again.

She downed the last of her drink in two gulps and pushed away from the table. As she stood up, another wave of despair swept over her but she pressed forward, driven by the image of her empty apartment, toward the lone figure at the bar.

She had chosen a sexy skirt, her only sexy skirt. It was made of silk, red with yellow flowers, and it hit her two inches above the knees. She knew her legs were good, probably her best feature. She'd chosen the top carefully, a clingy shirt in a pale color that went nicely with her hair. It dipped into a V in front, showing a small amount of cleavage but not too much; she'd picked it especially for the way she thought it made her breasts look nice. Rather than the usual braid down her back, she'd pulled her hair up into a topknot and escaping hair fell; unmanageably around her face and down the back of her neck.

She took a deep breath, averted her gaze from the stares of men around her and focused on him as she moved across the room. His back was to her and as she wove between tables, she kept her eyes trained on him. He was turned away from her now, his drink sitting in front of him, a pack of cigarettes at his right hand.

Someone grabbed at her skirt as she passed the last table but she avoided the sweaty hand and kept moving. She was trembling slightly by the time she made it to the empty bar stool on his right and she sat down. He knew she was there.

"This occupied?" Her words were almost inaudible against the background din of voices and music but he answered with a grunt and a shake of his head. He was drinking straight shots of something and he smelled of whiskey, leather and male.

*Now what?* She thought. The rules for picking someone up in a bar were so far outside of her sphere they were nonexistent.

The bartender came over, raised an eyebrow at her and pointed silently to her empty glass.

"Stoli on the rocks, please." She watched him pour her drink, place it in front of her and turn away. It was her mother's favorite drink and she tried to picture her mother's surprise at her daughter throwing back Russian vodkas in a bar. As she reached into her shoulder bag to pull out some bills, a hand reached over to stop her.

"I'll get it," his voice more sound than words against the background noise.

"Thanks." She reached for her glass, saw her hand tremble, and hoped he didn't notice. He held out the crumbled cigarette pack to her and she shook her head. "No. Thanks. I don't smoke."

"Hard to avoid in this place."

His voice was louder this time, resonant, almost pleasant, and she turned her head and smiled. "I suppose so. Do you come here often?"

"Not often." He pulled a cigarette from the pack and held it out. "You mind?"

She shook her head and stole a glance at him. There was something about him, she couldn't read it in his face, but felt it instinctively, a sense of safety with him that was completely at odds with his appearance. He looked rough, dangerous even, a dark shadow of stubble obvious even in the darkness. She'd never known anyone remotely like him. The few men in her life had been safe, academic types with thin, aesthetic faces, or the smiling nephews of enthusiastic neighbors, determined to find her a man. They'd always been casual and uncomplicated affairs. She'd never wanted anything more.

How had she come from that to this night, sitting in a dark bar filled with people she didn't know and would never know, hoping for something from this man?

"Jack Roselli." He put the unlit cigarette in his mouth, turned and held out his hand. It was callused and warm against her cold fingers.

"Sofie Dorcet." She'd picked the last name off a CD and said it quickly as she took a sip of Stoli. Two drinks were her limit; she was on her third and already feeling slightly dazed.

Apparently he didn't have the same problem, she thought, and watched him toss down another shot. Neither his speech nor his movements indicated he was fazed by the liquor. "So, what do you do?" She asked.

"I'm a cop." The words were hollow and he didn't smile when he said them. He lit his cigarette and turned to her. "You?"

She'd spent time weaving a plausible story about herself as she sat waiting for Claire and she retold it to him now. "I live on the west side, with my sister, I'm a student at Henry Ford Community College." She tried smiling but it felt like a grimace. "I work in a dance club Downriver, in Southgate—part-time, you know. To pay for school."

He nodded, watching her, impassive, but something resembling pain passed over his face and she wondered if he was listening.

"What brings you to the east side?"

"A friend—who stood me up."

His eyebrows went up. "Is he a good friend?"

She shrugged. "She. She suggested this place. I guess she found something better to do."

He took a deep drag on his cigarette and turned his head away to exhale. "So, what are your plans now? It's a pretty rough bar to be hanging out alone."

"I'm not sure." He watched her closely now, as though waiting for some sign. She took a deep breath and smiled back at him.

"You want to get out of here? We can go get something to eat." Without waiting for a reply, he stood up, pulled out some bills and threw them on the bar.

She forced another smile, nodded and downed the rest of her Stoli in one gulp before she stood up. Her legs trembled as she wove her way out of the bar ahead of him and she hoped he didn't notice.

They ended up at a rib joint off Woodward Avenue. The place was filled with boisterous customers, a mixture of street people and theater goers looking for adventure in downtown Detroit. She kept her eyes focused someplace beyond his head as they ordered, conscious of his narrowed gaze, assessing her under the garish fluorescent lights. She was grateful that the noise kept conversation to a minimum and saved her from answering in anything but monosyllables.

He ordered another round of drinks with the food. It was her fourth and she sipped warily at it, eating little, afraid she's be sick in his car.

She toyed with her food until finally, he grabbed the check and laid down some bills. She exhaled in relief, pushed away a grease-laden plate and stood up. She must have swayed slightly because he reached out and caught her arm, his grip steady, almost gentle as he steered her to his car.

He didn't speak as he started up the car, did a sharp U-turn and headed back north. She watched the blue haze of lights streaming past the car and tried not to think.

"You okay?" His voice came to her after what seemed like a long time, from a long way off.

"Fine," Her response was automatic. The entire evening seemed surreal, like something from a B-movie, not her own life, and her feelings, like the lights flying past the window, vacillated between terror and exhilaration.

His apartment was dark, a duplex on a small side street off Six Mile Road. The piles of clothes and stacked dirty dishes made her think of a life halted midstream, suddenly abandoned in a fit of despair, and for a moment Sofie was afraid.

He led her to a worn leather couch in what must have been the living room, barely furnished with a TV, computer and stacks of books and magazines. The CD he put on was unfamiliar, something dark and moody that fit with the place. She sipped at her fifth drink and watched him continue to down straight shots.

The alcohol was doing its work now, suspending her mind some place with no past or future. Abruptly he stood up, removed his jacket and shed his holstered gun without a glance at her. He strode over to the chair where she sat, reached down and pulled her up to him. The kiss was hard and fast, a warning and prelude to what was coming next.

Still holding her, he steered them into another room, this one uncluttered, with a small lamp in the corner, the only light, casting shadows as they moved. There were some indistinguishable pictures on the walls, but the large bed dominated the room.

Through the haze of alcohol, a voice in her head yelled at her, *Leave, leave now!* but the specter of her empty apartment rose up in front of her and she ignored the voice. She needed this night to escape the loss that threatened to suffocate her.

Heat vibrated off his body close behind her, and without a word, he pulled her up against his chest, purposeful, focused. He turned her head and directed his mouth to hers. The sudden assault of his tongue shocked her, but she refused to pull back.

She watched as he removed her clothes, his mouth never leaving hers. Hands moved over her almost gently, as though separate from the pain she saw in his face. In a brief flash of clarity, she saw the outcome of this night of insanity and that it might threaten her world as she knew it, but she chose to ignore the warning and went instead for the pleasure. It justified all doubts and took away all fears in the moment.

His eyes dark, he scanned her naked body before lowering himself over her. She wanted him.

~ * ~

It was still dark when she rose, silently and dressed, the evidence of her guilt sticky between her legs, their futures now as inevitably intertwined as their physical bodies had been on the rumpled bed. She called a cab and went home in the growing light of dawn.

## *One*

*Four Years Later*

He'd been sitting at his desk, staring at a printout of bomb fragments when Sofie called. Four years had passed but he knew who she was immediately. She'd asked him to meet her at a coffee shop near the precinct and he'd refused, but she'd been adamant and he'd reluctantly agreed to meet her.

He arrived just after noon and saw her sitting at a table near the back. She was easy to spot. Although he'd been blind drunk that night, he still remembered her fragile, heart-shaped face and the hair, with gold lights in it, that had come undone. That night she'd been wearing something sexy, but today she wore baggy sweats and had her hair pulled back carelessly from a face devoid of make-up. Not the kind of woman he would have picked up in a bar, but there was still something about her, something elusive, almost compelling, that he'd refused to dwell on after that night.

As he walked towards her, he was struck again by that indefinable quality. Four years ago she'd worked at being sophisticated, even a little brazen, but he'd seen the nervousness behind it. Today, although she had a slight smile on her lips, he read fear in her eyes.

Without speaking, he sat down opposite her. She began with an apology, ridiculous in the face of the circumstances they'd last been in together and it caught him off guard. She launched into her reasons for requesting a meeting, but he stopped her after only a few words, not understanding what she was saying.

She began again, slower this time but still he didn't understand, until she came to the part about a little girl, a daughter, three years old, named Katya. "She's your child," she said quietly.

He heard the words, but their meaning escaped him and he stared at her, angry, not wanting to understand. "You asked me here to sell me some goddamned story that I got you pregnant after you picked me up in a bar? We had a couple of hours of drunken sex four years ago and all of a sudden I'm a father, right? You've gotta be kidding!" He was too loud, even in the noisy restaurant and her face blanched, but he didn't care.

"I'm telling you that you have a daughter. And I think she's in danger." She spoke forcefully and he heard her, even over the clattering of dishes and loud conversation from the next table. She sounded almost confrontational, something he didn't expect from her.

"I don't know what your game is, lady, but I'm not playing. *You* picked me up—in a bar, for God's sake! What the hell would make me believe any kid you had was mine, especially since you never contacted me or bothered to tell me about it until now?" He looked around the restaurant; it was a cop hangout and he lowered his voice.

"I know. I'd never have come to you at all except I couldn't think of anything else to do. I think she's in danger and you're a cop. Since she's your daughter, I came to ask for your protection—for her." The words were quieter now, but she threw them at him like a challenge, and it got to him, despite his anger. "I think she's being stalked. I didn't know where to turn." Her glance darted around the restaurant. "Please. Just hear me out before you decide. That's all I'm asking. If there's even a slight possibility she's your daughter, wouldn't you want to protect her?"

Without waiting for an answer, she reached into her bag and extracted folded papers. "I have her birth records with me, and I have her medical records, her blood type. I know it's not much, but that's all the proof I have." She paused, waiting for a response, and when he didn't speak, she went on. "I could get some proof for you, DNA, if you're willing. I'll do whatever it takes to convince you. I need you to do something. This isn't a game. She may be in danger and she needs you." She sat back, the movement jerky, a contradiction to the graceful way she held her body. "I know it probably sounds insane to you but believe me, until that night, I'd never picked up a man in my life. There is no other man who could be her father. You were the only one. I was..." She stopped again and he waited, watching for some sign, something she wasn't saying. "We were both drinking, I was careless, and I had Katya."

The restaurant was filling up with people, many of them fellow cops. Someone from his precinct called out a greeting, but he ignored it and kept his eyes on her face. She could have a variety of motives: money—what little he had; blackmail; some sort of nasty practical joke; she might be mentally unbalanced. Or she could be telling the truth—or what she believed was the truth. "So you're saying it was a one-time thing. You got drunk, came on to me and wanted to get laid? And there you go, a kid, right?" She shrank back further from him, but he didn't care. He wanted to give her pain, to see how she responded.

"You can be sure I would never have contacted you except I'm desperate. Katya's in some sort of danger and she needs your protection. I don't care what the hell you think about me or my actions that night."

The waitress came over and he ordered automatically for both of them, without taking his eyes from her. Her eyes were gray blue and an unwanted image from four years ago sprang up in his mind, of staring down into them as they widened in pleasure. And he sighed, suddenly resigned to whatever she had to say. "So let's hear the story."

"It started a month ago. I got a letter from some insurance company asking me to contact them about a claim. When I called, I was told it was in reference to Katya. They wanted information about her, the name of her father, her birth information. The man on the phone kept asking so many questions. I've never heard of the company, so I got scared and refused to tell him anything. But he kept after me, he kept calling. At first it was just a couple of daytime calls, polite, not rude or anything. Then he started calling at night about two week ago, always asking questions about Katya. And then he mentioned you."

Her last few words fell like a stone into a suddenly silent room and he scanned the restaurant automatically. "Go on."

"I tried star-six-nine, but nothing. He said his name was Robert Arnov and that he was with Lexington Life. I found the company on the Internet and called them, but they never heard of this Robert person. Then it got worse. He started calling two or three times a night, so I called the phone company about an unlisted number, but they said it would take at least three weeks to get one. A week ago, I found a letter in my mailbox with no stamp on it. I brought it with me." She shuffled through the papers in front of her and produced some folded sheets with small, neat writing on one side.

"So did you report any of these incidents to the police? The harassing phone calls? The letter?" He reached out and took the letter, knowing the answer he'd get.

"Yes. At least, I reported the calls. They didn't seem to take the threats seriously and didn't want to do anything about them. So, I didn't go further with it. I was afraid I'd drag you into this inadvertently, since you're a cop. I decided the best thing to do was to warn you and ask for your help."

He raised an eyebrow at her. "And that's what this is all about? A warning?"

She'd been holding her coffee and she sat the mug down abruptly, spilling liquid over the rim, leaving a dark puddle on the table. "No, I told you. I want to protect Katya but I also wanted to warn you, in case I have to go to the police." She glowered at him and he almost laughed, her attempt at fierceness so inane. "At first I tried to convince myself it was all a hoax, something I could handle. But then yesterday, someone tried to pick up Katya from daycare. Luckily, her teacher was alert and wouldn't let her go with the man. Instead, she called me. I panicked and called you."

He didn't want to care, didn't want to get involved with this, but he thought about his sister and guilt overrode common sense. Dinah. She'd only been nineteen when she'd died, in his car, his fault, and he thought about this small child, maybe his. "Where is she now?" he asked tersely, a capitulation for the child, but without sympathy for the mother.

"She's staying at a friend's house. I told her not to let her go outside or to leave her alone until I pick her up. My friend doesn't know the specifics, just that I'd been having some problems with someone harassing us."

He sighed and pushed away the unwanted food. Sofie's sandwich sat untouched in front of her. "When can I see her?"

Relief spilled over her face and he looked away as she spoke, not wanting to care. "As soon as possible, right now if you can."

"I can't leave right now. I'm working." He ran his fingers through his hair. "I need something else from you, some ID or something." *Christ.* He at least had to do some checking on this woman before he ran off half-cocked with her.

She opened her bag and pulled out a small card. "Here's my card. I own a bookshop on Mt. Elliott. You can call there and talk with my business partner. Or I can give you the numbers of some of my neighbors." She handed him the card and pushed the rest of the papers across the table at him. "Katya's birth certificate and her health records. Is that enough?"

He stared down at her card and the papers. "This will be enough for now. I'll need an hour or so to straighten up some things at work. Where can I reach you? At this number?" He held up the card. At her nod, he stood up and grabbed the check. "Wait for my call. I shouldn't be more than a couple of hours." Without another word, he turned and strode out of the restaurant, refusing to look back.

~ * ~

He saw the little girl first. She had curly blond hair and was dressed in a sun suit covered with blue flowers. His throat tightened at the sight of her; she looked like Dinah. But the little girl also looked her mother, with her heart-shaped face and full lips. As he got closer, he saw something else—the little girl had his brown eyes.

Sofie had changed into some sort of sundress, a pale yellow color that reminded him of the smell of flowers that had lingered in his bed after she'd left. She'd tidied up her hair and it hung down her back in a braid, loose strands framing her face. She held her daughter's small hand and watched him, unsmiling, but the little girl smiled shyly. She held onto her mother's bare leg with a free hand and Sofie bent down, disentangled her leg and picked up the little girl in her arms. "This is Katya. Katya, this is Jack."

He stared intently at his child and forgot to smile. "Hello, Katya." He held out a palm and watched as she carefully placed her own small hand in his. She reached out and touched his face lightly with fingers like a butterfly.

Sofie turned a quick smile on her daughter before shifting her gaze back to his face. She was as uncertain of him as he was of her. His memories of that night were like syrup, concentrated and trapped in a small bottle, then put away. For him she'd been desire and her scent blended in his mind with the taste and feel of her. He'd been consumed with pain and she had absorbed it, taken it from him and given him a few hours of oblivion. And he had given her this little girl.

~ * ~

Sofie had insisted they meet at this ice cream shop and he leaned against a wall, waiting as she ordered something for Katya. Such an innocent activity, he reflected, in the midst of all the uncertainty of what was to follow. Fear reached out suddenly, clawed at him, and he took a sharp breath and turned to scan the room, as though the mere act of looking for the danger would cause it to appear. He wanted to move to a less public place, to hide them. "Let's go," he barked.

Katya had a chocolate cone and ate it sitting in the back seat of his car. It was hot for October, a late Indian summer, and he watched Katya's cone leak pale brown liquid down her chest and onto the blue cornflowers of the playsuit. She sat without speaking, licking her cone with a slight smile, showing dimples.

"I'm taking you both to my place. We can talk there, at least. And if need be, you can stay the night, until I do some checking and figure out what the hell's going on." His words came out rougher than he wanted and Sofie looked uncertainly at Katya.

He wondered if she too was flooded with unwanted memories from his place. He hadn't slept that night, but had repeatedly come back to take more from her. He hadn't shaved for three days, since Dinah's funeral, and his heavy beard had left red scratches over her throat, her breasts, the tender skin of her inner thigh.

He blinked away the image and turned to start the car, expecting protests about staying at his place but she said nothing. "I have a spare room you can use if you need to stay a day or two."

Friday late afternoon and the street was filled with cars, people leaving work early to enjoy the last of the warm weather or auto workers finishing their shift at the nearby Cadillac assembly plant.

He drove quickly through familiar streets, constantly checking his rear view mirror, but no one followed. The east side of Detroit, once a colorful mix of cultures and nationalities, was more homogeneous, less ethnic these days; the small Italian, Polish and Russian communities were all that were left, determined holdouts against the rush to the suburbs started in the sixties. Here and there, two- or three-block areas persistently held on with small, locally-owned shops, fighting a losing battle to keep the old world intact for the aging immigrants.

After joining the Force, Jack had saved for three years and bought his house in the same Italian neighborhood where he'd grown up, near enough to his parents to see them often, but far enough to have his privacy. The house was small by East Side standards, started in 1940 before the war and finished in 1945, newer than most of the other houses in the neighborhood. The important thing was his brothers, two of whom were cops, as well as many of his friends on the Force, lived in the area and it was probably the safest neighborhood within a three-mile radius. Right now he needed safety, some place to stash Katya until he could figure out what was happening and come up with a plan.

He unlocked his door and stood back for them to enter, watching for Sofie's reaction. It had been Friday night when he'd brought her here before, but later, closer to midnight.

The last rays of the day shone through a window, casting an unwanted spotlight on the disarray inside, like a metaphor for the despair and anger he'd sunk into with his sister's murder. He didn't want Sofie to see it now. He didn't want her to invade what was left of his life. He flipped on the overhead light and moved them quickly through the entry way and into the kitchen, picking up as he went.

Sofie and Katya stood watching him, a sharp contrast to the clutter of the room in their bright sundresses, the scent of flowers and ice cream clinging to them. He threw down his jacket and pulled off his shoulder holster automatically, glancing over quickly at Katya to see if she'd noticed the gun, but she merely smiled. Piles of dirty dishes sat on the chipped linoleum table and he shifted them to the dishwasher, making space for Katya and Sofie. He wiped off the table and was struck by the notion that this small act was the beginning of something that would change his life forever.

"Have a seat." He pointed to a chair. "Would you like something to drink? Or something to eat? It's dinner time." Without waiting for a response, he turned to search for something suitable. "What would you like, Katya? I have soup or—a peanut butter sandwich?" A wave of anger hit him. *Hell, she was three years old and he had no idea what his daughter liked to eat!*

"Peanut butter and jelly," she whispered.

He fixed the sandwich and without turning around, called over his shoulder, "Do you want one too, Sofie? Or can I get you some soup?" It was the first time he'd said her name and it felt strange on his tongue, too soft, like her.

"Soup's fine. I'm afraid I've never developed a taste for peanut butter." She picked Katya up and put her in a chair, getting out a juice box from her bag. "Jack, it's getting late. I need to check on my store. My business partner's working late tonight." He turned, hearing tension in her voice. "She's alone. I just want to be sure everything's all right." She glanced over at Katya. "Are you really thinking of having us stay here tonight? If so, I'll need to get some things from my place. I live upstairs over the store." She added.

"I think the best thing to do right now is have you both stay over. I'll put in a call and have a patrol car stop by and check on things there. They can probably pick up whatever you need." He pulled out his cell phone, turned away and spoke for several minutes to someone before handing the phone over to her. He waited until she'd given instructions on how to get to her place. "Put in a call to your partner and warn her someone's stopping by to pick up your things. Ask her to pack what you need for tonight and have it ready." It was an order, said with the authority of a cop.

~ * ~

So here they were, strangers, bound together in the quiet, darkness of his house. Sofie had refused the offer of his spare bedroom, filled with the memories of happier times in his life. He'd gratefully acquiesced and instead, she and Katya were bedded down for the night on his sofa. Katya lay curled up under a quilt and he stood in the doorway of the dimly lit room, watching her tiny lips opening and closing slightly in sleep. The darkness of her eyes, like his own, was the only contrast to her light hair, so much like her mother's, and he wanted to reach out and touch a curl.

Sofie lay in back of Katya, one arm looped around the little girl. Conscious of him suddenly, she shifted and opened gray eyes to meet his. He held her gaze for a brief moment, turned around and headed back to the kitchen.

He sat staring at his mug, knowing he'd had too much caffeine, but unable to think of sleep in the face of the day's events. He'd already made up his mind to get them out of Detroit, at least for a day or two, up to his family's cabin. It would give him some breathing space and time to think about what was next. Aside from being the same blood type as he was—AB—he had no real proof Katya was his child, but looking at her, he knew. Or maybe on some level he wanted it to be so.

A half dozen questions ran through his mind: What was the real threat to Katya? What was he going to tell his parents? How was he going to deal with Sofie and their past? He pushed aside his mug, stood up and turned towards his bedroom for a sleepless night.

## *Two*

The pale morning light shone on Sofie's slender legs, illuminating them against the backdrop of the darkness. Jack stood in the doorway and watched her cross the living room, lean down and check Katya before turning towards the bathroom. He returned to the kitchen and was in the midst of cleaning up last night's dishes when she finally emerged, face scrubbed, her hair again in a single braid down her back. "You alright?"

She jumped at the sound of his voice. "I'm fine." A whisper only and it brought an unbidden image—a whispered word, a look of amazement as she stared up from beneath him. He pushed the memory away.

"Your things were dropped off after you'd gone to sleep last night." He pointed to two small duffel bags sitting on the kitchen table. She turned back to the kitchen, strode over to the bags and began sorting through them. "Anything else you need for now?"

She looked confused and he realized she'd expected hostility rather than concern from him after yesterday's confrontations. "No thanks." Closing a bag, she looked directly at him for the first time that morning. "Actually, Katya could use something to eat for breakfast."

"Well, there's always peanut butter." He smiled in resignation, bitterly aware of how little he knew about being a father.

"Yeah and I'm sure she'll eat it again. I wish I was as easily satisfied."

Her face reddened with her words and he was glad. She could damned well be as unhappy with unwanted memories as he was. "We need to talk," he said and motioned her to a chair opposite him. "I'm taking you and Katya to my family's cabin on Lake St. Clair. You'll be safer there right now. Just for a day, maybe two, until I get word back on some things I'm checking. Do you have a cell phone on you?"

"No, I don't own one. Still resisting." Her attempt at humor slid over him and the slight smile on her face died.

"I'm having your home and work phones checked, tracing all incoming and outgoing calls, and doing a quick check on your friends and acquaintances. I'll have someone talk with Katya's teacher first thing Monday, about the man who showed up at daycare. It'll take a day or two to get some of that done before you go back to your apartment. Your business partner—can she take care of the bookstore for a day or so?"

She nodded

"I'm probably going to be staying at your place for a few days at least, until I determine what the threat is." He sighed. "It may be that'll be enough to scare whoever it is off, if it's some crank. If nothing serious shows up, I'll have someone watching your place and Katya's day care for the next few weeks, but I'll try and keep things as normal as possible for her. If need be, I can hire someone to watch you both."

"I'll pay for it." There it was again, the challenge. It seemed faked to him and he wondered about the disparity.

He waved away her words with a shake of his head. From the description of her ramshackle apartment and bookstore, it was obvious her income was barely subsistence level.

"What else?" She leaned forward, as though she wanted to yank a promise from him that Katya would be safe.

"I need more information from you," he said. "What about other family? Any at all? Sisters or brothers, uncles, aunts?"

"No, I have a second cousin who lives in Northville. I see him once in a while. My family passed away a few years ago, before I had Katya." Wariness crept back into her tone.

"Until three weeks ago, you felt no sense of danger, any unusual incidents happen? Anything that might indicate someone watching you?"

She shook her head. "Nothing."

"How long have you had your store?"

"Three years. I bought it with Monica, Monica Berkholz, my business partner, about four months before Katya was born."

"Have you always been so careless about security?"

"What do you mean?" Her face colored.

"Last night, the cop I sent to check things out and pick up your stuff, he found your partner there alone at night, late, the doors unlocked, customers wandering around the place. The inside access door to your apartment from the store was unlocked. Hell, anybody could have gone up and hidden!" Anger at her resurfaced. Sitting there, her freshly scrubbed face, she looked almost fragile, a sharp contrast to her words for him. Yet, he felt the same desire he'd felt four years ago and he cursed himself for his weakness. How in the hell could he possibly still feel attracted to her? She'd had his kid and kept it from him. She'd used him and cast him off without a thought. He shuddered, thinking about her raising his child.

"I have a business! I have to keep it open. The door was unlocked because the book store is open for business at night and I leave the door to my apartment open when we're doing business. We have stock stored upstairs, things we need. We always lock everything up when we leave."

She'd pulled herself up as she spoke and again he got a sense of seeing a pretense she was showing him, some sort of damned independent woman thing. He didn't respond, but watched, fascinated with the show of strength.

"Think whatever you want about me, but I'm a good mother, a cautious mother. I take good care of my daughter and I don't take risks with her." She stood up and paced around the table, searching for something, and not finding it, turned back to him. "We live in a very close neighborhood. It may not look safe to you but we all watch out for each other. The shops around my store are owned by friends, people I've known since I was a little girl. It's a close-knit Russian community. Monica knows that and she'd never feel unsafe there either."

He saw real annoyance now on her face, for the first time.

"You aren't going to make a lot of fuss, checking things out, are you? My customers and my neighbors? Please don't make accusations or frighten them. Even Monica doesn't know much about the threats. I told her about the calls but I haven't mentioned the day care thing yet. I didn't want to alarm anyone, not her and not my neighbors."

"I don't plan on alarming anyone. But don't you think you should at least tell your business partner what's happening? It seems only reasonable to have her on guard." He said.

"I don't think she needs to know. Not yet. She has a daughter herself and she'd go crazy if she knew Katya was being threatened." He knew his face showed only disbelief and she went on. "I know what you must think of me, but I'm not careless, especially now, where Katya is concerned. That's why I called you. I'm asking you for protection. In normal circumstances my neighbors and friends would support me, I'd go to them for help. But I don't want to worry them. They're mostly old, a lot of them don't even speak English. If they thought there was some threat to Katya, it would terrify them.

That's why I called you and I don't want you turning around and upsetting them."

It was a long speech, not what he expected from her, and any residual anger he felt fled. "I see." He got up and poured water into the coffee maker, not looking at her, uncertain and suddenly curious about her. He wanted it to be simple, her motives straightforward and selfish, but she wasn't what she seemed to be.

Katya chose that moment to call out from the couch and Sofie went to her. Jack followed, driven by a need to watch her with his daughter. Katya sat quietly, holding three dolls, each dressed in some sort of ethnic costume. They looked well used and he wondered if they'd belonged to Sofie. Katya sensed his gaze, looked up and gave him a quick smile. He smiled back and headed to the kitchen to pack.

With Katya awake there was no more discussion. Jack threw together an overnight bag and waited for Sofie to get Katya dressed for travel. The weather had turned cold, a return to normal for October and Sofie dressed herself and Katya in sweats. She pulled jackets from the duffels and he stood waiting as she tugged a warm cap over Katya's curls. He turned to collect his shoulder holster and jacket, their three bags, and followed Sofie and Katya out the door.

Outside, his sense of urgency returned and he shepherded them to his car, keeping an eye out for unusual activity on the quiet street. It was less than an hour's drive from the east side of Detroit to the cabin and he drove in silence, listening to Katya's singsong humming drifting up from the backseat. They pulled into the dirt drive leading to the cottage just after ten a.m.

Jack hadn't used the place in four years, not since Dinah's funeral. He'd spent five days there, in a drunken stupor, before giving up and driving back into the city, defeated but resigned to living. He'd returned for one more visit a week later—the night after he'd met Sofie.

It was a typical Michigan cottage: a few small rooms with worn, knotty pine walls, heated with propane, bathroom fitted a septic tank toilet. Its one redeeming feature was a fireplace made from huge stones hauled from miles away. The cottage sat a hundred yards off Lake St. Clair, sheltered from the highway by pine trees bent by years of gales blowing off the lake. The cottage belonged to Jack's Grandmother Lucci and, by unspoken agreement, he and his three brothers used it almost exclusively.

Jack stepped out of his Cherokee, squinting against the cold wind, and scanned the barren landscape around the cottage. He saw no one and nothing out of place. He grabbed the bags and motioned Sofie and Katya to follow him into the shuttered cottage.

It was cold inside, almost as cold as outside, and he lit the heater quickly. The place wasn't meant for use in winter. It was meant for summer weekend getaways, leaving the place with a feel of abandonment about it, smelling of mildew and dust. He turned on lights and hurried back outside to get wood to supplement the meager heat from the propane.

He plugged in the refrigerator, put away supplies and made up beds, and watched Sofie settle Katya. She laid out a blanket for Katya in front of the fireplace with a picture book and turned to the coffee waiting on the counter. By the time Sofie got her coffee poured and turned to sit down, Katya's blond head lolled on a pillow, eyes shut, thumb to mouth. Up too late last night and too early this morning, she was asleep. Sofie covered her and came back and sat down opposite him at the enormous wooden table. He offered her a plate of rolls and she raised her eyebrows at them. "My mother makes them and I freeze 'em. I brought some along." He waited a beat for her to take a bite of roll and launched his assault. "I still want to know why the hell you never contacted me about Katya."

The suddenness of the attack startled Sofie. She spoke slowly, wary of him now, weighing her words. "I never contacted you because it had nothing to do with you. It was my responsibility. I should have told you that I wasn't using some sort of protection."

"That's a pretty flimsy excuse for not letting me know."

She ignored him and went on. "It was a bad time for me and I wasn't thinking clearly. My mother had just died a couple of weeks before—my grandmother a month before that."

He started to say something, but she kept talking.

"I got drunk and picked you up. In a bar, for God's sake. You're the one who so kindly pointed that out yesterday. Why would I even think about contacting you?" She glanced at him. "But when I found out I was pregnant, I was glad. I wanted the baby. It gave me something to plan for, a new family. It just never occurred to me that someone I picked up in a bar would want to be told he was going to be a father." What she didn't say was that she'd felt grateful to him for that night, grateful for Katya.

He looked skeptical, as though she was hiding something important from him, *a cop look,* she thought.

"Raising a child alone wasn't strange to me, you know. My mother was a single mother, and her mother. I never even considered the idea of a man being part of it, especially someone who was so drunk he probably didn't even remember he'd had sex with me. I didn't really want a father for Katya."

"I *AM* the father!"

She looked over at Katya who slept on. "I'm not denying that. You asked me why I never contacted you and I'm trying to explain why. I knew I could handle being a single mother. After all, I'd had years of watching how it was done. I had no idea in my head you could handle being a father, someone blind drunk who picks up a stranger, takes her home for sex and never thinks to look her up or see if she's all right. Why would I want you involved in raising my child, financially or otherwise? I never thought of contacting you—until now." *Liar,* she thought.

She had thought of contacting him—many times. When she was pregnant, she'd spent hours daydreaming scenes where he turned up at the hospital, bringing flowers, smiling. She'd replayed that night she'd gotten pregnant in her head so many times she could write a book about it. And she called herself a fool for all of those daydreams.

"So you never thought about that night again?" It was as though he'd read her mind. "Basically then, you used me as a sperm donor? A good fuck—and an instant family!" He was getting louder and she leaned back away from him.

"No. It wasn't like that. I'd just lost my mother. She was the only family I had left. I didn't set out to get pregnant. I'm not even sure myself what I did want." She sighed and sank back in her chair. "Maybe you're partially right. Maybe all I was looking for was some comfort and an offer of sex was the best I could find."

"Yeah, well have you ever thought all that crap you're throwing at me is just an excuse? You can justify the hell out of getting knocked up, but don't have to deal with me or any guy. You say you grew up with women only? It sounds to me like you're clueless and scared shitless having to deal with men. It was easier just to use me for a night and avoid any serious responsibility."

He was too close to what she feared about herself and, instead, she focused on her actions. "I saw you sitting at the bar and you seemed lonely, as desperate as me." She forged on, knowing there was no going back or fixing it for him. "Accuse me of whatever you want, but it's done and now there's Katya."

She felt an emptiness in the pit of her stomach, as though someone had carved out a piece of her. She wanted to elaborate, to explain, except she couldn't even explain it to herself. "I didn't just forget about you. After Katya was born, I thought about telling you about her. I thought about it a lot. I even called you at the Precinct from the hospital, but I hung up before you came on the line. I convinced myself you'd make accusations, that you'd just be angry I'd gotten pregnant." She paused. "And I was right."

He took a deep breath. All he wanted right now was to get away from her. The scent of burning logs mingled with the musty smell of the place. It reminded him of being a child here, he, his four brothers, Dinah, all crowded into the one small bedroom, his parents in the other, all of them laughing, happy. Suddenly the air felt suffocating to him and he felt defeated. "And you were never going to tell me about Katya, were you?"

She swallowed, but didn't meet his eyes. When she spoke, it sounded muffled, as if the walls absorbed her words. "I kept thinking that some day I would." She paused and finally looked up at him. "You're right. If it hadn't been for this threat to Katya, I probably would never have told you." She looked away. "I don't know why. I can repeat all the things I've been saying to you, that you seemed unreachable, maybe even dangerous. Whatever answers I give, you won't believe me, anyway." She shrugged. "And it doesn't change anything." Her last words were faint.

He knew she was right. He'd been insane those weeks following Dinah's death. He'd pulled it to him and wallowed in it. He'd cared about nothing and no one but the pain, his own and his family's. But he didn't want Sofie anywhere near the truth about how it had been. "If you thought I was some sort of sociopath, why in the hell did you pick me up that night? You get some sort of kick out of danger?" The question was rhetorical. He stood up and paced the room, afraid he would get louder if he didn't move. "I would have helped you, you know."

"No, I didn't know. And I didn't think you were a sociopath. What I thought was that you were alone, and in a lot of pain. And you were drunk. At first I was afraid, but you seemed almost..." She swallowed. "I don't know, more desperate for someone than me. It made me feel..." she shrugged again, "I don't know, useful, almost grateful, Jack. And because of that, I did think of you again."

He flinched at her words.

"And then there was Katya. I saw you constantly in her face. I don't know. Maybe it was being selfish, more than I thought. You were obviously unhappy and I didn't want that added to my own, I didn't need more complications in my life."

He stopped in front of her. "You're right about one thing. I wasn't in any shape to deal with anything that night, that's for damned sure." He said. "What I'm pissed about is the fact that I have a daughter who's three years old. You robbed me of the opportunity to be part of her life, something that belonged to me as much as you. What's worse, you robbed my parents of knowing their only grandchild." He ran a hand through his hair. "But, I suppose that's a moot point now."

He stood for several moments and finally sat down in front of her. "So, how did you find me? Have you been keeping tabs on me for the past four years?"

"You gave me your name that night and told me you were a cop. I just called the Detroit Police and asked for you." She looked up quickly, and he could see what was coming. "Did you try to find me after that night?"

He shook his head. "I wondered about you, maybe even worried some, but I never searched for you. I didn't make any attempt to see if you were okay." It was the closest thing to a confession of guilt she'd get from him.

She smiled sadly, "So where do we go from here?"

He leaned back, relieved to not further pursue the mistakes he'd made. "Right now we sit tight. I have some feelers out and we'll hang here for a day or maybe two. It'll take a few days to get the results of the traces, but I have someone watching your place, keeping an eye out for anything suspicious. Tomorrow we'll check with Katya's teacher. And I have someone working on the letter. We'll start checking around on any contacts you've had with strangers in the past month. And your neighbors, of course." He raised a hand to halt her protest. "We'll be tactful. We're just trying to get at whether anyone's been asking questions about you, anything suspicious. I'll get on the phone in a while and see where we're at right now. If nothing turns up by the end of today, I'll decide where to go from there." He stood up. "Right now, let's make some lunch."

They worked side by side and when Katya woke, they all sat eating together, neither he nor Sofie saying much to each other. He was patient with Katya, answering her questions about the cottage, about the lake, telling her about the pictures on the walls of kids romping on the beach. Katya eventually ran out of questions and the cabin was silent, the isolation intensified by the howling of the wind outside.

After lunch, Katya begged to go down to the lake and he refused all pleas, relieved when she finally gave up and retreated with Sofie to the small bedroom. He spent the next few hours alternating between his laptop and his cell phone, talking to her neighbors, going over the list Sofie had given him of her acquaintances. He checked twice with the Precinct for updates on anything new.

It was late afternoon when he gave up and sat, legs sprawled out in front of the fire, pulling on a cigarette. He was disgusted with himself and the bitterness that lingered from his talk with Sofie. He tossed the butt in the fire, stood up and wandered to the door of the bedroom.

Sofie was curled around her daughter, both asleep, and he stood watching, wondering how he could have come to pick her up that night. She certainly wasn't his type. She was slight, with a ballet dancer's body. He liked his women tall, voluptuous, full-blown. Sofie's hair had come loose from its braid and lay around her face. She wore no makeup and she looked defenseless. He liked strong women who were sure of themselves, sophisticated, independent but sexy, who knew how to dress for a man. The sweats Sofie wore were faded and rumpled, as though she'd had them in her closet for years.

But he couldn't forget how she'd looked that night, walking ahead of him as they left the bar. He remembered she'd bounced a little when she walked; it had seemed optimistic, an approach to life he hated, then and now. He'd downed four straight shots before he became aware of her at his elbow. She had plopped herself next to him and although she was clearly nervous, he couldn't miss her invitation. He didn't pick women up in bars—he wasn't that desperate. There were plenty around if he wanted one. He'd never done one-night stands and never picked up strangers—until Sofie.

One stupid night and his life had changed forever. He watched his daughter sleep and felt a tightness around his heart, as though something inside him was trying to work its way out. He moved his gaze to Sofie. She'd been different from the other women he'd known, but he knew how she'd ended up in his bed that night. He'd been drunk as hell, but there'd also been something about her that had appealed to him and he'd grabbed at that.

Hazy images floated up, her pale body lying beside his, shiny with sweat, a strange mixture of sensuality and innocence. He remembered a fleeting sense of guilt as he stared down at her. She had lain dozing, exhausted and he'd reached out a hand to touch her slender thigh, sticky with his semen. He'd had a moment of panic that even the haze of alcohol couldn't disguise, but he'd pushed it aside until the next morning when he found the single condom he always carried in his wallet, unopened, lying on the table. He'd cursed himself for a goddamned fool and spent the next week working to erase any memory of the night and the woman.

When Dinah died, his life had stopped, any future he'd been planning had been put away. That night after they'd buried Dinah, he'd stumbled into the Mariner's Bar, to Sofie. Now it had come full circle. He had a child and someone was threatening her, but he pushed away the fear that it had something to do with his job.

~ * ~

The wind continued to howl around the cabin, the dark outside alien, the fire inside a refuge. Sofie knew he was watching her and she knew he was confused. He didn't trust her, maybe even hated her. But tonight, isolated here, she knew on some level he wanted her, just as he'd wanted her four years ago. She needed him to protect their daughter; she wasn't sure what else she wanted from him.

Perhaps every person was led to one moment in time when the best of life was possible, and the rest of the time was spent in meaningless activities to hide the void. That moment for Sofie had been when she'd had Katya and anything that didn't involve protecting her right now was superfluous.

Katya lay huddled against her belly, asleep, when Sofie wakened suddenly, startled by something. The fire was burning down in the living room, sending an eerie light through the open bedroom door. It was colder in the cabin now and the darkness felt ominous. She lay still, listening, but the only sound was the wind, still howling.

Sofie eased up and out from under the heavy blanket. The door to the small bathroom was closed and light shown under it. She grabbed a quilt from the foot of the bed and went to stand in front of the door, listening.

The door opened and Jack came out, dressed in sweats, bare-chested, a towel wrapped around his neck. "Something wrong?"

"Something woke me." She whispered.

He moved quickly, grabbed his holster, and strode to the door of the cabin, easing it open slightly. She stood back against the wall, waiting.

Nothing was out there, but the wind and leaves that whirled about the car. He eased the door shut and turned to her, pulling her against his bare chest with one arm, and covering her mouth with his. She said his name and the sound startled him. He thrust her away, expression tight. "Shit! That was a stupid move on my part. Adrenaline rush probably." He shrugged, as though to excuse his behavior. "Nothing out there. Probably just the wind you heard."

"Or, maybe I just heard you." She turned and headed into the bathroom, confused, shaking slightly.

He was standing at the bedroom door when she came out, watching Katya. She'd pushed back the blanket further and lay exposed. Without a glance at Sofie, he went to the bed, bent down and gently pulled the covers up. He inhaled sharply and headed to the other bedroom, calling over his shoulder, "Get some sleep. We're leaving early in the morning."

Sofie lay down next to Katya, wide awake now. How had she arrived here? She'd lost her virginity at 22, later than any of her friends. A tall, lanky teaching assistant, who played the piano for her, plied her with gin and tonic and wooed her into his bed. She had let him take her, watching like a spectator as he pulled off her clothes. Her first sexual encounter in the end had been only mildly interesting and she'd never seen him again.

How had she gone from that to this man who was Katya's father? She'd had so few moments of intimacy and nothing worth remembering, until Jack. She lay awake in the dark and tried to convince herself that what had just happened between them was of no consequence. In the past four years, if she'd learned anything, it was that she was strong, and she didn't need anybody, especially a man. But, he was Katya's father and for now, he would keep her safe.

## *Three*

Sofie felt Katya crawling over her and turned to see the clock—6:15. A foot hit her in the belly. "Awgh!" Katya turned and grinned, her face lighting up like a Christmas elf. "Have some mercy, sweetheart! Give me a few more minutes, please!"

Katya scrambled across the bed and onto the floor, running, her baby bear t-shirt and matching panties twisted around her small round body. Sofie shivered under the covers and squinted through one eye at Katya, who danced around the room in the thin watery morning light, unaffected by the cold damp of the cabin.

"I gotta go potty!"

"It's out there, sweetie." Sofie pointed blindly towards the open door.

"I'll ask Jack!" Sofie smiled as Katya turned and headed out to the other bedroom, dragging her bear. Apparently Katya's shyness with Jack was gone.

"You do that." She murmured the words into the pillow and sank back into sleep, smiling at the thought of big tough Jack handling potty issues. She hoped he would realize how cold Katya was and either turn on the heat or wrap her up in something warm.

~ * ~

Jack surfaced from deep sleep swatting at something insistently lighting on his cheek. He batted it once, twice, and finally flung his body over, arm outstretched. The thing cried out and he opened one eye and stared into the dimly lit room at the small person on the floor holding a stuffed bear. "Katya!" He bolted out of bed and swooped her up awkwardly into his arms. "Did I hurt you?"

She shook her head, stared up at him, serious now and threw her small arms around his neck. "I got to go potty." It was a declaration that confounded him, but he instinctively moved to the bathroom, quickly now, juggling her in his arms. *What the hell age does potty training happen and what am I supposed to do now?*

He didn't have to worry; she knew exactly how to deal with him. She squirmed out of his arms and without giving him a second look, pulled down her bear panties and climbed up on the toilet seat. He turned to go, but only made it two steps outside the bathroom door when she called after him, "Jack, can you wipe me, please?"

The toilet paper roll was empty and he grabbed a new one from the shelf above the toilet, pulled the paper off and grabbed a wad. He handed it to her with raised eyebrows and grimaced with relief when she took it and did her own job.

But before he could escape, she smiled up at him again. "Jack, will you help me down?" Her bear panties were around her ankles and he reached down and pulled them up over chubby legs. Resigned now, he lifted her up and turned to the sink, holding both her small hands under the faucet.

"Thank you." So polite.

Sofie lay staring at the ceiling, frowning as she listened to the two voices blending from the bathroom. She'd had the baby alone, no one there holding her hand and urging her on; no one laughing and crying over her beautiful little girl. In the end it didn't matter. Katya was everything and Sofie's loneliness had disappeared. Whatever fears she'd had about being weak or needing a man in her life seemed trivial. But that wasn't the point now. It was Katya who needed a protector, and just maybe, she needed a father as well.

~ * ~

The wind continued to whistle through the pine trees behind the cabin, whipping the dull gray lake into a frenzy. Katya was the only eager person this morning and she ran around in circles outside the Jeep, chasing leaves from the lone maple by the dirt drive. Sofie watched her laughing, happy to see Katya so pleased with life, whatever the adults around her felt.

"Katya, come on, honey. Get in." Sofie held the door for her and watched as Jack strode over and scooped her up, gently but firmly, and placed her in the backseat of his car. He looked older than she remembered, older than what four years could account for, especially in the harsh light of the day. She stared at him, tracing his fine eyebrows that seemed in complete opposition to the rest of his rough-hewn features, as though two sides of his character were at war on his face.

It was almost noon and Jack had gotten an all-clear on her apartment an hour ago. The plan was to go back to Sofie's and let her handle some business. They'd agreed Jack would stay with them, at least for now. The entire discussion took place without eye contact and she sensed in him the same wariness she felt. She vowed there would be no repeat at her place of last night's dance with desire.

They rode to Sofie's silently, listening to Katya's running commentary on the passing scenery, interspersed between her bites of peanut butter toast. Jack stared straight ahead; he seemed far away. It was after eleven and the morning rush hour over; there were few cars on the road, but he kept checking the rear view mirror, frowning each time. She glanced back at her daughter and caught her scowling at the mess the peanut butter had made on her hands and Sofie smiled at the similarity of expressions.

Jack glanced over at Sofie and raised his eyebrows. She knew what he was thinking. *What in the hell do you have to smile about this morning?* She was beginning to expect his moods and almost found his scowl endearing today. He was going to be in her life, and hard to ignore, in the next few days, but it couldn't be helped. She tried to picture them bumping elbows in her small apartment, or imagine his large bulk wandering the narrow spaces of her bookstore, glaring as her eccentric customers tried to get past him. She'd already given him a quick sketch of her life. It was a world of casual acquaintances and strangers, with very few close friends. He'd looked at her list but it was insufficient for him, he wanted more information, a deeper look. He knew she had no men in her life and she cringed at the thought of being laid out, completely open, for his inspection and harsh judgment.

~ * ~

Jack scanned the street where he'd parked before motioning for Sofie, who held tightly to Katya's hand. They made their way past the front of the store, closed up tight on a Monday.

Jack surveyed the stickers plastered over the large windows: announcements about the homeless shelter, women's rights meetings, PETA protest notices. *Shit! She runs a freaking left wing feminist bookstore and every character in the city is invited to make this place home!*

The alley was barely a car width across and ran along the north side of the bookstore, the kind of small thoroughfare common in older Detroit neighborhoods. He followed her down the narrow alley to a nondescript, heavy metal door, directly opposite a red one, the back door of the bakery.

Sofie unlocked her door and stepped back, waiting for him to lead the way up the dark wooden stairs, eight well worn steps leading to a landing before dividing into a Y, one arm leading down to the front of the store, the other up to her apartment. At the top of the stairs Sofie unlocked a wooden door painted with bright colors and they stepped into the sunlit kitchen.

She motioned him to put down the bags and have a seat. She moved around doing the things he knew she did every day when she came home, hanging coats on pegs, placing Katya's little backpack on the table so her daughter—his daughter— could reach her toys, putting on the kettle for tea. It was surprisingly quiet in the apartment, at least in this room, away from all street noise. He took in the solid wooden table, the clean lines of the cupboards, the shiny hardwood floors, and was caught off guard. If asked to predict her design style, he would have bet on sweet, flowery, too cheery for his taste. Instead, the place was straightforward in its simplicity with a touch of bright color that declared real people lived here. It went against all of his notions about her.

~ * ~

Sofie moved around, trying hard to ignore any sign of censure of her home by him. She'd owned the wooden framed store and upstairs apartment for four years. Monica and she had met in graduate school; they'd liked each other immediately and had formed a working partnership that had evolved into trust. Monica had been there when she'd found out she was pregnant. She'd offered her humor and been a friend when Sofie had no one.

Sofie's share of the building had been purchased with the small amount of money left from her mother's estate. The store was on Mt. Elliott, within the few blocks left of what was once a thriving Russian community. It was where Sofie had grown up and where she was at home. All that remained was contained within a two-block area, and this was fading fast with the passing of each elderly store owner. She'd brought Katya to the apartment as a baby and had created a home for her here.

Once the bookstore was open, Sofie and Monica set up a schedule and took turns working and their daughters grew used to lives that revolved around it. Sofie loved the musty smell of used books mixed with the scent of coffee always ready for their customers. Katya loved the place and she loved the people, sitting in the back of the store with piles of picture books or moving between tables, passing out homemade cookies.

The dark, lonely months when Sofie's mom lay dying were replaced with the laughter of her daughter. Katya's intense, deep brown eyes were the only reminder of that night with Jack. Sofie had done a good job of pushing away her memories of him along with her feelings of guilt, but unexpectedly she'd find herself wondering if he were happy yet. And sometimes she'd dream about him, wakening from sleep to imagine Jack holding Katya in his arms. She'd never known her own father, but Sofie imagined him sometimes, as elusive in her mind as Katya's would be. She could picture both of them, perfect fathers, insubstantial and no real threat to the balance of their lives. Now all that would change.

~ * ~

Katya hummed a sing-song little tune as she played, stopping often to say something to her dolls and laugh. She was engrossed with one doll particularly, a tattered Raggedy Anne she'd found at the cabin, digging around in a closet. It had belonged to Dinah and Jack had given it to Katya.

Jack sat watching her now, mesmerized, trying to think back to a time when he'd laughed like that. Over the past couple of days he had never seen her sad or angry, she never whined, she rarely complained. Had there been a time when he had been as happy as that just with life? He'd buried not only Dinah but all his memories with her as well. Now Katya was resurrecting them. Aware of him suddenly, she looked up, giggled and offered up her doll. He bent over to look and inhaled her little girl scent, a sweet mixture like flowers and strawberry lollipop. He breathed her in for a moment and eased back, afraid he'd frighten her.

Unaware, she smiled again and tried his name. "Jack." Her shyness was disappearing but it was too soon to tell her he was her father. For now, the way she said his name was enough.

~ * ~

Sofie stood at the door of Katya's bedroom, her heart racing, watching him bend over his daughter. She couldn't help smiling at the picture—their two heads, dark and blond, were bent over the doll. He touched Katya's curly hair briefly and Katya laughed up at him, with his same dark eyes. Jack turned and caught sight of Sofie in the door. She knew she'd seen more than he wanted her to and she watched his expression change from a smile to a frown as he shifted his gaze from her.

Sofie headed for the kitchen and scanned her refrigerator. There was barely enough for her and Katya, let alone a hulking male. She reached for her coat and turned to tell Jack she'd be back in a few minutes.

"Where the hell do you think you're going?"

He was standing so close behind her she could feel his heat. She smiled defiantly at him; he might have a big gun, but he wasn't so scary. "We don't have enough food. I'm just running down the street to pick up a few more things."

"We'll all go, then." It was an order.

"No need to. You can stay here with Katya and I'll be fine. No one's threatening me. Really, I'll be fine, Jack. I'm just going next door to the bakery and then two doors down to the grocery." She ignored further protests, shrugged on her pea coat and called out to Katya. "Honey, Mommy's going to get you some cookies. I'll be right back, okay? You stay with Jack."

Katya nodded, checked Jack's face, and gave him an impish grin. "You want Mommy to bring you a cookie, too?"

Sofie didn't wait to see how Jack handled this maneuver, but ran down the steps, two at a time, and out into the alley.

It was Monday midday and Mrs. Ivanova's bakery was busy, full of Detroit Edison workers in hard hats, gray-haired ladies in black dresses, and a couple of small boys, in line for the bakery's famous kulebiak, a small meat and vegetable pie, or vatrushki, a sweet pastry filled with jam.

Sofie took her place in line and chatted with Mr. Korovkin. She'd lived next door to him growing up and he was really old now, eight-five at least, thin and bent but as mentally agile as he'd been twenty-five years ago. She stood behind him and listened, struggling to interpret his jokes, thrown at her in Russian, and laughed, whether she understood or not.

Mr. Korovkin's turn came, and Sofie suddenly felt the hairs on the back of her neck stand up. She turned towards the back of the line and tried to focus casually on who was there. There were at six people behind her, two women and four men, some talking, some silent. Two of the men had their backs to Sofie, one of them in a knit cap pulled tightly over gray hair that straggled out below. The other man was younger and wore a baseball cap. He was slightly built with light hair, curling around the edges of the cap. She watched them for a few minutes, saw nothing out of the ordinary, and turned back to the counter.

Her errands took longer than planned and she hurried down the alley. She struggled briefly with her key as she juggled bags of food, a sack of cookies dangling between her teeth. Jack met her at the top of the stairs and she knew he was unhappy with her, again. "Okay, I'm sorry I took so long. Did you have any trouble?" She mumbled the words around the cookie sack in her mouth and without waiting for a response, breezed past him and dumped the bags on the kitchen table. It was ornate, round, and old, one of a handful of things she'd inherited from her grandmother. She grabbed the sack from her mouth and turned to Katya. "Hi, sweetie! Have fun with Jack?"

"We played hide and seek, Mommy. But he doesn't hide very good—he's too big. Can I have a cookie now, please?"

The hand she held out was wet and Sofie turned to take a closer look at Jack; his hair and face were dripping water. "What happened?"

"I was hiding in the shower and she turned it on." He sounded bemused and he made a face at Katya, who laughed at him and grabbed the sack of cookies. "Gimme one of those!" he yelled, his unshaven face darker than usual, but Katya only giggled and ran to hide.

*Amazing*, she thought. *He's actually playing with her. He must save up his bad moods for me.* As she put away groceries, she remembered the sense of someone watching her at the bakery and shivered, but the sound of Katya, laughing as she ran from room to room, dissipated her mood.

Sofie moved around the apartment, restless, aimlessly putting things away. She checked her voice mail and shook her head when Jack paused from his game with Katya to look over. *What in the heck am I going to do the rest of the day, trapped here with him?* Resigned, she pulled out a pen and paper, dropped onto her couch, and went to work on a more detailed account of her life for Jack, basically everywhere she went and everything she did.

She mapped her days out, including every errand she might make and every person she might encounter. She was still at it a half hour later when he lowered himself into the worn leather armed chair opposite her.

"Katya still hiding?" she asked.

He shrugged. "She got bored with our game, so I pulled out my bomb squad kit and gave it to her."

Sofie's eyes widened.

"It's okay. There's nothing there she can hurt herself with, except a small knife and I removed that. She's busy investigating a bomb scene at her Barbie dollhouse." He gave her the closest thing to a grin she'd seen and pointed at her notepad. "So you got anything more for me?"

She handed him the pad and stood up. "Let's do this while I'm making some lunch. Katya needs something and I'm starving. You hungry?" She asked, heading to the kitchen. "How about tomato soup and kulebiaka?"

"Sure, whatever you like. You didn't happen to pick up any beer, did you?"

She reached into the huge refrigerator, circa 1960, and pulled out a long-necked Strohs. She passed it to him, unwrapped the kulebiak and placed it in the microwave. "Katya, come and get ready for lunch, sweetheart!"

Katya was into the kitchen before she got the entire sentence out, dragging three dolls tied to her waist with scarves.

She lifted Katya up and put her in the small booster seat that had belonged to Sofie when she was small. Katya grabbed her spoon and attacked her soup, without interrupting the flow of words she addressed to a red-haired doll with no clothes on.

Sofie spooned the pastry onto two plates, gave one to Jack, and sat down to eat as she worked on another list. He wanted more details on her friends and she sketched out brief descriptions and background information, elaborating on the characteristics of each person.

He reached out and took the notepad, skimmed it and pushed it back to her, frowning. "Just give me the basics, Sofie. I know they're your friends, but you don't need to sell me on how wonderful they are."

When he asked her about boyfriends, she hesitated, smiled ruefully and shook her head, "No one really."

"No casual dates?"

"No, I don't like leaving Katya too often." She looked over his shoulder, giving the sheet a final glance and started going over it with him, a view of her life that looked too simple to her. As she read, Katya looked up to add remarks about the places she liked.

"So you spend most of your time in the immediate neighborhood? No longer trips anywhere in the past couple of years?"

"No, I've stayed mostly around the east side. I'm not much for daring adventures."

"Well now, I don't know about that," he drawled, "you were pretty daring four years ago. But then that was another Sofie, or so you said, earning her way through school dancing at a club as I recall." He raised his eyebrows. "All B.S., right?"

She nodded and looked at Katya, who, unconcerned, turned and slid down off her little chair, dragging a parade of naked dolls. She held one lady wrapped modestly in a napkin with sticky, soup-covered fingers. "Mommy, I'm done."

Sofie leaned over, wiped her hands and waited until Katya wandered out of the room before going on. "So that's it. My life's pretty routine, as you've probably noticed. I stay in this neighborhood, have a few friends from the east side, Monica's my one close friend, and then, of course, new customers who wander into the store sometimes." She thought a moment. "Oh, and my Internet customers."

He glanced up sharply from her notes and pushed away the dishes in front of him. "Hell! You have Internet customers, too?"

"Sure. We sell on E-bay and Amazon Z-shops and on a couple of other small bookstore web sites. And we have our own website, of course, but we don't get much direct business from that, except a few people specifically looking for feminist bookstores. Or social activists, since we do some promoting of groups on our web site, too."

"How long have you been doing Internet business?"

"A few years. We started selling a few things on E-bay two or three years ago and then decided to put up our own site." She saw skepticism in his expression. "Look, Jack, it's really no problem. People do it all the time. The number of Internet or stranger stalking incidents is exaggerated, it's really pretty low." She pushed a stray strand of hair off her face. "Anyway, I'm so protected around here and it's impossible to believe anyone I know, or see on a regular basis, is a threat."

"Famous last words. You think you've cornered the marked on safety or something? Or is it you just don't pay attention to the news?"

She kept her eyes on the paper and ignored his sarcasm. "I've thought a lot about this in the last week or so and I don't think whoever's harassing us is a stranger. He knows too much. And I don't think it's about me. I think it's someone who knows you, especially since the man who called mentioned your name."

"How the hell would someone even know Katya existed, when I didn't know?"

"It seems possible someone found out, somehow. The news is always reporting about identity theft. It must be easy to get information on somebody. Someone with the know-how might be able to find even a little piece of information about Katya."

"Did you put my name on the birth certificate?"

"No. I've thought a lot about this. The only places I can think of where I ever mentioned you were times when I needed emergency numbers. Maybe at the hospital when I went in— I'm not sure. I did give the day care center your number, but I told them it was confidential and asked them not to keep it in their records."

"Anywhere else?" He asked tersely.

"No. At least I don't think so. But it is possible the information's out there for someone to find, if they look hard enough." She narrowed her eyes at him. "And since you live in a world where threats are an everyday event, don't you think the most likely thing is that it's someone from your life?"

Jack stood up and strode to the refrigerator to grab another beer. He didn't speak until he opened it and took a swipe. "Sure, there's always a slight chance it's related to me some way. But the odds that someone searching finds information like that is hit and miss. It's way more likely the threat's directly related to your life. Especially since you're in contact with strangers a lot, and you have no idea who the hell they are."

Another of his judgments assigned from on high. She frowned but refused to respond.

"You live in a fantasy world, Sofie, if you think you're in no danger from your customers or the Internet. That store of yours is a public place, a feminist bookstore, for God's sake! There are bound to be weirdoes hanging around just because of the nature of the store. And I suppose you think nothing of having Katya spend time there with you? The idea that your community will protect you is stupid and it's setting you up for a disaster."

"That's a pretty strong indictment of my life when you don't even really know me, Jack. I've done okay for almost thirty years with my stupid muddling along."

He smiled slightly and she knew what was coming. "And you *called* me because?"

"Because I can't take the chance I might be wrong—not with Katya, that's why. It may sound ridiculous to you, but I don't have the kind of life where bad things happen, for whatever reason. But when that man tried to get Katya from her day care, I knew I needed help, especially since the police already had refused to do anything about the calls. You were the only person I could think of who might actually care and could do something about it." She did need his help and hated that she needed him.

"You're living in an illusion, Sofie, if you think some aging Russians, clinging to their past, in the middle of a big city can protect you. Maybe you've been lucky so far, avoiding 'bad things' as you call them, but, Baby, I can tell you it's everywhere. Just by shutting yourself off and saying you don't attract it is foolish, even goddamned stupid!" He sat down and took another swipe at his beer. "Hell, not only do I work every day in that world, it's eaten up my life for the past four years. It's not some fantasy to be gotten rid of by wishful thinking or hiding from life."

His face was drawn with pain and she had to look away. She felt the unfairness of his accusations in her stomach but couldn't blame him for his views. She absorbed the punch and responded more gently. "All right, Jack. Assuming I'm living with danger that I'm unaware of, what should I do next? You're not asking me to stop selling books online are you? I can't give up the E-bay and Z-shop sales. That's where most of our income is right now—until we get the store well known. And as far as the store itself goes, I'm not going to put up a sign saying 'Strangers not welcome'."

She flicked her braid over her shoulder and stood up with that pronouncement to clear away lunch. He didn't answer, but instead reached around her to grab the dishes.

"Let me do them."

"Thanks." She let go of them, turned and began clearing the rest of the things off the table. It was almost three in the afternoon and the midday light was gone, leaving the room cast in shadows. She hadn't turned on the heat yet and shivered in the cold of what used to be her safe, cozy kitchen.

~ * ~

He'd sent someone to talk with Katya's teacher at the day care center but tomorrow he'd call her and set up guidelines for Katya's safety. For now, he sat in Sofie's living room, laptop open on a table, waiting while the duty officer forwarded an email attachment of all incoming calls to Sofie's store and apartment over the past month. He'd also requested a permanent tap be placed on her phones until further notice. Sofie was giving Katya a bath and he could hear the sounds of laughter and splashing water coming from the back of the apartment.

Frustrated with no results, he abandoned his laptop and wandered around the living room. It was dark now and he reached for the switch on a lamp. There were photos everywhere—sitting on the table, hung on the walls—all photos of women—some with a very young Sofie and some with women who looked as though they could have been her twin, but forty years earlier. Her mother, he assumed, her grandmother, her relatives—all living with her every day, watching over her. It gave her life a continuity that was not unfamiliar to him, coming from a large Italian family where everyone kept track of everyone else. Although his family would deny it, he knew he'd been the cause of a break in that trust.

He stared at the room, trying to make sense of the owner through the style of the place. The apartment walls were pale blue, trimmed in a thin gold line circling the entire room just below the ceiling. Three windows looked out on the street and as he watched, the streetlights came on, casting faint blue shadows in the early evening gloom. The world outside to him was just another Detroit street. He'd grown up only a few miles away, but this place was a world away from all he knew.

The room contained rows of shelves filled with books, mostly old and well used. He wandered over and pulled one out, *Lord Peter*. He knew it would be something unfamiliar and he wondered what the hell he was doing in this strange apartment, watching over this woman and her child. He turned and spotted a picture of Katya, dressed in an elf costume, big paper ears stuck to her head. She grinned out of the picture at him, dark eyes like his and Dinah's, and he knew why he was here.

It was after midnight when he closed down his laptop and looked up to see Sofie stepping out of the bathroom into the dark hall. He'd watched her moving around her apartment after

Katya had settled down and eventually he'd heard the shower running.

She looked up at him now and motioned him to follow her into the small bedroom that belonged to Katya and was his to use during his stay. As they passed the larger bedroom, he looked in and spotted Katya sprawled out on Sofie's bed. A faint table light sat by the bed and cast enough light for him to make out teddy bears that dotted the pajamas she wore, twisted around her round body, one dimpled leg exposed. His gaze moved from his daughter to Sofie, her damp hair pulled up in a messy pony tail, the ends falling over the pale skin of her neck and he stared at the spot where her skin met her collar. Without turning to look at him, she pointed towards a dresser and handed him a pile of towels.

"Goodnight, Jack."

"Goodnight." He wanted to say something else, but he could think of nothing.

## *Four*

Jack's cell phone rang as he stepped out of the shower. He made a grab for it, in the process knocking over a bottle of perfume sitting on the counter. It was after midnight and the call was from Central Dispatch, a 10-85, all officers respond to the scene at Poletown Assembly Plant off Mt. Elliott. He rang up the duty officer and was informed five Cadillac SUVs were blown up in the New Vehicle Lot, a possible 10-31, crime in progress. The twelve detectives on the Bomb Squad did an on-call rotation and it was Jack's week. He had to respond.

He pulled on his shorts and jeans with one hand without taking time to towel down and put in a quick call to his backup. First on the scene would secure the area and as highest ranking, Jack was responsible for overseeing the site. With a large crime scene like this, the dispatcher automatically put out a general call to the squad but he dialed Garrison and Karetta to reconfirm.

Bare-chested, he grabbed a towel and stepped out of the bathroom, straight into Sofie.

"What's going on?" Sofie whispered. He had on the same worn jeans and was rubbing at his wet head with one hand, holding his cell phone in the other. "I just got the call—yeah, the Poletown site." He spotted her as he turned, still talking into his phone. "I need someone to back me up for a couple of hours—yeah—2115 Mt. Elliot, a bookstore and residence..." His voice trailed off as he listened to someone respond.

She pulled her eyes away from the droplets of water running off his chest and waited for him to finish his call.

"Yeah, right. The party is Sofie Novakoff. And her daughter. I should be gone about two hours or so. " He kept rubbing his head, watching her. "Stalking—across the street is fine. Just make sure you get a good view of the alley adjacent— Yeah, okay. You've got my pager number. Thanks, Tony. I owe you."

She followed him into the living room where he grabbed up his abandoned sweatshirt. "What's happening?" She asked.

"I'm on call. I've gotta go. I should be back in about two hours, but I've set up someone, an off-duty cop, to watch this place. His name's Tony Lubchek. He'll sit out front in his squad car till I get back. If anything happens, anything at all, you get any weird calls or anything unexpected, call him. I'll leave the number for you." He pulled out a notebook and scribbled something on it. "Don't let anyone in! But answer the phone if it rings. I may call to see that you're okay." He didn't wait for an answer, grabbed his holster and leather bomber jacket and headed down the stairs. He yelled, "Lock the door!" over his shoulder and left.

Sofie stood staring at the bottom of the stairs for long minutes and finally wandered to the window. The rain added to the misery and isolation she felt when the door slammed shut behind him. The heat had been turned on hours ago, but was the apartment was still cold and she wrapped her arms around her body and shivered.

Jack's Cherokee pulled away as the squad car drove up. All the lights were out and the car sat dark, nothing moving, except a period flick of ash onto wet pavement from a pale hand that emerged from a window.

Restless, feeling a desperate need to talk to someone, she headed to the kitchen, pulled out the rest of the kulebiak and grabbed a cold beer. She backtracked to her room, checked to be sure Katya was asleep, and headed down the stairs, throwing her raincoat over her shoulders as she maneuvered out the door.

Outside, she stopped. The overhead light was out, leaving the alley in complete darkness. She pulled the door tightly closed behind her and checked to be sure it was locked. Taking a quick deep breath, she set off at a run towards the street.

She watched the taillights of a car disappear around the corner, leaving Mt. Elliott deserted except for the lone squad car. Stuck in the middle of Detroit, the neighborhood still had a small town feel after dark when her neighbors sought the safety of their homes, most of them in bed by ten.

Sofie darted across the street to the darkened car. She pounded on the window with a fist, juggling the beer and food. "Hi! I thought you might be hungry so I brought you something."

The window came down slowly, and a homely, twisted face looked up at her. "What the hell you think you're up to?"

"I'm Sofie, Sofie Novakoff, Jack's friend. He sent you to keep an eye on us, right?"

The man fit her pictures of an undercover cop, in beige car coat, pulling on the cigarette dangling from his lips. "Yeah, and like I said, what the hell you think you're doin' wandering around the street?"

She held out the bag and beer to him. "I brought you some food." She felt completely stupid. He obviously wasn't hungry and didn't care to have a conversation. And she sure as hell shouldn't be running out here, leaving her sleeping child alone inside. It was the kind of thing that would only reaffirm Jack's opinion of her, both as a person and a mother.

He sighed, rubbed his face and worked unsuccessfully to hide a grin. "So you're Jack's lady, huh? Well, sure. I guess I could use something to eat. Jack called before my nightly pizza delivery showed up." He reached out and took the bag, but hesitated before taking the beer. He opened the sack, took a whiff. "That smells great! Piroghis, right?"

She shook her head. "Kulebiak. My neighbor makes it. Russian." She pointed to the darkened bakery.

"I really shouldn't be drinking, you know, sort of on duty like, but I guess since it's a gift, I can make an exception."

"Jack said you were off duty tonight."

"Yeah, but Jack'd shit a brick if he knew I'd touched anything while I'm on stake-out." He smiled broadly and stuck out a hand, a huge claw that engulfed her fingers, but squeezed her hand gently. "Tony Lubchek. Glad to meet you." He took a bite of pastry. "So, how'd you meet Jack? He's not one for socializing much." He shrugged. "Except casual-like, you know?"

Sofie frowned. Yeah, she knew, or could easily guess. Jack liked his women a night at a time, only. Beyond that, he wouldn't bother. But what in the heck had Jack told this guy to get him out here so late, sitting in the rain? "We met a few years back and I was in some trouble, so I called him."

A car came past and she stepped closer to the squad car. "I need to get right back. My daughter's upstairs sleeping. I just thought maybe you'd be hungry out here. And I wanted to thank you. It's nice of you to do this on your time off." She stopped. Jack would hate any attempt she made to get friendly with his fellow cops.

"You left your kid inside by herself? You locked your door, right, when you came out?"

"Of course. The neighborhood is pretty safe, generally." She nodded but glanced back at the entrance to the alley. "I'd better go. Thanks for sitting out here and watching out for us."

Another car approached as she crossed the street, slowed and moved on. She couldn't see the driver and didn't recognize the vehicle.

The glare from the street made the alley seem darker but she forgot her fear in a rush to get back to Katya. Groping her way to her door, she reached out to feel for the lock. The sound stopped her momentarily. It came from a short distance behind her, causing her fingers to tighten around her keys as she listened. It was a raspy sort of noise, like someone had been running. The alley extended beyond her building and opened behind her store in a Y, onto another alley. It was all in complete darkness now, every light extinguished—the bakery light, the back alley light and her own above the door. She held her breath, waiting, debating whether to grapple with her lock or race back to the street and the safety of Tony Lubchek.

The thought of Katya, asleep upstairs, alone, decided her. She found the lock with her key and pushed the door open quickly, her heart pounding. Thank God, she'd left the stairwell light on and the apartment door open, allowing faint light to shine down from the kitchen. She panted as she took the steps two at a time, made for the open door and turned to slam it shut against whatever threat, real or imagined, lurked in the alley.

~ * ~

Jack had the siren and flasher on before he hit the freeway. As he drove, he grabbed his back-up .38 and reached over to lock it the glove compartment of his Jeep. He'd already put out a 2040 for the Roving Inspector. Arnold McMillan was a tough-as-nails cop who answered only to the Chief of Police. He'd expect to be called in as advisor on a blast of this size.

They'd had six major unsolved bombings in the past four years. Since 9/11 the focus around all bomb attacks had shifted from drug-related to international terrorism, with Canada only a bridge or tunnel away, and the large Arab community in nearby Dearborn. The other bombings had been random, the only link between them the fact that they all had something to do with cars. And this one fit the pattern: brand new SUVs. While the thinking was mostly around foreign threat, Jack wasn't convinced they were dealing with international terrorism.

Arnold McMillan didn't see it that way, but he'd defer to Jack, as sergeant and lead detective on this crime scene. It was Jack's show; he'd own it, give all the orders, call the shots.

Jack always wanted to be a cop and it had to be the Detroit Police Force or none; it was nothing fancy, just tough cops doing a hard job. Four years ago and ten years on the Force, he'd made sergeant on the Bomb Squad, something he'd coveted. Two months later, Dinah died and he began questioning the choices he'd made—not enough to quit, but just enough to be eaten up by self-doubt and guilt. It had been four years of hell.

He was sure the car bomb that killed Dinah was meant for him. He'd been working a case involving an auto executive's upscale house on East Jefferson and they had no leads. Dinah's murder was still unsolved and after four years, the case was stone cold.

The proximity of Detroit to Canada, the large population of Shiite Muslims in adjacent Dearborn, the importance of the automotive industry to the American economy, all these factors pointed to international terrorism, but Jack was skeptical.

He tracked communications as he drove the two miles to the site, trying to keep his thoughts away from Sofie and Katya, trying not to worry. Sofie was an enigma to him. He wanted to follow his instincts and treat her like a loose canon, with her crazy notions about family and her liberal do-gooder ideas. But there was something else about her that confounded him. She talked a good game as an independent woman, but it was at odds with something fragile and helpless about her and it drove him crazy. He liked his women aloof, but available, up front about their needs and not afraid to demand what they wanted from him. And then there was Katya.

It was 12:13 when he reached the New Vehicle Lot entrance. Squad cars were scattered along Mt. Elliott and inside the outer parking area, near the guard tower at the factory entrance. The fifteen-foot-tall fluorescent lights in the parking lot made it as bright as day, illuminating the broken fence roped off with CSI tape.

An EMS was sitting beside the gate and Jack pulled his car off to one side behind an unmarked PD car, opened his trunk and grabbed his orange jumpsuit and bomb kit. Beyond the fence, his team had already set up police spotlights that shone on pieces of what had once been SUVs, strewn over a wide area. The charred and twisted metal was surreal and out of place beside the shiny, untouched Cadillacs nearby. The bomb had been powerful enough to destroy five SUVs.

McMillan was already there, feet widespread, head up, teeth bared, reminding Roselli of a black bulldog yanking at its tethered chain. He was past fifty now, had started as a street cop and been promoted through the ranks to Inspector, second in line only to the Chief of Police.

"Roselli! Where in the hell have you been?" He yelled, barely nodding in Jack's direction.

"Glad to see you here, Inspector." Jack jerked his head towards the EMS loading a victim. "Looks like they're getting braver, doesn't it?" Each bombing had gotten a little wider in scope; Dinah had been the only fatality to date, but tonight they'd fucked up again.

"The night watchman. A retired cop, seventy-five years old, a grandfather." McMillan spit out the words. "Making his rounds. He's alive—just. Lucky he was caught on the other side of the fence. If he'd been ten feet closer, we'd be picking up pieces of him with the frags."

They stood together behind the eight-foot barrier fence with two more uniforms and Mike Karetta, another member of the Bomb Squad. The entry fence was bent down with sections twisted at odd angles above their heads, probably broken in a hurried exit, once the charge was set.

"Looks like your standard electrical fuse, hooked to det cord. Probably used a blasting cap and some sort of battery-driven receptor. We already found the receiver—a garage door opener, about fifteen feet back, over there." Karetta pointed behind them.

It had been triggered from some place within a fifty- to a hundred-foot perimeter. It would have to wait for a lab analysis to get the type of explosive, but any residue sampling would only happen after the Tech Team finished photographing and laying out the grid over the scene.

Jack pulled two uniforms aside, gave them instructions to search the abandoned eight-story building across Mt. Elliott and get some panoramic photos while they were there.

He put a quick call into Dispatch for a helicopter to take aerial shots using a night lens. From the lay of the det cord, he already knew it was probably some type of plastics. The type would give them some information, but since 9/11, Semtex, the plastic explosive material favored overseas, was as available in this country as C4, the American-made stuff.

ATF was automatically notified by Central with any large scale bombing and would do the residue analysis faster at the national lab than it could be done through the local crime lab at 2600 Brush. Once his team gathered the samples, they'd air express it and within twenty-four to forty-eight hours they'd have results back. Given the extent of damage, there'd be no samples taken until sometime late tomorrow.

Jack stepped over broken fencing and worked his way through debris to what was left of the SUVs: five charred skeletal chassis, with det cord still lying beneath them, almost pristine, running from the central cord with separate tracks. He noted some of the surrounding vans had dents and broken windows but many vehicles looked untouched.

McMillan followed and watched as the uniform first at the scene pointed out "Save the Earth" spray painted on a slightly damaged SUV that sat fifty yards behind the smoldering vehicles.

It took an hour and a half for Jack to make the rounds, interviewing the first on the scene, talking with the photo and surveillance people and setting up teams to scour the surrounding neighborhood for witnesses.

Jack zipped up his jacket inside his jumpsuit against the cold wind that blew through the immense parking lot and waited for McMillan's thoughts. "Whatta think? Any similarities to the Auburn car bombing?"

Jack shook his head. "The extent of explosive power looks similar," he said. "But the signature raises lots of questions."

"Yeah, too pat," McMillan mumbled. "Makes life too easy. Well, hell. Our friends are gonna be showing up any moment."

No city cop wanted the FBI's interference but, since 9/11, they made their presence known at every bombing, especially anything that shouted terrorism like this site.

McMillan pushed his hands deep into his pockets, and threw back his head in defiance of the wind. The photo team walked past, shoulders hunched, pushing cameras into bags. "You through?" McMillan barked.

"Naw, the fingerprint guys are still there photographing." The voice coming out of the parka hood was young and high, of indeterminate sex.

McMillan frowned at the sloppy reply, a fresh kid with no respect, but he let it pass.

Jack had spent three months in DC training for the Special Teams Bomb detail. He'd seen them all, the standard home-made, garden variety bombs, fertilizer bombs, like the one used in Oklahoma City. And then of course, there were the sophisticated devices that cried out international terrorism, usually made with products purchased or stolen from the military or their suppliers.

The problem with the four cases, now five, they'd been working over the past four years was that the majority of them looked amateur, drawing suspicion away from any organized terrorist group. Tonight's bombing looked like a chemical fuse or maybe electrical, both effective when used with one-hour delays, giving the perps plenty of time to get in and out, past the security guard. The four unsolved bombings had been with basic pipe bombs, crude but effective, destroying a small fishing cottage of a Ford executive on Lake Orion, the garage of an advertising agent from Auburn Hills, and a failed attempt to blow up an auto VP's car.

On the other hand, the bomb that killed Dinah had used an ignition fuse, set to go off the second the car was started. She'd been playing a prank on Jack, probably meaning to take his car for a joy ride and leave it parked at their parents. He'd been on the night shift and had been asleep inside his place when he was awakened by the explosion.

He didn't see the connection with this. The simplicity of the pipe bombings pointed away from the more sophisticated electric- or chemical-fused type of bomb used tonight. And the bomb that killed Dinah had used an ignition fuse. And then there was the graffiti. It raised new questions that were hard to answer, since ecoterrorism hadn't been a local concern in the past four years. There were no cells that he knew of closer than the UP of Michigan or southern Indiana.

The bombs ranged in size from fifty to one hundred fifty pounds, big enough to blow up a small house or five SUVs; nothing larger had been used to date. The ambivalent signature of the bombings had left the Bomb Squad nervously juggling multiple theories, hinting at international terrorism, but no leads—until tonight.

Jack pulled a cigarette from a crumpled pack of Camels, cradled it in his fist for a few moments and lit up. He stood staring into the pile of blackened metal on the other side of the fence, thinking about Dinah. After she'd been killed, he had come close to chucking in his law enforcement career and heading back to school permanently. In his undergrad years, he'd briefly toyed with the idea of going into law, but the enforcement side of justice was in his blood and called too loudly to him. His father had been a beat cop, his dad's brother a detective, and two of his younger brothers were cops, one in the Academy now.

"Roselli, anything you see?" He could hear the rare patience McMillan granted him and knew he was being given more space to maneuver, because of Dinah, even after four years. He'd also been granted priority clearance and consultant status on all statewide bombings as part of his caseload.

"My gut feeling says it's gotta be a group this time, too many details for a damned Unabomber."

McMillan nodded but didn't speak.

"Anything else I should know about this, Arnie?"

McMillan looked at him a moment before stepping closer and leaning forward. "It was called into Central about nine tonight, the bomb threat—no time or place given, no way to trace the call."

Jack turned and stared at his boss. "Any mention of responsibility?"

His nod was barely perceptible inside the parka drawn up around his face. "They said one word: CUR—Coalition of Urban Responders. Mean anything to you?"

Jack's thoughts slid over various terrorist groups, ranging from survivalists to religious but came up with nothing. "Never heard the term before. Anything in our databases or the web?"

"We're checking it out. I've heard it once before, the buzz on it was a small sub-cell of Earth Liberation Front. You'll find whatever we dig up on your desk in the morning, Roselli."

Jack sucked in his breath sharply. *Hell, not now, with Katya!* "Yes, sir." He did some fast calculations. "Inspector, I have a situation, personal, that I'm dealing with right now."

He filled McMillan in on the background of Katya's stalking, leaving out details about his relationship with Sofie. "The little girl is my daughter. I'd appreciate it if you kept it under your hat, Arnie."

"Christ, Roselli. You never mentioned you had a kid!"

Jack scanned the darkened lot beyond the crime scene lights and shrugged. "She just reappeared in my life—her mother called me a couple of days ago. Worried about threats she'd received."

"Shit, Jack. So what do you need? Backup? I don't have any extra men right now. The best I can do is assign an extra beat cop to watch the neighborhood. Where does she live?"

"Near Six Mile and Mt Elliott. The Russian area."

"Well, I can probably give you Mac for a few hours here and there, if you need drudge work." Mac was desk clerk upstairs at Central Precinct. "Listen, I'll make sure it doesn't go any farther than him."

"Thanks, Arn. I appreciate it." He knew McMillan was being generous on this, Dinah's death again. That, and his family's history with the Force. "I took the liberty of asking Tony Lubchek to sit watch tonight, but I'll take any help I can get."

"So you're camping out at the kid's house right now?"

"Yeah."

"Well, get the fuck out of here now. We're just about done for the night, but I wanna see you on this first thing in the morning. I'll have Karetta dump everything we get tonight on your desk, along with the other stuff." McMillan turned back to the scene.

Jack pulled his jumpsuit closer, staring at what had been five, family dream vacation vehicles. He shuddered and tried to push away the image of what was left of Dinah, lying in the rubble. He'd gotten there before they could push him back and the image was burned into his brain forever. The image was replaced by one of Katya, running to climb into his Jeep this morning. He cursed and turned to leave. There was nothing to be done until the evidence team finished up here.

It was past two before Jack got back to Sofie's and after three by the time he got to bed. Sofie had moved Katya in with her, leaving him the smaller room. He lay on the narrow bed, the octopus lamp throwing out changing patterns on the ceiling. The bed was two feet too short, leaving his bare legs sticking off the end. It was too hot now in the apartment and he tossed aside the Pooh Bear quilt and lay in his shorts, legs and chest bare.

It wasn't the bombing that was keeping him awake; it was Katya. He had nothing so far on the stalker—no traces on any calls, nothing unusual reported from friends or neighbors, and no sign of strangers, other than customers to the bookstore. He had nothing but the word of a woman who had kept his daughter a secret and he didn't trust her motives. Even the day care teacher was vague, no clear description or even a clear memory of exactly what the man had said.

In the past three days his life had been turned inside out, as though he'd been driving along a broad highway and someone had jumped out and flashed him a detour sign that led off into a wilderness.

But with all that, there was Katya. However much he suspected Sofie was up to something, he knew Katya was his. He looked around the room at the treasures of a three year old and smiled as he fell asleep.

## *Five*

Sofie's life was arranged carefully around Katya and the bookstore. She planned her work activities—the book fairs, auctions, garage sales, anywhere books were to be found—around Katya, but often included Monica and Chrissie as well. She worked tirelessly with Monica to improve the image of their store, and it might have gone under in the first year but for their more lucrative Internet book business. But the bookstore itself was Sofie's real love and when necessary, when things got really tough, she was willing to clean houses to keep her business together.

Her life was consumed with her daughter and her business, broken up very infrequently with a rare friend or two from grad school, usually single women with small children in similar circumstances. Except for Monica prodding her, for the most part Sofie did not date or even allow herself to think about men. Her memories of Jack were vague and romantic, but shrouded in danger. The real Jack was too real and too demanding to fit her fantasies and all she could do was grit her teeth and hope to survive his intrusion.

~ * ~

Jack moaned as he rolled off the small bed and checked the time, ten o'clock. He was due at the Precinct at noon. He wandered out into the hall and was greeted with silence. He showered, dressed quickly and sprinted down the back stairs to the bookstore.

Sofie sat at a small table, between a woman and her shopping cart, pouring coffee into dainty china cups. Two more people sat in armchairs nearby, all of them dirty and obviously homeless. *Christ! Here she is inviting every vagrant from the street in to make himself at home while some nutcase is stalking our daughter.*

The coffee bar sat in the back part of the store, within view of the front, and he ambled over to grab some coffee. He glanced down at the counter and spotted a stack of bumper stickers that said "Question Gender." *What the hell does that mean?* He watched Sofie waiting on the disheveled woman with the shopping cart, smiling benevolently and nodding at her, as though she were serving the Queen of England. Her hair was pulled back in some sort of top knot and she wore her usual sweats. She glanced over, the look she gave him one of defiance mixed with gratitude, and as usual, her appearance and her attitude both confused and annoyed him. Why the hell did she have to dress like she could care less what anyone thought of her and be so goddamned sexy?

Sofie bent over and said something to the older woman, stood up and came back to where he stood. She eased the carafe back onto the hot pad beside him and moved papers away from the counter. "I thought you wanted to sleep late today," she said conversationally and motioned to a small white cup sitting on the counter. "Want some?"

He nodded. "Where's Katya?"

"Day care—Tuesdays, Thursdays and Fridays at 8:30. I took her. I was careful and I made sure they understood the instructions you laid out for them. That she isn't to leave for any reason unless I'm there to get her and that anyone showing up other than me or you, they call one of us. I gave them your cell number and your pager." She hesitated. "We agreed, right, that she'd be safe there for now?"

He pulled out his cell phone. "It's over on Chalmers, isn't it? What's the street address?" She gave it to him and watched as he relayed it to someone.

"What are you doing?"

"I'm sending some backup to make sure the place is secure." He hesitated. "One of my brothers—he's a cop." He motioned towards a booth. "You have a minute to sit down and talk?"

He took his cup and followed her to a booth that had a good view of the room. He made a sweeping gesture towards the three people sitting two booths away. "To start with, what's all this?"

"You mean my customers?" She asked.

"They're customers?"

"You think I should be more careful about the people who come into the bookstore, right?"

"Not just in the bookstore, everywhere you go. You're worried enough to call me in to protect her, but think nothing of exposing her to anyone and everyone who waltzes in off the street." His words echoed in the quiet store and he cursed himself for the ridiculous situation he'd been put in.

"Jack, most of these people have been around the neighborhood most of my life. We get a few strangers each day,

69

but for the most part the people who come to my store are a part of my life—and Katya's. I can't just ignore them."

"I thought this was a woman's bookstore. Why in the hell are those two men sitting over there?" He gestured towards a table where two unshaven men sat quietly eating cookies.

She shrugged. "Some men actually like women's writing, you know."

He rubbed his face, feeling stupid. Not only now was he a cop, but a sexist one in her view. "Look, I'm gonna need to do some checking on your regular customers, you know, as well as your friends and neighbors." He juggled the little china cup, trying to take a sip without spilling liquid down his clean t-shirt. "How many people do you get in here each day coming in for handouts? Not your buying customers."

"The homeless ones? Probably two or three, some days more, depending on the weather. Most of them I know, a few are just passing through. They usually rotate, every couple of days different people. They all have their regular stops, places they're welcome to sit a while. I'm on their route. They like the predictability of being able to have some place to go mornings after the shelter closes and before the center opens."

He rubbed his face with a hand, trying hard to tone it down. "Sofie, the people you know are one thing. We can at least check on them. But you're so casual about the strangers who wander into this place. When she's not at day care, she spends most of her time here at the store, right?"

"Jack, look. She's been spending time here all of her life. I can't refuse to let people into the store if I don't know them or they look less than respectable. And I can't suddenly refuse to let Katya be down here. It would upset her. These people don't have the means or the interest to threaten us, they're just trying to survive."

"So do you know their names? Or what they do? What do you know about any of them?"

She shook her head, frowning. "I know a few of their names—mostly first names. I wouldn't intrude on their privacy by asking for information they don't want to give."

He was angry with her but at the same time, oddly moved by her, and irritated with himself for feeling either of those things. He didn't want to care about her, one way or the other. She was Katya's mother and that was all. He reached up automatically, about to brush a strand of hair away from her face, but pulled back instead, and she blinked up at him. *Shit,* he thought, *now I'm touching her.* He liked women who touched him. He sure as hell had no interest in a woman who didn't want or need men. Or, even worse, a woman who seemed to need him too much. He wasn't sure which of those two categories she fell into, probably both, he decided, and stood up abruptly. "We've gotta come to some agreements around here, Sofie, about the security issue."

Sofie stood up as well, nodded absently, and turned casually to talk with a middle-aged woman in a heavy man's coat, striding up to the counter.

When the woman had gotten her coffee and gone to a table, Sofie turned back to Jack, who frowned at her. "Well? That woman you were talking with, what's her story?"

"Her name's Mary DeVault. She has a Master's Degree from Earlham College, in Indiana. She was a writer for the

Detroit Free Press for a while, doing a city news column. Five years ago she lost her job, her husband left her, her son had died five years before that in the Gulf War. She's basically alone. She lives at the Shelter, but spends her days at the Center, talking with people. She's got a lot of ideas for promoting the bookstore and I like her." She delivered the litany as a challenge.

"You like everyone." He stopped. "Except maybe me." His words sounded like a backhanded attempt to get a compliment but they came out before he could stop them.

"Is that bad? I don't see anything wrong with that." She stood up again. "And I don't dislike you. Would you like some more coffee, Jack?"

He suppressed an urge to reach across and shake her. "No, not now. And sit down! Listen, Sofie. Either we do this my way or not at all. You've got to make some changes around here with your security. At least until we get this thing resolved."

"Okay, then, tell me what you need me to do."

"First, for now its best if you're not alone in the store with strangers. If you're going to have people wandering around, I'll come down when I can or maybe your business partner?"

"That's crazy! I can't call you or Monica in every time someone I don't know comes in. You have to work and Monica and I have our schedules synchronized."

"Isn't there anyone else you can get in—some high school kid, to do stocking or something? Just to have someone here with you."

She shook her head. "Jack, I really can't afford to do that. Chrissie, Monica's daughter, is here a lot with Katya when she gets home from school, but I don't have anyone else."

"I'll pay for it—just get some neighborhood kid to be here with you. How much can it cost? Minimum wage, right?"

"I can't allow you to do that. You don't have the money to shell out for me."

"It's no problem. At least it'll save me from going nuts when I'm at work, thinking about no one here with you and Katya." He finished his coffee. "So can you get someone for backup today? I'm on call and I need to get into the Precinct in about an hour."

"You were called out late last night." She said it as a question.

"Yeah, Poletown. It probably made the morning news—some idiots blew up some SUVs." He checked his watch. He needed to stop by the Crime Lab to pick up the preliminary frag reports before noon.

The comings and goings of a Bomb Squad cop was a mystery Sofie didn't want to pursue. "I'll call and see if I can get someone to keep me company. Mr. Belady's son usually helps out at the grocery. He's sixteen—a high school drop out. I can probably get him—at least for today. Will that work?"

He reached into his jacket and pulled out his cell. "Gimme a break and call him now, okay? And ask him if he can be available on a regular basis. Even if you feel it's a waste of my money, it'd give me a little piece of mind."

She took the phone and went over to a counter to search for the number. He watched as she talked on the phone, smiling, then looked back over at him and nodded her head. She was pleased with herself.

"His name is Peter Belady. He can come. I told him it would be for a couple of hours, sometimes less. I thought it might be best if he's here nights when we're open. During the day there are so many people walking past, I don't think it's a problem. I usually work Mondays, Wednesdays, and Fridays with alternating Saturdays. Okay?"

Jack nodded and took back his phone. "I need to get going. You can reach me at my Brush Street office or on my cell." He pulled out a notepad and jotted down his numbers for her. "I'll probably be gone today at least five hours, maybe more. I'll try and swing back by here. I'm going to set up things at work so that I can do most of my paperwork from here on my laptop."

"Thanks, Jack."

"While I'm gone, can you see if you can get any information on your customers? Especially the strangers. You don't have to be obvious—just ask some questions, okay?"

She nodded.

"If you really want to know a lot about these people, the kindest thing might be for you to have someone talk to the people at the Shelter or the Center. They know everyone." She took his coffee cup and watched as he zipped up his jacket. "Jack, listen, really, these people are fine. If anything, think of them acting like Katya's watchdogs. They care about us, just like we care about them. If anything threatened Katya, they'd be the first ones to help out."

He looked down at her, conscious suddenly of how much shorter she was than him. "All right. I'll have someone make a couple of calls to the Center and the Shelter later today. Will that suit you? You don't have to disturb them here."

"Do you want to take some coffee with you?" She held his cup out to him.

"No, thanks. That cup wouldn't even survive the drive to work."

"I've got some take-out cups stashed under the counter." As she bent over, the back of her sweats slipped down, exposing a dimple, causing a sudden tightness in his groin. He waited as she poured his coffee, saying nothing.

"What time did you say you have to be at work?" Sofie asked.

"Dammit! In about ten minutes! I need to go. When's that kid coming over?"

"He said he'd be here in thirty minutes. I'll be fine until then."

He scanned the room as two more women came into the store. "All right, but make sure someone you know is here always, okay? I've set up some backup and from now on, whenever I'm on call, someone will be watching the place. Don't be alarmed if you see a squad car sitting outside when I'm gone."

She nodded and took a sip of coffee. "I met him last night, your friend, Tony. He was sitting outside in the squad car and I brought him something to eat after you left."

He stared at her, speechless.

"Jack, I want you to know how much I appreciate all you're doing. I know all this has completely disrupted your life and I'm sorry."

"What the hell did you think I would do? She's my kid."

She reddened. "Of course. But thanks, anyway."

"Sorry. This is difficult for both of us."

*God,* he thought, *how in the hell had she gotten through life this far?* She was clueless, a bleeding heart liberal who loved the notion of good deeds—and a walking invitation to danger.

He turned back again, juggling the paper cup. "I'll need to go with you later today when you pick Katya up at day care. To give them the heads up from you that I'm okay to pick her up, if need be. What time does she get out?"

She wrote it down for him and he felt her watching him swagger out the door.

When he wasn't out at a crime scene, his place of work was the 1500 Brush Street Building, where he usually struggled through mounds of paperwork. The balance of his job involved either ballistics matches at the firing range or attending autopsies. And once a month he lectured on bomb squad procedure at Oakland, Detroit or Macomb police academies. Today, he was going to spend tedious hours going over the CSI data from last night.

He waded through four hours of data and was cutting it close to get to the day care center by 4:30. Sorting through the reports was mind-numbing, rifling through the pages and pages of measurements and statistics required for police work documentation these days. He got himself cleared to work from Sofie's over the next few days, shuffled the balance of his papers together into a briefcase and set off for East Gratiot, the wind whipping around the Cherokee like a toy.

The day care center was on Seven Mile and Beckham, both roads heavy with traffic at this time of day. Jack double parked in front of the Center, set his light atop the Jeep and climbed out to look for Sofie. She stood inside the door, searching the street, and he caught her eye as he jogged up the steps.

They spent some time signing the necessary papers for Jack to pick up Katya when necessary and were the last to leave the

Center. Jack followed Sofie's dented Honda back to the bookstore and waited as she parked in a small space in the alley.

Monica sat at a counter reading and looked up when they came through the back door. Sofie waved at her as she and Katya headed upstairs. Jack headed for Monica.

She looked a little older than Sofie, mid-thirties maybe, average height, stocky in build, but leaning more to voluptuous than overweight. Her dark hair was styled and she was attractive in a silk shirt and snug-fitting pants.

Jack held out a hand. "I'm Jack Roselli." He waited, wondering how much information Sofie had given her.

"I know. Sofie told me about you." She smiled at him. "Want some coffee or a bagel? Just brought a bag in, fresh."

He nodded and she poured two coffees, handed him a cup and the bag of bagels. "You know why I'm here, then?" She nodded, but said nothing. "You and Sofie have known each other a long time?"

Monica took a bite of bagel before answering. "About six years. I met her in grad school. Then her grandmother got sick so she finished her course work, sort of hit and miss. Then her mother suddenly died. We became business partners around that time. She finally got her degree right around the time Katya was born. And we were going into business. Believe me, it wasn't easy for her, with her mom dying, pregnant, starting a business and her classes." She squinted at him. "Is this just idle conversation or part of a background check on everyone hanging around?"

"Both. So, how much do you know about the situation?"

"Well, at first Sofie just hinted at being harassed. But today she gave me the lowdown on the business with Katya." She grimaced. "And you're checking out all her acquaintances, right?"

Jack looked around the nearly empty store. "Right now, I'd say I'm more concerned about her customers than her friends." He gestured towards three disheveled looking men, each carrying a bundle, heading out the door. "Is the social club happening here her idea or yours?"

"Oh, that. I suppose it's Sofie's. She likes to take care of people. She's always been like that. In class, she was always coming to the rescue of some student, offering to take notes or tutor him, things like that. But don't get me wrong. She's not neurotic about it or anything. She thinks people should help each other out, especially women. It's natural to her, coming from her background."

She paused, and when he didn't speak, went on. "She hasn't told me the whole story, though. I mean, what's between you and her. But it's hard to ignore what's in front of my face. You're Katya's father, right?"

"Yeah." His tone was neutral, offering nothing more.

"How serious is this stuff that's happening?"

"There's always danger when someone is being stalked. We're not taking any chances right now, that's all. I'm going to be around until I'm sure Katya's safe."

"Well, if you're thinking it might be one of the regulars from here at the bookstore, I don't get it. Some of them may be poorly adjusted, socially that is, but I've never seen anyone show any weird attention to Katya. And Sofie isn't the kind of person to draw a predator to her. She may be generous but she's not stupid. She's nobody's pawn." She paused again. "I'd say your life style fits more with the predator scenario."

"What in the hell does that mean? I didn't even know she was mine until three days ago and unless Sofie's lying, no one else knows she's mine either."

"You're pretty suspicious, aren't you? Even for a cop." Monica refused to back down. "She hasn't told anyone, as far as I know. She never even told me who Katya's father was, and I'm her closest friend. I just think maybe it's too easy to blame Sofie's lifestyle. She's gone through a lot in the past four years but she grew up normal, you know? Nice people, nicer than most, a mother and grandmother who worshipped her. She doesn't have enemies."

He let it go. Obviously, he wasn't going to get any place with Monica. If there was anything Sofie was hiding, Monica wasn't going to tell him.

~ * ~

The sky had turned gray and it had gotten colder, too cold to sit outside much longer. The three of them had gone in over two hours ago. The little girl, the woman and Jack. It was important to go slowly, the pleasure of tormenting him, making him suffer, making him wonder what might be coming—or not. Go slowly, draw out the game, play until there was nothing left to wring from it. Show them the danger, withdraw it, then show it again, and again. More pain, more suffering.

It was working. Jack was in the net now, struggling, trying to get away, but unable to leave. It showed on his face. The woman was pretty, in a low-key sort of way, too pretty. She and her daughter—and Jack. And then there was Jack's job—an open door, easy to maneuver, easy to use. Jack would be punished.

It would be nice to go into the bookstore, to talk to the woman and his child, maybe become friends. But not yet.

## *Six*

Wednesday was Sofie's day off and Katya stayed home from day care. Jack spent an hour and a half at the Precinct, gathered up everything he needed and headed back to work at the apartment.

He walked in to find Sofie doing dishes with Katya chattering away at the kitchen table. She clutched the doll he'd given her to her small chest and the sight of it made his throat constrict. He turned away, preoccupied with shedding his jacket and holster.

"Jack, look. I made a dress for Suni!" She handed him the doll and he took it, conscious of the trust in her smile. *Thank God she didn't inherit my disposition.* But then, probably at one time he'd been like her, full of love and trust, instead of the cautious, disillusioned man he'd become.

"Did you make this?"

He turned the doll over in his hands and examined the material she'd wrapped around the doll. She'd hung things with safety pins from the doll's clothes, his keys being the major ornament. "Where'd you find those?"

"Your coat. I was lookin' for gum. Was I bad?"

"No, honey, but next time ask me and I'll look for you, okay You know, Katya, I'm gonna need these."

She didn't look offended, but merely took back the doll and removed the keys. "Okay. I wanted something nice of yours for her dress."

He reached into his pocket and finding nothing worthy, reached for his wallet and pulled out things until he found a picture of himself at 18 with all his brothers. "Will this do? It's not very sturdy but if you're careful, it should last a while."

She took the picture in her small hands, studied it and gave it back. "Okay."

She watched him turn the doll over on its back, unfasten a safety pin and pin the picture flat to the material. He gave the doll back to Katya, caught her small face in his hands, bent down and brushed his lips over her forehead. She smelled of baby powder and flowers. He looked up and found Sofie, watching, coat in hand, face unreadable.

"You going out?" he asked.

"Katya and I need to do shopping this morning. Just on the street here, not far. This afternoon, we're going go-carting, remember?"

"Oh yeah." *Another crazy scheme of Sofie's.* He'd discussed it with her briefly and loudly yesterday. When Katya joined in with her own pleas, he gave in. "I'll get my jacket." He picked up his shoulder holster and slid it on, eyes fixed on Katya, then pulled on his jacket.

They walked the street like a normal family, Katya holding Sofie's hand. Within a few steps, she grabbed Jack's hand as well and swung along, humming to herself. The picture was so incongruous and out of step with his normal life. As they strolled along, he scanned the street, their blond heads standing out too much for him to relax.

The bakery must have been a normal stop since Katya expectantly stood in line and received a bear-shaped pastry from a beaming old lady. He watched her politely thank the woman who, in turn, reached down and patted Katya on the head.

From the bakery, they moved on to the butcher's, the fish store, a small produce market and finally the drug store. At each stop, Jack watched in astonishment as Sofie was greeted by name and Katya given hugs and kisses which she accepted without argument. She trotted along beside him, trying to keep up with his long strides. He looked down at her and sighed. He knew he'd had it; no matter what happened, there was no way he could go back to life without her.

They'd finished all their errands and loaded down with bags, the three of them strolled towards the bookstore when it happened. Despite the cold weather, Katya had begged for an ice cream cone and she dragged behind, holding her ice cream high to keep from dripping onto Suni's dress.

Without warning, Katya stopped, pulled her hand from Jack's and reached down for Suni at the curbside, where she'd fallen from Katya's sticky fingers. The bicycler was coming fast and hit the doll seconds before Katya could grab her, tossing it into the air and out into the street.

Without pausing, Katya stepped off the curb. The car was coming slow, but too fast for the busy street. It happened in slow motion, Katya's small voice crying 'Suni,' Sofie's horrified shout. The car served at the last instant, just as Jack reached Katya and yanked her up hard by her arms, away from the car. The screeching of tires were followed by a moment of eerie silence, everyone immobilized as though fixed in time, the doll still lying, torn and dirty on the street.

Katya began to cry and Jack hugged her against his chest. "Suni! Suni!" she sobbed.

"Katya, oh God, Katya," Sofie cried, rushing to her daughter.

"She's all right. I have her." He kept repeating the words, to reassure himself as well as Sofie, unsure if she really was all right. He scanned her face and body, looking for signs of injury. He held out her legs, Her jeans were dirty and had a long tear down one pant leg, revealing a thin line of blood trickling down her small calf. He tore back the material further and examined the cut, not deep but long.

Jack held tight to Katya, refusing to let her go. "She's all right, Sofie. The fender scrapped her leg but she's all right." His voice sounded weak. He pointed towards the street. "Sofie, get her doll."

Shaking, Sofie turned to the street and saw a passerby run out and grab up the doll. The man came back to Sofie and handed her the crushed doll.

The dazed driver climbed out of his car. He was only a kid. "Is she okay? I couldn't see her, honest. Is she all right?" He looked about seventeen or eighteen, skinny, shaggy-haired, and trembling.

Jack handed Katya to Sofie and strode over to the kid. "What in the hell were you doing? Let's see your license and registration," he demanded.

The boy stared at him, but didn't move until Jack pulled out his ID and flashed it. "I said your license and registration!"

A small crowd began dispersing, leaving the boy alone to face Jack. Katya held tightly in her arms, hugging her dirty doll, Sofie came over to Jack and the boy. She was obviously on a rescue mission. "Jack. It was an accident. He's sorry and no one was really hurt. I don't want to press charges or anything like that."

Jack looked incredulous. Katya held tightly to her doll, tears streaking her face. "Suni." She smiled and hugged the doll closer. She worked with tiny fingers to straighten out Jack's picture, now bent and dirty but still pinned to the dress.

Jack stood open-mouthed as Sofie exchanged information with the boy.

"I'm Sofie and this is Katya. And Jack." She smiled.

"I'm Zachary. I'm really sorry. It was an accident. I'm sorry."

"See, Katya. Zachary didn't mean to make your leg hurt. He's sad about it." Sofie kept up a stream of conversation as she watched Jack.

"All right, that's enough. I still need your ID and registration." Jack held out his hand with a sigh, exhausted. It was hopeless where Sofie was concerned, intent as she was on trying to befriend the world. He gave the boy a warning and Sofie gave him an invitation to visit the bookstore any time he wanted for free hot cocoa.

Jack watched, eyes narrowed, as the kid drove off, fighting off the urge to at least take the kid down to the Precinct and give him a scare. It was becoming increasingly clear to him that Sofie was only going to keep coming between himself and his better judgment.

With the morning accident, Jack assumed the go-carting was off. He was wrong. Both Sofie and Katya were determined to keep their plans for the afternoon. With her leg bandaged, Katya had her lunch and a nap and was ready to go.

It had turned colder, was blustery this afternoon and the fairgrounds were empty now. Only a few weeks before they'd been filled with tides of people wandering the State Fair, but the rest of the year the place was used only for minor events, with a few small-time midway rides struggling to get by with local drop-in customers. In another month the cold weather would shut down the rides completely.

Jack let his gaze roam the fairgrounds before returning to Sofie who placed Katya into a cart and fastened her helmet. It was too big for her small head, engulfing her, leaving her ponytail sticking straight out below.

The guy who ran the go-cart concession was in his sixties, gray-haired, pot-bellied, a vague family friend of Sofie's. Another of the strange mixture of characters who made up Sofie's life, it seemed that the man's cousin was a neighbor of hers. The neighbor owned the produce store two blocks down from the bookstore and had suggested Sofie take Katya to ride the go-cart, his treat. Sofie and Katya were thrilled; Jack was not. He hated the open spaces that made the place accessible to any and everyone.

The SUV investigation was stalled out after only three days and he was restless. The results from Washington had been delayed and that left him shuffling through the maze of data he had, juggling his hours between the Precinct and Sofie's place.

More frustrating still was the lack of a lead in the threat to Katya. He'd stayed up late the past two nights, going over background checks they'd made on Sofie's friends, finding nothing. He also found no direct paper trails that pointed to him as Katya's father. The birth certificate didn't list him, there was nothing permanent in the hospital records, no references linking him to Katya in any databases he pulled up.

The interview of Katya's teacher had drawn a blank as well. She could give only a vague description of the man who'd come to pick Katya up, and the note he'd given her. But it was typed and signed by Sofie, with Sofie's signature verified. The tracers put on the phone calls in and out of the bookstore and apartment turned up nothing, no unaccounted for calls on record, either business or personal. He was getting impatient.

His instincts said to stay calm and keep close to Katya, yet a part of him struggled with the notion that the whole thing was a hoax, something cooked up by Sofie, the motive beyond his comprehension. He'd stuck to them like glue since last Friday.

It was now Wednesday afternoon and still he was stuck at her apartment, with no leads. The time was coming when he was going to sit her down and talk about what the hell was going on.

Jack watched Katya weaving around the go-cart track, as he kept an eye on Sofie who strolled towards him. She had on a navy pea coat against the cold, jeans and loafers that, from a distance, made her look like a teenager, with her hair pulled back in a ponytail like Katya's.

She looked up, gave him a wave and he felt his chest tighten; he looked away without responding. *Why in hell can't I at least be civil to her? She's done nothing to me.* Nothing except get pregnant and not tell him. Nothing except give him the best night of sex he'd ever had. He knew damned well why he couldn't be civil to her. Because he still wanted her, and he didn't trust her. He thought about the feel of her body under his, the sounds she made, her fingers clutching his back, hanging on desperately as he pounded into her. There he was, hard as a rock, standing in the middle of this goddamned deserted fairground. He cursed himself for a fool.

He shifted his focus to Katya and her small hands clutching the wheel. He zipped up his jacket and walked along the fence, watching her. She drove slowly, wobbling along the track from side to side, intent on the moment, this morning's accident forgotten. Her blond ponytail, below the helmet, bobbed up and down as she bumped along. She was his, he thought, a part of him.

She caught his eye and gave him a smug little smile, pleased with her newfound driving skills. He turned and scanned three hundred sixty degrees, stopping at any untoward activity, before sliding on and finally coming back to rest his gaze on Katya. She had picked up speed now, her smile broader, and he could almost feel her exhilaration in his own body.

Sofie worked her way around the fence to Jack. He had his back to her and she came up behind him and touched his arm, causing him to jump and curse under his breath. "I'm sorry, Jack. I just wanted to go get something to eat for Katya. Do you want anything?" Her face was red, embarrassed at having touched him when she knew he didn't want her touch.

"No, I'm fine. Don't go far."

"Just that stand we passed on the way in—it's the only one that seems to be open." He reached into his pocket to get some cash but she shook her head. "I have money."

She smiled again and he wondered how in hell she could be so cheerful on such a bleak day, hanging out with a man, barely civil, and a child who might be in danger. She strode off, looking back to wave at Katya and moved out of his sight around the shrouded merry-go-round.

Katya finished her ride and Jack headed over to the gate to get her, looking back where Sofie had disappeared. The man who ran the ride lifted Katya out of the little car and turned her towards the gate. She came running lightly, on tiptoe in her scuffed sneakers. He expected her to pull up short but she kept coming and barreled into him, grabbing hold of his knees with arms that only reached part way around his legs. "Jack! Jack—I did it! I did it!"

He bent down and caught her chin in his palm, wanting an excuse to touch his child. He steadied her with one hand while he unfastened the clasp of her helmet. Unconfined now, her hair stuck up on top in wild disarray. He dropped the helmet and swept her up in his arms, inhaling the smell of her.

She put her arms around his neck, laughing. "Where did Mommy go?"

"She went to get you some food, scout. She'll be right back." He leaned her back to look into her face, watching for fear of him but she seemed unconcerned. Her matter-of-fact approach to the order of things in her life was mystifying to him.

Still holding her, Jack strolled over and thanked Oscar for the ride.

"No problem. Come back any time. I knew Sofie's mom and grandmother for years. Sofie's had a hard time since her mom passed on and I'm glad to do anything I can for her." He reached out and shook Jack's hand. "I'm glad to see she has a man to look out for her now." His words hit Jack like small invisible darts and he cringed. "It isn't right that she has to take care of her little family all alone. She deserves better than that. Especially now." Oscar glanced at Katya, appearing afraid he'd said too much.

Katya and Jack headed for the Fair entrance and Sofie. They found her standing next to a hot dog stand, talking with a man dressed as though it were summer, in shorts and t-shirt. He held her hand and she was smiling up at him.

Jack tightened his grip on Katya and jogged over to them, a feeling like hot lead coursing through his belly. Sofie turned and smiled.

"Jack. Katya, this is Steven Szcepaniak. He lives around here."

Jack merely nodded without offering a hand and watched the man's response.

Katya lisped, "Hello."

The guy was young, in his mid-twenties, maybe a little older, slightly built, clean cut, with pale hair and eyes, now fixed on Sofie.

"Steven is down on his luck right now and needed some money for food, so I gave him some. Can I borrow a couple of dollars, Jack, to get Katya a hot dog and drink?" She said it casually, as though giving her money away was an everyday occurrence.

Without taking his eyes from the man, Jack reached into a pocket, pulled out a wad of bills and handed them to Sofie.

Steven's gaze shifted from Jack to Sofie and then to Katya, causing Jack to tighten his hold on her. "So did you ride the go-cart, Katya?" Steven's voice was quiet and hard to hear in the wind.

"Yes. I rode by myself—fast!"

"I'd like to see you ride some time. Are you going to come again?" Steven asked.

"Can we, Jack?" Katya's breath was warm on his face.

"Sure, we can. One of these days we'll do it again."

Sofie came back, hotdog in one hand, soft drink in the other. "Let's sit down over here on a bench." Jack ignored Steven and sat Katya down and handed her a hot dog, leaving Sofie to deal with her charity case.

"You'll probably find a job soon. I know it's tough right now and if I can help you in any way, come by my store." Sofie held out her card to Steven, then came over to the bench and handed Katya her drink. Steven was out of sight before Katya finished her food.

"You know that guy?" Jack asked.

Sofie shook her head, not looking at him.

"Then what the hell do you think you're doing, giving out information to some guy on the street?"

"Jack, it's all right. He's just a kid. He doesn't even have a winter coat to wear. He's fine. He's from around here, he already knows my store." She reached down to wipe mustard off Katya' chin. "Besides, you're here. I probably wouldn't have talked to him in a place like this normally but you're our watchdog." She smiled and he frowned in response.

Jack waited until they were heading back to the apartment, Katya already asleep in her car seat, to bring it up again. "Sofie, you can't keep doing this. It's stupid to start up conversations with strangers right now."

"I'm sorry you feel that way, Jack. I'm really not stupid, you know." She looked away from him, but he saw her hands were trembling.

"Shit!" He reached over and caught one of her hands as she tried to pull away. "I'm sorry. But you drive me nuts!" The words hung in the air between them.

She pulled her hand away. "It's all right. I know. You don't need to apologize."

He could think of nothing to say in response and turned his attention to the road.

When they got back to the apartment, Jack rang up the station and spoke with Jackson, the p.m. duty officer on the information desk. "Listen, can you do a trace for me on a Steven Szcepaniak?" He spelled it phonetically. "No exact spelling, about five foot ten, sandy hair, mid to late twenties, eyes gray or maybe blue. Hangs out around the fairgrounds area, says he's unemployed right now. Might be homeless. Try the shelter on Seven Mile or the Homeless Center."

"Sure thing, Roselli. Where in hell have you been lately? You on a stakeout?"

"Sort of. I'm doing some work from home these days. A personal problem with the family." Jackson didn't probe further; they all knew about Dinah.

Jack hung up, aware of Katya behind him, turned and smiled down. "Come here, scout. Let's see if you got your hands warm yet." He reached out, took her hands and turned them over to engulf them in his own. They were red, chafed from the wind and he blew on them, then bent down and kissed her knuckles. She laughed, watching his face. "So what's up now? You have plans, young lady?"

"I want to play but Mommy wants me to take a nap." She sniffed.

"Well, your mother is probably right. I could use a little sleep myself." He stretched and stood up. "Where's your mommy?"

"She's washing my clothes. And checking things in the store." She yawned. "Do I have to lie down?"

"If your Mommy says so. How's your leg?"

"It's good." She held up her leg and stared down at it. "Can you lie down with me then?"

"Sure thing. Come on." He took her hand and let her take him to Sofie's room.

The shades were partially drawn, but faint light shown in from outside. She settled down in the double bed and he drew a light cover over her. "Jack, are you going to lie down with me until I fall asleep? Sometimes Mommy does that."

He kicked off his bootes and lowered himself onto the bed. She surprised him by snuggling close, rolling over with her back against his chest, her thumb automatically stuck in her mouth. In five minutes he heard her even breathing. Two more minutes and he was asleep as well.

## *Seven*

Monica had a parent-teacher conference on Thursday and Sofie took her shift at the bookstore. People roamed the aisles, stopping regularly to paw through piles of books, oblivious to anything but the pursuit of *the* book.

The bookstore attracted few upscale types, but rather women who were more interested in feeding their minds than decorating their bodies, ideas always winning out over accessories.

A woman in a long-sleeved, white cotton shirt and baggy, torn jeans turned into the magazine row. Her hair was dishwater blond, dark at the roots and pulled back haphazardly into a strange sort of ponytail, her face devoid of makeup. Moving beside her, like an appendage, was a smaller-framed woman with gray-streaked dark hair, protecting her friend's *keeper books,* like sacred treasures. Sofie watched them and tried to picture Jack's response to her female customers; she knew he'd despise them.

The few men wandering the store were older, most of them from the neighborhood or the Shelter. From time to time, younger men turned up, there to support their cause or to demonstrate their political correctness by supporting a feminist bookstore.

Sofie didn't discriminate with her causes, and the walls and windows advertised PETA, Green Peace, Habitat for Humanity, Amnesty International, The Hunger Project. The counters were stacked with leaflets about upcoming meetings and recently published books.

Contrary to appearances, though, heavy-duty feminist literature was more in Monica's line while Sofie was more eclectic in her tastes. She supported one and all causes. Whatever their fans or critics might think about it, a rundown Detroit neighborhood was a most unlikely place for a feminist bookstore.

Sofie didn't recognize Steven Szcepaniak when he came through the door until he stepped up to the counter to order a cup of tea. His hair was shoved back under a dark blue cap, his skin so pale she wondered if he'd been sick.

"Steven. You really meant it when you said you'd stop by and see me sometime. I'm glad you dropped in." She held out her hand and he took it. His fingers were slightly damp and he barely squeezed hers before dropping them.

"How are you today?" His voice had a nuance to it she hadn't heard before, a distinctive, almost melodic quality that was pleasing to her.

"Are you looking for anything particular or just here to get in out of the cold?"

"I'd like something about the bombing that happened a few nights back—the one at the factory." He spoke the words fastidiously, his grammar perfect. "You have anything about ecoterrorism? You know, those radical environmental groups who want to protect the earth and go around bombing lumber mills? I'd like something about ecoterrorism, in general, what they hope to prove, where they focus their efforts."

She looked around the counter, searching for anything related to Green Peace. She'd hidden an ELF flyer under a pile of Outward Bound applications yesterday, after Jack had lectured her on promoting terrorist organizations. The flyer had disappeared and she sighed. With the Bomb Squad working on something less than two miles away and the lead investigative cop hanging out here, she didn't want to touch the ecoterrorism issue.

"I don't really have anything from any environmental group now except Green Peace—and an ELF flyer that I seem to have misplaced. There's a pile of this week's newspapers over on the magazine rack. You can probably find the story about the SUVs some place in there. I read something in the article about an ecoterrorist group being under suspicion for that."

He looked over vaguely at the magazine rack. He was so earnest and seemed so helpless, she dropped her inventory list and led him to the pile of newspapers, then pointed him towards a section with books about the environment. He stayed for fifteen minutes, but she saw him often darting glances towards the door, and she was relieved when he finally waved goodbye and left. Something about Steven Szcepaniak was very sad.

Jack was working late, stuck there until ten and Sofie was uncharacteristically nervous. She was also dusty, tired of books and hungry. Jack had insisted she get someone in to be with her tonight and Monica had agreed to come over. They spent the evening cataloguing a shipment of books from an estate sale, plying Chrissie and Katya with snacks and computer games to keep them quiet.

The phone rang twice before Sofie got to it. She pushed back her hair as she picked up the receiver. The voice was low and sexy. "This is Kim Barber. May I speak with Jack, please?"

"I'm sorry, he isn't here right now. Can I take a message?" Sofie asked.

"Yes. If you see him, tell him I'll meet him at the Convention Center Saturday; he doesn't need to pick me up. I should be there by six." She hung up without a goodbye. Sofie mentally shrugged and turned back to the last box of books.

"It was for Jack?" Monica asked casually, noticing Sofie's discomfort. "A woman?"

"Yes. Someone named Kim Barber."

"Kim Barber? I went to high school with her, if it's the same one. She was prom queen senior year. One of those girls who look like they never went through adolescence. And sexy as hell! She's a vice squad cop now so it probably is her calling. Asking for Jack, huh?" Monica tapped her lips with a pencil. "Funny thing. Jeff and I saw her a few months ago, at a fancy fundraiser. Jeff mentioned she was dating some guy on the Bomb Squad. Hmm, so it was Jack." Monica's current boyfriend was with the Public Defender's office, a social climber and good for any and all gossip in the City's bureaucratic legal system. Sofie kept shelving.

"Strange, someone like her going into police work. Her daddy was a fancy plastic surgeon and they lived in a big house on the lake. Who'd have thought she'd become a narc, or whatever the hell she is." Monica was from Grosse Pointe and knew myriads of information about anyone from that opulent suburb.

Sofie shrugged, closing off further discussion about Jack. She felt suddenly irritated, but didn't care to explore the causes. She pushed the empty box under a table and went over and grabbed Katya up in a hug. "Monica, I have to go fix Katya some supper. Can you close up?"

Monica nodded, distracted, still thinking about Kim Barber, but wary of saying anything more about her to Sofie. Instead, she loped over and planted a kiss on Katya. "Sure thing. I'll put the boxes out in the alley before I leave. Are you okay with working tomorrow?" It was Friday, their busiest store day.

"I'll be here. I can't really go anywhere right now. I might as well do some uploading of our web site files while I'm stuck here." The complaint was only a way for her to push against the feeling of being constrained by Jack, since she loved being at the store.

"Don't forget Saturday night—the Bolshoi."

"Oh, God! I forgot all about that! Monica, I don't suppose I can get out of it this late, can I? Jack is going to think I'm insane if I go out on a date right now."

Jeff had been selling Peter Isaac to Monica for six months as the perfect man for Sofie, and Monica was determined Peter and Sofie get together. Three weeks ago Sofie had agreed to a blind date to the ballet and had promptly forgotten about it. The tickets were for this Saturday.

~ * ~

The bookstore was quieter than usual for a Saturday. It was raining now, in cold, unrelenting torrents and the abandoned buildings scattered throughout the neighborhood looked more desolate than usual. Jack had come in late the past three nights and Sofie had found no opportunity to mention her date for tonight. *Coward!* It was getting late now and the only thing to do was to call and let him know. He had plans himself for tonight, that thing Kim Barber had referred to, and Sofie set up her neighbor to baby-sit Katya with Chrissie's help.

She dialed Jack's cell phone, praying she'd get his voice mail, and she did. "Jack, this is Sofie." *Of course, stupid, as if he wouldn't know who I am.* "I need to go out for the evening. It's something Monica arranged weeks ago. I forgot all about it, but I can't let her down. I set up my neighbor to watch Katya, with Chrissie." She paused, knowing he'd be irate. "Since there's been no sign of any threat for over a week now, and since you're busy, I felt all right about having my neighbor stay over with Katya. I won't be late, I'll be back probably before you are." She hoped. She called his pager and reluctantly left a message for him to call her. He might be upset, but he must feel there was no real threat. Otherwise, why was he weaning himself away from constant surveillance of Katya? In the past few days he'd been around only during the night. He'd probably even be moving back to his apartment soon, she reasoned.

As soon as Monica arrived, Sofie closed the store and hurried upstairs to fix supper and get the girls settled. Then came the unveiling. Sofie stood in the center of the room as Monica did a circuit around her new dress. It was a plain red sheath with spaghetti straps, a retro sixties' number, with sling-back pumps, her hair pulled up in a loose knot that made her look almost sophisticated.

"You look nice. You really do."

"You sound surprised!" Sofie made a face at her in the mirror. "I've been known to look pretty good sometimes." She turned and grabbed a pair of pearl earrings, jabbing them in as she looked around. "Where's Katya?"

"They're in the front room, watching a video. Mrs. Ivanova called to say she's on her way."

Ms. 'I' was seventy-five, had lived above the bakery most of her life, and Katya loved her to baby-sit since she always brought cookies.

"Don't worry, Sofie. She'll be fine. We'll leave both Jeff's and my cell phone numbers and Chrissie is great with Katya. You've left her with Mrs. Ivanova lots of times and no problem." Monica paused. "Jack's working tonight, isn't he?"

Sofie made another face in the mirror. "He's at some sort of banquet—probably with *Kim Barber*," she emphasis the name.

"And you're jealous."

"I am not. He can have a life. Just because he's the father of my child doesn't make him my property."

"Just because you had the best sex of your life with him doesn't make you want him for more?" Monica had coaxed and wheedled, but gotten only a few details about the infamous night out of Sofie, who wasn't going to go any further into it; she'd already said too much.

"No! He's too damned critical of me and my life, there's no way we'd never fall into bed again. Anyway, he doesn't need me for sex, since he has Kim and according to you, she's *hot!*" she countered, grinning. "And I have my date. Who knows, maybe I'll get lucky tonight!"

"Ha! How many men have you gone out with in the past three years? One or maybe two? And you didn't get lucky with either of them. Or rather, they didn't get lucky with you. Now that I know you've been holding out for a bad boy cop all this time, when are you going to get over Jack and find someone who, not only can give you great sex, but knows how to laugh once in a while?"

"What makes you so sure it was great sex? It was just a one-night thing. Or more like a couple of hours."

"Yeah, right. For one thing, I can tell just by looking at the guy that he'd be great in bed. You know, the way he moves—and his hands."

Sofie screamed in protest. "That's such a crock. Or at least, you'll never know if it's true from me."

Sofie wandered around the room, stopping first at the mirror, then the window, as Monica sat and watched. Hopefully this night out was a good thing and would ease the tension between her and Jack. He probably would even agree. He'd made it clear, both by actions and words, that he was sticking around to protect Katya only. The apartment was too small for two adults and even Katya had noticed them trying to avoid bumping into each other and did her best to maneuver them together whenever she could.

Katya skipped into the room and ran over to rub her small hands down the soft material of her dress and Sofie reached down and drew her up into her arms. "How does mommy look? Good, huh?"

"Where's Jack?"

*Damn! Jack again!* "He's out tonight, sweetie. I told you, Mrs. Ivanova from the bakery is going to stay with you, okay? You like her! And Chrissie." Chrissie dug through the videos and pulled out a Disney movie. It was amazing to Sofie that Monica, whose every thought revolved around sex, had a thirteen-year-old who preferred Disney to MTV.

Katya leaned forward until her small nose was centimeters from Sofie's and frowned. "Will she bring me cookies?"

"I'm sure she will. Doesn't she always? She's going to put you to bed, all right? You'll be a good girl and do what she says?"

"Okay. But I hope she brings me two cookies." She made a face. "Are you going to say goodnight to me when you come home from your date?"

"Of course. I never miss that. You and Chrissie can sleep in my bed tonight, okay?"

"What about Jack? Will he say goodnight to me when he comes home?"

Sofie sighed. "I'm sure he will. He did last night, didn't he?" Sofie set Katya down at the sound of the doorbell and went across to let in Mrs. Ivanova.

~ * ~

They had agreed to meet Jeff and Peter at the Masonic Auditorium, and the two men stood on the marble steps, scanning the crowd. Jeff, who had a face that could have doubled for Harrison Ford, glowered at them as Sofie and Monica walked up. "Monica, I told you 7:30 prompt! Where in the hell were you?"

Monica merely grinned at him and turned to pull Sofie forward. "Sofie, this is Peter Isaac. Peter, this is Sofie."

He was blond, lean and muscular, with a face like a young Robert Redford. He was dressed like a high-class lawyer, not the lowly public defender he was. *Wal-Mart meets GQ*, Sofie thought, looking down at the dress she's been so eager to purchase from the resale shop. At least her expectations were minimal—a little adult conversation that went beyond single, terse sentences.

Jeff and Peter had both attended University of Detroit Law School, but had lost touch until Peter was hired earlier in the year by the Public Defender's Office. Jeff, whose aspirations were higher, was conscientiously courting a law firm at the New Center and hoped to leave the PD office in his dust. Knowing Jeff, Peter was probably of a similar bent.

Sofie shook hands with Peter. His hands looked manicured, and she stifled a sudden attack of dread at facing the evening ahead. Not only was this guy dressed way out of her league, he worked for the City, an amazingly inbred bureaucracy. She saw her lurid history with Jack spreading like wildfire throughout the entire justice system.

Peter Isaac was the perfect date—and Sofie was bored. At ten years of age, Sofie had dreamt of the Bolshoi. That, at least was lovely. Afterwards, they headed to an R&B club on the River and Sofie sat nursing her drink, stifling yawns, as the men traded inside jokes and quips about cops and the city.

"So, Jeff tells me you've been having some problems lately and have called in one of Detroit's finest as a bodyguard." Peter smiled over at her.

She barely nodded her head, wondering what Monica had said to Jeff. "It may be nothing, but I had a scare a few weeks back with my daughter and I thought we should be careful for a while."

Peter frowned. In his world, things had to be pretty bad before someone would pull in a cop for private protection. "Jack Roselli, right? I don't know him well, except to say hello. But from what I know of him, I don't think he's prone to giving out favors. What's the catch? You got something on ole Jack we oughtta know about?" He leaned towards her. "Is he getting paid for this?"

Sofie raised her eyebrows at Monica. *This is your doing, now you get me out of it.*

"Jack is an old friend of Sofie's, and he offered to help out. You know, the thing with his sister? Well, he may not be Santa Claus, but he does care about kids."

"Jeff tells me Jack's spending nights at your place. I'm surprised Kim Barber is putting up with that. She keeps a pretty tight rein on the men in her life, from what I hear. If Jack's wandered into her universe, ain't no way he's going to escape without a lot of struggle."

Monica glanced over at Sofie and shrugged, and the conversation moved on, leaving Sofie to absorb what they'd said about Jack's personal life.

For two hours Sofie repeatedly checked her watch until just before midnight, yawning, she dragged herself up the sagging staircase to her flat. She'd talked them into dropping her off first, avoiding any attempts from Peter to prolong the goodbye. Since Chrissie was staying the night with Katya, it gave Monica a rare night alone with Jeff.

The lights in the apartment were all on but the flat was silent. "Mrs. Ivanova?" Sofie whispered. She moved from one room to the next, searching frantically in her mind for rational explanations. The place was empty.

She stood unmoving, terrified, then turned and ran for the door, where she slammed into a hard body.

"Sofie! Damn it! What's going on?" Jack grabbed hold of her hands trying to fight him off.

"Katya's gone! I left her with Mrs. Ivanova. They're gone!"

"What the hell do you mean you left her?" He was too close and his voice was too loud.

"I went out for the evening, a date. I tried to let you know, I put in a call to your pager, but you never picked it up. I left a voice message for you, though, and I left Monica's cell phone number too, in case you had to reach me. It had been arranged for weeks. I forgot all about it until yesterday and there was no way I could get out of it. Monica set it up weeks ago." The excuse sounded pathetic in the face of the empty apartment.

"You had a date! Christ, that's perfect! Why am I not surprised. I thought you said you didn't date? It looks to me like your life's nothing but a series of one-night stands that you don't call dates." She cringed and yanked her arm away from his hold on it. He ignored the response, whipped out his cell phone and dialed. "Detective Harkins. Roselli here."

Sofie moved around the apartment, looking for some sign, trying to think, his voice still ringing in her ears. Before they did anything, she needed to call over to Mrs. Ivanova's apartment. Maybe she had an emergency and took Katya and Chrissie with her. Maybe. Sofie turned and ran down the steps, heading out the door before Jack could catch her.

The layout of the building next door was almost identical to the bookstore's, the upstairs apartment entrance directly opposite her back door. Sofie plunged into the dimly lit alley.

Someone had replaced the bulbs over both doors, and a green shield above the bakery door cast a sickly green arc around the entrance. The rest of the alley was in darkness.

Sofie pounded repeatedly, calling out, "Mrs. Ivanova!" When it opened, Sofie fell forward, gasping like a long distance runner. "Mrs. Ivanova! What happened? Where's Katya?"

"She's fine, dear. Now don't you fret. I got a little worried, the phone kept ringing and no one was there when I answered. I was afraid it would waken Katya, and it kept interrupting Chrissie's video, so I just called my nephew, Eddie, over and he helped me get the girls up to my place. I told Eddie to write a note; didn't he do that?" The old lady pursed her lips.

Sofie shook her head, mute.

"I'm so sorry to cause you worry, my dear. They're fine, really."

Relief replaced irritation and Sofie reached out and hugged Mrs. Ivanova. "That's fine. I'm just glad I found you and everything's okay."

Jack stepped into the open door behind her and placed his hands on her shoulders, forcefully. With a brief nod, he pulled out his cell and placed a call. "Roselli here. 1040. The problem is handled. I'm signing off for the night. Night, Maxine." He snapped his cell phone shut, but kept his hands on Sofie's shoulders.

Sofie herded Chrissie across the alley to her place with Jack close behind carrying a sleeping Katya. Sofie's legs shook so much she had trouble making it up the stairs. She settled Chrissie into bed beside Katya in her bedroom, dreading the words she knew were coming from Jack. He stood silently in the door until she finished, turned and strode ahead of her as she shut the door gently behind her.

"Sofie, come in and sit down." His voice was flat.

She dropped into the nearest chair, her legs giving way.

"Sofie, this has got to stop! I'm busting my butt juggling my regular job while trying to manage the security around here while you go off and leave Katya for the night without even letting me know. What the hell are you thinking? What kind of mother would go off on a date when her child's supposedly being stalked?"

*Supposedly.* Sofie heard the word inserted carefully into the sentence. Due to this evening's mess, he was questioning everything Sofie had told him. "Look, Jack. I know it looks bad, but I did put a call into your pager, to let you know I needed to go out tonight. And I left a message on your cell phone."

"I didn't get your message. Did you try calling me at the precinct? I was there until six. Or you could have told me last night, you know. I'd have arranged something."

"I'd say that I'm sorry but that's not going to make it with you, is it? I know you think it was a stupid thing to do. To me, it seemed reasonable. I couldn't get out of this evening gracefully. Like I said in my message, this was planned weeks ago and I was letting other people down by not showing up. I've used Mrs. Ivanova a lot for baby sitting Katya and she's very reliable. I gave her your cell phone and pager numbers, I told her how to reach me on Monica's cell phone." She shut up then. Whatever she said, he'd made it clear what he thought. She was a fool and a liar. And a bad mother.

"You know, Jack, I've been thinking things over and since there's been nothing happening since you moved in, maybe it was nothing but a hoax, someone just trying to scare me. Maybe we should reconsider this arrangement. Whatever I do seems to make you mad and it's driving both of us crazy. It might be for the best if you moved back home. Just knowing you're available if something does happen is enough." *Liar,* she thought.

He stood up and strode over to her, stopping too close. He smelled like cigarettes and soap. "Sofie, look, I'm sorry about what I said, about being a bad mother. It's just that you piss me off at every turn." He sighed. "Hell, maybe you're right. Maybe I need to back off right now. I know you'd never intentionally put Katya in danger, but dammit, just tell me if you want to go out and I'll change my plans."

"Jack, I know it's been difficult bumping into me at every turn in this apartment, never having any privacy or space for yourself." She said. "It's pretty awkward for me, too, needing to have you close by. It might work just as well if we set up some sort of calling system, where I report anything unusual to you. And maybe you could have someone check up on us from time to time, for a few weeks." She stopped an urge to wring her hands and shoved them into her pockets.

He shook his head. "No. It's too soon. I need to do some more investigating before I back out of this that far. Nothing's turned up, but I'm not ready to write it off as a prank just yet."

Nothing, he had nothing. Even the thinnest links were dead ends. He'd put traces on that homeless guy they'd run into at the fair grounds earlier in the week, nothing there. Nothing on any of the names he'd gotten from the Shelter or from Sofie. But, dammit, he wasn't backing away from this yet. "Let's give it a few more days, maybe a week more and see if anything else shows up, okay?" He gave her a slight smile. "So, you had a nice time, I hope? With all this, it would be too bad if you didn't enjoy yourself."

"Not particularly. The ballet was wonderful, but I probably would have preferred it by myself. Monica set up the evening, with a friend of hers and this guy from the Public Defender's office—Peter Isaac." She stopped, aware she was giving him way more information than he cared to know.

"Yeah, I know Peter." Whatever else he was thinking, he wasn't going to share with her. He pulled off his jacket and shoulder holster. "I'm really beat. We'll talk some more tomorrow. I'll go over with you what little I've got and we can start looking at backup plans for the future, okay?"

He headed toward Katya's bedroom but turned back. "Where are you sleeping tonight with the two girls in your bed?"

"I'll just make up the sofa here for me. It's pretty comfortable." She grabbed up the pillows and started to pull the bolsters off.

"No. You take Katya's bed. I'll bunk out here tonight."

"I'll get you some bedding." She was too tired to argue further.

"Hey. That dress looks great on you, by the way." He smiled slightly as he said it and Sofie felt a wave of desire roll over her.

"Thanks. I appreciate the compliment, especially since I'm sure my dress didn't get a second glance from anyone else tonight."

## *Eight*

Sofie rolled over and opened her eyes for a moment then shut them quickly. The sun shining in the one small window was blinding. Sofie remembered last night and groaned. She stumbled off the small bed and went to check on Katya and Chrissie.

Jack was lying sprawled out, face down, legs spread-eagled on the coach, a hairy calf sticking out from under yellow sheets. She stared, unable to pull her eyes away, remembering the feel of those legs against her own. Disgusted with herself, she turned and headed for coffee.

She felt rather than heard him behind her, the heat of his body causing the hairs on the back of her neck to stand up.

"Can I help?"

"I'm just making coffee. What would you like for breakfast? French toast?" She scooped coffee grounds into the filter and pushed the pot under the drip spout.

"That's fine—whatever you're fixing for yourself and Katya. How can I help?"

"You can run next door and get some fresh bread—ask them to slice it for you—one-half inch slices, okay?"

"It's open on Sundays?"

"Just a couple of hours—it's a tradition around here—fresh bread every day."

He nodded as he pulled on his boots and jacket, grabbing his shoulder holster on the way out the door.

He was gone less than ten minutes and returned with enough bread to last Katya and Sofie a month. She dipped slices of bread into the egg mixture and put the first batch on the grill, conscious of his eyes following every move. Searching frantically for something to talk about that wasn't inflammatory, she asked, "Are you off today? Or is there never an off day for you guys?"

He took a sip of coffee before answering. "I need to go in this afternoon for a couple of hours, but that's it." He hesitated, weighing his next words. "Look, my parents are having Sunday dinner—it's a ritual of sorts in our family. That and Wednesday drop-ins. I usually try and make it Sundays since my brothers usually show up. It's the one time we're all together. Since I couldn't make it last Sunday, I thought I'd stop by tonight. Maybe you and Katya would like to go along? You're guaranteed great Italian cooking."

"We'd love to have dinner with your family." In light of last night's fiasco, an invitation was the last thing she expected this morning.

"I'll pick you two up around six, all right?"

"Should we dress up or casual?"

"Casual's fine. I should warn you, my family's pretty big, what with my three brothers, their families and all. It can be pretty intimidating." He frowned into his coffee mug. "I want Katya to meet them. I haven't said anything about her to them yet, but I think it's time they start getting to know her."

A wave of panic spread through Sofie. She'd called him to protect Katya, not move her into his life. At this point, it sounded far too proprietary.

He apparently read something in her face as he said, "Sofie, look, I'm not sure how this is all going to work out, once we handle the immediate problem, but I want my parents to get to know Katya."

"I understand. I just hadn't thought that far ahead."

"Let's play it a day at a time and see where we go with this."

"Okay." At least he wasn't pushing her off the scene—yet. He took a sip of coffee and looked around the room and she wondered what he thought of her kitchen with its fifties memorabilia. She'd put up photos of family members as far back as great-grandparents, taken when they first came to America in the early twentieth century. They comforted and reassured her in a way she could never explain to anyone.

He stood up and wandered around, taking time to look at each photo. Was he looking for some clue to Katya's background or merely being polite?

"Those pictures are my family on my mother's side. I never knew my father or his family."

He raised his eyebrows and she added, "My mother never told me anything about him, except his name was Richard and he was French Canadian."

"So you grew up on the East Side of Detroit? With your mother?"

"And my grandmother and aunt. We lived in a small house about two blocks from here. Years ago, this area was entirely Russian, even in the late seventies, when I was born. Now most of the ethnic flavor's gone, except for two blocks either side of the bookstore. That's why I decided to open the store here. It's familiar to me. And gives me a sense of belonging. Sort of a substitute family, now that my mother and grandmother are gone."

"No sisters or brothers? Cousins?"

"No, just me—and Katya. I'm an only child, raised by my mother and my grandmother, sort of a matriarchy." Why in hell was she telling him all this? She waited for a smirk, but his face remained impassive. "Actually, my grandmother was a single mother, too. Her husband died in World War II and she raised my mother and my mother's sister by herself. She was a teacher." She shrugged. "So you might say I'm carrying on the tradition."

"No boyfriend? And you have no plans to marry and give Katya a father?" His tone was neutral, hard to judge. "This guy you went out with last night? Nothing serious?"

"Peter?" She shook her head. "I never met him before, a blind date. You don't even need to bother looking into his background. The evening wasn't very successful. I was home before midnight. I doubt if I'll ever hear from him again."

"So your plans are to raise Katya yourself? Seems like a hard choice to be making. It can't be easy financially. It's obviously been a burden."

"Katya isn't lacking for anything she needs. I give her the important things." *Why*, she though, *am I always defending myself with him? Who made him the judge of the world?* She narrowed her eyes at him. "Maybe we should stick to the point here. You're looking for any men around who might be a threat to Katya. That's what you're digging for, right? Well, there are none."

"Don't get so offended. I need to check. It's part of my job. And, I wasn't trying to pry. I would like to know what kind of life Katya's had, what your plans are for her. It seems only reasonable to get some background, since she's part of both of us."

"In that case, how about telling me something about your life? You come from a big family. You grew up on the east side?"

"Yeah, my parents still live in the same house where I was born. Not far. Seven Mile, bordering on St. Clair Shores. It's not that different from around here; almost everyone below fifty has split for the suburbs, but a three- or four-square-block area is still mainly Italian. I have a pile of relatives living within a mile of where I grew up, mostly in St. Clair Shores."

"Did you always want to be a cop?" she asked, shoving aside glasses to make room for the platter of French toast. She wondered how far she could push him for answers to personal questions.

"Yeah, pretty much as far back as I can recall. My dad was a cop and I just always wanted to wear a gun, like him." He smiled and she blinked involuntarily in response as she dropped down opposite him. "Two of my younger brothers are cops, too, or will be. One's with the narcotics. The other's finishing up at the Police Academy next month."

"So you're pretty satisfied? You aiming for Police Chief or anything like that?"

He took a bite before going on. "I had a plan to move up in the justice system, the DA's office and then maybe even go for a judgeship. I finished one year of law school at U of D."

"You know Jeff Carpenter—Monica's boyfriend? He went there to law school."

"The name sounds familiar. I know Peter, the guy you went out with." He chewed slowly, weighing his words. "Anyway, after Dinah died, it all seemed pointless. My parents needed me around and school took too much time."

She nodded and put all her attention on cutting her toast. He was too big for her kitchen. He seemed to dominate everything, a contrast to her own compact life. Was it too small? Too insular, if not for herself, then for Katya?

With this first mention of the impact of his sister's death to her, Jack had moved the conversation into unfamiliar territory and she carefully eased away. "So, about dinner tonight. Won't your parents think it odd that you bring a strange woman and her daughter to a family-only event?"

"No. My younger brother brings a different girl each week." His laugh eased the tension in the room. "He's either trying them out with my parents or just testing the water for some future woman. I'll just introduce you as a friend and they'll accept you. They'll love Katya."

He took a swallow of coffee. "They love kids—anybody's will due. They started working each of us over, as soon as we hit our twenties, for an heir. My brother Vincent's wife is expecting, the first..." He paused at the word *first*. "...as far as my parents are concerned. I need to make this right by them. They've missed the first three years of their first grandchild's life and never even knew it."

Some sort of apology might be required, but it was irrelevant at this point. "Jack. Feeling bad about keeping them in the dark is useless now. The only thing I can say is that it never occurred to me to think about your family, or what Katya might mean to them. I'll do what I can to make it up to them."

He reached out and flicked a loose strand of hair off her face. "I'm not the complete bastard you think I am. You're pretty damned careless sometimes, or maybe the word's thoughtless, but you're not mean. And I must have been pretty intimidating that night, unshaven, drunk as a skunk."

It was an awkward explanation, and backhanded compliment, but she took them, wondering just how far he really could trust her. "You're a little scary sometimes."

"Katya's a great kid," he said. "You did a good job with her."

Love wasn't a word she associated with him, but she could see he felt something strong for Katya. She leaned forward, feeling a momentary bond with him. "You've made a big impact on her, you know. I might even say she's turning into a Daddy's girl, if I had a clue what the heck that means myself."

"Sofie, look, I was angry at first, pissed at being used. I'm trained as a cop, with automatic reflexes. Let's see if we can stop fighting over what happened and do what's good for Katya. Right now, all I want is to be with her. I want her to be a part of my family. I think she can give my parents something I haven't been able to, some healing."

She wanted to touch him but knew he didn't want that.

He stood up and moved to the sink with his dishes. "I've got some things to do around here this morning. Then I'll probably be leaving around noon. I'll be back by six. Have you got someone to stay with you and Katya today?"

"I'll go over to Monica's this afternoon. We'll be fine. Everything's so quiet, it seems silly to call someone in for a couple of hours."

"Okay, I'll call if I'm going to be later than six, okay?"

"Sure. I'll tell Katya we're going to meet your family."

~ * ~

The Rosellis owned a two-story duplex, similar to the rest of the houses on the block. Jack's brother, Vincent, the second son, lived upstairs with his wife. They were expecting their first child in four months. A carbon copy of Jack with a major difference, Vincent approached life with a smile and a nonchalant attitude. Tony Roselli at twenty-eight was the youngest of the boys and still lived at home while he finished up at the Academy. He was handsome, charming and shared himself generously with a revolving door of women. Marcos, Jr., was the only Roselli male not in law enforcement. He ran a limo service with his wife and lived nearby.

Maria Roselli stood at the door, waiting for them. Too impatient for polite introductions, she threw open the door and pulled her oldest son to her small frame. "Jack!"

"Hi, Mama." Jack shifted Katya in his arms, leaned over and kissed Maria's cheek. She ignored the flowers he thrust at her and stared at Katya.

Jack reached behind him and drew Sofie through the door, nudging his mother out of the way. "This is Sofie. And Katya." Jack added. He turned Katya around in his arms and watched his mother work to control her face. *Shit, she knows. I should have known she'd spot it right away.*

Maria took a deep breath and stared into round black eyes under the mop of yellow hair. She gave Sofie a brief nod, but all of her attention was fixed on the child.

"Katya." Maria said the word quietly, as though she were afraid the child would disappear. She held out her arms.

The foyer, covered with numerous hooks and many coats, was too small for the group, but no one moved. Through the archway, Sofie spied six people, staring as Maria took Katya from Jack. They were all silent, caught up in a drama that left Sofie out, but the pain in the room was almost palpable and it washed over her like a flood. Katya tightened her small arms around Maria's neck, burying her face in the dark navy silk covering Maria's bosom.

"Katya, this is my mother, Mrs. Roselli." He said and reached out briefly to touch the small head bent against his mother's shoulder.

"Call me Mama Roselli like everyone else around here does, okay?" The invitation was simple but her voice trembled.

Katya raised her head and lisped, "Mama Rosey?"

A broad smile lit Maria's face and spread to the others in the room. "Mama Rosey is good. I like it." She shifted Katya in her arms. "Let's go see what we can find you for a treat, okay? Are you hungry, sweetheart?"

Sofie watched the two bent heads exchange whispers and move through the doorway beyond.

Jack steered Sofie towards a large man standing next to a much smaller, red-haired woman. "Sofie, this is my brother, Marcos and his wife, Pauline."

Marcos grinned and pulled the woman in bright red pants tighter against him. He caught Sofie's hand and pumped it.

The introductions went around the room: Anthony, who grinned at her and smirked at Jack; Vincent, a smiling, wider version of Jack; his pregnant wife, Beth, a lawyer, with the kindest face Sofie had ever seen. They exchanged hugs around and included Sofie, making her feel awkward. There were no other children.

The volume of sound went up with the introductions and kept rising as they talked about mundane events, throwing nonstop quips and jokes at each other. Someone motioned Sofie to a gold settee where she sat down gratefully, out of the center of action.

Katya was brought back into the room, now in the arms of a balding, rotund, and very tall man who held her as though she might break.

"Dad, this is Sofie, Katya's mother. Sofie, this is my dad, Marcos, Senior." Jack's voice was unsteady.

Katya seemed perfectly content to be passed around to every person in the room as Sofie sat watching, trying to absorb the sense of the family that hummed around her. Jack may not have told them Katya was his, but it was clear they all knew.

"Sofie, you want something to drink?" Jack asked.

"Please. Whatever everyone else is having."

"We usually drink wine around here. My dad makes it in the basement." He raised an eyebrow at her. "It's not bad, really. My dad's been perfecting it for thirty years, so he's learned some things along the way." He smiled and she grinned back, a truce called, for now at least.

It was two hours and many glasses of wine later before dinner appeared on the table. The large Rosellis and their small women crowded into the dining room. Maria sat at the head of the table, gathering praise for her cooking. It took two more hours to eat the huge meal of homemade raviolis, followed by veal, and topped off with cannolis. Slow food all the way.

As soon as coffee was served, Sofie excused herself. Coatless, she sat on the front porch, glad to escape the warm room for the quiet cold outside. She didn't hear Jack come up until he sat down next to her on the stoop.

"So what do you think?"

"You mean the dinner?" She knew he didn't mean that.

"What do you think of my family? I'm hoping Katya will be spending a lot of time with them from now on."

"They're wonderful. And Katya's clearly already taken with them, all of them." She stopped, unsure how to ask what she needed to know. "Did you say anything? To any of them, I mean? About Katya being yours, ours?"

"No, but they know. I should have guessed they'd spot it right away."

"How? I mean, other than you'd probably never bring someone else's child around to meet them?"

"Katya looks exactly like Dinah did at that age."

Silence.

"Say something." He said.

"I'm not sure what to say. I know she died four years ago. Was that why you were in the bar that night?"

"Yeah. That's why I was drinking myself into oblivion. And that's why I picked you up." He glanced over at her. "That's why Katya's here tonight."

"What do you mean? Are you being literal or are you implying it was some sort of fate?" She glanced behind her, but the front door was shut tight.

He stood up and moved down the three steps, turning to face her. "I don't believe in fate, but if Dinah hadn't been killed that week, I'd never have been in that bar and there'd be no Katya. I don't know what the hell that means." He shrugged. "I'm not trying to find some mystical explanation. I'm just stating a fact. I'd say it's more irony than fate, but hell, a cynical bastard like me loves irony, right?" His laugh was without humor.

"My parents have been struggling since Dinah was killed and now Katya's here and it's the first time I've seen my mother really smile in four years. I'm the cause of all the pain so why the hell not bring them some comfort?"

"If Katya can do that for them, I'm glad. I'll do whatever I can to help you so she can be part of their lives."

"Yeah, I'll make sure she is. My mother's got four brutes for sons who've fallen short so far in the grandkid department." He paused. "I'm not sure when to actually come right out and tell them. They know she's a Roselli, but I can just hear the reproaches coming, especially from my mom. Tonight's probably not the best time to get into that." He reached into his pocket and drew out a limp package of Camels, thought better of it and stuck it back.

Sofie didn't answer. She was torn between wanting to stay the center of Katya's life and wanting to help these people deal with their loss. "I'd like it if you told them soon, Jack. It's too weird for Katya the way it is. And maybe it's a two-way thing. Maybe she needs them as much as they need her. It's always just been the two of us. She could use some more family." The wind suddenly whipped up a whirlwind of leaves that circled between her and Jack. "Somehow, we'll work things out." She tried to sound enthused, but it cost her something. A houseful of strangers, a man who vacillated between accusations and kindness to her—she wasn't sure where she stood and she was afraid.

"Yeah, we'll work it out. As far as telling my parents about Katya, the only reason they haven't jumped down my throat about it is because you're here. I'm sure they'll give me an earful the first opportunity they get. Don't worry about it. Right now, we need to focus on getting to the bottom of the threats."

She shivered and he took off his sports coat, leaned down and threw it around her shoulders.

"What's stopping me from telling them is our relationship. I don't know how the hell to explain what happened. Any way I say it, I'll look like shit in their eyes. The other problem is that we're basically strangers and I don't want them worrying about you disappearing and taking Katya with you. My mother couldn't take it if she got to know Katya and then she was gone."

"I wouldn't do that, Jack, I promise you."

She stood up abruptly, her head hitting him under the chin hard. "Oh, sorry." She reached up and patted his chin absently, as though he were Katya.

"Come on, it's too cold out here. Let's go in."

The men settled down in the living to watch football. Katya lay against her grandfather's chest, sound asleep, her blond curls brushing his nose when she stirred. Jack sat opposite, throwing barbs at his brother, his eyes repeatedly straying to his daughter and his dad.

Sofie sat in the kitchen with the women, listening to them talk as Maria packaged up food for each of her sons. "Mrs. Roselli, can I help you with something?" She studied the woman's features. She was the heart of the Rosellis and Sofie wondered how Dinah had fit into the picture. More importantly, how would she herself fit in?

"Sofie, call me Maria, please. I made you a package to take home, with a special treat for Katya. She liked the cannolis."

As paper sacks filled with food, Maria and the other women threw questions Sofie's way. They were innocent enough, where she lived, what she did, who her family was. She told them about the bookstore and about her mother and grandmother. No one asked about her relationship with Jack.

It was almost eleven when Sofie came into the living room, her arms filled with bags of food. She nodded to Jack who was already getting into his coat. He reached down and gently gathered Katya up in his arms, wrapped her coat around her small body and handed Sofie her coat. They did another round of the hugs and kisses, and this time Sofie saw the tears.

The car was parked across the street and down a block. The houses were all two-story, many were rental duplexes, all built before 1930 and typical for Detroit. Cars lined both sides of the street but the traffic was slow and sparse.

The nearest street light was halfway down the block from the Rosellis', leaving the street dark except for faint light coming from nearby houses. Jack walked ahead of Sofie, holding Katya while Sofie struggled with the bags of food. The wind was colder, no stars were visible. Sofie plodded on automatically, deep in thought, Maria's face fixed in her mind, thinking about her own mother who never knew Katya.

Three quick pops rang out behind Sofie and startled, she turned to look for the source of the noise. Before she turned halfway, Jack grabbed hold and threw her to the ground, his body falling heavily over hers with Katya wedged between them. He pushed an arm under his coat and she saw him draw his pistol.

"Stay down" His voice was rough.

He eased up a few inches, taking some weight off them, and scanned the dark. As he moved, Sofie eased her hand under her daughter's head to cushion it against the solid muscle of Jack's chest.

"Mommy!" Katya whispered. "Are we playing hide and seek?"

"Shhh, sweetheart. Be really quiet and don't move, okay? Until Jack tells us we can get up."

"You okay, Katya, honey? Just lie still for a few minutes for me." Jack whispered as he eased back further. As he scanned the perimeter, he switched his gun hand and pulled out his cell phone. His whispered something indistinguishable into the phone, snapped it shut, and tightened his grip on them.

"You're doing good, Katya." He whispered and shifted to give more breathing space. "Stay quiet, all right? Just a little while longer, until some friends come for us."

It seemed like a very long time before Sofie heard a car pull up and Jack eased upright, pulling them to a sitting position on the cold pavement. He hugged them briefly and passed Katya over into her arms. "Wait here, Sofie. I know it's cold, but can you sit a few more minutes?"

Without waiting for a response, he got up and edged his way towards the uniforms getting out of the squad car.

"Mommy?" Katya's voice was anxious now. "Is Jack going to find some bad men?"

"Honey, those are policemen friends of Jack's. They're here to make sure we're okay. No bad men are going to hurt us. Jack will make sure of that."

Jack was gone a long time and returned with an officer in tow. "Sofie, you and Katya can get up and we'll get you into the squad car." He reached for them, caught hold of her arm and pulled her up. Using his body as a shield, he herded them the few feet to the car. Once inside, he leaned down. "Are you all right? I fell pretty hard on you. Do you need a doctor?"

"I'm all right. We're fine, aren't we, Katya?" She kept a smile pasted on her face, both for herself and Katya. "All we want to do is go home."

He reached out and touched Katya's face. "How about you, scout? You okay?"

Katya nodded at him, her face solemn. "Were we playing a game?"

"Not a game, sweetheart. I was being careful. Sometimes bad things happen and it's my job to protect people, especially you."

"And Mama."

"Yes, and your Mama."

Jack was again the cop, and Sofie remembered why he was with them and she was afraid.

He ordered them to sit tight and he turned and headed over to the uniformed cops. One of them had a flashlight pointed to the ground, searching the area. Sofie shut her eyes and let a mind-numbing lethargy overtake her. Katya was quiet now, asleep, and she pulled her closer.

Sofie awoke with a start as Jack climbed in beside her. He leaned down to peer at Katya. "She okay?"

Sofie nodded and pulled herself up straighter. The two uniforms climbed into the squad car and without saying a word, drove the half-block down the street to Jack's Jeep.

"Wait here." Jack spoke over Katya's head and the men got out and went over to the Cherokee.

Sofie watched as they searched the car, shining flashlights under it, opening the hood and trunk, inspecting the bumper. At last, satisfied, Jack jogged back, bent down and took Katya from her arms. He placed her in the car seat, turned and motioned for Sofie to follow.

Once they were secure, Jack turned back again to the officers, exchanged more words and climbed into the Jeep. As he drove through the darkened streets, Sofie stared straight ahead, her mind rushing with the events of the night, trying to absorb the abrupt shift from a sense of security to one of danger.

They parked in the alley, a few yards from the back door and she sat waiting as he searched the alley. When he was satisfied, he moved them up the stairs, Katya in his arms, Sofie lagging behind still toting the bags. He did a quick search of the apartment and gave Sofie the all clear.

The heat generated by the afternoon sun was long gone and the apartment was cold. With Katya tucked in bed, Sofie sat at the kitchen table, exhausted. She heard Jack's voice, coming from the other room, but couldn't make out the words. He'd been on his cell phone since they'd arrived, offering her no information or explanation.

She looked up as Jack strode into the room and sat down opposite her. He's tossed aside his jacket but still had on his shoulder holster. "So far it looks like an unrelated incident, a drive-by. They caught a couple of kids a few blocks away. All indications are it's just a coincidence."

"You're sure? How do you know it was those kids?"

"The bullet casings we found near where we went down. They found a revolver in their car—the same caliber—we just need to get a lab match on it." He leaned over and caught her hand. "I know, a coincidence like that seems too damned unlikely. But so far, Sofie, we've got nothing. Not a thing that points to a threat to Katya. It's starting to look more and more like some nasty prank, maybe some neighborhood kids."

"But what about the man who called for Katya at daycare? And the phone calls I got?" She left her hand in his, absorbing his warmth.

Instead, he let go and eased back. "It could have been a misunderstanding. Maybe the teacher got the name wrong. I saw all those kids when I went to pick up Katya the other day. They're crawling all over that teacher. She may have misunderstood."

"And the letter?"

"I can't explain that away so easily, but so far, everything checks out negative. Nothing on the tracer calls, no strangers lurking from your past. Aside from me." She smiled at the quip, the first he'd shared with her.

Sofie had showered and gone to bed when his mother called. The apartment was silent and he headed for the living room, where the sound of his voice wouldn't carry. He'd been expecting the night duty officer, calling to get his statement on the drive-by. Instead, his parents' number showed up on caller ID and he debated whether to pick up. He sure as hell didn't need to talk with his mother tonight. "Yeah, Mama? What is it? Did I forget something?"

"Yes, Jack. You forgot to tell us you were a father." The accusation leapt out of the phone at him, the words staccato.

"Mama, please. I can't get into that right now. It's late and something's come up. I'm waiting for a call. Business." He sighed. He should have known she wouldn't let it go, even for an hour.

"Jack, that's your usual answer to my questions. But this time it won't fly. I'm not going to be put off and neither is your father."

"Mama, this isn't something to talk about over the phone. Listen, I'll stop by tomorrow, all right? I'm on duty at ten—I'll come by on my way to work."

She made a sound of disdain; he recognized it and cringed. "Whatever the story is, it better be good. I can't believe you've had a child all this time and haven't told us." She paused and he heard her swallow. "Jack, she looks like Dinah."

He watched the traffic below, his throat tightening. "I'll see you tomorrow morning, Mama. I love you. Goodnight."

He lay on the small bed, adrenalin still pumping, too wound up to sleep. Sofie moved quietly into the dark bedroom, like a ghost in white, but he knew instantly she was there. "Sofie?" He whispered.

"I… uh, I wanted to…" She stood in front of Katya's small bed, the light from the hallway outlining her body. He stood up, watching for some sign from her. She gave no ground but stood, waiting, and he moved within inches of her, reached out and took hold of her shoulders.

Her hand came up and he felt the touch, lightly skimming his bare chest, moving down to his arm. Damning himself for a fool, he pulled her towards him, lust overriding reason. She had on some sort of white garment that left a great deal of her legs bare. He felt their smoothness against his own. He bent down, intending to reassure her, but the heat between them erupted and their mouths fused, tongues darting, probing, and settling hungrily. He felt both her hands now, move around his shoulders and to his bare back, cool against his overheated skin. He let his hands roam around behind her and down over her thin cotton panties as he pressed her to him, warning her with his erection.

When she didn't shrink back, he deepened the kiss, repeatedly thrusting with his tongue, tasting her. Their hands moved restlessly in unison over each other, remembering the feel and touch of four years ago. When she threw her head back and gave him access to her throat, he trailed kisses down, only stopping at the sound of her gasp, startled into momentary reason.

"Get the hell out of here now, Sofie, or you'll be naked in that bed in ten seconds!" He pushed away, waiting for the response that didn't come.

When she didn't retreat, he cursed, picked her up in his arms and deposited her on the small bed, joining her under the covers. There was a child's lamp beside the bed and he reached out and turned it on. It cast a low pink light on the bed, throwing out shadows of ducks around the room.

"Sofie." He said harshly as he reached out and pulled her tightly against him. He ran hot fingers down the line of her back and under her panties, absorbing the feel of her firm buttocks. She made another sound, unfamiliar to him, but he knew it was the sound of surrender.

Her hand came up and captured his as it slid around to her belly, and she held it there. He inhaled sharply, swamped by desire. "Do you want me to stop? I can let you up now and you can go back to your room. This is your last chance." His voice was hoarse.

She shuddered and whispered, "No, don't stop."

Still, unresisting, she lay beneath him. His erection was rock hard and it nudged her belly. He pulled down her panties in one motion, cursing as the elastic caught on her heel. She gave no help but lay passively, breathing fast, watching. He felt dizzy, the blood rushing to his head. He stopped to gaze at her round breasts, her erect nipples, then on down to the pale skin of her stomach, and to the dark triangle between legs still drawn together.

He looked up at her face. It was unreadable in the pale light. He pulled the covers up and over both of them, wanting to shield her, even as he pulled his shorts down and rolled over onto her body. She fit into his arms easily, without a word, as though she were a part of him he'd recovered. They lay still, as if by mutual agreement, soaking up the warmth and smells of each other, breathing fast, in unison.

Trying to read her face, to get a reading on the situation, he pushed himself up on his elbows and stared down. Both of their bodies, nude now, stood out in stark contrast against the bed sheets dotted with teddy bears. He wanted to draw back, even as his erection quivered against her thigh, but her hips arched up and instead, he pushed her legs apart further and settled himself between them.

Still neither of them spoke. He lowered his head and took one tender nipple in his mouth, sucking gently at first, greedy for the taste of her, all reasonable thought overridden by need. She whimpered his name and her hands caught in his hair and drew him closer, cradling his head as if he were a child at her breast.

One hand slid down her belly and as he probed the wet folds beneath the soft hair of her mound, her whimpers turned to muffled cries. He explored her with trembling fingers, lingering over her until he could bear it no longer and plunged one finger deep into the small opening.

She cried his name, pushed up her hips and pulled her legs back wider for him. Frantic now, he withdrew his finger and reached blindly for his wallet on the nightstand. Fingers awkward, still trembling, he sheathed himself and turned back to Sofie, legs spread, waiting for him. As he moved to position himself above her, she raised her hips to receive him and gasped as, with one thrust, he penetrated her.

The sound of flesh meeting flesh blended with repeated wordless cries. She gasped as he sucked feverishly at her distended nipple, blurring the line between pain and pleasure. He worked to hold back, but the end came abruptly, his body bucking, going rigid over her. Amidst his own cry of release, he heard what sounded like sobs as her body contracted and shuddered with his.

He lay atop her, his head turned into the pillow, unable to confront so much spent emotion. Her face was turned into his damp neck and he inhaled the intoxicating smell of their sex, as their bodies continued to shudder and contract. There were no sounds coming from her now, but he felt her tears running down his neck, an interruption to his sense of euphoria, making him feel confused and uncertain.

He pulled himself up but she gasped and caught at his shoulders, holding him.

"I'm too heavy, Sofie."

She was slow to release him and when he finally stood, the sensation of separation was almost painful. Unsteady, he turned and looked down at the outline of her body under the teddy bear sheet, covered with the shadows of ducks. She had turned her head away but he saw the tears running down her cheeks.

He stayed in the bathroom for a long time, standing under the shower, struggling with what had happened. *Goddammit*, he thought. *What the hell am I doing?*

When he came out, she lay on her back, watchful. She'd pulled the sheet up tighter around her but had left the light on. He walked over beside the bed, leaned down and whispered, "Sofie, get some sleep. I'll sleep on the couch in the living room."

"Jack, it's all right. Don't beat yourself up for this. We've both been under a lot of stress. Blame it on that, or adrenaline or something."

She reached down, gathered up her t-shirt and panties, and pulled them on. "Can you move Katya in here beside me, please?"

Without another word, he went into Sofie's room and lifted Katya into his arms. The apartment was silent and cold. He moved quickly to the smaller bedroom, laying Katya gently down beside Sofie. A blanket lay on the on the floor, tossed aside in the heat of the moment. He bent down, picked it up and placed it over them. Sofie gathered Katya against her, cradling her where he had lain minutes before. He turned and went out into the dark living room.

## *Nine*

Monday traffic was sparse; the few people of working age in the neighborhood were assembly line workers who did the seven a.m. shift at Poletown. Jack stopped at Marconi's Bakery for a box of donuts, stood in line patiently with the older people who made it their daily ritual, then headed for his parents' place. It was eight o'clock in the morning, way too early for a heavy conversation, but there was no avoiding it. He'd crept out of Sofie's without encountering her, unwilling to confront the mistake they'd made last night. It was bad enough he had to face his mother this morning, but he knew *she* wouldn't wait.

Last night he'd been overcome by lust, something on which he usually had a strong rein, unlike his younger days, when he'd ride it and let it rule him. Finally, too many meaningless morning-after conversations had left him with a bad taste for empty sex and he'd left it behind.

Now he wasn't so sure he'd left anything behind. It had jumped out at him unexpectedly, only this time he couldn't blame alcohol or youth. It left him reeling, confused, and wanting more. Worse, he felt trapped by his own desires and desperate to escape from whatever Sofie wanted from him. He shoved the whole thing aside and stiffened his resolve for the painful conversation he knew was coming with his parents.

Maria Roselli met him at the door, her face unreadable, something it rarely was for him. "Hi, Mama. Here." He pushed the donuts at her, needing to postpone questions until he got some coffee in him. He followed her obediently to the kitchen. His father sat in suit coat, as he always did at the table, even for breakfast.

"Hi, Dad. How are you?" His dad raised his eyes and glanced towards his wife in response to the question. *Oh shit.* Jack cringed. *Here it comes.*

"All right, Jack, sit down and while I'm getting your coffee, you'd better be getting your speech ready. And I don't want any vague answers from you this time."

The coffee came too fast, plopped down in front of him, sloshing over the rim of the mug. He'd been awake most of the night, first having sex with Sofie, then working on a reasonable explanation for his mother about Katya. He sure as hell didn't want to go into the stalking thing right now and he was goddamned certain he didn't want to discuss Sofie, either, right now. The only thing for sure was that Katya was his daughter and he had to start there.

"Mama, I'm sorry. I was hoping I could ease Katya into the family slowly, so it wouldn't upset you."

"Upset me? Jack, have you gone crazy? How much more could you upset me than not telling me about my own grandchild?" Without waiting for explanations, she launched into the tirade he knew was coming. "What did you think, Jack? That we'd reject her? Or was there something wrong with your family that you didn't want Sofie and Katya to meet us?"

"You know that's not true, Mama." He protested. "Sit down. I'll tell you about her." He motioned to a seat beside him, caught her hand and pulled her down. "I just found out about Katya two weeks ago. At first, I wasn't positive she was mine." This was the part he dreaded: how to tell his mother he'd picked up a woman in a bar, took her to his house, had sex with her and never saw her again.

"I met Sofie four years ago. It was a week after Dinah'd been killed. I was drinking a lot. I went to a bar and met Sofie and..." He searched for words, but none came. His mother just stared at him, refusing to help. His dad, who usually was willing to come to his aid in these confrontations, ran fingers through his thinning hair and kept his eyes cast downward at the table. "I... we only had the one night together—and I didn't see her again after that. I didn't know she'd gotten pregnant that night." His mother glared at him. "I know. It was stupid! So damned stupid! The only excuse I have is that I was drunk, too drunk to even remember much of what happened. The next morning it was all a blur. Anyway, I never saw her again. Until I got a call from her two weeks ago, asking me to meet her."

This was the next part he wanted to skip over. "She didn't bring Katya with her, but explained how someone had been calling and making some threats towards Katya. She told me that since I'm a cop and Katya's my daughter, she called me. She asked me to help keep Katya safe." His mother blanched and he hurried on. "That was two weeks ago. At that point I still thought maybe the whole thing was some sort of a con. I didn't know Sofie at all, I had no way of knowing for sure Katya was mine." He swallowed. "Then I met her and I knew she was mine."

He ran a hand over his face, looking up to find both pairs of eyes trained on him. "You saw her! She looks just like Dinah. I should have realized you'd spot it right away, but I was hoping I could get by with introducing her to you gradually, and once we got beyond this threat thing, you could get to know her."

"Jack, I can't believe you'd be so dense as to try something like that. Thinking we'd be so blind. You've never even brought a date to dinner, let alone a woman and a child. And I can't understand your reasoning in trying to keep her away from us."

"I wanted to spare you the pain of—she looks just like a Roselli all right but I don't have any hard evidence, no DNA or anything. And I still don't know what Sofie wants from me. Beyond the protection bit. I've been staying at her place—in a separate bedroom," he added, feeling ridiculous for having to explain his sex life to his parents—especially since, as of last night's escapade, he was lying about it.

"So far there've been no more threatening phone calls, nothing." He didn't mention the shooting last night. "Mama, I was trying to spare you more worry. I was hoping I'd get to the bottom of the threats before you got to know her. But I wanted you to meet her. I guess on some level, I wanted your confirmation that she was a Roselli. Well, I got it." He mumbled the last words.

"Oh, Jack! I can't believe this! I'm so mad I could easily throw you out on your tail! Jack! She's our granddaughter! Our first! And she looks exactly like Dinah." The last words came out in a whisper.

He reached for her hand, she withheld it momentarily but finally gave in. "I know, Mama. I know." He sighed. "Katya's my kid."

"But, Jack, why...why has Sofie been keeping her from you? From us? It's so cruel. How could she do that?"

"She wasn't being cruel, she just didn't know. When I met her I was drunk, she didn't know anything about me, about my family. From that night, she was sure I wasn't the kind of guy who'd want to have anything to do with a kid. Hell, I don't blame her. She says she never thought about my having a family who'd want to get to know Katya." He played with the cup handle, avoiding their eyes.

"She's a single mother. She was raised by a single mother. And her mother was raised without a man around. All she's ever known are families without fathers. She just never thought beyond that. Until she got back in touch with me—and met you." He stopped and waited for them to absorb his words, watching their faces as they worked to understand. Jack picked up a piece of donut and unconsciously took a bite.

"When she met you last night, I think for the first time she realized that Katya had a real family, with uncles and aunts and cousins. Sofie's mother, her whole family is dead. They died not long before she met me. Katya's never known anyone except Sofie."

"Oh, Jack." This was too much for his mother, for whom family was everything.

"She's ready to share Katya with you." He was working way harder than he'd planned to get them on Sofie's side, and he wondered where he was headed with this. When he left this house last night, his only thought had been to bring Katya to his family. Now, whatever the hell it was that had happened between Sofie and him last night had changed all that.

His mother began bombarding him with questions, about Sofie, about what happened that night, about Katya's life so far.

His dad sat quietly, taking it all in until, at last, he interrupted, "Maria, listen to yourself. You're harping on old news. We got what we got now. Jack says he didn't know anything about the little girl until two weeks ago. He brought her over here to us as soon as he felt she was pretty safe. That's good. He did what he had to do, being a cop. And now he's doing what's expected of him as a son, a good son. So give it a rest now, okay? Just take God's gift to us and stop worrying about the circumstances."

His mother sucked in air and stopped talking. Marco Roselli rarely spoke his mind, but when he did, she listened. She wiped her eyes and got up.

Jack took a deep breath, stood up and turned to meet the hug he knew was coming from her. He said nothing more but instead, let his dad's words do the work.

~ * ~

It was after ten before Jack made it to work. It had been eight days since the Poletown bombing and McMillan called a meeting for 10:30 to review the findings, leaving him only a few minutes to scan his desk for messages before gathering the ballistic reports from over the weekend.

He saw Sofie's name first, that's what caught his eye. It was from McGill downstairs in records. The message was short but grabbed him in the gut.

"Information gathered on tracer on calls during the past month from 555-3631 and 555-1690 showed no unaccounted for calls. All calls placed to nursery school on 09/15 were from the complainant's business phone." *Jesus Christ!* He swore viciously, grabbed the note and stuck it in his pocket.

It only got worse as the day went on. Scanning the list of calls for the month, he found five to Central Precinct, two to the annex building on Brush and three to his home phone. He hadn't received any calls from Sofie himself in the past month except the one she'd made two weeks ago to his office. He went over the phone list slower this time, and found two more phone calls placed to his parents from the bookstore number.

By the end of the day, he sat at his desk, staring at the numbers, struggling to understand what he was seeing. Everything so far pointed in one direction—to Sofie herself. He thought about last night, cursing at himself for being pulled in so far. A leap into a stranger's bed and life, someone he'd briefly encountered four years ago. *Introducing her to his parents, goddammit!* The sense of betrayal was raw and burned his gut. Was Sofie playing some giant game with his life, using Katya as the pawn? He swallowed the bile that rose in his throat, trying to control his rage. He felt like a fool, enmeshed in something he didn't understand, something that seemed sicker than anything he could have imagined.

Jack didn't get back to Sofie's apartment until after nine, three hours later than usual. He hadn't called and the meal she'd painstakingly worked over for two hours sat solidifying in the pans. When he walked in the door and she saw his face, she knew the dinner was a mistake, an assumption on her part of something that had not happened last night.

She stood up as he dropped his jacket and holster on the counter. "Jack, I, uh, made dinner. I guess you had to work late?"

"Yeah, I got held up." He didn't smile. "Is Katya in bed yet? I need to talk to you, privately." He didn't even use her name.

"She's already asleep. She tried to stay up until you got home—she drew a picture for you at daycare, but she finally gave out and I put her down."

He rubbed his face with his hands and dropped heavily into a chair. She knew whatever he had to say was going to be bad. Instead of sitting down, she grabbed a mug, poured him coffee and sat it down in front of him before roaming back to the stove.

He said nothing, waiting, as she moved around the kitchen picking up, organizing until finally, she threw the gray looking mess that had been potatoes au gratin down the disposal.

She'd attempted to dress up a little, not really clear herself what she wanted from Jack. If anything, she should be relieved at his coolness, given the chance to back away from something she really didn't need in her life. But she still felt stupid for letting him see she cared anything about last night. She'd put on a silk shirt, had added a light touch of make-up, and curled her hair. Now she was dressed for some imaginary masquerade ball. The look of disgust on his face was too much for her.

It hadn't passed his notice she'd dressed up—probably for him. A pale blue shirt matched her eyes, made them almost shine. Her pants accentuated her slender hips. *She's too damned skinny*, he argued irrationally, waiting for her to sit down. She continued to avoid him, busying herself putting away toys, shuffling newspapers into a pile, throwing food down the disposal. Suddenly, exasperation boiled up in him. "Oh, for God's sake, Sofie, sit down so I can talk to you!"

She didn't answer, but she stiffened and she moved to a chair. He'd had all day to process the situation, to mull over all the facts so far. He was calmer now, less irate, but still pissed at her, all the more because he'd ended up in her bed last night.

"Sofie. I got back the reports on your phone trace and there were no unaccounted for incoming calls." He waited for his words to sink in before continuing. "But there were a goddamned bunch of unexplained calls coming out from your numbers. Both the bookstore and your apartment. What do you have to say about that?"

She stared at him. "What do you mean unexplained calls? What kinds of calls?"

"To my parents for one thing. Multiple calls to the precinct over a period of a month. And calls to my home number." He waited.

"What are you saying? I don't understand."

"I'm saying it looks damned fishy that you say you never tried to call me, except the time you called and asked me to meet you. But there are all these calls to the station, calls to my place. Even calls to my parents, dammit! Why? And why did you lie about all this?"

"You think there was no threat? Is that it? That I set all this up in order to ensnare you?"

"Well, it sure as hell looks that way."

She stood up and glared at him. "You egotistical gorilla! You think I planned all this to get you somehow? Oh, boy, I'm starting to get some idea where you got that reputation as a womanizer. It's part of your pathetic image, right? And I had the nerve to come around with a stray kid of yours and disrupt the game. Last night must have really galled you. Getting it on with someone who's set a trap for you."

"Hold it, Sofie. Sit down and let's talk. I haven't accused you of manufacturing the whole thing. I just want to know how you would explain the calls?"

"I can't explain them. And what do you think I would gain from all this? You can't think after four years I've decided I can't live without you?" She sat down, sucking in big gulps of air to calm herself.

"So let's calm down and back up. I'm just telling you what I have so far; a lot of calls you can't explain coming from your phones, no record of any other calls, no unexplainable calls in the trace on the daycare. Nothing. The note to Katya's teacher even had your signature on it. Can you explain all that?" He wanted to reach over and shake her.

She sighed, looking resigned to all of it. "I can't explain any of it. All I know is I did get calls for three weeks, I only made one call to you, none to your place, and none to your parents. I never signed any note for Katya to be picked up by someone else at daycare. If you want to believe I made all of it up, be my guest. I'm tired of fighting with you."

He sighed this time, less certain of the facts and his own position now that he sat in front of her. She just didn't seem to have what it took to be a con artist. And he couldn't see the motive. "Look, you're right. I'm too tired to fight this out now. Maybe I was a little out of line, jumping on you like that." He stood up and took off his holster, dropping it on the table. "Let's leave it tonight, no more words. I'll be moving back to my apartment, probably tomorrow."

She merely nodded, saying nothing.

"Once I get back to my place, I want to set up some sort of weekly schedule to see Katya. And for my parents to see her regularly. Is that agreeable to you?" He sounded deliberately impassive now.

"All right. Give me some possible options and I'll work on a schedule."

He stuck his hands in his pockets. *How in the hell did we get from last night to this place?* He cursed silently, searching for some common ground to have a civil discussion with her.

He tried to wrap his mind around the idea of Sofie plotting this whole thing, using Katya, and couldn't. Standing here facing her, he found himself wanting to give her the benefit of the doubt, but everything pointed to a dead end. *What motive could she have? Money?* Shit, he was happy to give her child support. In fact, he'd be happy to take over partial custody of Katya if Sofie was agreeable. He knew she would never agree to that. If it was all some sort of plot to snare him, last night had worked well for her. Even if he was an egotistical prick like she'd said, he wasn't self-centered enough to think she'd go to all this trouble, just for him.

"If nothing turns up this week, we'll have to conclude it was all a hoax. But I want her in my life, Sofie. I'm going to provide child support for her." He'd expected anger at this and he got it.

"Jack, I already said you can see her as often as you want. We can plan to have you over to eat at least once a week and maybe your parents would like to have us over another night."

"Sofie." He sighed. "I don't mean you and Katya, I mean I want to see Katya alone." The words cut like a knife into the sudden silence and he looked away. There was nothing left from last night, no tenderness, no caring.

She wanted to get away from him, for him to leave. Instead, she pulled up her chin and looked directly at him. "You can visit Katya and you can take her to your parents. We can set up some sort of weekly schedule. But I'm her mother and I'm staying in her life. For all I know, your accusations about me may be just a feeble attempt to get her away from me. Well, accuse all you want, but where Katya is concerned, I won't be pushed aside."

He stared at her, realizing what she was getting at. "I'm not planning on trying to take her away from you, Sofie. I really don't want to get into all this. Katya needs us both. I'm not trying to get rid of you." But he was. He didn't want her around, didn't want to be tempted by her, seduced, tricked. Especially after last night, he didn't want her. He couldn't trust himself and he wanted to be rid of her now, before he was drawn in any further.

She tried to match his words. "Okay. Let's leave it for now."

The air was thick with a distrust caused by two strangers who'd shared something too intimate. "We can work out the scheduling details in the next few weeks. In the meantime, I'm probably going to be clearing out of your way in a day or so. I'll keep a watch on your place another week or so, check into continuing the drive-by patrol cars. And you can always call me in any emergency."

He stood up. Neither of them said anything about last night. "I've got a few calls to make tonight. I'll do them in the kitchen, so I don't disturb you. Goodnight."

Her face stiff, she sat, not moving, until he was out of the room. Finally, hearing him on his phone, she pushed herself up, turned off the light and went to her room.

## *Ten*

It was Wednesday afternoon and the store was quiet, too quiet for Sofie. She sat in front of her computer, unblinking, reviewing web sales, facing the empty store. Katya sat next to her, working on a drawing for Jack. The ringing of the phone in the quiet store was startling and Sofie grabbed it, knocking over what was left of her cold tea. It was Kim Barber.

"Yes?" Sofie heard the low voice and braced herself. She didn't want to have a conversation with Jack's old girlfriend about anything.

"Ms. Novakoff? Sofia, right? I was wondering if you could possibly meet me at my office? Perhaps this evening? I'd really like to talk with you about something."

Sofie stared down at her order book, not seeing it. *Damn*, she thought, *what does she want*? After the past two nights, Jack's old girlfriend was the last person she wanted to see. The pain of his cold distrust was too fresh.

"Can you tell me what it's about? I'm working until five and it would be difficult after that, with my daughter."

"I've been discussing your problem with Jack and I have a few ideas about it. I could meet after five. My office is in the Annex, 1200 Beaubien—5:30? Room F204. Second Floor."

She didn't want to go, it was stupid, but Sofie agreed. Could Jack possibly have told her about Katya?

Monica turned up right at five and raised her eyebrows at the mention of a meeting with Kim but Sofie shrugged it off. What the heck, she could endure some embarrassment for anything that might be evidence for her side of the story. She arranged for Katya to eat with Monica and promised she'd be gone no more than a couple of hours.

~ * ~

The sun filtered through the dirty windows. It pierced the stale cigarette smoke that lingered in the air and turned it into shafts of light. Kim Barber wore a blue suit that hit four inches above her knees, leaving enough leg showing to impress anyone. Her jacket crossed midline at her ample chest, drawing further attention to it before anchoring on either side of her narrow waist with gold buttons. She looked more like a centerfold model than a narcotics investigator. Except her face, which fit neither stereotype. She had a sweet smile, better suited to the girl next door than to vice cop, a face that didn't belong with a porn star body.

She came forward with her hand extended and Sofie noted her beautifully-kept red fingernails. Being a cop must not be hard on manicures.

"Thanks for coming on such short notice, Sophia. May I call you that?" Without waiting for a reply, she turned back to her desk.

"Sofie."

"Pardon me?"

"My name's Sofie, not Sophia." Sofie felt like a child, unsure whether to sit down without an invitation.

"Of course." Kim shuffled some papers around her desk, watching Sofie. "Sit down." She motioned to a chair and Sofie chose to ignore it. "I'm not sure whether Jack has mentioned it, but he and I have a thing going. We have had for some time. Since I know him so well, and believe me, I know he can be a real bastard sometimes, I really felt like it was my duty, as a woman, to let you know what was going on, since it concerns your child."

She stood up and reached across the desk for a satin bag and retrieved a cigarette. She lit it, without asking permission, came around and balanced herself on the edge of the desk, swinging one long leg.

"To get straight to the point, I thought you should know that Jack is getting ready to press forward for custody of your daughter. While I can understand why he might want to do this, I'm not really thrilled about this complication in my relationship with him."

Her leg swung faster and she paused only to exhale a stream of smoke that rustled blond wisps of hair lying on her forehead. "In the circumstance, you can understand that I don't want this conversation to go beyond us, but I wanted to speak with you, just to let you know I'm on your side. I've had my own run-ins with him, you know? I know how he can be and I feel it's very unfair of him not to be straight with you about the situation. Loyalty is highly overrated, you know, when it comes to men. One woman to another, we need to support each other." She smiled.

"I'm not sure I know what you mean. And I don't think anything between you and Jack is really any of my business." Sofie said. "And what's between Jack and me has nothing to do with you."

Kim stopped smiling. "Look, I'm sorry to hear you take it that way. But whether you like it or not, since I have a relationship with him, what's between you and Jack concerns me. I happen to know that Jack is the father of your kid and that he didn't know about her—until recently. I also know he's planning on using that, your withholding her existence from him, along with the fact that you haven't provided a safe environment for her, to get custody." She blew out a long stream of smoke. "Sisterhood aside, I'm not looking for unwanted complications in my relationship with him right now—like another woman's child." She flicked another ash. "Don't get me wrong. I understand why it's so important to him, his family situation and all, but it really doesn't work for me." This time she flicked the ash into a small cloisonné box on her desk.

Sofie didn't know what to say. She'd accused Jack of scheming to take Katya from her night before last, and he'd sworn to her he had no plans to do that.

Kim's eyes narrowed. "He hasn't told you, has he? He isn't going to say anything—until the papers are in motion. I'm sure he'd deny he has any such plans."

"It's ridiculous! He can't be meaning to do that. Why would he? He can visit any time he'd like to see her. He can have all the time he wants with her!" Sofie tried to stop the outburst but the words kept pouring out of her.

"Well, he's planning on showing you're an unfit mother, that she's being raised in an unhealthy environment. You can't really expect him to be normal about this, you know. I mean, all the circumstances being what they are. You never even let him know he has a daughter. And there's the way his sister was killed and his guilt about that. He's a cop, in a different position than most men. Especially since he thinks you set up the whole threat thing." Kim paused. "And then, of course, there's his mother. She's very protective of all of her children and with the loss of her only daughter, she's putting pressure on Jack to make sure she keeps her only grandchild."

Sofie was suddenly exhausted and dropped into a chair facing Kim's desk. Absently, she stared at the bottom of the desk and noticed the scuff marks, as though thousands of feet had kicked at it. She was just one of the many accused who'd come through this office. "Jack would never do that. Or Mrs. Roselli. I've met her. She was very kind to me. She wasn't vindictive or angry."

"Well, that's probably true at least on a superficial level. She wouldn't throw a scene in front of Katya or her family, you know. And I doubt Jack would say anything. He's too clever for that. He's been watching, weighing the circumstances, I'm sure. It's like him." Kim flashed another smile, lips barely moving.

Sofie was having trouble picturing Jack withholding that kind of information from her. He'd had no qualms about accusing her of setting up the threat to Katya. He might be reticent and uncommunicative, but in the past week, he'd never hesitated to let her know what he thought when he was upset. She'd even thought she was beginning to understand him. She knew now she had no idea what he might do. She'd barely seen him in the past two days. He was still living at the apartment, but managed to avoid her, coming in late and leaving early. Their only exchanges were written schedules, who was picking up Katya, where he could be reached. The only thing she knew for sure was that he was moving out in a day.

Sofie watched Kim, trying to see beyond her words, looking for some truth in her warning. She was certainly not the kind of person who'd care about the sisterhood of women or even the best situation for a child. That was obvious. If her relationship with Jack was serious, she'd hate the constant presence of another woman's child around. Was there something else she wasn't saying?

It seemed ludicrous to Sofie that two days ago she'd considered the possibility of being friends with Jack, maybe even continue being lovers. He'd made it clear the next day they were going no place together and he was further from her now than any time in the past four years. She was no threat to Kim Barber. Except perhaps through Katya. As long she was struggling with Jack over Katya, Jack and she would be involved.

Kim stood up and moved around behind the desk, searching for something on it. "Sofia, you know, I'm not sure what your game is with Jack, but if it's really just that you want protection for your daughter, you should make sure you get some real evidence. While I don't doubt your word on this, Jack clearly does and he's at the point where if something doesn't turn up, he'll be ready to set the custody thing in motion. If it were me, I'd be damned sure that I got some evidence—get this thing settled at least. Then maybe we can both get on with our lives."

Sofie wasn't sure she'd heard it right. Was she advising her to falsify evidence? To make something up? That was insane. "I thought the harassing calls and the threatening letter were enough, especially with the attempt to take Katya from daycare. I can't believe anyone would doubt that it happened. Why would I make something like that up?"

Kim shrugged. "From what he says, Jack seems to think you were either setting him up for some sort of financial gain or you've designed this story as a ploy to get into his life, some stalker scenario of your own."

He thought so little of her he believed she'd use her own child that way? Sofie moved restlessly, the darkening room closing in around her. She wanted to escape, to get away from Kim's questions. "I'll have to think all this over. I'm not sure what to do at this point. I really need to go." She stood up and moved to the door.

The halls were empty as she left and she ran down the backstairs, afraid of a chance encounter with Jack or someone who knew him. She stumbled as she went, checking back over her shoulder for anyone following. It was dark outside, but the downtown holiday lights, recently hung, cast garish illuminations on the abandoned buildings around the station.

~ * ~

Thursday was a replay of Wednesday with inventory at the bookstore and no sign of Jack. He'd shown up late again the night before, and she'd heard him using the bathroom, but hadn't see him. The next morning he was gone before seven; she'd feigned sleep rather than face an early morning encounter with him when he'd cracked open her door.

He phoned midday and they had a cool, two-sentence exchange and again that evening, he merely called up the stairs to let her know he was dropping Katya off from daycare. He came in late again Thursday night. There was no word from him on when he was moving out, the only evidence of his continuing presence the bomber jacket hung on a peg by the door.

By Friday Sofie was desperate for answers. Monica was at a two-day bookseller's convention in Chicago, leaving Sofie to face her worries along with another day of inventory. She'd sent Katya to daycare for a second day in a row to spare her boredom with Sofie busy at the store. Jack would pick her up later this afternoon.

The call came just after five, a low voice, sing-song, gender neutral. "Katya isn't coming home." That was all it said.

Sofie sat staring at the phone, replaying the words, trying to focus on something familiar about the tone. But the call had been different than the others. The voice sounded nothing like the man who'd called before, the one named Robert Arnov. This sounded like a woman. She stared blankly at the wall. Kim Barber refused to leave her thoughts. She searched her mind for some reason for Kim to place the call. Maybe giving Sofie the motive she suggested? A cop would never place a threatening call, would they? Even in some pretense of assistance?

When Katya and Jack didn't appear at 5:30, Sofie began pacing the floor, making repeated calls to Jack's cell and his pager, leaving messages. She moved from the bookstore up to her apartment to check her voice mail.

She was desperate, and close to hysteria when she heard them trudging up the stairs just before eight o'clock. "Jack! Thank God you have Katya!" She rushed to grab her daughter, but pulled back, afraid she'd scare her. "It's okay, sweetheart. I was just worried about you, but it's okay. I forgot Jack would take care of you."

"I took her over to my parents for dinner. Did you forget? I told you yesterday morning."

She stood up, pushing back her hair, loosened by her nervous fingers as she had waited for them. "Oh, God, Jack, I completely forgot. I called your pager and your cell and left messages. I guess I should have thought to call your parents' house."

She reached down and unbuttoned Katya's jacket, easing her out of it. "Why don't we get into the bathtub, okay, sweetie? And then bed. You've had a long day."

"I want Jack, Mommy. Jack will help!"

Sofie sighed and nodded her head. "Jack will help, won't you?" She swallowed down a protest and turned Katya towards the bathroom. Her legs were still trembling.

It took almost an hour to get Katya settled down in bed and Sofie waited impatiently in the living room. Finally, he ambled into the room, unrolling shirtsleeves, coat in hand.

"Jack, I got another call tonight. That's why I was so frantic when you arrived so late. The voice was strange, almost high pitched. He said Katya wasn't coming home." She said. "When I couldn't reach you, I got frantic."

Jack rubbed his face with his hands, laid down his jacket, resignation crossing his face. "Okay, let's have it. Where did the call come in? Up here or down in the bookstore?"

"The bookstore. I was alone, working on accounts. Monica's away, remember? She's gone to Chicago for a couple of days. I'd closed the store at 5—the call was probably only a few minutes after I'd locked up."

He pulled out his cell and dialed. "Hi, Lacey. Roselli here. Can you run a trace for me? Yeah, we're tapping the line."

Sofie waited while he gave her store number, hung up and turned back to her with an unreadable expression.

"Sofie, if this doesn't show anything, I'm going to have to get rid of the tap on your phone. So far nothing's turned up and along with all the personal time I've been pulling, the Chief is riding me."

"What are we supposed to do, just ignore the calls?"

"Look, right now I'm tired. I don't know what to say about the calls. It would be nice if Monica or someone else could listen in one of these times. It would give me something to back up the claim. Right now, I'm starting to get strange looks at work about this." He didn't need to add that she was the one whose sanity was in doubt.

"Jack. Do the people you work with know about Katya—that she's your daughter, I mean?"

He frowned, his patience wearing thinner. "No, no one. Except the Inspector, and the Chief. I told them about the threat to Katya and that she was my daughter. What with my family's history, they aren't going to question me too much about needing to protect her. Why?"

"I've been trying to think who else might know about Katya. Besides your family," she said. "What about Kim Barber? You told her about Katya?"

"Kim Barber!" He exploded. "What's she got to do with this?"

Sofie paused, not wanting to venture where he'd hate her to go. "She called me yesterday and asked to see me. She said she had some information for me. I went to see her."

He was stone-faced. "What the hell did she want? I haven't said a word to her about Katya. There's no reason for me to mention her. She asked you to come and see her about what?" He glared and she took a step back.

"She asked me to stop by her office. She said she wanted to discuss the problem of Katya. She said she wanted to help me, that you'd asked her to call me."

He cursed softly. "Look, I haven't told Kim anything about this. As far as anyone else at work knows, I'm dealing with a family issue, doing some personal bodyguard time, for friends. Some of the guys are starting to get curious, with my working at home so much last week, but it's none of their goddamned business. No one—except my boss, has the right to dig into my personal life."

He pushed his fingers through his hair, working for control. "There may be some gossip around about what I'm working on, since all the leads have fallen through, but that's the extent of what anyone knows." He stood up and walked over to her. "So what did she want?"

"When I got there, she changed her story. She told me she wanted to warn me about you. That you were getting ready to proceed with a move to get custody of Katya." The words fell heavily into the quiet room. "She said since there was no proof of a real threat, you were operating on the assumption I'd planned the whole thing, and that I'm an incompetent mother. That I was just after money or something."

"Anything else?" His voice was taut.

"It seemed plausible to me, since you've already accused me of as much. She said she was doing me a favor by telling me.

She even hinted at the idea that I should try and get some real proof. She said that since she had a relationship going with you, she didn't want it jeopardized by whatever's going on with us."

"I'll speak with Kim and find out what the hell's going on." He paused, his next words softer. "It's not true you know, Sofie. I'm not just hanging around here trying to gather evidence against you. I don't work that way. I'm here to get this cleared up and keep Katya safe. I'll do whatever it takes to make sure no one hurts her. That's all I'm doing."

He stopped and weighed his next words. "If nothing turns up on this trace tonight, I think it would be best if I move back home, especially after what happened Monday,"

"You're probably right, Jack." She answered, avoiding looking at him.

"For now, I'm doing the best I can to clear up this thing. In the meantime, just take it easy, okay? Don't go running off on your own to try to deal with this."

His pager went off and he pulled it out and read it. "Let me handle things. I'll talk to Kim and see what's up with her. I've gotta do some things tonight. While I'm downtown, I'll check on that trace too, okay?"

He was trying to placate her, to put her off rather than give her any answer. Sofie sat a long time after he'd gone, staring down on the street, wondering what to do next.

It was after ten when she finished killing time, straightening up the apartment, roaming around picking up the last of Katya's things. She spotted Jack's sports jacket lying over the back of a chair, grabbed it up, and took it into his room.

When she shook out the coat, papers fell out of the inside pocket onto the bed and she glanced at them automatically. They were blank legal forms, the words on the top said "State of Michigan, Application for Custody." She dropped to the bed, shaking.

The words caught her by surprise, stunned her, a complete contradiction to what he told her. Turning on a light, she sifted through the papers, searching for anything. He'd lied to her, he'd already had the papers, even as he said he'd never do it. There they were, in his pocket, not filled out, but ready.

She didn't hear the apartment door open, didn't hear his footsteps until he was outside the room. She turned quickly and saw the quizzical look on his face. Before he could speak, she bolted past him, heading for the safety of her own room.

He caught her before she made it through the door, wrapped his arms around her and pinned her against his large body. His arms were like steel, the hard barrier of his chest impenetrable. "Let me go, Jack!"

"It's not what it looks like, Sofie. Let me explain."

"What's there to explain, you bastard? It's crystal clear. You said you weren't going to try and get Katya from me, but here's the proof you are. I'm in the way and you want me out of the way so you can have her."

He took a deep breath. "No. It's not like that." He drew back, releasing her arms. "You're right, I do want Katya—but I'm not planning on stealing her from you. We're strangers. Aside from the weird chemistry between us, we don't know each other at all. At this point, I'm just trying to cover all my bases, I can't afford to just let it slide and operate from hope. The lust thing between us is confusing things, making me unsure as hell of my own feelings."

She tried to edge back from him.

"You can't deny it's confusing, Sofie. We're going to have to find some way to work through this and share her. I did get the papers, but you must have noticed I haven't filled them out. It was just a precaution. In case."

"What do you mean?" She said. "In case? Of what? What could possibly justify getting custody of her from me?" She narrowed her eyes at him.

He still had his jacket on, revealing a black t-shirt beneath, his usual working outfit. He had a day's growth of stubble on his face and he looked exhausted. Sofie leaned against the door, defeated. "I know you're tired, but Jack, I need to know what this is all about!"

"All right. If you're determined to drag this out of me now, here it is. Like I told you the other night, everything we have to go on from you so far has fallen through. Even the letter can't be traced. There are no fingerprints on it, there's no such post office box. Katya's nursery school teacher only saw a note signed by you and this man." The words tumbled out of him, accusatory.

"The only thing she can tell us is that the man stopped by and tried to pick up Katya, but he claimed to be someone sent by you. There's no evidence that he wasn't, except you say he wasn't. So you're the only person who has any real knowledge that someone is after Katya."

"And since I'm a lying, scheming bitch, you've decided to get custody of her."

"No. In fact, the investigating officer working with me hasn't ruled out the stalking scenario, but all evidence so far points to you, Sofie. My boss is starting to ask questions. If he gets wind of anything weird about the threats, he won't hesitate a second to call in Social Services on this and throw Katya into protective custody. As her father, I'm the alternative." He was breathing now as though he'd been running.

"That's absurd! They could accuse me of being a threat to my own child, on no evidence? And take Katya from me?"

"Yes, they could. I'm doing every thing I can right now to back up your story and check out the evidence myself. If they can come up with some motive on you, they won't hesitate to look into it. In the meantime, they'll take Katya out of the home."

"What motive?"

"For one, me, Sofie. They'll be looking for a money motive. If they start investigating and find any evidence you're in dire straits, anything that points to a desperate need, that can be motive enough. If it gets to the point where they call in SSI, I want to make sure I've got clear custody. Right now, especially for Katya's sake, I'd prefer not to do that. I don't want her in the middle of this." He stated bluntly. "But if I have to, I'll step in—we'll send her to my mother. You wouldn't object to that, would you, if things get that far out of hand?"

Her throat tightened. "No, but that can't be. It won't go that far. How could they think I'd endanger my own child?" She choked back a sob and glared at him. "And how does Kim Barber fit into all this?"

He made a move towards her but didn't touch her. "I don't know, but I'm going to find out." He still had on his jacket and he yanked it off, exposing his holster riding one shoulder of his black t-shirt.

"Look, Sofie, it's late. Let's get some sleep, okay? I'll put a call in to Kim and get to the bottom of it. Right now, I'm beat. I promise you it's going to be all right. I won't let anything happen to Katya."

She resisted the dismissal. "You keep saying that. But it sounds to me like the investigation is just stalled out, that until whoever is harassing us does something real, maybe even harms Katya, there'll be no more investigation?"

"I'm saying that we'll keep on this, that I'm here and I'm going to make sure she's okay, even if I have to hire private protection to back me up." He hadn't said he believed her though. "And I promise you I'm not going to take Katya away—permanently."

He reached out and touched her cheek briefly. "I won't do anything that will hurt Katya, I promise, or you, Sofie. There are so many factors at work in this. Keeping an investigation going, trying to work out some sort of protection arrangements for her, and then there's my mother. She's so afraid of losing Katya, she's begging me to do whatever I have to as long as Katya's safe." He grimaced at her. "She wants to know why I didn't marry you."

She stared back at him, her expression so like Katya's when she'd lost her doll that he almost hugged her to him. "I know." He said. "Crazy idea, huh?"

He stood in the dark hallway, watching her go into her room and turned back to the kitchen for a beer. *Jackass*, he thought. He didn't trust her, but he told her he did. Basically he'd lied to her. He said he wouldn't hurt her, but he was pretty damned likely to do just that. He didn't know who the hell to believe.

Taking long swigs from the bottle, he stood in the doorway of the living room, staring at the faded pink light from the street, off, on, off, flickering in the dark room and thought about Sofie in bed, curled up.

*Goddammit!* No matter what she'd done or how she'd roped him into her life, he wanted her. He downed the rest of the beer and went to bed.

## *Eleven*

The squad room was full of Friday night business, anything and everything illegal occurring on the east side of Detroit. The bomb squad had a meeting in ten minutes and Jack sifted through reports, looking for similarities in his files to unsolved bombings over the past five years. He had a hard copy of the recent trace on Sofie's phone from last night and, like all the other traces he'd run, nothing had turned up.

He was frustrated enough to pull out his hair. Added to that was the ambivalence he felt over the heat they'd generated four nights ago and his distrust of her since. He found himself thinking about her at odd moments in the day and cursed himself for it. Instead of evaluating the findings on the frag data, he replayed Sofie's words, trying to recall their conversations and whether there was anything he'd missed, some sign that she wasn't being up-front with him. He wanted to stick with his natural suspiciousness; he knew it and trusted it well, but something about Sofie made him want to believe her. And no matter whichever way he ran it, he couldn't see her using Katya as a pawn in a game she was playing.

It was an all-team meeting and the situation room was full. After an hour, he still had nothing but frustrations, only more of them. There were no leads, nothing concrete from the CSU and except for the too obvious message on the SUV, nothing to distinguish this case from the last. All connections between CUR and ELF had been investigated and led no place. Following threads in the National Crime Database regarding ELF groups around the country showed no active cells in the Detroit area and, unlike the LA Hummer bombings, there was no chatter on active ecoterrorist groups in the lower peninsula right now. On top of that, he had to go back to Sofie's and deal with her and where to go from here. He'd threatened to move out in a day or two. They were now coming on two days and he either needed to shut up about it or move his ass back to his place.

Kim caught him as he threw on his jacket and shut down his laptop for the night. She had on one of her usual "fuck-me" outfits and he knew, without looking, every male eye in the place was focused on the action of her ass as she headed to his desk.

He waited, knowing where the conversation would go and pissed that he had to be having it. She'd made it clear to him for the past few months that all she wanted was for things to get back to where they'd left it six months ago—sweaty sex and no conversation. He had no desire for more of either. Much more appealing and harder to stifle was his urge for sex with Sofie, something he damned well wasn't going to do again. It was crazy, since, of the two women, it was Kim who fit his MO for bed partner. Yet, as she swooped down on his desk with her firm backside, he felt not even a twinge in the groin area.

"Jack, I'm glad I caught you."

"Yeah? I'm glad you stopped by. I wanted to talk."

"Good, I'd got something for you. I got your page last night, but I was on a stakeout." She made a quick motion to shoot him with a cute finger and thumb move. "Your friend Sofie called me the other day and asked to see me. She stopped by my office Wednesday evening." Kim raised an eyebrow at him. "She was a little unclear about what she wanted. She seemed to think I might help her get some evidence. Around the thing you're investigating with her daughter."

"Sofie told me she'd seen you. But she said you called her. I'm a little confused here, Kim. Why would she ask you to assist her? She has me working on the case."

"Well, Jack, you know, you can be a little scary at times. Especially when you're mad. She seemed to feel you didn't believe her story and that she needed to get more evidence so you would." She glanced up at him. "You know, don't you, that there's a rumor going around that little kid of hers is yours. I wanted to see what she had in mind, so I didn't discourage her visit. Anyway, she asked me not to mention it to you. I hate to butt in on this, but she seems a bit irrational, you know. If she were a parent of my child, I'd be a little worried."

He scanned the room but no one was near enough to hear her words. "Yeah? As far as the speculation on her daughter's paternity goes, I'm not interested. I'm only interested in protecting the kid. And getting things cleared up as soon as possible. So what exactly did she say to you?"

"Well, she went on and on about calls and some letter that you didn't believe were real. And then she asked me a lot of questions about evidence, like what was admissible, what a cop needed. All pretty strange, you know?"

He watched one crossed leg, swinging rhythmically as his thoughts moved back and forth in synchrony with it.

"She seemed desperate to get something for the record. She even asked me if I'd back her up, if she found something. It almost sounded like she wanted me falsifying evidence. I really think you need to put a leash on her."

She frowned and flicked something off her lapel. "Look, Jack, I know you want it kept quiet, but you know, she told me

Katya's your daughter. She admitted it. And she pretty much said the three of you were together, a family. She's got something cooking in that strange little head of hers. I just thought I should warn you. You know I'm on your side, Jack."

What the hell was Sofie up to now? And why go to Kim? She was asking for trouble. Kim was a friend of his, but she wouldn't hesitate to report Sofie if she thought there was some sort of illegal set-up going on. And why the fuck had Sofie lied to him about setting up this meeting with Kim? Where was reality here? It felt like a cold hand squeezing his heart and he shuddered at the thought of Katya in the middle of all this.

His mind leapt back twenty years. He'd been thirteen and considered himself head of the family after his father. He was the Zorro, the Long Ranger, the Terminator of his neighborhood while Dinah was a fearless little girl of six, always in need of his protection. He'd swooped down repeatedly to save her from the neighborhood bullies who'd grabbed her ice cream cone or from the three Roselli brothers, whose main pleasure in life was to make her cry. He swore he'd always be there. He had to keep Katya safe, no matter what.

"Let me handle this, Kim. I'll talk with Sofie and get it straightened out. It was probably just a misunderstanding. She doesn't have a clue how police procedure works. She probably assumed you were working on this with me." He looked away to hide the lie in his eyes.

"Jack, I don't think it had anything to do with a misunderstanding. She pretty much asked me to falsify a report for her, about the calls she says she's been receiving. She wanted me to pretend to listen in on a call and then document it for her."

She stood up, lifted her arms and pulled on her suit jacket. Jack could almost hear the spontaneous groans as the men in the room grabbed their crotches. "I don't want to say anything to the Chief about this, Jack, so I'm counting on you to deal with it. If you care about that little girl she claims you fathered, you might want to look into some legal help at this point, just in case things deteriorate with your friend." She patted down her shiny hair, grabbed up her bag off his desk and strode with long-legged action out of the room.

~ * ~

It was after nine when Jack got home and Katya was waiting at the top of the stairs for him, holding the book she'd chosen for him to read her. He leaned down and kissed her on the top of the head, pulled off his holster and dropped in on the shelf.

Sofie sat at the table, watching as he turned back to Katya, his expression so different from the one he'd just flashed her. Tonight there was something else there that Sofie couldn't read, something like fear. "Would you like a beer, Jack? I bought some today."

"Yeah, thanks, I could use one." He pulled out a kitchen chair and dropped heavily into it. He took the beer from her carefully, avoiding touching her. She winced and turned to put the kulebiak into the microwave, not looking up until she'd composed her face. She knew whatever he had to say was going to be painful.

"Sit down." He said it without inflection. "I talked with Kim Barber this evening. She stopped by to see me." Her face gave nothing away. "She said she'd seen you Wednesday, but her story was a little different from yours, Sofie. She told me you'd called and asked to see her." He spoke slowly, then stopped.

"She said I called her? I can't imagine why she'd say that. She actually asked me not to mention to you that she'd called me. I have no idea why she'd come to you with a different story but it's a lie, Jack." She saw disbelief in his face and swallowed, knowing she was pleading a losing case. There was no way he'd believe her, her word against a fellow cop and girlfriend. Kim had months, or even years, with him to back up whatever she said. She had nothing but a night of drunken sex four years ago, and the claim of a daughter they shared.

"Sofie, look, whatever the fuck is going on, throw me a few crumbs of the truth here. Why the hell would Kim make up a story like that? What's the point?"

"I have no idea." Sofie looked around as Katya came into the room, still carrying her book. "Katya's waiting for you to read to her. Why don't you do that and we'll talk after."

Jack pushed back from the table, most of his food untouched. "Come on, Katya, let's go get you into bed. What's your pleasure, tonight?" He took the book from her and headed for her bedroom.

"Night, sweetie." Sofie kissed her daughter, pushed her after Jack and sat down to eat, tasting nothing. She restlessly paced the floor until he returned and without ceremony, she started in where they'd left off. "Why would you think I set up a meeting with her? What did she tell you?"

He sat down heavily in front of his warm beer and cold kulebiah. "She says you called her looking for ways to get evidence, that you asked her to help falsify evidence." He stared intently at her face. "Well? What do you have to say?"

"I say she's crazy! I didn't call her and I never asked to see her. She called me. She asked me to come down to the precinct. She said she wanted to warn me about what you were up to, with Katya." Sofie absently took the pastry out of his hands and put it into the microwave.

"What the hell does that mean? Warn you! She said she'd heard rumors about Katya but she didn't really know the facts, until you told her yesterday. No one knows at the station, except my boss. Or they didn't, until you went down there."

"She did know! She told me you were planning on getting custody of Katya and that I should be careful." She pulled the hot food out and plopped the plate down in front of him.

"Well, if that's the story, you're damned close to the truth at this point! I am thinking of calling a lawyer now, after what you pulled with Kim. Either you're a liar or you're crazy, and I don't want my daughter around this!"

"Your daughter! All of a sudden, she's your daughter, not mine?"

"Our daughter then! I don't want her exposed to whatever crap you're scheming up and if you don't quit it, Sofie, I will start trying to get custody. In the meantime, I wanna have full access to her. I want to be able to see her any time and I want my family to see her."

"You're putting out a lot of contradictory threats here suddenly, Detective. And just yesterday you were assuring me you had no intention of going after custody of Katya. As I recall, you promised me. Some promise."

"Yeah, well that was before I found out about this thing you pulled with Kim. I can't believe you actually tried to get away with saying she called you. What in the hell were you thinking of that I wouldn't go and ask her."

"I told you. She did call me!" Sofie stood up and took her dishes to the sink, fighting an urge to throw them at him. "As far as custody goes, you have no claim on Katya. She's my daughter. I did everything for her. Your name isn't even on the birth certificate as the father. You'd never even have known she existed if I hadn't trusted you enough to let you into her life!"

"That's my fucking point! The sort of world you're exposing her to here, with all those weirdoes in your store, your financial problems, and then you never even came to me. I don't see much of a problem to show just cause, at least for partial custody of her." He ran his fingers through his hair.

"Christ. I don't want to get into a shouting match over this, Sofie but I'm damned confused here. I thought we were starting to have some sort of understanding. You promised me, just the other night, you'd stay out of the investigation and let me handle things. I even had some hope we might become friends."

"Is that what you call Sunday night? Is that what friends do with each other?"

"Dammit! You know that's not what I mean. I'm talking about a trust broken. I was beginning to really think we could work something out, maybe even like each other. A good situation all round, especially for Katya. Instead, I catch you in this lie. And as far as I know, it's just the tip of the iceberg. How do you expect me to react? And as far as what happened Sunday, we both agreed we were upset and it was a mistake."

"That's an easy out for you, Jack. Is that how you explained away four years ago? It's fine to have a night of sex with some stranger just because you're upset? You got what you needed and never bothered to find out if I was okay afterwards?" He blanched at her words.

"It's easy now to throw that in my face, four years later, isn't it? Is that what this is all about? Getting even with me for that night? And what about your role in it? What about your responsibility? Are you playing some sort of sick game using Katya like a carrot, to wave her in front of me and then disappear with her? Or to scare the shit out of me, so you can see me dance around like a fool, trying to protect you?"

Sofie picked up his dishes with trembling hand and carried them to the sink, afraid if she said another word, she'd burst into tears. He sat, watching her, his eyes narrowed. Crying would get her no place with him. The situation was new for her, but the challenge was familiar. It was the daily struggle she lived with, her fight to be strong, like her mother and her grandmother. She fought a constant battle with that fear that at her core, she was weak. This time the fight not in her mind, but real, an opportunity to call on something within herself. She felt a burst of optimism, a certainty in her that, if she could deal with this, she could deal with anything in her life.

She filled the tea kettle and made coffee, her trembling evaporated. "So what are you going to do, Jack? You throw around these accusations so righteously, even though you've known me barely three weeks. Your sense of fairness sucks. You've been waiting to get the goods on me and Kim gave you the opening." She pulled out a mug and some cookies. "It sounds almost as though you're relieved. You don't have to bother with me, don't have to deal with whatever happens between people other than sex." A mental image of beating on him with her fists gave her renewed energy and she pressed on. "You've got a simple explanation for the whole thing now and that gives you an easy out—just make me the bad guy here, without a trial and then go after what you want. In this case, Katya. If that's how it's going to go, you can get out!"

He stood up without speaking, paced to one end of her kitchen, turned and took a deep breath. "Calm down, Sofie. All right? This is going no place. Let's see if we can find a way to discuss this sanely, all right?" He shrugged his shoulders, easing the tension, and came back to the table. "You're right. I decided before I got here you were guilty. Here's your chance to explain, let's hear what you were doing. Why did you go to Kim?"

"I told you. She called and asked me to stop by her office." She held up her hand as he started to protest. "This is useless. If you aren't going to at least consider what I'm telling you might be true, there's no point in going further with this discussion."

"Okay. Tell me your side of it."

"As I said, she called me on Wednesday and asked that I come down and see her. She said it was something she was working on for you, about Katya. It was after 5:30 when I got there and no one was around."

"Convenient."

She glared at him and went on. "Anyway, when I got there, she said she wanted to help me out, by giving me information. She started out with some story about the sisterhood and all that, but when I didn't buy it, she switched to her own agenda. She said Katya and I were in the way of her relationship with you." She fortified herself with a bite of cookie. "She wanted the whole thing finished, out of her way. She said you were getting ready to go for custody, and that you were gathering evidence against me and biding your time."

He frowned. Sofie's story had a familiar ring to it; it sounded like something Kim would say.

"She repeated what you told me, that there's no evidence anywhere so far that the threat to Katya's real. She said if it were her, she'd make damned sure the evidence did stand up. She implied I should get evidence, whatever the cost, even if I had to manufacture it. She seemed so strange and over-the-top, I got nervous. I told her I'd think it over, just to have an excuse to get out of there, and I left. I was in her office a total of, maybe twenty minutes."

He fiddled with the salt shaker, watching her as though he found the truth in her face. "I can't see it, Sofie. The whole thing's so far-fetched. A police officer would never suggest you manufacture evidence. Christ! It's ludicrous."

She had stated her position and refused to argue further.

He rubbed a hand over his face. "I've already told you I'll do whatever's needed for Katya. What ever you want. What I want from you is to drop this crazy story you're telling about Kim."

That was it, then. He'd decided against her. "I can see this is pointless. I don't want you here now. If you want to contact an attorney, be my guest. If you want to see Katya, you can see her. I'll set up some sort of schedule for you. But you'll never get custody of her. You've made up your mind, based on the word of a girlfriend. Or maybe it's that blue line thing or whatever they call it. Anyway, I know when I'm beat. Please, just get your things and leave. I'm going to bed."

She didn't want to see or hear him leave so turned on the shower, full force and stood under it until all thought was beaten out of her. She climbed out and was toweling herself down when he knocked on the door. "Sofie, please, I can't leave like this. Come on out. I promise I won't throw any more accusations at you." It was the closest thing to a concession she'd get from him.

Throwing on her clothes, she yanked open the door. He stood, hands stuffed deep into his pants pockets, looking almost contrite.

"It's late and we're both tired. Give me a list of times and I'll write up a schedule. I'll drop the Kim story, but in return what I want a promise from you there'll be no custody attempt. I won't bother you about anything else. Your job will be just to be there for her." She went over and took down his coat and handed it to him. She left him no opening for further questions and he asked for none.

"I'll set someone up to continue the protective drive-bys. Call me if anything turns up that might be a threat, all right? I'm not dropping this completely, you know. If we get anything else, I'll follow it. That's the best I can do. If you promise to leave Kim Barber alone and drop whatever plans you had with that, I promise to throw out the custody papers."

"I can promise that easily enough, since there was no plan. Call me tomorrow with your schedule and I'll give you

Katya's. Of better still, email me at the bookstore. That way you won't even have to come in contact with me again." She said it without rancor.

He sighed and ran his fingers over stubble on his chin. "Sofie, I'm not trying to avoid you and I'm not going to do this through email. Ideally, I'd like us to be friends, if possible. I'll call you tomorrow and then we can set some things up." He headed towards the bedroom. "I'll get my things."

Within minutes he was back, his duffle in hand and heading for the stairs.

"What shall I tell Katya? She expects you to be here in the morning."

"Tell her I'll be by tomorrow early to talk to her. Don't upset her about my moving out. I'll explain to her tomorrow that I'll be seeing her just as often. I'll make sure she isn't upset by this."

He moved down the stairs, calling over his shoulder, "Come down after me and make sure the door's locked tight, okay?"

~ * ~

Sofie sat staring at her mug. It was after midnight and she couldn't sleep. She'd thrown away the last of the coffee and brewed some herb tea. He'd been gone over two hours and his words seemed to still hang in the air. She sat in the darkened room and watched as a squad car drove by, slowed down, and moved on, leaving the street empty again. It was Friday and a few blocks away, the late night bars would be crowded, like the night she'd met Jack. People laughing, talking, eager to forget the pain of their lives and find a moment of pleasure, as she had.

*God*, she thought, *what happened?* How had she been so blind? His distrust of her was impenetrable. She'd pictured them becoming friends, laughing about things Katya did during the day, almost like real parents. It had been nothing but a damned illusion. She'd been blinded by how he felt about Katya.

She was almost glad he'd trampled over those illusions of hers tonight. It left her with a sense of purpose, a new confidence in her ability to protect Katya. She no longer needed to depend on Jack. She could do whatever was necessary to make sure Katya was safe.

Kim Barber. That was the first thing she had to do, find out what she knew, what she was up to. She'd promised Jack she wouldn't repeat what happened. That didn't mean she had to stop looking for the truth. Kim knew something, and Sofie wanted to know what it was. How could she find out what was going on? There was only one way.

## *Twelve*

The twenty-minute bus ride down Woodward Avenue was painfully slow and Sofie sat idly, playing with her flashlight, wondering if Katya's red plastic toy would give enough light. It would have to do. Kim's office was in the annex building next to Central Precinct. Cold Case Investigations on the first floor, Ballistics and Chemical Assay in the basement, the Vice Squad office, Kim's domain, on the second floor. The third floor housed the Bomb Squad.

These were offices only, and labs. The chaos and noise that was part of every waking moment across the street at Central was missing here and Sofie entered through the side door unobserved. She moved quickly up the stairwell to the second floor, encountering no one. The dim hall was empty except for a lone cleaning person at the other end, making Saturday night rounds. Sofie glued herself to one side of the hallway, dropping into doorways to avoid being spotted. She'd taken Katya to spend the night at Monica's, hung around for two hours until the girls were in bed, and left at ten, with the understanding she'd go home and spend a quiet evening in bed with a good mystery. Instead, here she was, committing a crime.

Sofie stumbled over something, maybe a pail forgotten by the cleaning lady. She fell to her knees, and lost a shoe in the process. She didn't dare to go back to get it, and instead stumbled forward, past the second door, the third, stopping at the fourth.

She tried the knob and it turned, the door was unlocked. The place smelled like Pinesol, which meant the cleaning people had already passed through, probably planning to lock up when they finished with all the rooms.

Sofie edged the door shut behind her and shone her light around the room. It looked smaller by night, the two windows on the far side letting in a faint glow from the jail behind. Red and green Christmas lights reflected off the street below, shimmered off the walls. The desk and four sets of file cabinets dominated the room, and she sighed and hopped, minus a shoe, over to the desk to begin her assault on the drawers.

*Is Jack on duty tonight?* Sofie didn't let the thought linger for more than a moment. If he found out she'd broken into Kim's office, he'd probably be pleased; it would only confirm what he already believed, that she was a liar and crook. What he thought was irrelevant at this point, except as it related to Katya. That was a real problem. If she was caught and arrested, Jack wouldn't hesitate to renege on his promise and go for custody of Katya.

Limping around the room, she wished she'd worn something besides her Birkenstocks, something nailed to her foot. The second desk drawer was the one she wanted—she'd seen Kim throw a set of keys in there Wednesday night as she'd come into the room.

She found the ring, studded with little semiprecious stones, 15 or so keys hanging from it, at least six of them small, file-cabinet-size.

It took endless minutes to go through all the keys and she wiped sweat from her forehead as she worked. She kept an ear out for the cleaning woman, stopping from time to time to peer out the door and identify her location. She tried every key, working her way through each cabinet, every file, looking for anything about Katya, anything about Jack.

In the fourth cabinet, the bottom drawer at the rear, she found something; a folder containing pictures of Jack, his medical records, and a copy of Katya's birth certificate. She flipped through it quickly, suppressing the urge to stop and read the files on Jack.

She shoved the entire file into her purse, knocked the drawer closed with a hip and returned the keys to the desk.

Flashlight off but still in hand, she stepped out of Kim's office and into the darkened hall. The door closed with a click behind her, just as she heard footsteps, running, towards her. The dark figure loomed large, and grew, a shadow, distinguishable only by the small beam from a flashlight fixed on her.

*Oh, God! I've got to get out of here!* She turned to run and, as though in a dream, her feet seemed stuck in place. She willed them to move, and still they resisted.

"Police! Stop! Put your hands up!" She turned back and looked at him, a uniformed cop, gun drawn in one hand, juggling a flashlight and her shoe in the other.

"Down! On the ground now!" He yelled the words, but gave her no time to act. Instead, he pushed her face down, cuffed her and patted her down. She lay breathing hard, ribs hurting from the fall, afraid to move. He reached down and roughly pulled her bag from her shoulder. She looked up, silent, as he rifled through it.

"Stand up!" Catching hold of her cuffed hands, he pulled hard until she staggered upright. "Move!" He pushed her ahead of him down the hall and down the darkened stairwell.

She didn't speak as he prodded her down the two flights of stairs. She kept her eyes fixed on the steps, afraid she'd trip and fall into the darkness below.

Her breath came out in a hiss as she hit the cold air of outside. Still holding tight to her arms cuffed behind, he pushed her across the deserted street and through the back door of Central Precinct.

The building was crowded with people, uniformed cops dragging in disheveled criminals, like herself, cuffed, unruly, smelling of violence and fear. Each of them was steered into the same brightly lit room, cluttered with desks and benches, where they'd all be booked and led off to jail for the night. Including herself.

The bench he shoved her down on was hard, the air overheated and smelling of unwashed bodies, lights merciless after the darkness outside. People around her cursed or cried, accompanied in the background by the continuous ringing of phones. She sat mute, waiting for her paperwork to be finished, when she would be booked and taken away.

No one spoke, other than the arresting officer, who Mirandized her and turned her bag over to someone in plain clothes. He sat at a desk, eating a bagel with one hand and rifled through her bag with the other, unconcerned.

It took more than an hour to get her fingerprinted and booked. Someone took her to an empty desk and told her she could make one phone call.

She phoned Monica, who listened between uttering expletives. "Sofie, my God! You can't be serious! They caught you breaking and entering? At the precinct? What in God's name were you doing? I thought you were at home in bed!"

"I can't explain now, Monica. Please, just promise me you'll keep Katya. Don't say anything about where I am. Just tell her I had to go on an overnight trip." She took a deep breath, trying to think. "No, don't tell her anything. She thinks I'm at the apartment. Leave it at that. Just get someone over here as early as possible to get me out."

"Don't worry, Sofie. I'll handle it."

"I have a little money in the safe. Use that. Or if it's not enough, I have some jewelry of my mom's in there. Take it."

"Sofie, what about Jack? Why don't I call him? He could probably get you out of there tonight."

"Please, Monica. Don't call him. That's the last thing I need. He's just looking for an excuse to get to me. Just call Jeff in the morning, okay?"

"I can call him tonight, you know. He'd come down."

"No. Don't call him. I can take a night in jail. Just take care of Katya until I can get out."

Sofie hung up and let them escort her back to her bench. It was 1:30 in the morning and she sat down to wait. It was going to be a very long night in jail.

~ * ~

Jack was on-call, working late at his office. Anything to keep from going home to his apartment, where he'd spend the night second-guessing himself about his exchange with Sofie. The rest of the Poletown frag reports sat in front of him, finally back from DC, but it was useless, he kept reading the same paragraph over and over.

He did cull from the report something about a chemical signature on the explosives. The stuff came from a naval munitions center in Southern Indiana. First thing tomorrow, he'd contact them, get a list of their suppliers and find out the likelihood of tracing stolen explosives from the naval base. How in the hell had it gotten from there to Detroit?

He was on-call this week, working nonstop, getting only four or five hours sleep a night, then getting up for another sixteen-hour shift, all the while worrying about Katya. And then the blow-up with Sofie last night.

The call came in just after two a.m. and he cursed into the phone as the duty cop identified himself. They'd found a folder with personal information about him on a perp taken into custody tonight, a Sofia Novakoff. *Goddammit!* She'd been picked up for B&E at the annex, coming out of an office in Vice, a floor below where he sat right now.

*Shit!* Furious, both at her and at himself for caring, he grabbed his jacket and ran across the street, throwing on his shoulder holster as he went.

She was sitting on a bench at the far end of the room, leaning forward, hands behind her, cuffed. He kept his eyes fixed on her as he stormed the bench. She had on a dark sweater and pants, minus a coat and minus one shoe. "All right, what the hell is this all about?"

He was too close, much too loud and she pulled back. The one person she didn't want to see tonight was here. "Since you've put the threat to Katya on hold, I decided to do some investigating on my own. I got caught." She pulled herself up, ignoring her hands cuffed behind her.

"You got caught? Well, what the hell? Too bad, huh? Otherwise, no problem, right? You feel completely justified breaking into the police department, do you?"

"Actually, I was. I found the evidence I was after, that your cop friend knew something."

"What cop friend and what evidence?" He stared at her. "I got a call that some personal papers of mine had turned up on a perp—that's you."

"I got those papers from Kim Barber's file cabinet."

"Kim Barber! Shit! You broke into her office? I should have known it. You couldn't leave it alone. I'd almost think this was some sort of high school prank you're playing—except Kim's a cop and she sure as hell won't let this pass."

She glared at him. "What does that mean?"

"It means I think you're jealous of Kim and doing your damnedest to incriminate her in some crime you've dreamt up."

"I am *not*. She told me some things that she shouldn't have known, about Katya. After mulling it over a couple of days, I decided I wanted to know what she's up to. Especially since you're not interested." She pulled her one unshod foot beneath her. "She had some reason for calling me in to see her. She had information in her file cabinet you said you never gave out. I had no other real leads and I just did what I needed to do" She shrugged.

"What information do you claim she had?"

"She had the file in a drawer, with things in it about Katya, where she was born, things like that. Why would she even care? She had it pushed into the back of a file cabinet with things about you. Is it normal for a cop to keep personal information on another cop? Even a close friend?"

"Hell no, but I still don't know that she didn't get it from you. And by the way, where's Katya while you're out on this little adventure? You claim you want protect her so badly, then you go off on some insane escapade and leave her some place? While you spend the night in jail?"

"She's staying with Monica. She's safe."

He saw the look of dogged determination in her face and made a sound of disgust. "Even if you didn't give Kim that information directly, you probably made her curious enough to go digging after you met with her. Whether she had any business looking into it or not, you probably set her up."

"This is hopeless. Why are you here? Just leave me alone and I'll deal with this. I broke into Kim's office. Why should I bother to defend myself? Why don't you just go on home, Jack?"

He sighed. "Because you're going to jail and whatever I think about this shit, I'm not going to let that happen." He spotted the detective nearby sifting through papers, and stood up. "Don't move and don't talk to anyone. I'll be back as soon as I handle this."

*Shit,* he thought, *I can't believe I'm here doing this! Goddammit!* He dropped into the empty chair next to the booking desk and started the process of extricating Sofie from jail.

It took 45 minutes of everything from threats to butt kissing, but he finally got the B&E charges dropped from her record. *At least she wasn't caught with a weapon on her! Thank God for small gifts.*

He walked back to Sofie, who sat with her head resting against the wall, still cuffed, still minus her shoe. The situation was so nuts, he would have laughed out loud, if he wasn't so pissed. His head throbbing, without a word for her, he grabbed the keys off the desk, bent down and uncuffed her. He tossed the keys and cuffs across the desk and pulled her up, not gently.

"Come on, let's go." Without a nod at anyone, he ushered her out of the station.

She stumbled along beside him, limping, and he slowed down. "I'm free?" she asked, incredulous. "They're not going to arrest me?"

"I got them to drop the charges. You sound like you're unhappy about it. Where's your coat?" They'd reached the steps out front and the wind cut a path in front of them, howling. "And where's your shoe, dammit?"

"I lost the shoe going into the building. The other building. I think I dropped my coat when the cop grabbed me." She hugged herself, for a moment, preferring the idea of jail to dealing with Jack. "Where are we going?"

"Next door. Come on." He yanked off his jacket, threw it around her shoulders and put an arm around her. Feeling his heat, she swayed slightly against him and stiffened. He made another sound of disgust, but didn't speak.

The rain had started just after midnight and had changed to cold pellets, coming down fast. He sheltered her with his body as he steered her across the street to the Annex.

She stood alone in the dark stairwell as he took the steps two at a time and disappeared. Endless silent minutes passed before he returned with her coat and shoe. He'd found the coat lying in a heap in a darkened corner of second floor, the shoe lying on the first landing.

"Here." He thrust his cell at her but kept steering her forward, out the door and down the street. "Call Monica and tell her you're out of jail. I don't want her frightening Katya with this."

She made her call, hunched over, sheltering the phone, as they struggled down the street together, fighting the wind.

In the quiet of the car, she passed him back his phone but said nothing. He drove fast and she shut her eyes, not caring anymore what he thought. She dosed off, startled awake when he pulled up to a bus stop and parked. "Where are we?" She'd assumed he'd dump her at home.

"Some place where we can talk. And I need coffee."

It was another all-night diner, this time on Woodward off Six Mile Road, similar to the place he'd taken her four years ago. Not a cop haunt, but familiar to him. He'd put a lot of late nights in here, studying, when he'd been working on his degree at U of D. The glare of fluorescent lights burned his eyes and he scanned the room for a private booth. The place was filled with regulars. Thank God, no one he knew. The clubs around Detroit were closed and many of the customers in the place leaned over coffee, working to get sober before driving back to the suburbs. It was hot in the place, a sharp contrast to the cold sleet falling outside.

She ordered tea and he watched as she sipped it, the heat of the room and the hot liquid bringing color back to her cheeks. Her hair was pulled back tonight, pinned up in the center. It had fallen down, maybe in her scuffle with the cop, and loose strands hung about her face. Whatever makeup she'd on was long gone and she looked worn out and defenseless.

He took a gulp of coffee. "I'm not gonna get into it tonight with you, I'm too tired. Let's just see if we can avoid accusations right now and come up with some sort of agreement on how you're not going to do anything else stupid."

She glared at him. She was unfathomable to him, definitely confusing. Who was this woman? The kind of predictable female he thought she was had morphed into a blend of protective mother/female crime fighter.

"You want me to promise never to break into Kim Barber's office again?" She muttered the words as if they burned her mouth.

"I want you to promise to stop doing anything illegal and leave crime investigation to the cops. If there's something really threatening Katya, I'll find it."

She frowned down into her cup. "I can promise I won't break into the police department again. That's about the best I can do for you right now, Jack. I'm not promising there won't be something else you won't like."

"I suppose that's the best I can get from you tonight? I thought we had an agreement you'd contact me the moment there was a threat to her and I'd be there." He pierced her with his usual narrow look.

"That's not good enough. You made it clear you don't believe there is a threat, and since, according to you, there is no real evidence, I need to do something myself. You're asking me to treat the symptoms when they arise, but what I'm going to do is find the cause."

"Shit, Sofie. What in hell do you think you can do? You've demonstrated tonight how bad you are at this."

"I may be an amateur, but I have determination on my side. And as far as Kim Barber goes, I don't care what you say, she's involved in this somehow. Your girlfriend's the one making up fantastic tales and manipulating the circumstances, not me."

"She's not my girlfriend!" he spat back.

"Fellow cop then. Whatever she is, you're taking her word over mine, and I'll never convince you I'm telling the truth."

"There's nothing about Kim's background, either work or personal, to make me doubt she's telling the truth. She has no reason to lie about all this. I'm sorry." He finished off his coffee and glanced at her. "Let's get out of here and I'll call you tomorrow."

The street was deserted as he pulled up in front of her store, went around and waited. Against her protests, he escorted to her to her door, took her key and opened it. Keeping her behind him, he scanned the stairwell and finally led her up the stairs.

The apartment was cold and dark. It felt bleak, desperate, like her face tonight. Without thinking, he placed a hand on the back of her head and pulled her against his chest, a momentary truce. Sighing, he pulled away and turned to go. "Lock up after me, Sofie. I'll call you in the morning."

## *Thirteen*

Sofie rolled over and opened one eye to check the time. It was after ten in the morning and the apartment was quiet. Then she remembered. Katya was at Monica's for the night. With a moan, she also remembered she'd broken into the police department and gotten arrested last night.

She pushed her reluctant body up to sitting, surveyed her clothes lying in a pile in the center of the floor. After Jack left, she'd turned the heat up full blast, a desperate attempt at comfort in a rancorous world.

She got dressed, intent on escaping her empty apartment for her bookstore, closed until one o'clock on Sunday. Today, her books were her comfort, safe and inviting, while the apartment was only a metaphor for a lonely future.

She made the coffee double strength and stared down at the street where neighborhood regulars were heading for the bakery to get their Sunday morning pashas.

The thought of seeing Jack after last night's encounter made her stomach burn. The word 'betrayal,' never a part of her vocabulary until Monday, had become a recurring theme in her head, growing steadily louder. He'd promised her nothing but protection for Katya, yet she felt duped by him. Worse, she felt deceived by her own expectations. He was no different than how he'd always been, but she'd wanted to believe he was something more. Instead, all he ever gave her were accusations—and sex. She waited for him to arrive, another opportunity for betrayal.

Katya was staying with Monica, who'd promised to bring her over after breakfast. Sofie promised Katya they'd go to work on decorating the store for the holidays as soon as she got home. Thanksgiving was a week away.

The phone rang. Jack, distant but speaking at least.

"Sofie, I'll be delayed a couple of hours. Can I drop by later?"

"Whenever you want. I'll be downstairs in the store. As soon as Katya gets home, we're going to start working on decorations."

"Where is she? Still with Monica?" He hesitated.

"Yes. She's taking the girls out for a treat and dropping her off after they eat. Will it work if we have our discussion after I get Katya settled down for her afternoon nap? We'll just keep the body blows to a minimum, okay?"

"That'll work." He ignored her humor. "Want me to pick anything up?"

"You could stop by the bakery next door and get a dozen Christmas cookies, if you would. I'd appreciate it." He murmured something and hung up without saying goodbye.

A box of Christmas decorations was sitting on the back counter, waiting to cheer up the dreary day. Sofie usually looked forward to hanging the stuff and she made a point of turning it into a festive occasion for Katya. She began pulling out the strings of lights blindly, focusing on untangling each knot as though it was the solution to the world's problems.

Katya arrived at the same time as Jack, carrying her little reindeer tote bag. Jack carried her in, holding her as though she might slip away from him.

"Mommy! Hi! Look! Jack's got me! He can help us decorate the store!"

"I see, sweetie. If Jack wants to, we can sure use his help." She looked inquiringly at him, his face open one moment, closed the next.

"I can stay for a while. I'm good at reaching tall places, at least." He set Katya down and turned her around to unzip her coat. She smiled at him and Sofie watched his face soften.

"We could use you for putting up our lights. It's the thing we hate the most, isn't it, Katya?" The little girl made a face and ran across the room to climb up on a stool and peer into the decorations box.

"I can do that, for sure." Jack eased out of his jacket and his holster at the same time, placing them on the counter within reach. "Where do you want me to start?"

They worked for an hour, *like a family*, Sofie thought, fool that she was; he wasn't here for that. He was here to chastise her and get a promise from her to stop interfering in his life.

They tested and strung lights for an hour, fortified by Katya's chattering. By the time the last box of decorations was hung, Katya's enthusiasm had been replaced by yawns and Sofie settled her on the little cot in the back of the store.

"She'll sleep for at least an hour and we've got about that long until we open. We can talk." She pointed to two stools and sat down on one, waiting for his lead.

"I got your record wiped clean. There'll be a report of the break-in but it won't go anywhere. Your name will be in the report but you won't be charged and there's going to be nothing in the public records."

"Thank you." There didn't seem to be anything else she could add.

"Yeah, well, I want your promise that this is it. No more going to see Kim, no calls to her, no more contact with any one in the department, okay?"

"I can promise that. But Jack, I would like to know what happened to the file?"

"The one you say you stole from her office?"

"Yes. Would you at least take a look at it?"

"I have, Sofie. I intend to talk with Kim about it. But leave it alone now. I'll get on it with her and find out why the fuck she has it, and deep-six the file. But I want you to leave it to me."

She nodded, relieved. Last night's anger had cooled, he had shelved his suspicions and was making damned sure they didn't keep ragging on each other today. Well she could play it that way. "So now what, Jack? Where do we go from here with Katya?"

He sighed and leaned back on the stool, stretching his long legs out in front of him. "Well, for one thing, I'd like to take her to visit my parents next week. It's their anniversary, their fortieth."

"That would be fine. What day?"

"Wednesday. We usually eat around 6:30 so if she could be ready by five o'clock, I'll pick her up then."

So this is how it's going to be, Sofie mused. We'll have these brief discussions about Katya's schedule, she'll gradually become a part of his life and I'll slowly become the outsider, separate from them.

"We need to set up a weekly schedule." He said. "Maybe I can pick her up from daycare some days and take her out to eat or do something with her. A couple of times a week?"

"She'll like that, Jack." Sofie took a deep breath and pursued what she most feared. "What about your plans to contact a lawyer?"

"I told you, I'm going to hold off on that, Sofie." He paused. "As long as you don't get yourself into further trouble..."

She refused to defend herself, a useless exercise that only left her powerless. "All right, I appreciate that, Jack. Let's leave it at that for now. As far as Kim goes, if you make sure she isn't using that file against Katya, I'm willing to not pursue anything further there." She picked up the mugs and placed them on a tray. "And if you feel you want to avoid further contact with me, I can understand that. We can work out some system."

He sighed and his face softened. "Sofie, it sounds like I've imposed a life sentence of exile on you. I'm not trying to extricate you from my life. I just want us to do what works for Katya."

Something turned over in her chest with his words. It sounded civil at best. She doubted the words were more than something to placate her. But one small show of concern out of his mouth and she was ready to lay her head on his chest. She was disgusted with herself. Both her mother and grandmother had managed to raise their daughters alone. Sofie had heard no complaints from either woman about the situation. She couldn't recall a time when they'd ever discussed the need for a man around. They were women who knew how to take care of themselves. Was it some sort of genetic weakness in her that made her susceptible to Jack?

She pulled her shoulders back and spoke directly to him. "You're right. If I seem a little uncertain about all this, it could be due to my lack of experience with a male role model. I really have no idea how this father thing works, you know. But give me some time and I'll be fine with it." She went over to the desk, pulled out her weekly planner and thumbed through it. "Let's set up the schedule for the next week or two, okay?"

He stood up and came over beside her, pulling out his PDA. "My schedule is pretty unpredictable. I'm on-call one week out of the month. The other three weeks I usually work days. Could I see her, maybe a couple of times a week, and then maybe have her overnight once a week? Except the weeks I'm on-call, that is."

She smiled. He seemed so uncertain himself that she wanted to reassure him. "That'd work, I think. We'll have to get the okay from Katya on the overnight part, just so she's easy with it. Maybe we can try it out one night next week and see how it goes"

"How about next Wednesday? After the dinner at my parents? Do you think she'll be okay just with me?"

"She'll be fine. She trusts you, Jack." She wandered away from him, wanting some space to bring up a more difficult subject. "Jack, there's something else." She stopped and turned. "I think it's time to tell her you're her father."

"I know. I've been thinking about it, Sofie. It keeps circling around in my head, wanting to tell her, trying to figure out the best way, worrying how she'll take it. I need your support in this. My parents really want me to tell her. What do you think? Should I tell her today? With you there?"

She swallowed, surprised that he wanted to include her. "I'd like to be there. And I think it would be a good thing for you to tell her now."

"All right, as soon as she wakens."

She reached out and touched his hand. "Thanks, Jack, for asking me rather than just doing it, pain in the ass that I am, making your life one big problem."

"My life was already a problem, Sofie. If anything, Katya's brought some sanity to it, a peace I never expected." The words were almost a personal confession, and she held her breath. He sat, saying nothing as she busied herself getting the store ready to open.

"Mommy!" Katya wandered towards them, wearing t-shirt and panties, dragging the doll Jack had given her. "Can I get up now?"

Sofie took her back to the cot to find overalls and shoes. "Jack wants to tell you something and I think if we all had some cocoa and cookies together, that would be nice. What do you think?"

Katya nodded, liking the idea of being included in adult business. They sat around the table, sipping cocoa, Jack's face drawn.

Katya went to the heart of the matter. "Jack, are you sad?"

"No, scout. I'm not sad. I'm a little nervous is all. I have something to tell you." He swallowed and Sofie waited, letting him lead. This was his show.

"Katya, how would you feel about having a daddy?" The words leapt from him, ragged and too fast, but Katya showed interest. "I know we've only known each other for a few weeks, but what would you think about me being your daddy, sweetheart?"

He looked almost like a boy, vulnerable and eager. Sofie held her breath as Katya stared at him. Gradually, a smile took shape, first in her eyes, then moving to her mouth, opening out into a grin that animated her entire body. She turned to Sofie. "Jack's going to be my daddy?"

Sofie nodded and Katya laughed and turned to Jack who began to laugh with her, hesitant at first, then louder until finally he reached over and grabbed Katya up into his arms and swung her over the top of the table onto his lap. She turned towards him, and threw her arms around his neck. The pain in Jack's face disappeared, the transformation so blinding, Sofie turned away.

~ * ~

Jack awoke Monday morning to an unfamiliar, precarious world where things looked like they were working out and he was almost happy. He planned his week to include the process of introducing Katya into his family, slowly, so as not to frighten her with their flood of affection. On Wednesday night he'd bring his parents with him to the bookstore to pick up Katya for dinner. It would be the first time she'd meet them as grandparents, the only grandparents she would know.

His state of mind lasted until he got to work and Kim Barber showed up in front of his desk, minus her smile. He'd dreaded this meeting today, but he knew it was coming and something he had to deal with, the sooner the better. *Shit,* he thought, *here it comes!*

"Jack! Have you got a minute?" She leaned on his desk, straining her black leather skirt against her rump. "This is a distasteful situation, but you know why I'm here. I just got the report of the break-in at my office Saturday night. Really, this is too much, Jack. It's not just some silly girl's prank, you know. She broke in! Went through my files—they're a mess! There are files missing!"

He let her spew it out, waiting for her to finish.

"Then I couldn't believe what I heard. You managed to lean on everyone involved and get the charges dropped. I won't have it, Jack! I want her charged."

"Look, Kim, I know you're upset, but there aren't going to be any charges. It was a stupid move on her part, but it's over. It was a one-time thing, a misunderstanding." He pulled the file out of his drawer and threw it down on his desk. "What I wanna know is what the hell you were doing with a file about Katya and me in your office?"

Kim frowned down at him and turned her attention to a speck of something on her pale sweater. "Jack, what are you talking about?"

"The file that Sofie got from your office. This one." He pointed down at the manila folder. "Someone has done a hell of a lot of research into my private life."

"I have no idea what you're talking about. Is this a file you picked up off your friend? If you're trying to say it's one of the missing files from my office, you're crazy. I don't know anything about a file on you. This is ridiculous. You're just stalling. I want something done, today. It's breaking and entering, and I don't care if you're fucking her brains out, I want her arrested!"

"Kim, calm down, for God's sake! I'm not sleeping with her!" At least not now, he thought. It was a little over a week ago she'd lain panting beneath him for at least a few hours.

"There was nothing taken from your goddamned office except this one file. You, or someone, has been prying into my personal life and I want to know: why? Do you wanna tell me what it's all about or do I have to go over your head?" To go over her head meant he'd have to go to the Inspector or the Chief.

She stood, hands clenched, as though trying to keep herself from reaching out and striking him. "You can do whatever you want. I don't give a damn about your fucking private life. So what if you're like a dog in heat, Jack, sniffing around after your next bitch. I happened on that information accidentally, going through some files, and since you've no problem getting into my panties as often as you want, without a 'thank you, ma'am' on your way out, I felt no compunction when I found the stuff on your daughter."

"What in hell does our relationship have to do with Katya?"

"Well, I'm sort of doing my own private survey, on your moral character, the baser side of you. I wasn't surprised at all to find out you'd gotten some stupid woman pregnant and never bothered to find out a damned thing about that kid of yours!" She spat the words at him, her familiar smile still pasted on her face.

"Look, Jack. I don't want to fight with you. I'm still your friend, even though I feel that you've treated me, and probably all the women in your life, like shit. But, hey, who am I to complain? Just a man thing, right? We had some fun. Any bitterness on my part is my own responsibility, I suppose? Isn't that what you guys usually say?"

"Kim, give it a rest." He looked towards the hallway, aware of her voice echoing off his bare walls and out the door. "Whatever your personal grievances are with me, that's a separate issue. If I hurt you, I'm sorry. I thought we were on the same wavelength. Shit!" Looking for a way to cool down, he stood up and went over to shut his door, came back and sat down to face her.

"As far as I knew, what was between us was clear from the beginning. We both said there'd be no strings. I'm sorry as hell you feel ill-used but I never intended for it to be anything more than what it was, some fun, a little pleasure for each other. That's as far as I ever saw it going. I assumed that's all you wanted. If you wanted more, I'm sorry." He argued, "You have no right, though, to pry into my past. What was between Sofie and me was a long time ago and it's nobody's business."

He thought of the accusations he's thrown at Sofie and his stomach recoiled. The description she gave of her meeting with Kim was probably true. "Whatever business you thought you had with Sofie, I'm damned if I'll let you harass her. You said she called you, but she says otherwise. You called her and set up that appointment. I'm inclined now to believe her. I don't know what you thought you'd get out of her, but you can drop the pretense with me about it." He paused to let his words sink in, his next almost a whisper. "Kim, whatever the hell is going on, I'm gonna get to the bottom of it. And it'd better not be some scheme you've cooked up to get even with me. Or was the whole thing some plan to get my job? I know you've been putting out feelers for the Bomb Squad for some time now. Was that what this is all about?"

"Jack, Jack." She smiled and he wondered how he'd ever found her desirable. "I'm not after your job. And if you want to believe her over me, that's up to you. I should remind you, though, who the creditable person is in this situation. I'm not the one who got herself booked on a B&E charge. I have five years on the force behind me and a good record."

"Yeah, well whatever credibility you had with me is shot. Between the file you've gathered on me and your conduct today, I wouldn't trust you to answer my phone!"

"All right. Take her word over mine if you want, but you can't prove anything. I admit I did some digging into your past and I did have the file on you and that kid, but there's nothing more to dig into, Jack. We're done here." She stood up from his desk. "I'm willing to forget the whole thing this time, but if you pursue this further, Jack, I'll make sure your little Sofie ends up doing some time for her part."

He left her threat hanging in the air, unwilling to go further into the tangled accusations lurking behind her words. "Sofie'll stay away from you, Kim, and you stay away from her and Katya. I'm warning you!"

She shrugged, gave him a slight smile that didn't reach her eyes and sauntered out his door.

## *Fourteen*

Almost three weeks of the roller coaster ride with Jack; and Sofie was tired, and sure he was as exhausted as she was. While it was probably a good plot for a romance novel, the details of the past weeks didn't get anywhere close to the reality of the living the situation. Their very different approaches to life, so contradictory of each other, overrode whatever attraction they felt. They were two strangers, trying to cooperate in a situation with adrenaline running rampant. Her feelings about him were so predictable, they were almost humiliating. She watched him go from wariness to concern to friendship to lover and finally, to betrayer. While she kept trying to reframe it, the outcome was the same and the reality was painful. She and Jack had no future.

She tried to think of him only as Katya's father rather than the man he had sometimes become in the past few weeks. The last way she wanted to see him was as someone she might need in her future. There *was* no future with him, except as Katya's father. She wanted to go back to the Jack of four years ago, the distant, uncommunicative cop, but she'd seen another Jack, a man who loved Katya and who'd rearranged his life simply because a strange woman asked it of him.

She hated where she stood with him now, weighing every word she said. He saw her uncertainty; she could read it in his eyes, in his wariness. But part of her still wanted him and she hated that, too.

Katya was with Jack and his family for dinner, a natural way to bring her in as a family member, and Sofie refused to feel left out. She'd planned to go out herself, with Monica and Chrissie, then come home early, take a hot bath, and pull out a good book.

She was getting dressed when the phone rang. The voice sounded male, speaking so fast she had difficulty following him. He muttered vague words about her being set up, she caught the word stalker, and he gave her instructions to meet him if she wanted more information. Cursing herself for a fool, she agreed to go.

~ * ~

Sofie glanced down at her watch; it was late, after eleven. They were coming to the end of the line and the bus was empty. They'd just passed the Connor Water Treatment Pumping Station, sitting regally at the corner of Conner and East Jefferson. Across the street, once an old schoolyard, a huge lot was now home to hundreds of brand-new Chrysler SUVs, waiting to be shipped. Just in back of them, the huge old Chrysler plant, now Daimler-Chrysler, loomed ominous under fluorescent lights.

She stared at the SUVs and shivered. It was too much of a coincidence with Jack investigating a bombing at the only other assembly plant in town. Jack had dismissed a link between threats to Katya and his job, but an image of Dinah was fixed in her mind.

East Jefferson ran parallel to the river, struggling to maintain its past gentility, as crime and industry threatened to overrun it. A block further and the street would transform from gritty to affluent, as it turned northward through the elegant suburbs along the lake.

The bus pulled to its final stop on the east side of the street, in front of a Coney Island and Sofie emerged, prepared to blend in with the night in her dark pea coat and black leggings.

Her instructions had been to turn towards the river on Connor. She stood at the corner, keeping an eye out for squad cars or anyone suspicious. No one noticed her, all activity focused instead on the liquor store that sat adjacent to the darkened post office. She'd been told to head down Connor and when she reached the river, someone would meet her by the fifth berth at the second row of piers. She checked her watch again and looked down the length of street disappearing into darkness. She began to walk.

It took fifteen minutes to get to the river and find the dock. It was November, too early for ice breakers, and lonely lake steamers passed silent as cats in the night, heading upriver through Lake St. Clair, then Lake Huron, and on north to the Upper Peninsula. At Katya's age, Sofie had walked with her mother and aunt out on the solid slabs of ice that cobbled the river in the winter, staring across at the alien world of Canada. She'd had no dad to hold her hand, had never met him. The only thing she knew about him was he'd been in the war and he'd died. Had Jack ever walked across the ice holding onto his father's hand? She pictured Katya's small fingers engulfed in Jack's and smiled.

The street was deserted. It was narrow, but two-way, with old houses on one side and broken sidewalk running along the water treatment plant on the other. She stopped and stared out at the dark emptiness that was the river, a few small bobbing lights indicating a rare boat passing quietly.

Vessels of all shapes and sizes littered the marina, some in the water, many in dry dock. They lay inert and shrunk-wrapped against the cold weather, deserted until spring. As she passed the second pier, she heard footsteps, muffled, coming up fast behind her. She paused and looked around, her heart pounding, before ducking down under a tarp-covered hulk. More sounds, voices this time, came out of the darkness two or three docks beyond her, muffled like the footsteps. She crouched down and waited, sweat trickling down her face even in the freezing air.

The sounds seemed to go forever, more voices, more footsteps. She felt a push to follow instructions, no matter what, and strained her eyes, trying for a sense of direction that would head her to the second row of piers.

It was insane to come down here alone. Four days ago she'd been picked up for burglary and here she was, at it again, doing exactly what Jack had warned her not to do, probably right in the middle of some crime. Too bad, she thought, that no one was taking her fears for Katya seriously. If they had, she'd be home, warm and safe, as would Katya. Instead, it was up to her.

The men's voices continued to waft over her, mesmerizing in the darkness, blended with the continuous slapping of waves against the pilings.

The men were moving faster now. She could hear what sounded like metal against metal, dull thuds of large objects being dropped onto the wooden pier, reverberating under her feet. The sound of a car engine broke the continuity, moving closer in the darkness but without lights. She stood up and listened. It was very close now, coming from the same direction as the voices. Car doors opened and closed, a trunk creaked. Then again, the sounds of heavy objects being dropped, the rattling of the car springs.

She was well hidden and blended in with the hulk of the boat, leaving her safe, she thought. Suddenly, spotlights flooded the area, the bizarre scene in front of her flashed, like something from a nightmare, men running everywhere, many in uniform, guns drawn, scurrying out of every structure.

The light shone on her also, she realized, no longer hidden but standing out in startling clarity against the white bulkhead. She turned, blindly and began to run, instinctively, away from the cops, away from the frantic movements of men in slow motion under bright lights. She headed down the pier in the opposite direction, but it was a repeat of the other night, running in slow motion, her legs refusing to respond. Behind her, she heard shouts, "Stop, police!" barely discernible over the pounding of her heart.

She headed for the darkness beyond the marina, a group of buildings beyond the spotlights. She almost made it, got as far as the last pier, beside a low white building with a closed sign in the window, shut down for the winter. Then felt the sharp stab in her low back, to one side. It was slight, a pinpoint of pain, like the bee sting, but it knocked her flat.

She landed face down, sprawled on the cold wooden slats of the boardwalk, arms outstretched. Her body vibrated from the impact and sent shock waves from head to toe. The sensation of pain followed quickly, focused on her left side. It muted the bright lights and harsh cries circling around her.

"Don't move!" Even amidst the confusion, she recognized Jack's voice. Hands patted her down, moving up each leg over her hips and at the sound of her gasp, he paused. "Sofie! God damn it! Roll over and stand up, slow!" When she didn't move, he grabbed hold of an outstretched arm and yanked her roughly around. She cried out again, louder, and he paused, searching her face. "What is it? Are you hurt?"

"My side!" She whispered, clenching her teeth as his hands moved over her more. When he drew back, she saw his fingers, covered with something dark. She knew it was her own blood.

"Lie still. You've been shot." He reached into his pocket and pulled out a handkerchief and pressed it into her side. "Can you hold this?"

She murmured a reply that seemed to satisfy him, but her mind was growing fuzzy. She watched, dazed, as he pulled out his cell phone and barked instructions into it.

"An EMS is on the way. Don't talk, Sofie. And for God's sake, don't answer any questions right now!"

Time passed in a blur of voices and movement. She felt herself lifted up and placed on something. A frenzy of activities continued around her on the dock, men everywhere, K9's sniffing large metal cans, uniformed men crisscrossing the docks.

It was dark and quiet in the ambulance, a break from the chaos outside and she shut her eyes, blocking out the cop standing guard nearby. Jack had disappeared, but she knew he'd be back before she wanted to see him, this episode one more nail in the coffin of his trust in her.

They took her to Detroit Receiving, a place she'd been twice, both times too painful to think about, first her grandmother and then her mother, the visits preambles to goodbyes within months of each other.

The emergency room reverberated with moans and cries, just another Detroit night. Detroit Receiving was where they took all the accidents from downtown, all the drunks, all the shootings—and they'd brought her here. It must be Jack's decision, to have her within a few blocks of the city jail, where she knew she'd probably end up, again.

She lay in an examining room, waiting her turn, when she heard Jack's voice on the other side of the screen. He pulled back the white cubicle curtain and gazed down at her. She pulled the sheet draped over her closer, feeling naked. Above the blood soaked gauze pressed to her side, a few inches of skin and part of her breast lay exposed.

His voice drifted over her, as though from a great distance. "I spoke to the doctor, Sofie. He says the wound is superficial. The bullet passed right through, missing any bones or organs."

His voice was more dismissive than reassuring, as though being shot was no worse than a cut finger or sprained arm. She ignored his words and focused instead on her immediate concern. "Where's Katya?"

"She's with my parents. We were in the middle of dinner when I got the 1033. She's fine." The words were curt, followed quickly by what she knew was coming. "What in the hell were you doing at the river?"

"You aren't going to believe me, I know, but I got a call this evening. He said he had information about Katya's stalker and he wanted to meet me." She turned her face away from him and stared at the bottles on the counter beside her.

"Sofie." The word was a whisper. "Shit!" He reached out, took her chin between his fingers and turned her head towards him. "You've done it again! You'd better be telling the truth about why you were there, because there's no way I'm gonna be able to get you out of this, if you're lying. If you're implicated in any way in what happened there tonight, you're going to jail." He stood up, sighed and ran his fingers through his hair. "Hell! You're no terrorist, Sofie, but what explanation can you give me that makes sense? I gotta have something here, besides some vague story about a call." He rubbed a hand over his face.

"What was going on there, Jack? And why were you there?" Her words came out slurred.

"It was a stake-out. We got a tip on some trafficking of goods across the river, explosives, headed for the Daimler-Chrysler plant. I was there because they called me as soon as the call came in." He moved closer, leaning over her, and she shut her eyes, too dizzy to follow his movements.

"Listen to me, Sofie. Give me some answers, something, now, and I'll try and get further questions put off until tomorrow. The hospital's going to keep you overnight, in a twenty-three-hour bed. When you get called in for questioning tomorrow, just tell them the truth. And by then, if there's any God, we'll have gotten some sort of collaborative testimony from the perps, like they don't know who the hell you are or something along those lines."

She nodded without opening her eyes, his words washing over her.

"Rest, right now. Everything's going to be all right." He'd said those words to her before too many times over the past three weeks, only it hadn't been all right. Between reassuring her, he'd questioned her motives, betrayed the trust she'd placed in him, and threatened to take her daughter. She, on the other hand, had done everything but lied outright to him, gone behind his back too many times, undermined his work, and betrayed any trust he had in her. She sighed. Maybe it was even, neither of them trusting or trustworthy. With all that, she felt his hand against her cheek, rough and calloused, but cool, a fleeting touch.

"Look at me." It was an order, but gentler than his usual ones. She opened her eyes and focused on his face and their gazes held, assessing, measuring.

~ * ~

It had been more than an hour and the doctor still hadn't shown up. Jack stood, impatient, inhaling the imperceptible scent of flowers that came from her, mingled with the antiseptic smells of the hospital. Her eyes had been closed for a long time and he wondered if she were asleep. He wanted to leave but couldn't. The cubicle seemed quiet, isolated against the sounds of the busy ER around them.

Her hair had fallen from the tie that held it in place and lay spread around her pale face, clinging to her neck. He reached down and pushed back damp strands clinging to her face. She had on some sort of black leggings that outlined her body, revealing far more than her usual baggy sweats did. They'd removed her shoes and he saw her toes were painted a dainty pink, reminding him of Katya. He traced the lines of strain on her face and roused her. He needed some answers.

"Sofie, I know you feel like shit, but I need to ask some questions now, tonight, before I leave." He pulled up a chair near the examining table. "Tell me exactly the events leading to your being at the pier tonight."

Her eyes popped open. "I told you, I got a call. It was a man's voice. He told me I was being set up, that Katya was being used as the bait. He said if I wanted information, I should come to the second pier, the fifth berth. So I did."

The ER was too hot, but she shivered and he reached out for a thin blanket on the counter and spread it over her. Her face was drawn, probably shock as well as pain.

"So who shot me?" The annoyance in her voice almost made him laugh.

"Not the good guys! Looks like from a Smith & Wesson .38—we confiscated one when we took the perps into custody. Our guys didn't fire a shot." He paused, when a nurse entered the small space, checked Sofie's side and took her pulse, before leaving. "If you can give me a brief statement now, Sofie, it'll speed things up. Just tell me everything you can remember. Forget about trying to convince me or if I believe you or not.

I'm just a cop, getting a statement from you." He pulled the chair closer.

"I got the call this evening, around six maybe. You had Katya with you and I was supposed to go over and eat dinner at Monica's. I decided I needed to go and find out what this guy wanted. So I left Monica's around nine or so and took the bus. I had to change buses once and took the East Jefferson bus to the end of the line. I got there just after eleven. The guy said to meet him at 11:30 and I did." She said. "Or I tried to."

"You're sure it was a man's voice?"

"It sounded like one."

"Give me his exact words, as best as you can remember."

He had fifteen minutes to get a story from her before the ER doctor showed up, interrupted frequently by nurses and orderlies, doing labs on her or checking her pulse. He finished and she lay with eyes closed, when the ER doctor pushed aside the curtain, escorted by a nurse carrying a tray of needles, ready to suture up her bullet wound.

He sat outside in the waiting room, filling out the hospital's required forms for gunshot wound. She was staying overnight and wouldn't be released until morning. He needed to get back to work. And he needed to file some sort of damned report that would protect Sofie.

He called his backup unit, arranged to meet them at the lock-up downtown, and called his mother to check on Katya.

Sofie was paler now, any remaining color gone from her face. "Sofie," he whispered and reached out to brush her cheek with his knuckle. She wakened with a start, confused. "I have to get going. They're gonna keep you overnight. Katya's fine at my parents. I just put a call in to them a while ago and she's asleep in my old room. Don't worry, they'll take good care of her. Don't call her tonight. It's too late and it'll only waken them. You can call first thing in the morning." He pulled out a pad, wrote the number down and pushed it into her fingers.

"I have to go. You'll be called for a statement when you're up to it, but I've got your story and I'll do what I can to keep them from charging you right now. I just pray to God the perps we picked up at the scene will swear they had no fucking idea who you were." He paused. "Just rest and don't worry. You'll be released tomorrow and we'll get this straightened out."

He leaned down and kissed her surprised face, tasting her damp skin. Without another word, he turned and left.

~ * ~

She lay staring at the white curtain still swaying after his quick departure. His behavior surprised her, stunned her. She'd violated all the rules that ran his life, broken all the promises she'd made to him. Her actions tonight were reprehensible in his world, but instead of ranting at her, he'd kissed her. She had no idea what had caused this shift in him. She clutched the piece of paper he'd put in her hand, the slight sting of his beard lingering on her skin.

She floated in and out of sleep. They'd moved her to a room at last, dark and quiet, the only illumination from the single light shining over her bed. She tried to focus on what Jack had said, something about explosives, brought across from Canada. It was a set-up and the cops had been tipped off.

They'd given her some sort of sedative to ease the pain. There was nothing else to do tonight. Katya was safe with the Rosellis, it was too late to call Monica. Jack's words floated around her, strangely reassuring. Her life was out of control but she felt safe.

## *Fifteen*

Sofie sat in a wheelchair the next morning waiting for Jack. Outside, snow was falling, the first of the season, and Thanksgiving was a week off. She inhaled sharply, pierced by a sadness that was like a physical blow, the pain more real right now than any pain she felt from her wound.

Four years ago it had been snowing that day, her last Thanksgiving with her mother. Sofie had planned a small celebration, just the two of them, trying to make up for missing her grandmother who'd died two months before. She and her mother had laughed and planned for the future, with no idea that they were spending their last holiday together. Three weeks later her mother, fifty-five, was dead of a cerebral aneurysm.

"I need to get back. Will you be all right here by yourself until your ride comes?"

Sofie nodded at the nurse, turning to watch her disappear around a corner, grateful for time to think. This was Jack's doing again, always the cop issuing orders, probably not to leave her alone. She sat waiting for him, periodically peering around a Ficus plant, musing over the changes in her life. Four years ago, suddenly alone, she's been struck dumb with fear. Then, she'd met Jack and she had Katya. The fear hadn't left. It had lurked in the background, like a fatal flaw, waiting to pounce the moment she was vulnerable, leaving her with the notion that she was a fraud. But since Jack had come back on the scene, she'd found a resolve she hadn't known she possessed. Unwittingly, Jack had called it out of her. Jack, with his constant challenges and accusations, had forced her to take charge, to be bold. She laughed out loud, thinking about the perversity of him.

"What's so funny?" Jack stood in front of her holding a small bouquet of yellow flowers.

"I was just realizing that I love my life." The words were ridiculous in the face of the events of the past week. But her sense of freedom and power had absolutely nothing to do with the dire circumstances of her week. She shook her head at him, smiling.

He looked uncertain, but a small smile played around his lips. She reached out for the flowers. "For me?"

The grin broadened, his face flushed. "They're from Katya and me. She suggested it. She said you liked daisies."

She took the flowers. This was definitely a side of Jack she hadn't seen before. The new Jack from last night continued this morning and she didn't know what to make of it. "Thanks for coming to pick me up, Jack. And for taking such good care of Katya." She sniffed at the flowers. "I called her this morning. She said she hadn't missed me—or at least she missed me only a little bit."

He shrugged. "She's been distracted with all the presents and treats."

"Well, she's thrilled with your family."

"They love her." He said. "I know, they're probably spoiling her, but hell, they need to do it. After all, that's the job of grandparents." He smiled and his grim face softened. "How are you this morning?" He asked. "Pretty sore?"

"Yeah, but I'll live." She shrugged. "Jack, thanks again. I'm a meddler and a liar in your book, yet you keep bailing me out. Thanks."

He leaned down, his face level with hers, searching for something. "Roselli to the rescue, huh?"

She returned his gaze, wondering what was happening between them. "We should go, Jack."

He wheeled her out to the Cherokee, double-parked, cop style, at the curb. He held the door for her while she levered herself out of the wheelchair, up onto the cold leather seat. He went around and got in, gave her a quick look she couldn't interpret, buckled them both up and pulled off.

"You need me to stop for anything on the way? Prescriptions filled?"

She shook her head. Despite the pain meds, the pressure of the seatbelt caused her side to ache, and the motion of the car made her head swim.

"You can't go back to your place right now alone and try to care of yourself and Katya. You need some help."

"I'll be okay. I've got my pain pills and I can get one of my neighbors to come over and help with Katya." She eased her seatbelt away from her side and eased a hand over the wound site. "Don't you need to take me to the station? I thought you said they'd want to question me."

"We got what we need for now. The four guys from last night are sitting in the lock-up, doing their best to say whatever it will take to keep their asses out of doing hard time. They're definitely part of ELF, an urban ecoterrorist offshoot. We've got a definite match on the explosives with the Poletown bombing." He looked over at her. "And when asked about you, they don't have a clue who you are."

She noticed his red-rimmed eyes for the first time. He looked exhausted. "You've been up all night?"

He nodded. "For now, the statement I got from you last night will do. We can get a more thorough one in a day or two."

"Jack, you must be bushed. Monica probably could have picked me up."

"No problem. It was right on my way home and Katya's waiting for you at my parents. She may have told you she doesn't miss you, but my mother says she's upset." He glanced over at her. "Don't worry, my mother will give her enough comfort for ten kids." He hesitated. "There's something else I wanted to talk to you about. I spoke with Kim Barber yesterday." Sofie waited. "I confronted her about the file. She admitted she was doing something she damned well shouldn't have been, but we're at a stalemate right now. She's threatening to get you pulled in for the B&E if I make a stink about the file."

"Can she do that? That sounds pretty illegal to me—trading favors or something. Or is that standard cop practice?"

"Hell no!" He gave her a sideways glance. "Well, maybe, sometimes." He pulled onto I-94, heavy midday traffic claiming his attention. "I just wanted to make sure you knew I stood up for you." He smiled briefly. "You were right about Kim. I owe you one."

It almost sounded like an apology to her. She watched the snow hitting the windshield, falling faster now. "I'm sorry, Jack. It has to feel pretty nasty to you. You've known Kim, both as a cop and a friend for a long time. You've known me three weeks. Why should you believe anything I say?"

~ * ~

Katya stood at the door of the Rosellis', dressed in her red corduroy overalls, coatless. Somehow Jack had found the time to stop by and pick up clothes for Katya as well.

"Mommy! Mommy!" Katya jumped up and down. Then she spied Jack. "Hi, Daddy!" She said it softer, trying the word out.

Jack helped Sofie into the house and pushed her down in the nearest chair. "Come here, scout." He picked up Katya and lowered her onto Sofie's lap. The rest of the family hovered in the background, warned off by Jack's frown.

Sofie smiled up at his mother. "I'm sorry for all the trouble I've caused. I hope this hasn't disrupted your life too much."

Maria waved her hands and swooped down to plant a kiss on Katya's cheek. "No, no! Don't even say such a thing! She's part of our family! We love having her! And you, too!"

Sofie turned to see how Jack took this, but his expression was neutral.

"Jack told us you were sick." Maria glanced at Katya and bent down closer. "I hope it's nothing serious. Maybe you should lie down?"

Sofie shook her head, conscious of the question in Katya's eyes.

Jack interceded for her. "Mama, Sofie's pretty tired. Have you got Katya's things packed for her? We probably need to get them home." Jack leaned down and relieved Sofie of Katya.

As Jack gathered up the packages Maria pushed on him for Sofie, the other Rosellis passed Katya around, bestowing kisses that Katya willingly received. Vincent led Sofie to the car on his arm with Jack following, Katya in his arms.

"Remember—we're planning on having Katya for Thanksgiving still," Maria called out from the step, "and you too, Sofie." Jack waved at her as he put them into the car.

Katya sat in her car seat, chattering as she removed her doll's clothes with great care. Jack and Sofie didn't speak, responding automatically to Katya's questions. It was snowing harder, a white blanket accumulating on the sidewalks and parked cars they passed, forcing Jack to slow his speed.

He pulled directly into the alley behind the bookstore, went around and opened the back door to extract Katya. "Sit tight, Sofie. I'll be right back for you."

"I can make it myself, Jack." She released her seatbelt and started to rise, only to be gently pushed back.

"Let me do it for once, okay?" His smile took the edge off the words.

The apartment was cold and he pushed the thermostat up to almost eighty, before making a circuit of the rooms, turning on lights against the grayness of the day. He insisted Sofie lie down, and he and Katya worked together, stripping Sofie of her coat and shoes, down to her sweatshirt and leggings. "Keep your Mama warm while I find something for her to put on, okay, sweetheart?"

Katya climbed up on the bed next to Sofie and snuggled against her good side. He rifled through drawers until he found a long-sleeved gown, handed it to her and averted his gaze as she shed the sweatshirt.

He pushed another pain pill down her, got her settled under layers of blankets, and herded Katya from the room. "Let your mommy get some rest and we'll make lunch, okay?"

Thirty minutes later he was back, carrying a tray of food, but Sofie was asleep. He set the tray down and stood, uncertain, staring down at her. Something had happened to him, some shift. It started with his encounter yesterday with Kim and had gotten stronger as he sat watching Sofie in the ER. He was unsure exactly what had happened. Until now, he'd had no problem distrusting her and at the same time, lusting after her.

Like two separate lines of action. If he kept their relationship superficial, it was no problem. Just sex with the enemy. Last night, she'd moved from enemy to something else, something he didn't recognize and he wasn't sure how to deal with it. The cynicism and resignation he'd lived with since Dinah's murder had suited him well. It was dependable. He didn't know how the hell to handle this new thing with Sofie.

It took an hour to get Katya down for her nap. Jack lay down beside her, sighed and fell into a deep sleep, his feet sticking over the end of the small bed. He slept for over an hour, awakened by Katya moving restlessly on the bed next to him. He needed to get back to work.

Sofie was sitting up, pillows behind her, working on lunch. "Sofie. I've gotta go soon. Who can I call to help you with Katya?"

"Just bring me the phone. I'll get one of my neighbors. We'll be fine." He rubbed his eyes and she added, "Did you sleep at all?"

"I took a nap with Katya. I'm used to going on no sleep."

"Can you set Katya up with some toys here next to me?" Her nightgown was pulled tight and he stared at the outline of her nipples against the fabric, looking up suddenly to find her watching him.

"Caught me." Her face reddened and he laughed. "Sorry." Shit, he thought, just like an adolescent on a first date. "My mother sent a lot of food along. It's in the refrigerator, those stacks of Tupperware. You won't need to fix dinner, at least."

"Thanks, Jack. We'll manage okay. You should probably get going." Her hair was loose and she gathered it up and twisted it into a makeshift braid.

"Sofie." He stopped, unsure what else to say. He rubbed his forehead, searching for words. "I'd like to start over with you and me. Make another try. Neither of us is too sure about anything right now, but can we agree to work towards something? Friendship, at least?" The words didn't come easy to him.

"Jack, I don't understand this change. I thought after last night, you'd be calling the lawyer to start custody proceedings. Now you want to start over?"

He shrugged. "Yeah. Stupid of me, huh? I can be a real bastard sometimes. And you're a pain in the butt. But, hell, I don't know, maybe we kind of suit each other."

She frowned at him. "What do you mean?"

"I have no idea. I'm rambling. I not sure of anything right now." His flashed her another smile. "Maybe I'm punch drunk from lack of sleep. Let's leave all avenues open right now, okay?"

She held out her hand to him. "Okay. I'd like that."

~ * ~

Mrs. Alexandrovna agreed to come over as soon as her son got home. When Sofie heard her halting steps on the back stairs, she sank back into bed, relieved. Mrs. A would come loaded with goodies and Sofie could spend the rest of the day floating in the world of pain meds, drifting in and out of thoughts about Jack and what it all meant.

She hugged herself, secretly pleased he'd succumbed to her charms, at the same time uncertain exactly what she wanted from him. Right now, finding herself, what she really wanted, seemed the most pressing need, before she went further with Jack.

## *Sixteen*

Six days after the pier encounter, Sofie was on the mend, although her wound still throbbed at times, especially if she moved too fast. Jack was working eighteen-hour shifts, but spent as much time as he could with Katya. The day after Sofie's release from the hospital, he drove her downtown to give her statement. It was an exhausting hour and a half, but she'd been surprised at Jack's solicitude, even as he threw questions at her. It was clear she was there as a witness, not a suspect. Jack had gotten that done for her. The phone call she'd gotten that day had failed a trace and was dropped, a dead lead.

The four men apprehended sat in jail, awaiting arraignment on charges of terrorist activities. The investigation, to date, turned up no connection between this group, who operated out of the Upper Peninsula of Michigan, and Sofie. The men threw out vague references to someone else in the area, a supplier of the explosives and know-how, but on further questioning, it went no place.

Throughout the past six days, Jack had hinted at the future, but Sofie managed to dodge any discussion. As a result, he was annoyed and frustrated, with himself and her, unclear where to go from here. He couldn't help but notice a change in his own behavior; his predictably casual interest in women had shifted to an intense focus on Sophie and he didn't know what to make of himself. Even more baffling was the discovery that he actually liked Sofie and she seemed to like him.

Two days before Thanksgiving Jack dropped by, exhausted and depressed over the SUV investigation that had stalled out, again. Sofie gave him palliative spaghetti and surprisingly easy company. "This is a hell of a situation. I find myself begging for scraps." They were sitting around the table, Katya tucked away in bed for the night.

"What kinds of scraps?" She twirled leftover spaghetti on her fork and into her mouth.

He shrugged. "I'm afraid to say. All I admit to is, rather than going out for a few beers with the guys from work, I find myself here tonight." He grinned.

"So it can't be that bad if you're smiling."

"Yeah, well I haven't told you what the scraps are yet."

"You're referring to sex?"

"I believe it's been called that." He pushed away from the table. "Look Sofie, I'm confused. I don't know what the hell's going on here. I never go out looking for sex—well, at least not in the past four years—so whatever this is, it's a little more complicated than that."

"You're saying you want something from me, but you're not sure what it is?"

"Yeah. Hell, this is awkward." He stuffed his hands into his jeans pockets and strolled around to sit down beside her. "What do you think? Should I duck here or grab my jacket and head out the door?"

"Neither." She grinned at him, her eyes fixed on his. "I'm in a similar spot. I don't know what I want, but I know I want something from you. Maybe it's not so complicated after all. Maybe it can be solved just by some lovemaking."

He didn't smile back. "You think making love is a simple solution to something? Sounds way more complicated than what I had in mind. I've always called it having sex."

"Yeah, well it's just semantics, isn't it? You can call it whatever you want. I prefer 'a little lovemaking.' Sounds more human, less automatic to my mind."

He took her hand, pulled her up and led her towards her bedroom. Katya was back in her little bed, leaving Sofie's free and available.

She closed the door after him, shutting out any street noises. It was dark, except for a nightlight that threw a faint glow over the room. She drew him towards the bed, the aggressor this time. He reached out and cupped her face, searching it. Smiling up, her hands moved to his t-shirt, pulling gently at it, pausing to unfasten the single snap on his jeans before pulling the shirt over his head.

A sharp intake of his breath was loud, the only sound he made as she ran her hands over his chest, fingers lightly searching crisp chest hair for a nipple. He shuddered at the first light touch, moaned low when she repeated it, fondling him. She bent forward and pressed her lips into the matted hair, searching with her tongue until she found a nipple. He held himself still, but trembled slightly, as she licked, then sucked the flat nipple into her mouth, nipping at it with small bites. He drew back, it was moving too fast for him. "This is your idea of a little lovemaking, huh?"

"I think so. We'll see." She reached up, grabbed her jersey and pulled it over her head, careful to avoid the bandage.

"Is this going to be too much for you? With your wound?" He asked cautiously. She gave him a slight shake of her head as she reached behind her, unsnapped her bra and dropped it at their feet.

Still, he didn't move, but waited for her initiative. She leaned into him, standing on tiptoes, and pressed her breasts into the rough hairs of his chest. Putting her arms around him, she ran cool hands down his back. He felt her heart beating as rapidly as his own, and took a quick breath, then another, working to control himself.

Her hands moved around to his chest. He pulled away slightly to give her room as the hands moved down to his pants. Business-like now, she eased down the zipper and smoothly tugged his pants and shorts down to the floor. He stepped out of them, eyes glued to her hands, as she grasped his penis and brought it against her bare belly, the tip grazing her ribs.

"Jesus Christ!" The words were loud in the silence, but still he didn't touch her, letting her stay in charge.

She slid her hand down his shaft, exploring, spreading drops of moisture, lubricating him, as he throbbed and vibrated against her fingers. Too much now, he reached out to stop her. "Sofie. Please," but she pushed his hand away.

"No, let me." Her small hand encircled the base of his penis, exploring the dense hair. He was losing control fast, his breathing growing louder. His legs were shaking now and he sucked in large gulps of air. She moved her hand still lower, finding and cupping his scrotum.

"Sofie, sweetheart. No more. I can't stand it." He whispered. He caught her up in his arms and laid her on the bed, sinking down beside her. With her bare above the waist, he could make out the white bandage on her side. He turned and reached for the lamp beside her bed, flooding them in soft light, casting the room in deeper shadows.

He lay back, watching as her eyes moved down his body and stopped at his erect penis. Still without touching him, she lay back, facing him, clad only in the white leggings. His turn now, he feasted on the sight of her, feeling the heat grow between them.

"Sofie." He said hoarsely. He reached a hand across and ran fingers lightly over each breast, caressing, fondling each nipple, again, then again.

She hissed and arched her back, wanting more, her tight nipples begging for his mouth. He bent his head forward and let her pull him down. Her hand cupped around his head, fingers buried in his hair as he sucked first one, then the other breast. He was hungry, fierce now, the sounds of suckling mingled with her cries of his name, urging him on. With jerky movements, he pulled down her leggings, still sucking hard at a nipple. He pressed his fingers between her legs, testing her readiness and she cried out louder. "Jack, now!"

His pants lay discarded beside the bed and he grabbed blindly for them, pulled out the condom and ripped it open to sheath himself. He rolled back between her legs, pulled apart her thighs and penetrated her in one thrust.

She responded with a wordless cry and he paused, giving her time to adjust. Her cries turned to sobs and he cursed silently as he felt her heat tighten and constrict around his shaft. He withdrew, pushed her thighs further apart and pulled her legs up to rest on his forearms. He thrust again, harder, raising up to make contact with her clit. It sent her over the edge and she screamed, muffling the sound in his neck, her nails digging into his buttocks.

His control was gone and his body began to buck, unfamiliar sounds erupting from him, like an animal in pain. Their joined bodies gave out the wet, sucking sounds of each thrust and withdrawal, as flesh slapped against flesh, punctuated with gasps for air, and finally, cries of release.

The bed was damp under them, bodies shivering as they cooled. He rolled over and turned off the bedside light, leaving them lying illuminated only by the small nightlight. She pressed her body against his back, not allowing him to turn back to her, holding him there, spoon fashion. He relaxed against her, exhausted, unable to move, feeling her hand roam down his chest, exploring. In the past, she'd been a passive receiver. Tonight, she repeatedly took the initiative. Her hand trailed down over his flat stomach, lower, taking his semi-erect penis between her fingers, exploring and fondling him, until he grew hard.

He made a low sound in the back of his throat as she milked his shaft, squeezing lightly, running a finger over the twitching head. Finally, pleased with her results, she pushed him onto his back. He was panting now, ready, and she bent her head and pressed slightly parted lips to his abdomen, trailing her tongue down, finally to his penis. He held his breath, needing more. She licked delicately at the base and moved slowly up his erection, until she reached the throbbing tip.

"God, Sofie. Christ!" A shudder passed through his belly. "Sofie… Take me in your mouth… God!" She whispered words he didn't understand, opened her mouth wider, and took the head between her lips. She sucked feverishly, holding firmly as he arched up to go deeper. She began to sob, about to climax again herself, this time with him in her mouth. He swore violently, reached down with a hand and flipped her over to a squatting position in front of him. He was beyond worrying about her wound now, beyond all thought. He pulled her back against him roughly and thrust into her, hard and deep.

At last, they fell back, both depleted. "Hell!" He realized, too late now, that he hadn't stopped to put on a condom. He lay, helpless, unable to move, breathing raggedly into the back of her neck.

Finally, with great effort, he shifted off her, moaning. She turned her head up towards him, inches from his, their breaths mingling. "Shit, Sofie. I'm sorry!"

Her lips brushed his briefly and she laughed. "Hey, that's exactly what every woman wants to hear after her best efforts at lovemaking." She knew they'd forgotten something, but she refused to go down there right now. "It's all right. It was my fault as much as yours, Jack. And it can't happen a second time." She laughed. "Famous last words, huh?"

He turned and pulled her back into his arms. There was nothing more to say right now. She pressed her lips to his throat and fell asleep, exhausted.

He awoke to a cold room, the smell of sex still heavy in the air. She was curled up with her back to his chest and stirred slightly when he extracted himself, searching for body warmth before settling back to sleep. He stared down at her for a long time, unsure whether to go or stay. He slipped into the bathroom and he stood, staring into the mirror, looking for something reassuring in the familiarity of his own face, but his expression was foreign to him.

He returned to the bedroom and stood a long time, watching her sleep, tracing the lines of her bare back, over the white of her bandage visible on her side, down the gentle slope of her buttocks. He felt his groin tighten, cursed and eased under the sheet. When he drew her into his arms, she turned and pressed against him, her cheek pillowed on his chest. "Jack" she whispered. "What time is it?"

"After two," he said, "Try to get some sleep."

~ * ~

Sofie was awakened by faint light, seeping in around the drawn curtains. She rolled over at the sound of a door and Jack strode out of the bathroom, a towel hung around damp shoulders, his jeans unsnapped. Showered and freshly shaved, his face looked naked, almost innocent in the watery daylight and Sofie lay watching him, not moving, waiting to see if he realized she was awake. He picked up his shirt from the dresser, turned and came over to the bed. "Good morning. How do you feel?"

Shifting her body, she tried it out. "Well, I seem to have survived last night, wound and all." She sat up, leaning on her elbows, pleased with herself.

He sat down beside her and asked the question that kept resurfacing. "So, now what?" He buttoned his shirt slowly, but kept his eyes fixed on her face. "I'm at a loss, Sofie. How in the hell are we gonna proceed from here?"

"Where do you want to go?"

"Well, I think we missed a few bases a couple of years ago. I'd like to cover some of them. How about a date? There's the annual Policeman's Christmas Ball coming up—want to go with me?"

She grinned, pleased in spite of herself. "All right. That sounds like some place to go, from here, that is." She pulled the sheet tighter, but couldn't stop the grin that kept coming. "When is it? And what's the dress code? My sweats won't do, I suppose?"

He grinned back, the tension eased between them, and shook his head. "This Saturday night. The dress code is formal and no, I don't want to take someone to the Policeman's Ball in sweatpants. Any more questions?"

She tried to picture Jack showing up with a woman on his arm, one he'd had to save from jail, twice, and wondered what the heck he was thinking. "Can I have that towel?" She took it from him and he watched her maneuver and emerge from the sheet, wrapped modestly in the towel.

"You're feeling shy?"

She nodded, mute, but still grinning, and scrambled into the bathroom.

They were running late and she watched the three of them toss back breakfast, like a family. The thought unnerved her.

Jack was making calls with one hand, eating with the other, but he followed her with his eyes. Ignoring his looks, she tried hard to keep her hands steady.

Still in a rush, Sofie searched frantically through last night's castoffs by her bed, while Jack finished getting Katya ready. She looked for something easy to put on over a bandage, something that didn't smell like last night's sex. She ended up pulling on a clean sweatshirt, leggings and no underwear.

They drove silently to Katya's daycare, Jack no more eager than she was to discuss last night. Sofie was torn between embarrassment and fear over what it all meant for her future.

## *Seventeen*

It had snowed for Thanksgiving, gently, quietly, not the bitter, cutting cold that usually blew down the lake and took the city captive. Sofie made a valiant attempt to dress up for Jack's family gathering. He'd shared her bed again last night and she was tired. She grimaced at her reflection in the mirror, and frowned at Jack, standing behind her, whistling as he adjusted his tie. If he was tired, it certainly didn't impair his looks, or his energy. He caught her gaze on him in the mirror, moved up and dropped a kiss on her bare shoulder.

She smiled back, at the same time feeling pathetic at her response to any encouragement from him. Why bother with flirting, when faced with tonight's encounter with his parents? Jack would make it clear there'd been a change in his relationship with the mother of his child, and she had no idea what the Rosellis would think about that. She pulled on her simple white dress and stared in the mirror. Would they be upset that their beloved son was no longer just guarding his daughter, but sleeping with the mother?

Five minutes in the Rosellis' house and it was clear Jack intended to let it be known he and Sofie were having a very physical relationship. With Katya perched on one arm, he pulled Sofie against his side and steered her to his mother who stood by the kitchen door. Rosellis were scattered everywhere in the house, filling it with booming laughter.

"Hi, Mama." Jack, still holding tight to Sofie, leaned down to kiss his mother's cheek. He flashed his mother a look, like a shot across the bow, that said *no questions right now*.

Sofie reached out to shake Maria's hand, but found herself pulled against the woman's bosom. Sofie gasped as her wounded side was crushed under strong arms.

Jack stepped in and pulled Sofie away. "Forgot to warn you, Mama. Sofie's still pretty sore around the ribs from the other night."

Maria frowned. "So, why didn't you tell me this, Jack? Are you keeping more things from your mother?"

"Mama, you knew Sofie was hurt."

"You never said she'd been hurt. You said she was sick. I had no idea it was something bad. She has a wound?" Maria raised her eyebrows at Sofie, eyes questioning.

"She was hurt, but she's better now. Just a little less enthusiasm is all she needs, right now."

Maria smiled and reached for Katya, addressing her remarks to Sofie and ignoring Jack. "We missed you the last few times Katya was over. I hope you know you're welcome here, any time." She slanted a sideways look at her son as she spoke, an open challenge.

"Thanks, Maria. And thank you for taking care of Katya Thursday night."

"So that's when you got hurt? Jack just said you were sick."

"I had a slight accident. Nothing to worry about. I'm almost well now."

"Mommy hurt her side. Daddy said to be careful when I hug her." Katya included herself in the conversation. "Daddy helps Mama when she takes a shower so she doesn't get it wet."

*Oh, oh.* Sofie ignored Katya's remark and smiled blandly at the Rosellis, whose attention she now had completely. Jack lifted her coat from her shoulders, and slipped off Katya's. *Coward*, she thought, as she watched him retreat with the coats.

"Sit down and rest." Maria pointed to the couch. "Let me get you some wine. Jack's dad makes it, an annual event at Thanksgiving. We all have to taste it, at least." She brought out stemmed glasses and a small glass for Katya. Pouring out the wine, she turned to Jack. "To Katya—our newest Roselli."

Katya smiled, took a sip from her little glass and made a face.

The dinner was pure Roselli, loud and cheerful, nothing like the small Russian-style Thanksgivings Sofie had known growing up, and far more elaborate than the little tofu turkey dinners she and Katya were used to.

They drove home without speaking, Katya asleep in the backseat. They'd stayed longer than they'd planned and the streets were empty now, everyone home, overcome with food and drink. "That went pretty well, except maybe the part where Katya volunteered about my helping you shower." He said it without a smile.

She watched for some sign of what the 'that' was he thought had gone so well. His sudden change of heart towards her was exciting but disconcerting. Tonight, it was clear he meant to bring her into his family, but she wasn't sure it was what she wanted.

If she thought over what she and Jack had in common, besides lust, the idea that they might have a future together only left her wanting to run. While the nights were unforgettable, it was only when he left for work that she could take a deep breath and relax. There was too much uncertainty around him and what she felt about him, especially since whenever he touched her, desire replaced all logical thought. Was it ever possible to find that delicate balance between personal freedom and togetherness in any relationship? She had no model for it and wasn't even sure if that was what Jack wanted.

~ * ~

"The dress isn't me! It's too red—and too revealing. It feels like a costume, you know, the happy hooker, only I missed Halloween." Sofie stepped back from the mirror and Monica squinted at her. Two days after Thanksgiving, two more nights of sleeping with Jack, or rather not sleeping, but sharing a bed. No wonder she couldn't think.

At the worst times, she was certain, once the unfamiliar turned into the familiar, Jack would tire of his lust for her and ease back out of her life. Not that she was that great at sex. She'd had too little experience to be a great lover, but Jack seemed eager enough to keep her from sleep most nights.

She waited for Monica's assessment of the get-up. "It's great! You'll knock his socks off!"

"Whose socks?"

"Jack's, of course."

"Who said I want to knock his socks off?"

"Well it's obvious, Sofie. Not that you've shared the gory details with me, but anyone can see something hot is going on here! And from the looks of him, he's definitely got it for you. In fact, you're both pretty goofy looking."

"We are not. Jack's Katya's father—I need him right now. That's it. We have an understanding of sorts. As a result, we're both getting much more satisfaction out of a difficult situation."

"Yeah, right! You forget who you're talkin' to here. Getting much more satisfaction out of a difficult situation. That's the weirdest definition of getting laid I've ever heard. And, anyways, you look like you're on drugs."

"What does that mean? How do I look?"

"Like you've been run over by a truck. His. I have no doubt he's good at driving that truck of his. And I'm sure he takes it wherever he wants." She grinned. "So it's good, huh? You didn't share stuff with me four years ago and you're still being stingy. I need something to brighten my dreary days, since Peter's so preoccupied with school and work."

"Monica!" Sofie wandered over to the window and pulled back the curtain to watch for Jack. "I had nothing to say about what happened four years ago and I have nothing to say now."

"But I can fantazise, can't I? With Kim Barber so desperate for him, he's gotta be good."

"Why? What's so special about Kim and why is she the standard for good sex?"

"See, there you go. All I have to do is mention Jack's old girlfriend and you're off and running. You've got it bad. I rest my case."

Sofie ran her hands over her hair, catching at strands that kept falling out of her loose topknot. She made another trip to the mirror, stepped up close and rechecked her make-up, for the tenth time. "I look ridiculous, Monica. I've always been cosmetically challenged."

Before Monica could respond, Katya danced into the room. "Mommy—you look pretty!"

"See?" Monica said. "Katya knows best, don't you, Katya?"

"You look like my doll."

"Oh God, I look like a doll!" Sofie reached down and swung Katya up in her arms. "I hope you do know best, because it's too late now. I hear the door downstairs."

Katya turned and dashed to the head of the stairs, jumping up and down on her small tennis shoes. "Jack!" She put her hand over her mouth, mortified. "Oops! Daddy. Come and see Mommy."

Sofie gulped in air, feeling queasy, and waited for Jack's judgment. His eyes dilated when he spotted Sofie. He stared at her, not saying a word, his eyes focused on her bodice.

Conscious suddenly of Katya looking up at him, he turned and smiled at her. "I see her. There she is all right!"

"Isn't she pretty? She looks like Barbie, doesn't she?" Katya held up her doll next to Sofie's dress.

"Yes, she does look like Barbie." Jack's voice was impossible to read. He turned to Sofie. "You ready?"

She was sure the answer he wanted was 'no'. "Yes, I guess I am."

Sofie bent over Katya. "Sweetie, do what Monica tells you, okay? Go to bed when she says it's time. I'll come in and say goodnight, when I get home."

Katya nodded, pulled her two-foot frame up straighter and turned to Jack. "Daddy, can you come in and say goodnight to me when you get home, too?"

He lifted her up and gave her a hug. "Sure nuff, sweetheart. I'll come in and give you a big kiss, okay?" She nodded as he put her down, hugged Sofie's legs and wandered off to her toys.

Jack turned and frowned at Monica. "I have Jeff Kinski stationed outside on watch. You have any problems, just give him a shout."

Sofie grabbed up her shawl, frowning. "Are we back to needing guards?"

"Just tonight, Sofie, with both of us out for the evening, I feel better having someone watching." He turned back to Monica. "We'll be home by midnight. Sofie left you my cell number and my pager, right?"

Monica wagged her eyebrows. "Midnight, huh? Cinderella?"

"Sure," Sofie replied. "Cinderella, the Single Mother."

A long five minutes dragged by as they drove. At last Jack cleared his throat. "Sofie, that dress. It's a little over the top, isn't it?"

"What do you mean 'over the top'?" She croaked.

"Well, I mean it isn't really you. You know, you look like Katya said, like a Barbie doll. Too made up and too much cleavage. It doesn't suit you."

"Well, thanks a lot. That makes me feel really confident and ready to go face a few hundred people I don't know at a party." She turned and gazed out the window. After all, she couldn't expect him to be sensitive to what she was wearing; he was a cop.

Jack reached over and caught her hand. "I'm sorry. I'm an oaf. My mother always tells me I make the rest of the males in our family look sensitive. I didn't mean you don't look pretty. But it's too dressy, too pretty, it's not you."

"You'd better stop there. You're only digging yourself in deeper. So I should wear sweats all the time, is that it?"

"No, what I mean is, your looks are natural. You don't need to paint yourself up and wear a red dress and show your tits."

"My tits? Oh, God, take me back home. I'm not going." He kept driving. "I said take me home!" She pulled her hand away from his, on the verge of a meltdown. It was either sit nicely and pretend everything was fine, good ole Sofie, another female placating Jack, or she could proceed in the direction she was headed, hysteria.

"Shit." He had pulled over to the curb, in front of a strip club, turned, and caught her hand again. Forgetting her wounded side, he yanked her, not gently, and she landed sprawled on his lap. "Dammit! Did I hurt you? Sofie, I'm sorry. I forgot..." He eased her back against him, holding her shoulders instead. "Listen, you look beautiful. Hell, I don't know shit about make-up or clothes." He shut up, caught her chin and turned her face up to his for some nonverbal mouth work. Whatever retort was about to come from out of her mouth was silenced by his, his tongue searching and encountering hers.

She pushed him away ineffectively, his chest as unforgiving as a brick wall, and finally gave way and sank back against him.

Refusing to give ground, now that he had the advantage, he wove his fingers into her hair, causing her topknot to fall loose and cascade down over his hand. He worked her head sideways at a better angle and deepened the kiss. Groaning in unison, they pulled back and stared at each other.

The red spots on Sofie's cheeks grew brighter as a series of lewd noises erupted outside the car, made by three passersby. Before she could scramble back to her seat, he pulled her head down and kissed her again.

She squirmed against him and he felt his cock harden under the weight of her shifting rear. Hell, at least this approach was working better than talking. He continued the assault with his tongue as one of his hands found its way around to the front of her red dress and captured a breast. Sofie yanked herself back, staring at him. It was too good to last, he thought.

"So is that your way of making it clear to me I'm showing too much tit?" Her voice came out a squeak.

"Sofie." He struggled to push aside his desire, mingled with frustration. "I'm not trying to show you anything. I'm just turned on. I won't apologize for my mindless dick, and I am sorry about my blundering attack on your clothes. But I know the cops who'll be at this fucking thing tonight well enough to know you'll feel uncomfortable with them leering at you."

Her eyes were bright and he cursed himself for the oaf he was.

"So what do you want me to do, Jack? Go back home? Did you want to go without me? If you didn't think I was dressed right, why didn't you say so before we left?" She pulled back further but he caught her and pulled her back against his chest.

"Sofie," He tried again. "Look, I'm a jerk and I'm sorry. You look beautiful. I'm just not used to your looking like this.

I'm used to something lower-key, less flamboyant. Damn!" He shut up, took a breath and tried again. "Let's go to the dance. Nothing more will come out of my mouth tonight except compliments, I promise. You look wonderful."

He breathed a sigh of relief when she sat up and straightened her dress, reaching for her fallen hair. "All right. Truce, okay?"

He watched as she adjusted her hair, he pulled out his handkerchief and worked diligently at the lipstick he'd smeared over her face.

She waited patiently until he was done, then reached out and caught the handkerchief as he started to shove it back into his pocket, this time wiping his mouth. He flinched at the thought of the entire police department watching him saunter into the auditorium with lipstick all over his face.

St. Christopher's Hall was adjacent to Greektown and four blocks south of police headquarters. The place was like a curious blend of holiday and funereal spirit, the room decked out in bright Christmas reds and greens, most of the people dressed in black. Despite a techno-pop Christmas song the band attempted, the mood of the crowd reflected their attire more than the decorations.

Sofie watched Jack for some sign of correct behavior amidst Detroit's finest. People came up to say something in passing to him or called out a greeting, giving Sofie the once-over before moving away. *No one* had on red, but in style, her dress was very much like countless others in the room, many far more revealing than hers. She wondered what Jack's problem had been.

She stood near a large table littered with nametags while Jack handed their coats off. He took her arm and steered her towards a crowd of people gathered at an ornate bar, early twentieth century design.

"What would you like?" He draped an arm around her shoulder and he guided her forward.

"Stoli, on the rocks." The same thing she'd ordered four years ago, but his face registered nothing.

"Wait here." He pushed his way up to the bar.

As she watched his retreating back, she wondered why he'd wanted her to come to this event. It wasn't her style, nor was it his. And it placed her in the center of his life, something she could have sworn he never would want. She watched him juggle two glasses as he laughed with a couple in their forties, obviously more at ease with them than with her.

He looked over at her, turned to say something to his friends and they obediently followed him over to where she stood. As he strolled towards her, his eyes moved over her dress, resting momentarily on her semi-bared breasts and up to her face.

He handed her a glass. "Sofie, this is John Frazier and Katherine Weber—they live near my parents. John is on the Bomb Squad with me. Katherine is in Social Services—LaCasa, right?"

The woman nodded and turned to shake Sofie's hand. "Jack told us you have a woman's bookstore. I'd love to come by and see what you have. Do you specialize in anything in particular?"

Sofie shook her head. She liked the directness of this woman. "Anything by women, fiction or nonfiction. Lately, we've been spending some time expanding our social issues section—things women naturally take on—feeding the family, safety, peace issues."

Jack frowned. "Why do you say those are women's issues? Ask any guy and he'd say those things are important to him."

"I didn't mean it was our territory exclusively, only that women seem to have some inherent commitment to those areas. Probably a mother's point of view, rather than a political or moral agenda." Jack studiously kept his eyes on her face, avoiding the more dangerous parts of her body.

Jack and John shifted to talk about work, and Sofie and Katherine continued a discussion of writers. The words 'ecoterrorists' and 'factories' reached her ears, but she kept her attention fixed on Katherine, not wanting to know anything more about the dangers of Jack's job.

The techno music dissolved, replaced by something slow and easy. Jack caught Sofie's elbow, relieved her of her glass and tugged her onto the dance floor. They were the third couple out. A dance floor with three hundred plus people watching wasn't the sort of place she would have picked to present herself into his world, but it didn't seem to bother him.

She leaned into his chest, her forehead resting on his shoulder. They danced, ate, and danced some more. He introduced her to countless strangers, people he worked with, their spouses, city officials. She smiled and shook hands, wondering if any of the cops remembered her from the night she was booked.

Sofie had off her shoes and sat at a table, listening to another Bomb Squad wife talk about her husband. She looked up restlessly and saw Kim Barber winding her way between tables, towards her. Sofie searched for Jack and spotted him, angling his way back towards her. He'd seen Kim and was intent on intercepting her before she reached Sofie.

Kim, who beat him by seconds, turned to welcome Jack, as though they hadn't seen each other in years. Sofie was again struck by the purity of her features, so at odds with the staggering body.

"So, Jack, I never thought you'd have the nerve to bring your little criminal friend here to the Policeman's Ball, of all places. Aren't you worried she's going to pick pocket the Mayor and get towed off in cuffs again?" She said it with a smile for Jack alone. "Or are you going for a bit of irony? Is this your idea of a good joke on the police force? Or maybe just on me?" Kim's gown was black, tight, slit up the thigh, cut to a V in front that barely contained her heaving bosom.

"Give it a rest tonight, Kim. This isn't going to do any good. I invited Sofie tonight. That's all there is to it."

He grasped Sofie's arm and turned towards the dance floor, but Kim caught hold of her other arm. She aimed her words at Sofie this time. "Don't get your hopes up. That innocent wide-eyed look isn't going to get you far. Just because he accidentally slipped you a live one and now there's a kid doesn't mean he has anything to offer you besides his dick. He has a long history around the station of 'the fuck and run', don't you, Jack?"

Jack turned back and Sofie felt heat vibrating off him. "Kim, get out of my way and stay out of it. Otherwise, our next meeting will be before the Police Conduct Board."

Sofie's body trembled as Jack pulled her onto the dance floor. She prayed her knees wouldn't buckle. He held her tightly, his body calming her own. They danced, neither of them speaking, until finally, he pulled back, a question in his eyes.

"It's fine, Jack. I'm okay."

"You're sure? I've been dragging you around this dance floor as though you were a store mannequin. I completely forgot about your wound. Sure you're all right?"

She nodded and pressed her face into his shoulder. *Liar*, she thought. She wanted nothing more than to go home and fall into bed, just the two of them. They made it through two more songs and left.

## *Eighteen*

Kim was sporting a different look away from the precinct. Different, too, from the sophisticated look of Saturday night, with the long black sheath, slit up her thigh. She'd worked her impressive body into skintight leather pants, wraparound shirt, cut low enough to leave little to imagine, under a mid-length matching coat. The ensemble cried couture, as far from Detroit in style as miles. But there was something in the way she wore it that said *vice*, minus the appendage of *cop*. She had one of those bodies that would start looking a little chunky at forty, and without a lot of care, easily go to fat by the age of fifty. But at thirty-one she was a show-stopper.

The thing about her, Sofie decided, was the intriguing contradiction of face, as sweet as candy, with breasts that could fill a D cup. Sofie wondered how that all worked when pursuing a suspect. But maybe Kim's police work didn't require her to run around and get sweaty. Her skin was pink and white, her mouth round and slightly bow-shaped, nose short, turned up and very cute. Her hair was red bronze, long and curly. She flipped it back over her shoulder, from time to time, with a move Sofie found unfathomable.

Sofie had tried to ignore the persistent knocking at her back door, but it kept on. Finally, she'd given up and threw open the door, surprised to find Kim Barber standing in front of her.

Kim stood now facing her, and she wasn't smiling. "Where's Jack?" Her voice had a low resonance to it, the kind of voice most successful in the bedroom and Sofie tried, unsuccessfully, to erase the sound of it whispering dirty words in Jack's ear.

"He's probably at work. Something I can do for you?"

Kim ignored her and strolled around the room, the light from the table lamp casting long shadows behind her. "He's not there." She made no attempt at polite small talk or even normal civility.

It was late, after ten, and Sofie had no idea where Jack was. He'd dropped Katya off that afternoon from daycare and taken off without a word. Katya was in bed now and Sofie assumed Jack was either on-call and working late, or he'd decided to go back to his apartment for some much-needed sleep. She wasn't even sure if he was staying with her and Katya permanently, or if it had only been temporary, while she recovered from the gunshot wound. Their relationship seemed to be so unpredictable right now, she refused to ask him.

"He's probably on-call tonight."

She wondered why Kim hadn't just called the precinct and found out where he was. Was it common knowledge that Jack was spending most nights at her apartment? Why else had Kim come by, expecting to find him? The sex with Jack might be mesmerizing, but she wouldn't think of using it to gauge their future. She almost hoped Kim's showing up here would push things out in the open with Jack.

Kim roamed the living room, her face impassive, and her blank expression raised more alarms in Sofie's mind than all her shouting and accusations. *But, after all,* Sofie reassured herself, *however erratic she is, she's still a cop, an enforcer of the law.*

"Would you like to sit down?" She motioned to a seat, but was ignored. Kim moved to the window and stared down for a few minutes before turning back to Sofie, eyes flaring. "So this is the little love nest? This dump? You think Jack wants to live this kind of a life? He grew up in a house not much more than a step above this, but he's ambitious. He'd never settle for a lifestyle even worse than his family's."

Sofie had no idea what she was talking about. She'd never heard Jack mention anything about his hating his family's position. The one thing she was certain of with Jack was that he loved his family.

"And if you think having that little kid of his is going to do more than give you a temporary hold on him, you're dreaming. He may want that kid, but he wants lots more for himself. He's the big bad bomb squad stud. He can have any woman he wants, and believe me, he takes advantage of that. Why should he want someone like you? You're just a convenience to him right now. He can see his kid and get serviced by you on the side. But he won't have any problem with you being removed from the picture. In fact, once he sees the sense of it, he'll thank me. He's too afraid of looking bad to do it himself, but he'll be glad I've made it clear for him to get custody of his kid, without having to put up with some unsavory relationship with the mother."

The words were so blandly spoken, Sofie couldn't believe she'd actually heard them right. She sat and stared, working on the meaning.

A flash of something in Kim's hand stirred Sofie out of her thoughts and she jumped to her feet. She knew without seeing it clearly what it was. Kim raised the handgun slowly and pointed the nozzle directly at her crotch. She heard the click as the safety went off and held her breath, searching for an escape route.

The slam of the downstairs door startled both of them and Jack's voice called from the steps, "Sofie? Where are you?" He sounded upset, anxious. The urge to run to him was overwhelming, but the gun pointed at her didn't waver. Her side began to ache unexpectedly, reminding her she'd been shot once and wasn't ready to have it happen again.

Sofie's back was to the hallway, but she knew the moment Jack arrived, his voice quieter, slower than usual. "Kim. It's all right. Put the gun down. I'm here. Whatever your beef is, it's with me."

Kim looked from Sofie to Jack, confused, struggling between wanting to be rid of Sofie and wanting to talk to Jack. "Jack, I had to come. I had to stop her. I knew you'd never deal with this, but I can do it for you." Her words were quick, breathless, her eyes moving from Sofie to behind her, where Jack stood. "She's beneath you, Jack. Just look around this place. She's nothing but a fucking little schemer, trying to work her way into your life. If you can't see it, I can. Let me put a stop to her plans." Her eyes wavered, but she kept the gun focused on Sofie.

"Kim, it's all right. I understand. Put down the gun now. I'll take care of everything." He circled Sofie, moving between her and Kim, his eyes never leaving Kim's face. He had his gun hand inside his coat, ready.

Kim slowly lowered the gun and turned to face Jack. He made a quick move, snatching the gun from her with one hand, pulling her against him with the other. He stood for a moment, saying nothing, but holding tightly to Kim. He looked up at Sofie then, his face ashen, eyes blazing.

"Sofie, call the Precinct and have them get the Inspector over get here. Now!" Kim's face was pressed into his jacket, but she seemed limp now, almost lifeless, held up by Jack's body alone.

Sofie turned and went out of the room to make the call, her throat tight.

It took less than five minutes for backup to get there. Jack must have left the door open, and uniforms flooded the apartment, followed minutes later by a black man in plain clothes. Neither Kim or Jack had moved, he still held her against him, her head buried in his jacket.

Sofie automatically went to Katya's room, not wanting to see or hear anything more from Kim. She was far more frightening standing silently in Jack's arms than she'd been ranting at them, and Sofie couldn't face her. She stood in the dark, looking down at Katya, sleeping, unaware of the danger around her. Sofie listened to her light breathing. Who would have raised Katya if Kim had shot her?

Continuous sounds of people coming and going, voices raised, intruded on her and Sofie moved reluctantly into the dark hallway. She pressed herself against the wall, wanting only to disappear. People passed by, stopped and spoke to her, asked her questions. She answered them automatically and watched them write down her words.

Sofie looked through the doorway into the living room where Jack still stood beside Kim as they cuffed her, his arm still around her, reassuring. The black man stood on Kim's other side, exchanging words with Jack. Sofie shut her eyes and waited.

At last, they moved Kim towards the back stairs, Jack still holding her arm. He turned to Sofie briefly. "Lock the door after everyone leaves. I'll be back as soon as I can." That was all.

Sofie trailed them down the steps, double-locked the door and headed for her bedroom. She sat down on the bed, misery bubbling up from deep inside her, the kind of fear and hopelessness that usually awakened one in the darkest part of the night, but lived long in daylight.

After a long time, she stood, went to the bathroom to change into a nightgown. She waited, listening but heard only the comforting sounds of the apartment, the furnace, the refrigerator motor. She dreaded Jack's return. She didn't want to think, didn't want to answer any questions or know anything more right now.

She climbed into bed, switched off the bedside lamp and pulled the covers up tight. The bathroom light was still on, sending a thin beam into her room. She fell asleep watching the light.

She awakened confused, and cried out as a hand shook her. It was Jack. The bedside light was on and he sat on the side of her bed, concern in his eyes. It was cold in the apartment and she shivered. He reached out and pulled her against him and it reminded her of how he held Kim. Inhaling the familiar scent of him, wanting his heat, she leaned into him, smiling slightly. *Poor Jack, doomed to have women constantly throwing themselves on his chest.*

"I'm sorry, Sofie." He didn't say anything more for a long time. "Kim's had this thing about me for a time now. It had nothing to do with you. Any woman I was around was probably a threat to her. I never realized it had gone this far." He moved his hands restlessly against her back. "She wasn't after you especially, just anyone who disrupted her plans. The dance on Saturday, it must have sent her over the edge. Her fucking fantasy world wasn't going to happen. If I'd been alert, I'd have spotted it. I wouldn't have left her that way Saturday night." He sighed and held Sofie tighter. "They've taken her to Detroit Receiving, the Psych Unit, for tonight. Someone will come by tomorrow for your statement." He grinned for the first time tonight. "You should be able to do that in your sleep now. Next thing you know, they'll assign you a desk."

Sofie raised her head, keeping her eyes focused on the small tuft of black hair visible above his t-shirt. "Jack, what about Katya? Was Kim the one doing the threats?"

He rubbed his eyes. His face was drawn and he looked exhausted. "I don't know. It's a hell of a motive. And that file you got from her office? She's got a shitload of data collected, both on me and Katya. She's been up to something, for quite a while."

"But why would she go out of her way to set up something that brought me and Katya into your life? And how could she know about Katya, when you didn't? Was she around four years ago?" She reddened. "I mean, were you dating her then? Could she have found out about that night?"

He frowned. "I've known her for about six years. I can't remember when we actually started dating. It's been on and off for a few years now. Mostly off." He reached out a finger and aimlessly traced the outline of her bandage beneath her nightgown, weighing his words. "I can't believe there was any way she'd have known about that night. Unless she was following me. I didn't plan to go to the Mariner and I sure as hell didn't tell anyone I was planning on spending the night dead drunk."

Sofie pushed back to see his face. "It seems impossible she could have been planning this for so long." She stared off into the dark side of the room, searching for something. "The only places your name ever came up were in daycare; I broke down and put your name and address down along with Monica's. And then on an insurance policy I took out on myself, I used your name as next of kin with Katya." He stared at her, suppressing a burst of anger at the ease with which she'd left him out of Katya's life.

"Could she have gotten enough information in the past few weeks to fill a file like that?" Sofie asked.

He shrugged. "Hell if I know. A lot of it *was* recent. Records of when I was at your place. She must have hired a PI to follow me around. Some phone records, hospital data about Katya, her daycare." He stopped and frowned again. "There's really no way to know how long this has been going on, unless she tells us. Right now, she isn't talking."

He sighed dismissively. "Can I stay?" This was the first time he'd actually asked her, usually they went to bed and he just stayed. She nodded, unsure where the request had come from. There was nothing else to say tonight and he got up and headed for the bathroom.

She reached out, turned off the bedside lamp, and waited in the dark. She knew when he came in by the scent of his soap. His shadowy figure moved towards the bed, dropping his clothes beside it and climbing in. His arm came around her tight and he cupped the back of her head and pulled her to him. He was completely naked and his heat settled around her, enveloping her cold body like a sauna. She raised her face and his lips touched hers, lightly, searching, then opened and pressed deeper. With a groan, she flicked her tongue over his teeth and pushed deeper into his mouth.

They lay facing each other and for a moment she remembered the first time, four years ago. Then, she'd lain, passive, waiting. This time, they fought for position as each moved to touch and caress, her hands as eager and demanding as his.

It was hard and fast, more physical than emotional, more sex than love, but way beyond where they'd gone before. After a long time, he leaned forward on an elbow, reaching around to turn her head towards him. "Did I hurt you?"

"No, I'm fine. I'm just…" She stopped, searching for words to reassure him. "I can't—I—I'm not used to this," she finished jerkily. She felt a brutal need for him, wanted to be overwhelmed by him, and it frightened her.

He lay with the top of his head burrowed in her neck, his face turned away, as though he shared her conflicted feelings. Their legs were entwined, both bodies giving off too much heat. Her head spun with sensations. Was this what she had wanted? This wild exchange? One moment free, the next moment consumed? His hands moved over her shoulders, traveled down her spine, claiming her. His fingers cupped her buttocks and drew her closer, against his still hard penis and she took it eagerly between her legs, capturing it between her swollen labia.

They lay quiet, restless rather than peaceful, and she turned her head to look at him. His eyes were shut, as though to shut everything out. She reached up and touched his face, tracing the rough features with her fingertips. Her hand fell away and, legs intertwined still with his, she slept.

## *Nineteen*

They awoke staring at each other, the space as wide as possible between them in the narrow bed. Sofie pushed her loose hair away from her eyes and blinked at him. "Hi." Her voice sounded gritty, as though she's been asleep for years.

He grinned at her and she blinked again. He looked far too satisfied for someone with a few hours sleep and the night they'd shared.

"I suppose it's asking too much at eight in the morning for a quickie?" He winked and she glanced at the door. As he reached for his pants, Katya bounced in, oblivious to the sight of them in bed together.

"Daddy! I see more snow! It's on the cars! Can we go sledding today? Ple-e-ease!" She jumped onto the bed and Jack threw Sofie's nightgown across to her. He picked up Katya, swung her around once, giving Sofie time to dress, before plopping her back onto the bed. Wearing only pants and shirtless, Jack headed for the bathroom, tossing over his shoulder, "Ask your mother."

Sofie frowned at his back and turned to Katya. "Sweetie, it's a work day and you have school. Maybe later this afternoon, if things aren't too busy, I can take a little time and we can walk over to the sledding hill, okay?"

As it turned out, it was a Snow Emergency Day, rare in Detroit. There was no daycare and the store could not open. The urgency of the morning disappeared for Sofie and she made French toast as Jack called into the Precinct.

He leaned down, and grabbed a plate as he was patched through to his team. Waiting, he turned, made a face at Katya and started forking in the food. "Yeah? Ryan and Conant? I'll be there in fifteen minutes or less."

He plopped down his plate and turned to Sofie. "I have to go. I'll call you as soon as I get finished. Wait for me. I'll stop by and pick you and Katya up later on." He glanced over at Katya, her dark eyes meeting his. "Katya can come along with us to the Precinct."

He knelt down in front of Katya. "Want to come with me to work this afternoon? Would you like that, scout? Maybe a tour of where I work?"

Her eyes grew big. "Can I show Suni the jail and the bad guys?"

He shook his head. "Sorry, honey. Those bad guys are in a different building. You can show her the desk where I work sometimes. And you can try on the handcuffs."

She'd already used his on him more than once as he slept on the couch and she frowned. "Okay, I guess. Can we go sledding after that?"

Jack looked over at Sofie, who nodded. "The local hill is a little tame for you though, isn't it, Jack?"

"How about Middle Rouge? I'll call you." His eyes stayed fixed on her face. "You okay?" She nodded.

He reached out and grabbed hold of her neck, and pulled her to him for a kiss. With Katya's "Me too!" he turned and bent down to do the same for her.

~ * ~

Conant and Ryan was two blocks away from the huge Poletown factory and the bombing. The warehouse was deserted, as most were in Detroit these days and for the past twenty-plus years, since the riots of '67 had promoted the white flight to the suburbs. Jack pulled up to the building beside the empty squad car, the door open. He met his uniformed assistant, Polly Tenant, at the door. Polly was male, thirty and good looking. He'd been called Polly since elementary school when he brought a parrot to school for Show and Tell, but he couldn't say the name.

"Hey, Jack. How are you? Sorry to call you out on this but I thought you'd want to see it." Polly unlocked the door and they headed for the freight elevator. The place had giant holes in the structure wherever one looked, letting in cold air, snow piles on the cement floor beneath each hole.

"So, what have you got?" Jack pulled his jacket tighter against the steady wind blowing down the elevator shaft.

"We were doing a search, like you said, of all the buildings within walking distance. I happened on this an hour ago." He got out on the top floor and motioned Jack to a box of materials sitting in a corner. It was C4. The return address on the box was Crane Naval Base, Crane, Indiana.

Jack pulled out his gloves, bent down and began pulling out large quantities of C4 in small plastic bags, reams of det cord and boxes of caps. He dug through each of the bags and packages, looking for other IDs but there was nothing.

For the next hour they worked, getting photos of the site, setting up a grid, and watching as the lab team hauled the stuff down to the van.

He and Polly sat warming themselves in the squad car, going over what they had so far. He set up Polly to track the Crane stuff, called in to get an update on his suspects from East Jefferson and put traces on their past, looking for links to Indiana. He put one final call into Detroit Receiving to see how Kim was. She'd been transferred by her family to Ford Hospital Psych Unit. It was almost one o'clock before he put in a call to Sofie and headed for her place.

~ * ~

Sofie lingered over her breakfast as Katya roamed around the apartment, moving to a window every few minutes to check on the snow. Sofie swallowed the last of cold coffee and soggy toast, working hard to recall the blinding desire that had seemed more important last night than the uncertainties around her and Jack's relationship. A gnawing sense of unease, undistinguishable in the heat of passion, had reemerged this morning and threatened to swamp her.

Just after one, Jack called. He was heading back towards the bookstore, bringing pizza for lunch. They could eat it when they got to the Precinct. Sofie felt queasy at the thought of eating anything right now, particularly greasy pizza, but she didn't argue with him, knowing Katya would love it.

The Snow Emergency had interfered with criminal intent and the Precinct was quiet. Sofie felt eyes following them as they dodged between desks and headed for the fourth floor and the Chief Investigator's Office.

The Board of Police Commissioners was made up of civilians who established departmental policies, rules and regulations, approved budgets, and were the final appellate authority for employee discipline. As a police department employee, Kim Barber fell under the jurisdiction of this board.

The Chief Investigator was a black woman, fifty-ish, thin, fashionably dressed, her overall power second only to the Chief of the Detroit Police. Maya Douglas stood up and graciously held out a hand, despite being called in from her vacation. She greeted Jack, sat down and pointed to seats. Sofie glanced out the glass partition at her daughter, who sat in a large wooden chair, working diligently to handcuff a perpetrator, Jack's brother, Tony. Before Maya Douglas called her in, Sofie had given her statement to a stout man who never looked up from his computer, while three feet away, Katya and Jack sat eating pizza as though this was a daily event. If not a daily event, it was turning into a weekly one for Sofie and she prayed this would be the *last* time she'd have to give a statement to the cops.

Sofie and Jack sat down across from Maya Douglas. "Ms. Novakoff. May I call you Sofie? I wanted to personally call you in and apologize to you for the behavior of one of our officers. It's disgraceful and something we've never had to deal with before, with an officer of the police department. I can only offer you a promise that I'll do whatever it takes to ensure public safety as well as severely discipline Detective Barber. We are in the process of a complete review of, not only her case, but the entire department and its use of confidential information."

Her words were precise, like someone who demanded perfection, not only of herself, but of every other person under her charge. Without looking to Sofie for a response, she opened a file. "Since Detective Roselli has informed me of the threats to your daughter and his ongoing investigation into that, I wanted to fill you in on Detective Barber's access to your daughter's personal data." She stopped and glanced over at Sofie. "I thought you should know that at this point, Detective Barber's access to that specific information seems to be fairly recent. It may or may not have anything to do with the reported stalking incidents, which, according to Detective Roselli, started almost two months ago."

Sofie took a deep breath and waited.

"As far as we can tell, Detective Barber got the records on your daughter only in the past month and it appears they came from tracking insurance forms you recently filed. What led her to your insurance records is unclear since there's no paper trail specifically to that information. What we have determined is that she tracked you through Sergeant Roselli himself."

Sofie let out her breath with a hiss. "Are you saying Jack gave her the information?"

"From what little Detective Barber has told us so far, she was basically stalking him, having him followed, for the past few weeks. That led her to you and your daughter, whereby she made a concentrated effort to gather more information. She apparently was looking for information regarding your daughter's relationship to Detective Roselli." She pointed to Jack who sat, stiff-faced. "We have traced phone calls to your residence and your work, quite a few to Jack's cell phone and are following leads on other calls she made to your daughter's daycare."

"But how could you have missed these phone calls when Jack put a trace on every incoming and outgoing call I've had for the past month?"

The Chief Investigator grimaced, so briefly Sofie almost missed it. "A slip-up on the part of one of our investigators. It may have been dismissed as a routine call to Jack, while he was staying at your place. I'm afraid I can't explain that. I'm sorry to say I can't absolutely guarantee the threats to your daughter came directly from Sergeant Barber, but for now we may surmise that they did." She frowned and paused, apparently expecting a response.

Sofie looked at Jack and back at the Chief Investigator. "So what will happen to Kim?"

"She will be undergoing psychiatric evaluations and we will defer any decisions until after they are complete. You can be assured she won't bother you any more."

Sofie looked again at Jack who nodded at her, the only real reassurance he offered.

"For now, I recommend," Investigator Douglas continued, "you keep a vigilant eye on your daughter, inform us if any more threats or suspicious activities occur and we can only hope this will put an end to an unfortunate turn of affairs." She smiled, more fully this time, stood up and held out a hand. "Jack, please keep me advised of the situation."

Jack stood up, stiff-legged in front of the desk. "Investigator Douglas, I'd like to be kept informed on the outcome of the investigation of Detective Barber. Is that possible?"

"I don't have a problem with that, Detective Roselli. Anything else?" She tapped her pencil on the desk.

"I'd also like access to all files found in Detective Barber's possession relating to myself, Sofie or our daughter."

Maya Douglas flicked a glance at her wristwatch and nodded. "Yes. That seems reasonable in this situation. Is that it, then?"

Jack nodded, shook hands with the Investigator and followed Sofie out of her office. Outside the door, Sofie stopped abruptly and Jack grabbed at her shoulders to keep from plowing her over.

"You'll let me know anything they find, won't you?"

"Of course, Sofie." Investigator Douglas' words were meant to be reassuring, but he felt the return of a nagging dread, lodged in the pit of his stomach. He took Sofie's hand for a moment before releasing her, aware all eyes in the precinct were on them. "Don't worry. I'm not going to let this go. I'll make sure Kim never bothers you again. And I'll find out if there's any possibility she wasn't behind the threats to Katya."

They walked out of 1200 Beaubien accompanied by Tony, who was talking nonstop to Katya. Jack turned back to his youngest brother, a leaner, prettier version of himself, definitely with more charm. "Where you headed, Tony?" He watched Katya laughing up in Tony's face and a sudden image of Dinah laughing at Tony was like a punch to the stomach.

Tony wagged his eyebrows at Katya, "Going to check out the dead bodies at the Morgue. Want to come along?" He grinned up at Sofie's frown and turned back to an eager Katya. "It's okay, isn't it Katya? We already had a long discussion about dead bodies and stuff like that."

"What is it with you Rosellis' sense of humor?" Sofie waited for Tony to disappear and hissed the question to Jack.

He stopped in front of his Jeep, double parked beside an unmarked car, and gave her a dismayed look. "I can't believe it. You're accusing me of a sense of humor? That's a first!" He laughed and hauled Katya into the backseat of the Cherokee.

Sofie refused to respond but Katya's attention was caught. "What's sense of humor mean? Is that like cartoons? What about bodies?"

She was definitely more curious than shocked by Tony's words and as they drove, Jack questioned Katya about exactly what Tony had told her.

They continued their conversation past the Detroit city limits, through East Dearborn and onto Eddie Hines Drive. They were heading for the toboggan run.

~ * ~

The Snow Emergency left thousands of kids from the suburbs with no place to go on a Tuesday and the toboggan run was crowded. It took two hours to make four runs and Katya lost interest waiting in line, finding it more entertaining to pile snow on Jack. He lay at the bottom of a huge heap of the white stuff, while Katya and Sofie, both wearing embroidered mittens that looked like colorful Easter eggs, buried him deeper. Katya wore a matching hat but Sofie's head was bare and her thick braid was covered with snow. He lay still, watching their red faces, listening to the unfamiliar sound coming from his chest. Laughter. He tried to remember the last he'd laughed out loud and couldn't.

His stillness caught Sofie's attention and she stopped, holding a huge pile of snow above his head, and stared down into his eyes. He felt his chest contract. *God*, he thought, *Am I falling in love with her?*

She stood unmoving, eyes fixed on his, as though she could read his thoughts. She smiled briefly and dropped the huge snowball on his face.

"Damn!" He leapt up, lunged out and grabbed hold of one leg as she backed away from him. It took only a small tug to pull her down on top of him, an elbow to his solar plexus that knocked the breath out of him. Katya yelled loudly, dropped her snowball on them and threw her small body on top.

Suddenly remembering Sofie's wound, Jack extricated himself and pulled Sofie up. "You okay?"

"No, you big gorilla!" She laughed and, with Katya's assistance, pushed him back down.

The sun had come out and the snow was melting off their clothes, leaving them soaked through, as they staggered back to the Jeep. Jack carried an exhausted Katya, who refused to walk, and Sofie trudged behind, holding onto a handful of his sodden leather jacket.

He settled Katya in her car seat, turned the heat up full blast and headed back to the east side. As they pulled onto the freeway, he looked over at Sofie and smiled.

Neither of them noticed the vintage VW lagging behind them all the way back to the apartment.

~ * ~

It was almost six when they got home. Katya had missed her nap and was ready for bed. Sofie fixed a small dinner, gave Katya a quick bath, and put her to bed in the small room.

Holding mugs of coffee, they sat down on the overstuffed sofa, side by side, just out of touching range. He looked grave and she held her breath.

"Sofie, I've been thinking. I know we need to keep things low key right now and play it by ear, but I'm working on a way to spend more time with the two of you."

"What do you have in mind?" She asked cautiously.

"I'd like you to think about our making more permanent living arrangements." He gave her a side glance. "So what do you think?" *Dammit, where am I going with this?* Right now, she was his quarry and he wanted her. He couldn't think beyond that.

She squirmed as though the couch were a hot stove. "Jack, I'm not sure what you want. I know how difficult it's been trying to protect Katya and do your job at the same time. But if what Investigator Douglas says is true, it won't be a problem any longer." She looked over at him. "Or do you know something else about this you haven't said?"

He shook his head. The notion that she didn't need him was unsettling and it pissed him off; her uncertainty only added fuel to the hunt. He was used to getting what he wanted, and this time he was focused on her. He hedged his words, circling her in his mind. "I don't know anything more than you've already been told. It's a big leap to consider two different threats happening simultaneously." He stood up and paced across the room, as though distance would clear his mind. "But just to be on the safe side, I want some of the precautions kept in place, for a while." He looked directly at her now. "I want to make some changes in our relationship at the same time." He paused to give her time to absorb his words. "I thought you wanted that, too. Was I wrong?"

"I don't know, Jack. I'm confused right now. I do know I want us to have a relationship. I just don't know what it is right now. So much has happened in the last month." She pushed her hair back out of her face, giving herself time to find her words. "I don't even recognize myself as the same person I was a month ago. I need time to get used to the changes. I can't talk about the future."

He smiled at her. "Why do I suddenly feel like just another stupid, self-centered man? I assumed we both wanted the same thing. I guess I never thought to check it out with you." The words sounded self-effacing, but his demeanor reminded her more of a call to battle, one he was sure he wouldn't lose.

She took a deep breath. "Jack, for the first time in my entire life I feel like I have some control over the direction I'm going, like I have some options. I want to just sit back and think about what I want and where to go next. I need some time to do that." She reached out and put a hand on his arm.

He chose his next words carefully. "You're not the only one who's in a strange place right now. This is damned awkward for me. I think I might be falling in love with you." He held up a hand. "Wait, don't say anything. I just need to get it out. I'm not even sure I could spot love if it rose up and bit me, but it damned well seems to have done just that." He paused. "So, with all that, I'm not too far removed from where you're at right now. My usual MO is to take what I want, and if that doesn't work, to turn and get the hell out. But you've already heard those accusations, haven't you?" He smiled but didn't touch her. "So, let's just say we're in a new place, both of us, and see where we go from here."

She surprised him by leaning forward, her forehead just touching his chest. "Thanks, Jack." He slid his arms around her, applying no pressure and the silence between them was reassuring, almost comforting.

"As long as you don't ban me from your bedroom, that is." He laughed. "Well? Think we can manage that?"

She raised a flushed face and muttered, "Sure. We can do that."

## *Twenty*

The bookstore was open late Fridays since Thanksgiving. The regulars sat at tables or strolled the aisles, juggling mugs of cider.

Jack left early. He was working late every night this week at the crime lab on Brush, comparing findings on residue and frags from Poletown and Chrysler, cross checking with the materials they'd confiscated at the pier. He and Sofie had called a stalemate on their futures, but there'd been no stalemate on their bed time.

She looked up, wondering if the vivid images of sex with Jack translated into strange expressions on her face. The week of sleeping together had at least cooled off enough that they were getting some rest. Instead of only one to two hours sleep a night, they'd worked up to four or five; last night they'd had over six hours. In fact, sex was getting to be pretty routine. She could handle it, she thought, but wondered how old married couples ever got used to accidentally brushing up against a body part in the night that would suddenly set them off like firecrackers. She'd read some place that the average married couples had sex was once a week to twice a month. She tried to imagine being married to Jack and having sex as infrequently as once a week, but she couldn't get the picture in focus. The past few nights, they'd settled into a routine of sex upon entering and exiting the bed. It was a good thing her apartment building stood alone or she'd be worried about calls from neighbors complaining about sounds coming from her room. At least there was a closet between their wall and Katya's. She smiled and refocused on searching the web for book deals.

Katya sat on the floor, donut in hand, rearranging the pieces to a map of the United States puzzle. Every five minutes she called out a question to one of store regulars sitting nearby.

Sofie stood up with a sigh. "Sweetheart, it's time for bed now."

"Mommy, just let me finish these last two pieces, ple-e-ease!"

Sofie nodded and grabbed some books to reshelve. "Chrissie are you ready too, honey?"

Monica's daughter looked up, gazed at Sofie briefly as though she spoke a foreign language and, without answering, went back at her book.

Fifteen minutes later, Chrissie and Katya were settled down in front of a video in Katya's room. Chrissie was staying over to entertain Katya while Sofie kept the store open late for the holidays.

One more hour. Sofie sat at the counter, staring at the phone. Jack said he'd call but where was he? At last, three straggling customers bundled up and timidly stepped out into the blowing snow. Sofie wandered around the empty store, gathering up mugs and paper plates, wiping down the tables. She was at the sink in the back washing up, when the entire store went dark. She turned, took only a tentative step, before the floor began to rumble and move under her feet. Simultaneously, she was blinded by a brilliant flash of light and fell to the floor.

She lay stunned, her nose and lungs filling with acrid smoke. Her legs were sprawled over something, and she tried to feel what was under her. She'd landed on an unopened box of books. Something stabbed her palm. She remembered, she'd been holding a mug. It must have hit something as she fell and shattered in her hand. Her face stung, as though bitten by tiny insects.

She pulled herself up to sitting. The darkness was replaced by an eerie orange light that seemed to be alive in the darkness. It came from the front of the store, illuminating dust and smoke that hung in the air above her. She coughed and shook her head, trying to clear her thoughts, and pulled herself to her feet, as pain shot down her side. Wetness seeped through her t-shirt and she felt gingerly around the wetness. *Damn. Here we go again.* Something wet ran down her nose and dripped into her mouth. It tasted like cider, probably what was left in the broken mug.

The smoke was getting thicker now, pouring in from the front of the store, the air crackling with sounds of things being consumed by flames. Sofie pulled herself up, using a shelf for support. She took two steps towards the store front, but stopped. Katya and Chrissie were upstairs alone. Orange light, flickering and dancing, was getting brighter in the storage area; her sense of urgency grew. She dragged herself toward the stairs, crouching low against the growing smoke.

She stopped once, at the landing, and looked back. She could just make out the front of the store, filled with flames that covered the entire entrance and front windows. She dropped to her knees, and began the climb up the stairs, one foot, another, a third, endless steps in front of her.

The air was clearer higher up. Her side throbbed incessantly now, and she held one hand against it as she climbed. As she reached the final step, the door to her apartment was flung open, and two small figures stood, lit only from the flames below. "Mommy! It's dark!"

"Girls, quick, we have to get out! Come on! It's going to be all right. Chrissie, grab your coat. Feel behind you, hanging from a peg!" She groped for Katya's small jacket and her own pea coat, praying the girls had on their shoes. With Katya in her arms, holding tight to Chrissie, Sofie started back down the smoke-filled stairwell.

The stairwell was filling up faster now, obscuring the steps as they struggled down. At the landing, Sofie turned blindly and pulled Chrissie down to her knees beside her.

"Chrissie—crawl! Get on your hands and knees and crawl! Follow me! Hold onto my coat! Whatever you do, don't let go!" The last few feet were endless, crackling and crashing sounds punctuating their movements. She lowered herself down the last two steps, holding her breath against the smoke, Katya's face pushed against her chest.

When she reached the backdoor, she threw Katya's coat over her small head, stood up and pushed on the metal door. *Thank God*, she thought, *it's still unlocked!* She threw it open and cold air rushed in and hit her face.

She stumbled into the alley, dragging Chrissie behind her, sucking in clean air. She took deep breaths, overcome with momentary elation at just being alive. She uncovered Katya's face as she turned to grab Chrissie. "Come on! Let's get away from the building!"

The air grew cleaner as they moved towards the street, and she continued gulping in large quantities, soothing her aching lungs. "We're going to be okay, girls, it's going to be fine." Sirens screamed all around, in front of the store, fire trucks were pulling to a stop. *Thank God!*

Firemen jumped out and began pulling equipment and hoses from trucks, an unmarked car roared up and squealed to a stop behind the last truck. Sofie stood in the street, watching as a man headed towards them. As she stood there, a fireman dashed over and yelled in her face. "Anyone left in there?"

"No! It was just the three of us!" Sofie screamed back.

Her legs began to tremble and she struggled to keep erect, relieved when the man reached her, Tony Lubchek, their watchdog. He grabbed hold of one arm and took Katya from her.

"Come with me, ladies!" He turned and headed towards his car, looking back to be sure Chrissie and Sofie followed. Halfway there, seeing Sofie stumble, he turned back, encircled her with his free arm and dragged her with him.

The car was still warm inside. He pushed the three of them into it and reached for his cell phone. "Stay put, now. I'm putting in a call to Jack." He stood a few feet away, making his call.

She eased Chrissie and Katya slightly away from her, conscious of sticky blood trickling down her side. The cop had left the car running and the heater was blasting them with hot air.

"Jack's on his way. You girls sit tight!" She watched as he disappeared into the smoke and turned her head back towards the front of her store. It was engulfed in flames, smoke pouring out of the broken plate glass windows. Both girls were crying and she joined them. As tears ran down her cheeks, she whispered quietly to the girls, stroking Katya with one hand, favoring her cuts and holding Chrissie in the curve of her arm.

The door opened and let in a blast of artic air and Tony bent down. "You alright?"

At her silent nod, he turned away, saying nothing more. Sofie watched him head towards a gathering crowd, her neighbors. He herded them behind barricades being set up, shouting warnings at them to stay back. The streets had been cordoned off on either end now and there was no traffic. Spray from the high-powered hoses filled the air. A fireman raised a ladder and climbed up to an apartment window, broke it and climbed inside. Tears, mixed with smoke residue, stung her eyes.

~ * ~

Jack took the corner on two wheels, his attention focused half way down the block, where fire trucks were scattered randomly. He cut between two squad cars blocking off one end of the street, stopping only to flash his ID at them, before swerving down the icy street to the car sitting well back from the fire trucks. He leapt from his Jeep, loped over to the vehicle and threw open the door. Sofie looked up at him, her face streaked with black and pink lines, eyes brimming with tears. Katya and Chrissie sat on either side of her, crying.

"Sofie!" His voice shook. He leaned over to Katya, who came willingly into his arms. "It's okay, sweetheart, it's okay." He stroked her head automatically, hugging her close. He squeezed Chrissie's hand briefly and placed his free hand over Sofie's lying limply in her lap.

Her face buried in his jacket, Katya's question was so soft he almost missed it. "Daddy, where were you?"

"I'm sorry, sweetheart. I was working. I'm sorry." He took hold of one of Sofie's hands; she was shaking and he clenched it tightly, forcing her to look at him. "Sofie. Are you hurt?" In the darkness of the car, he could make out what looked like tracks of dirt and something pink running down her face.

"Scoot over." He said roughly, crowding in beside her. He pulled her up against his side, still holding tightly to Katya. "Chrissie? Are you hurt?"

Chrissie's face was streaked with dirt and tears, but she'd stopped crying. Instead, she stared, wide-eyed, at the flames and smoke still engulfing the bookstore. "I'm fine. Boy, that was pretty scary, though!" Her bravado sounded tenuous.

"We'll call your mom and she'll come and get you." He looked down at Sofie, who nodded. "Everything's gonna be fine." Jack reached for his cell and handed it to Sofie, watching her trembling fingers as she dialed.

Her voice was tight, hysteria just below the surface. "Monica, it's Sofie. Yes, we're fine. No, we'll all okay. The bookstore's still burning." TV news already had the story. "We're sitting across the street, in a car. Jack's with us. We'll wait for you here. The street's blocked off but just mention Jack's name and they'll let you through."

Jack listened, cursing silently. His instinct was to drag the three of them to his Jeep and put as many miles as possible between them and this scene. Instead he reached for his cell phone and dialed. This was a crime scene and he was needed; it was his job.

He called Dispatch first, relaying his position and what they had so far. Then he took a deep breath and pressed the speed dial for his mother. "Mama, yeah, this is Jack. Listen, there's been an accident at Sofie's bookstore, a fire. No! No, they're fine!" He gave her a minimum of information, holding back specifics. "I'm with them right now. I'm having them brought to your place. Is that all right? Yeah. No, they don't have anything with them. They'll need some things. Just for tonight, okay? Yeah, thanks. They'll be there in ten minutes." He waited for her to calm down. "No, I have to stay here. I'll call you when I can. I'll be there just as soon as I can get away." He hung up and drew Katya closer. She was quiet now, molded against him like a new appendage.

Sofie sat up. "Jack, listen, you shouldn't have called your mother. You know it will terrify her. We could have gone to Monica's." She shivered visibly. "The last thing your mom needs right now is to worry about something happening to Katya."

"Goddammit, Sofie. It won't help to keep Katya away from her now. It's on the news already. She already knew about the explosion." He stared hard at Sofie's face, trying to make out what the red streaks were. "Don't give out any specifics, just tell her what she has to know." Conscious of Katya, leaning into his neck, asleep, he bent to Sofie, "You okay?"

"Yes. As okay as I can be with my home in flames."

"You have streaks of something red running down your face."

She reached up and smeared one of the lines. "I think I got cut by flying glass or something."

"Do you need medical attention?" He tracked a red line trailing down her fingers. "Your hand is cut."

She shook her head. "It's okay. Just some scratches. Doesn't hurt, really." She didn't mention her throbbing side.

"Take Katya for a few minutes. I need to go check in. I'll get someone over here right away to take you to my parents." He lowered Katya onto Sofie's lap. "I'll be back in a few minutes, sweetheart." The endearment slipped out effortlessly and it shifted the tone of their conversation. Unsure if he was addressing her, Sofie nodded but didn't answer.

Paul Torreno was on-call and lead investigator at the scene, the back-up duties falling to Jack. Paul was new to the Bomb Squad, on the team for less than three months. Jack knew him only from one prior scene they'd worked together.

"Paul, what have we got? Anything?" Paul looked up, surprised that Jack had turned up so fast. "The place belongs to a friend of mine. I got the call and came over to help them."

"From the little I can get at so far, it looks like a mini-Poletown plan, way smaller. Det cord running from the rear door, probably triggered from the alley. We found the garage door opener and the receptor just inside the door." He pointed to some frags lying on the ground. "Probably a small quantity of C4 or Semtex again, maybe in a package or something placed against the front window." Paul pulled out a pack of cigarettes and paused to light one. "It did quite a bit of property damage but with the place closed, probably not meant to kill anyone."

Jack grimaced. "The bastards were lucky, then. There were three people inside the damned building. Any one of them happened to be standing by a front window, it could damned well have killed 'em."

"Sorry." He was young, too young for sympathy that came from life experience. "Anyway, the size of the bomb wasn't big enough to destroy the place. The fire's just about contained." They stood watching firemen pull back a pump truck to give room for the Bomb Squad van that had just pulled up. Torreno continued on with a description of the sweep he'd been able to do so far.

Jack listened restlessly, wanting to get Katya and Sofie to his mother's. "How much loss inside?"

"The front part of the place is pretty much burned out but, I could see plenty of boxes and shit in the back that looked untouched. Lots of smoke and water damage, of course. There's a door between the front and back areas. It was propped open but still did a fair job of containing a lot of the fire." He scratched his head and looked at Jack. "Had to be a fairly sophisticated job, maybe more so than Poletown, a lot of damage to a relatively small circumference. Looks like maybe something innocent, a bag or some shit, was left inside the bookstore, the det cord concealed."

Jack sighed and pointed towards the building. "I'm gonna take a look inside, okay?"

Torreno nodded. "Watch out for hot spots. The Bucket Boys are still roaming around in there."

Jack made a quick tour of the store, glanced into the back room, and dashed up the stairs to check out the apartment. The smell of smoke upstairs was strong, less so towards the back of the apartment. He did a perimeter tour and found the windows in fair shape, given the extent of downstairs damage, only three broken out in the front room. Below one of the broken windows, Katya's doll lay, discarded. He stood staring down at it for long minutes, turned and headed back downstairs.

The back of the store had already been laid out in a grid by the CSI people. One of his team, suited up in orange coveralls, was photographing and sweeping the back door for prints. He headed back to the front door, past firemen reeling in their hoses.

Jack sighed. The clean up would take days. He needed to tell Sofie, and made a quick decision to drive Sofie to his parents himself. Torreno stood by himself, working on his PDA. Jack strode over and relayed more information to Paul, informing him he'd meet back here at the scene in an hour.

He walked slowly, sloshing through melting snow towards the car where Sofie waited. His mind refused to confront the possibility that Sofie could have been in the front of the store when the bomb went off. He couldn't handle another death in his life right now. The ATF guys drove past slowly and honked at him. He'd be lucky if he got away from the scene any time before morning.

Monica pulled up behind Jack's Cherokee, leaping out. Jack hailed her over to the car where the girls waited. Upon finding Chrissie sitting, sleepy but calm and unhurt, she hugged her tightly and turned to Jack. He gave her a brief overview of the situation, implying accident rather than premeditated for her peace of mind at this point. Monica then had a brief exchange with Sofie, reassuring herself both Katya and Sofie were okay. He thrust a paper with his cell number on it and arranged for

Monica to call and update him on Chrissie the next day. He sighed in relief when she left and got Sofie and Katya into his Jeep.

He drove carefully, conscious of Katya, asleep in the back seat, Sofie leaning heavily against him. Her eyes were closed and she said nothing. He reached around her and he pulled his coat up to cover her shoulders. Still, she didn't stir. He'd asked her a few questions, got only one-syllable responses and shut up. Her face was ashen, probably shock, but her breathing was even and he let her sleep.

Maria Roselli stood watching for them in the door, her arms wrapped around her body in that familiar way he knew his mother comforted herself and allayed her anxieties. He pulled into the drive next to the house, went around and lifted Katya out of her car seat and passed her to his dad, who stood waiting in the cold.

He turned to Sofie and easily lifted her out. Used to her weight now, to the feel of her in his arms, she felt strangely lighter, as though the attack had stripped her of an essential part of herself. He dashed into the house and headed down the hall. His mother had lain Katya down in her bedroom and was undressing her quietly. He gave her only a silence glance and strode past into the small back bedroom.

Lowering Sofie onto the double bed, he felt something wet soak through his t-shirt. He swore and turned on the light beside the bed. The spot was dark, almost black. It was blood.

Sofie opened her eyes and watched him bend down to feel under the jacket for the source of her blood. "Don't worry. It's the same wound, not another one. I tore lose the stitches when I fell." Her calm voice didn't reassure him and he swore again as he pulled out her shirt and searched her side for the blood-covered bandage.

"What is it, Jack?" Maria was standing just inside the door.

"Sofie's torn her stitches out. She's bleeding some. Can you give me some help with it?"

"I'll get some things and be right back." She replied and turned away.

"Sofie, we need to get you to a hospital."

"No, Jack, don't. Please. It's fine. Get some gauze and tape and I'll bandage it up again. I'll be fine." She turned suddenly, eyes searching the dark. "Where's Katya!"

"She's okay, lie back. She's next door in my parent's bedroom, sleeping. Mama got her settled. She's fine." He pushed her back down and began pulling the shirt over her head. "Raise your arms."

She sat up and patiently waited as he unfastened her bra and dropped it on the floor. He placed a towel over her exposed breasts, another against her side. His mother stood beside him, holding a tray full of supplies.

Sofie looked from Maria to Jack, her eyes clearer now. "Jack. Your mother and I can handle this. It's not a man's thing. Leave. They probably need you back at the bookstore." She waved him away.

Uncertain, he stood up, watching her face. "All right. I'll call in a little while to make sure everything's okay. Sofie, do what my mother says. She always knows what's best." He bent down past his mother and kissed Sofie on the cheek, tasting the dried tears, tinged with blood, on her face.

Before leaving, he stopped at his parents' door and stood watching his daughter sleep. She lay on his parents' big bed, looking as though she'd always belonged there. She stirred slightly and he pulled the covers up over a pale arm flung over the blanket. He bent down, kissed her cheek and stroked her blond hair.

~ * ~

He didn't make it back to the house until after eight the next morning. His mother was in the kitchen, humming as she made cinnamon rolls for breakfast. She pulled out a chair and poured him one of her strong cups of espresso, asking him no questions, thank God. He dunked a roll into his coffee and thrust most of it into his mouth, not really tasting it but absorbing the quick energy. Just enough to get him into the bedroom, undressed and into bed.

"Mama, I'm beat. I've gotta get some sleep. If Katya wakens, are you okay with her or should I try and get someone here to watch her?"

She frowned and reached out to pat his cheek. "Don't be crazy, Jack. I love watching her. You go to sleep. Keep Sofie in bed, too. She needs the rest."

Jack stared at her, thinking he'd misunderstood. Had she actually given her permission for him to jump into bed with Sofie? In her house?

"Katya and I'll be fine. I have some shopping to do. When your dad gets back, we'll all go out and get some things."

"Mama, Tony's off today. Have him go with you guys, okay?"

She frowned at him. "Sure, but why? Tony hates shopping."

"I just don't want Katya without protection right now, after what happened last night. Okay, Mama?"

"Okay, Jackie. We'll drag Tony along." She pulled him up by an arm. "Go on, now. Get! Go to bed!"

He stumbled down the hall, pulling off clothes as he went. He glanced at Sofie, still sleeping, and went into the bathroom. He reeked of smoke and charred wood. Yanking off the last of his undergarments, he stepped into the shower and turned it on full force. Too tired to move, he just stood there and let the water rinse whatever it could of residue from his body. Finally, afraid he'd fall asleep standing up, he shut off the shower, grabbed a towel and staggered into the small bedroom.

Daylight shone in through one small window that looked out onto a tiny courtyard behind the house. The light looked pale blue in color, accentuating the shadows beneath Sofie's eyes. He dropped his towel and eased into the double bed next to her. She made a faint noise, turned and settled against him, then felt back into sleep.

When he awakened, Sofie was kneeling down by the bed, digging through her clothes, dressed only in bra. and panties stained with blood from last night.

He pushed himself up onto his elbows. "Sofie! Leave it. We'll find you something clean to wear." She glanced down at her stained clothes, as he rolled himself out of bed and caught hold of her arm. She moved automatically, allowing him to push her down on the bed, feeling stupid and confused. "Sit," he ordered.

His eyes lit on a small pile of folded things by the door, his mother had surreptitiously shoved them into the room sometime recently. He placed the pile next to Sofie and she searched it, coming up with a pink t-shirt and pair of cotton panties and leggings. She looked up at Jack.

"They were my sister's." He pulled on his trousers, his face impassive. "I'll go check and see if Katya's back. My mom was going to take her shopping this morning with them. They may still be gone."

"Jack, is it safe for her to be out? I mean, with the fire last night, maybe she's in danger."

"Tony went along. He'll take care of her." He aimed her towards the bathroom. "Get cleaned up and come out to the kitchen. I'll fill you in on the damage to your store." Seeing her face constrict, he added, "It's going to be okay, Sofie."

~ * ~

They sat side by side at the big round kitchen table, eating Maria's cinnamon rolls and drinking coffee. Sofie looked around, feeling as though it was the most natural thing in the world to be here with Jack, eating breakfast.

The sun shone in the large paned glass window, looking out over the small courtyard and fenced off alley behind. The room was painted yellow, small pictures covering every empty space—black and whites, larger colored photos, small Kodak snapshots. High school graduation photos, family vacations, family and friends some still around, some long gone.

Sofie glanced up as she ate, unable to keep her eyes from straying to another picture, another view of the Rosellis. The contrast to her own small family was astounding. Each photo was filled with large men and dark strong women, everyone smiling or laughing.

She felt his eyes on her as she surveyed his life in pictures. So secretive before, now, for some reason, he was willing to let her see the hidden places of his life. Conscious of his eyes on her, she glanced over at him. He had an almost feral look as he watched her, with barely suppressed resolution.

"What do you think? Pretty good-looking family, huh?"

She nodded, conscious of a hesitation in him. "It's okay, Jack. Give me the bad news. I can take it."

"Yeah, well." He rubbed a hand over the stubble of his heavy beard. "The good news is your apartment is in pretty good shape. Amazingly good shape, except for some broken windows and smoke damage. The store is another story."

He took a swig of coffee. "Since most of the damage was to the front part of the store, you lost all of your display inventory, all your furniture, everything in that room. The stuff in the back may be salvageable. At least anything in boxes."

He paused, weighing how much to tell her. "It was a bomb, probably a professional job, detonated from the alley." He spoke quickly, leaving her no room for questions. "The bomb may have been left in your store, in a bag of some type, probably sitting not far from the front door."

"What about the who, Jack? Who would want to bomb my store? Why?"

"Sofie, it looks possible it may have something to do with my work. The same MO as the case I'm working on." He leaned forward and stopped her hand from fiddling with her mug. "We can't be absolutely sure until we get some lab results, but it looks like I may be the link here."

He swallowed, frowned and turned up the uninjured palm, stroking it with his fingers. Her throat tightened as she watched his face. She wanted to comfort him.

"Can you tell me anything about who was in the store last night? Any time yesterday, actually." He squeezed her hand, a brief smile turning up his mouth. "Ever thought about writing a book about witnessing crimes and giving out statements? A whole new career for you."

She smiled at him, grateful for his attempt at a small joke right now, in spite of their circumstances. "And are you positive it had nothing whatsoever to do with Katya?"

He sighed and squeezed her hand tighter. "We can't rule that out yet, but it seems unlikely. Kim's still locked up tight. Her parents moved her to Ford Hospital for an extensive psych evaluation and long-term care. I called there last night to reconfirm it, she's been there for the past five days." Restless, he released her hand and stood up. "Until we get the residue samples back from DC, I can't be absolutely certain. But the similarities between your store bombing and the site I'm investigating are too close to be coincidence. It seems to rule out any connection with Katya. I'm the most likely link." He looked bleak.

"I'm sorry, Sofie. You came looking for protection from me. Instead, you've been shot, almost arrested, and now your place has been blown up. Rather than asking for my help, you should have run as far the hell away from me as possible."

"Jack. Since they bombed my place, isn't it possible the threat to Katya is still part of it?"

"I've thought of that, but I still can't see how they found you and Katya. Even Kim, who has access to all the databases, couldn't have found you until you appeared back in my life. There's no way I can think of that this group, if it is a group, could have gotten to you before me."

Sofie went to the sink and automatically started washing the breakfast dishes. "You're too hard on yourself, Jack. You're not king of the universe, you know. You can't take everything on yourself."

He stood beside her, watching her movements, without seeing them. "After you contacted me, they could easily have found you. I was at your place all the time, we were together. But I still don't get how they could have been calling you a month before that." He turned and grabbed another cinnamon roll sitting on the oven top. "You know, it's all speculation right now. Let's see what you can recall about anyone hanging around your store yesterday." His eyes moved from the small cuts on her forehead down to her side. "Do you need to see a doctor first?"

"I'm fine. Really. My side barely hurts this morning." She ran her fingers lightly over the cuts on her face. "And these are nothing, just a few scratches."

He frowned, about to say something more, but the back door sprang open and Maria came in, followed by Marcos, holding Katya by the hand.

"Mommy! Look, I went shopping and got a pig!" Katya held out a small stuffed animal. "And we're going to make some ice cream from the snow!"

Sofie bent down and caught Katya to her, easing her and her pink pig closer. "I like your pig. And what's this about snow ice cream?"

Maria set her bags down on the table and surveyed Sofie with a skeptical eye. "So you're looking better this morning. You found the things to wear, I see." She pulled off her oversized red coat and hung it up. "Katya, why don't you and Grandpa get a pan and go out and gather the snow?"

She waited until the door closed behind Marcos and Katya. "So, tell me what this is all about."

Sofie smiled at her. "Jack was just filling me in on things." She tried to keep her words light, but Maria frowned and turned to Jack.

"Someone blew up Sofie's bookstore. Right now we don't have much more than that, Mama. Her apartment isn't damaged too much, just smoke and some water. But the store is pretty bad. It'll take quite a while to get it up and running again."

Maria pursed her lips, not speaking, turned and put the water on for more coffee. "You'll need a place to stay, Sofie. You and Katya. You can stay with us." She was about to add something more but stopped as Katya came in, carrying a huge bowl of snow.

"Mommy, is our house gone now? It didn't burn down, did it? I left my toys there!"

Sofie reached out to take the bowl. "No sweetie. There was an explosion and a fire but our things are still there. We can't get them right now, until the firemen and the policemen finish making sure everything's okay. We'll stop by as soon as we can and get your toys, okay?"

"Katya, come over here and let's get the ice cream going before the snow melts." Maria drew Katya over to the table, her toys forgotten.

"Mama, don't make any more coffee for us, or lunch either. We'll catch something downtown." Jack turned to Katya. "I'm taking your Mommy out for a few hours, okay, scout? We'll be back after lunch. Do what Grandma Rosey tells you, okay?"

Katya smiled and patted his face with a cold hand. "Okay. But are we going to live here now?"

Jack looked up at his mother.

"Of course they'll stay here, Jack!" Maria turned to Sofie. "You stay with us now and Jack will straighten things out." She turned away, leaving no room for arguments.

"Mama, we'll be back in a couple of hours. I'll call you if we're going to be any later. I'm going to check and see if we can get into the apartment and get a few things. If not, can you call around and see if anyone can lend some clothes for Katya?"

"Of course, Jack. It's no problem." Maria poured coffee in a mug and brought it over to the table and sat down. "You're sure Sofie's up to going out right now?" She poured sugar into her large cup and stirred, her eyes on Jack's face.

"I'm okay. I just pulled a few stitches is all. I just want to get back to the store and see what's salvageable." Before Maria could argue further, Jack kissed his mother on the cheek reassuringly and drew Sofie towards the door.

## *Twenty-one*

The roads were wet but clear, the pristine whiteness of snow turned into undistinguishable piles of black blobs along the sides of the road. Sofie wore Jack's leather jacket still, and they'd stopped by his place to pick up an old coat from his days in uniform.

"I need to stop by the station, Sofie, for a few minutes. I thought maybe you could answer some questions while we're there." She nodded, resigned. She knew the routine.

They went directly to the Brush street station and up to Jack's cubicle. He sat Sofie down, rounded up some bad coffee for both of them, and plopped a small cassette in front of her.

During the hour he asked her questions, various members of the Bomb Squad came by, sat and listened for a while and wandered back to their desks. She drew Jack a picture of where she'd been when the bomb had gone off and gave him a list of people she thought had been in the store.

There'd been Mrs. Bergman, who frequently came in on Friday nights. She and Sofie had spent twenty or thirty minutes talking politics. Sofie had a brief exchange with Perry Greene and his checkers partner. At least three strangers had wandered in and browsed around the store. Steven Szcepaniak had been there, but he'd turned up two or three times in the past week. A couple of homeless regulars had stopped by to get apple cider and donuts. Beyond that, she couldn't think of anyone else. She recalled no packages left unattended, no last minute visits, nothing.

Sofie moved to a chair by the wall and waited as Jack and his team conferred at his desk. He ran his fingers repeatedly through his thick hair, shifting his gaze periodically to her, as though she might disappear.

Two cups of bad coffee later, he pulled out a tape from the microcassette recorder, handed it to one of his men and strolled over to her. "We can go now. We'll stop by your apartment." He held his jacket out for her. "Let's go, honey." Sofie turned to see if the last word had gotten a response. No one bothered to look their way.

The sidewalk in front of the bookstore was clear, charred and broken remains of her building lay like dead bodies in the gutter, ready to be washed away by the melting snow. Jack pulled up and parked. She got out and stared up at the blackened, boarded-up building. Trembling, she stumbled into the alley with Jack's arm around her shoulder to steady her.

Yellow crime scene tape had been stretched across the back entrance and Jack pulled it up to let her slip under. He unlocked her door and stepped back for her to pass, breathing in acrid air that burned their throats and noses. On the landing, she turned towards the store but he drew her back and aimed her up the staircase. "You can't go down there, Sofie, until we finish our investigation."

She peered over the stairs and watched a fireman pick his way around limp boxes, reaching down with a gloved hand to sort through something that he dropped into a plastic bag.

Apart from the smell of smoke, the kitchen and hallway were untouched and looked innocently normal. The living room was dark, the only light escaping in thin shafts under the boarded-up front windows. There was no standing water but there were dark spots on the couch and chairs and patches of discoloration on the hardwood floor.

Sofie knees threatened to give way when she spotted Katya's doll, laying a few feet from a boarded window. Fragments of glass lay scattered over the doll's sodden dress. Jack caught hold of her from behind and turned her around. "Anything you need in this room? Any papers? Insurance stuff? Bank information?"

She shook her head. "They're in the bedroom. In a small bank box under my bed."

"Come on then, get them and whatever you need for Katya. Get some clothes for yourself and let's get out of here. You can come back in a couple of days, once we've got the investigation wrapped and you're settled some place."

She followed him to her bedroom at the back of the apartment. "Monica! I need to call her! I can't believe I've left it this long."

"Hold it, Sofie. I spoke to her last night after I dropped you at Mama's. I gave her a quick take on the damage and told her you'd call her in a day or two."

Sofie looked horrified. "How did she take it?"

He shrugged. "Like she takes most things, with a quip. Something like, 'God, good thing I made it with our insurance guy last month!'"

Sofie made a face at that and they went into Katya's room.

"I told her you were fine and to leave you alone for a day. You needed sleep. I'm sending someone to her place for a statement."

Sofie roamed through Katya's room, picking out toys and dolls hidden away in drawers, things that had escaped the smoke. She pulled out a box of clothes from the closet and pulled articles out of the bottom. She did the same in her room, taking her bank box and grabbing things from her closet. She sniffed at each item and either discarded it or placed in a small duffle bag. They gathered up the boxes and bags and they headed back to his parents.

~ * ~

The Rosellis sat at the kitchen table, shoveling in piles of pink mush and laughing. Vincent and Tony were there, along with Vincent's wife. Dirty plates and leftovers sat on the side counter. Katya sat on Tony's lap, contented. Life looked amazingly normal, making Sofie pause at the doorway. She wanted things to stay the same here; she didn't want to be the one to bring more danger into this family.

They turned and looked towards the door. "Sofie! Are you all right? Mama called and told us about the bookstore." Vincent was effusive, coming over and hugging her tightly.

"I'm fine. Jack probably told you I hurt my side last week." She said. "I just re-injured it last night."

"What about your store?" Vincent asked.

Sofie shook her head. She didn't want to discuss the bookstore. "We stopped by there and picked up a few things from the apartment." Sofie reached over into the box Jack held, pulled out a couple of Katya's toys and set them down in front of her daughter. "Is this what you wanted, sweetie?"

Katya looked over the toys in front of her and turned to eye the box Jack held, as though it might contain Christmas gifts rather than her old toys. "My puzzles and Mr. Bear! And Lucy Locket! But Mommy, you didn't get my Barbie."

"Honey, I had to leave it for now. We're going to have to get it cleaned up. It smelled like smoke. Remember, all the smoke?" Katya nodded, dismissing Barbie in favor of the box in front of her.

Maria motioned for Sofie and Jack to sit. "So you've brought a suitcase, I see. You'll stay with us for now—you and Katya?" She sounded hopeful.

Sofie nodded. "I'd like that very much, if it won't put you out."

"No, of course not. You and Katya will take the back bedroom you had last night. It's a double bed so there's plenty of room for both of you." She looked over at Jack, challenging him to argue for his position in the bed. "So it's all settled? You'll stay here for now?"

"You'll need your car if you stay here, Sofie. I'll have someone drive it over later today. You won't be able to do any real work at the bookstore for at least a few days. Until we finish up there. In the meantime, you'll stay here, Sofie?" He waited, expecting an argument.

She nodded and said nothing, thinking about nights alone, without him. He'd be forced to go back to his apartment. She made a face at him and wiped the goofy expression off her face.

~ * ~

Two days later, Monica showed up at the Rosellis' to pick up Sofie. They spent the day at the store, putting calls into the insurance company, talking with the bank, sifting through the necessary papers to deal with the emergency. They'd work an hour or two, then stop to cry. Ten minutes of indulgence, was followed by hugs, deep breaths and more work. The rest of the time was spent planning how they'd rebuild the store, only better this time.

Sofie was sitting on the bed in the Rosellis' back bedroom when Jack called to check on them. He was on his way to his place for a couple of hours of sleep. "Hi, how's it going?"

"Okay. We're good." Sofie waited, waiting for some sign he missed her body beside him.

Either unfazed by it or feeling stoic, he didn't mention their separation. "How did it go today? Any problems getting in?"

"Nope. We waded around in the muck and mess, spending a lot of time being optimistic, between bouts of complete despair." She laughed, not really amused by any of it.

"Well, get some sleep. Let Mama take care of you and Katya for the next couple of days, okay? She likes doing that. I'll stop by tomorrow morning before I go to the lab. Take care, Sofie."

That was the most she was going to get from him tonight in the way of comfort. She sank into the small bed with Katya, pulled her warm body up against her good side and looked around the room. It was amply decorated, like all the Roselli rooms, with photos of the family and friends. She was suddenly wide awake, listening to her mind screaming surrender at her.

Her store was gone, destroyed. Where did she go from here? She thought of Jack, now in hot pursuit of her. He wanted them in his life and she wanted to hold back. She tried to imagine blending her strange bookstore and weird friends with Jack's cop world. She'd be gaining a father for Katya—and nights of great sex. But what would she be losing? The word 'surrender' kept reverberating in her head.

She knew now she could survive, maybe even thrive, in the world her mother and grandmother had made for her. So what was there to fear? It wasn't fear so much as a belief that being a strong woman was at odds with the world of men. There seemed to be no way to reconcile her own needs with what looked like the demands of a man. And worse yet, it was seductive, her own desires conflicting with her own best interests as a woman.

She thought about the Rosellis, with their huge men, but with a powerful woman as well. Sofie wondered how Maria dealt with it, amidst all those predatory males? Even their jobs reflected it. Not only did Maria survive, she managed them. It made Sofie smile.

Then she thought about Dinah, who had not survived, mowed down by the world of her brothers and father, and her fear returned. But she liked the Rosellis with their big family. She wanted Katya to be part of it. She didn't want her daughter to end up alone some day, living in a barren cloister of women.

Sofie fell asleep, thinking about Jack, about seduction, and about surrender. Right now, all she wanted to was give in and fall into his warmth.

~ * ~

The next four days were too busy to consider where she and Jack were going, or whether she wanted to go with him. She spent most of each day at her apartment, sorting through what to salvage and put it in storage and what to throw out. Monica came and went, dragging boxes for Sofie with her healing wound. On the fourth day, Jack met them at the store, and they did a final search through the downstairs, dragging out the last salvageable remnants.

It was late Thursday night when they got back to the Rosellis' and Katya was asleep in the back bedroom. Jack had followed her home. He tiptoed in to give Katya a quick kiss.

Unexpectedly, he turned and grabbed her. "Sofie," he groaned into her hair, "I can't stand this much longer." She was unsure of exactly what he couldn't stand, but hoped it was being away from her.

"I can stop by tomorrow after I drop Katya at daycare. I mean, if you can go in late to work." She felt ridiculously awkward in her attempt at simple seduction.

He swore softly and dropped a quick kiss on her lips, smiling in spite of himself. "I didn't mean just for sex. Although I won't refuse an invitation like that. I'll go in late tomorrow morning." He stopped smiling. "Actually, what I meant was that I can deal with shifting between my place, work and here for a while, but at some point, we've got to do something about this. I want to be with you two."

"Well, your mother is not going to put up with you sleeping here in the same room, no matter how she was that first night."

"Yeah, I know." He let go of her and lowered his two hundred pounds into a small chair that creaked under his weight. "I'll adjust for now, but think about the future, okay? It will be months before your store is going again. Whatever you and Monica decide about that, can you remember me in your planning?" He leaned back and pulled off his holster, easing it to the floor. "I want us to be a family. Maybe even start thinking about marriage. I wanna protect the two of you, but I can't do shit right now, with you and Katya in one place and me in another."

She swallowed and dropped down on the end of the bed, facing him. Her heart leapt at the word 'marriage.' *Traitor*, she thought. *The minute someone wants me, I jump to attention, like a dog!*

Jack's eyes strayed to Katya, curled up on her side with her thumb to her mouth. "Sofie, I know you're struggling right now, scared of all the changes. And God knows, this is an awful time for me to talk about marriage, when your whole life's been destroyed. But I know you feel something for me. And for my family. I can see if in your eyes. I hear it, mostly in the words you don't say. So think about it, okay? Hell, I think I may even be in love with you."

The words sounded painful, wrenched out of him. It made her laugh. "Jack. That's a heck of a declaration. Kicking and screaming, despite yourself, you think you might be in love with me."

He reached over and pulled her towards him, down on his lap. "I know. But give me a break, okay? I've never done this before." He pulled her tightly against his body and she inhaled his familiar smell. "I think I love you. I want you and Katya to move in with me right now. You can't stay at my parents' forever. It seems like the ideal time to give it a try." He flushed and laughed. "Think about it. And tomorrow morning I'm going to show you how much I love you the Roselli way." He grinned. "And have you begging to move in with me."

She heard something else beneath his laughter, an uncertainty about his ability to protect her and Katya. Like her, he was battling his past. She relaxed against him, for now, sliding her arms around his chest to hug him, loving the feel of his hard body. "All right. I'll see you tomorrow morning at your place and you can show me how much you Rosellis love your women. In the meantime, I'll think about the living arrangements, to try and figure out how it could work." She made a face and muttered something into his t-shirt.

"What was that?" He asked.

"You know, I'm going to have to change my entire belief system about family. My version is a male-less world. And the Rosellis are anything but that."

He pulled away so he could see her face, his now serious. "But my mother runs this family."

"Yeah. I know. But I'm not Maria Roselli. I don't quite see myself fitting into the role of matriarch of testosterone heaven."

~ * ~

Friday was cold and gray, weather in complete agreement with the state of Sofie's situation. She got up early and took some pain meds that cast a slight glow on her depression. She bundled up, got into her battered Honda and headed for Jack's place, her heart thumping with expectation. She kept doing this, succumbing to the pull of her body, when her mind wanted to shrink back and watch the scene play out slowly. She'd convinced herself after he'd left last night, that she'd call him first thing this morning and suggest they take a break from the sex and desire. Just for a week or two, ostensibly to give her body time to heal, in reality, to give her mind some breathing space. This morning, she just wanted him.

She turned onto I-94 and headed west, automatically watching the heavy, eight a.m. traffic speed by her. A new fear surfaced as she got closer to Jack's place. Lurking in the back of her mind someplace was the belief that Jack saw her and Katya as substitutes for Dinah, peace offerings to his parents for not protecting his sister. She wondered how long their relationship could last if it was based on her being a substitute in the family.

She found a parking place and sat staring at the dashboard. It was 8:20 and the street was empty. Most of the people in this upwardly mobile neighborhood were already at work. She heard someone at her car door and turned in surprise. Jack, in t-shirt and sweats, stood shivering at the curb. He raised palms up, as if to say *What the hell are you doing sitting out here?* She grimaced, grabbed her bag and got out.

His apartment was still dark; he hadn't bothered to turn on his lights. On the kitchen table sat a carafe of coffee with two cups, one half full. She threw off her coat without a word. He pointed to a mug and she nodded, waiting for him to fill it and hand it to her. Her body needed fuel and her mind needed time, something to stall the inevitable move to the bedroom. He picked up his mug and drank, standing a little too close to her, almost as if he sensed her urge to run and was blocking her way. Taking three large gulps, she looked up and forgot everything except wanting him.

The room was quiet enough to hear Sofie's breathing speed up as he steered her into his bedroom. She went willingly enough, but from the moment he saw her sitting outside in her car, staring straight ahead, he knew she was having second thoughts.

Giving her time for only one quick cup, he moved her quickly to his bedroom, knowing once there, he could silence her fears, at least for a while. And his own. Almost a week since her store was bombed, the investigation was stalled again, but the similarities between the bookstore and Poletown bombings scared the hell out of him.

He picked up a damp towel on the chair in his room and took it into the bathroom, wanting to give her a few minutes to adjust to his bedroom, but not too much time to start considering other options. He caught sight of himself in the mirror and stared. He had showered and shaved but it hadn't helped. *Shit! I look like hell!* He'd gone back to the lab last night and stayed past midnight. Back at his place, wired from too much caffeine, he'd been unable to sleep. He'd had about two hours of down time and he was exhausted.

She sat on the edge of his bed, as far as possible from him and he moved automatically to sit down next to her. He pulled her back against him, the feel of her body against his good, not only for getting aroused, but for instant energy. He slipped an arm around her waist, careful to hold her below the bandage. His other hand trailed over her flat belly and down to cup her, feeling heat radiate through the layers of material under his palm. He pressed his fingers into her and waited for a response. She fell back against him and he immediately recognized her surrender, both of her body and her mind. He pressed his lips against her arched neck, taking small bites as his free hand unfastened her jeans before she stiffened and pulled away.

He had to make his move now, before reason began to rage again in her. He slid his fingers quickly under her panties and into the heat between her legs. He stroked her pubic hair, and moved his finger down to part her folds, wet and ready for him.

She gasped as he inserted a finger, brought to alertness by the abrupt entry. She moaned involuntarily and arched up to take him deeper. He buried his face in the damp hair at the nape of her neck, he inhaled her smell, and let her body initiate the movements, watching as she pushed her hips up against his fingers.

"Jack." She whispered and he recognized it as a plea.

He withdrew his hand and turned her towards him, almost roughly. "Okay?" The question was rhetorical; they both knew he wouldn't stop at this point. Nor would she make any move to stop him. They were both beyond thought.

"Please." She implored.

His control snapped and he grabbed hold of her sweatshirt, raised her arms over her head and ripped it off. She wore no bra and her nipples were drawn tight, both from the cold of the room and desire. He bent his head and took her in his mouth, sucking hard, using his teeth to take her to the edge of pain.

She gasped and he redoubled his efforts, pushing her back down to his bed. Her fingers dug into his scalp with a pressure that equaled that of his mouth on her breast. Hoarse cries came from deep in her throat. Continuing to suckle her, he pushed down his own sweats with one hand and pulled off her remaining clothes. He pushed her legs apart, using his legs as leverage, and pushed her over onto her belly. He halted, suddenly remembering her wound. "Did I hurt you?" He was kneeling behind her, his erection quivering, waiting for entry.

"No! Jack, please!" Her face was pressed into the sheet and her plea muted, but he heard it. He reached across to the nightstand, grabbed a condom and turned back. Her legs parted further without urging and he guided his throbbing cock between her buttocks, spreading her labia with his fingers, searching for entry. The head of his cock barely inside her slippery folds, he pulled up her hips and thrust deeper, the contact of her buttocks against his belly forcing a guttural cry from him. The repetitive sound of flesh hitting flesh was followed quickly by hoarse shouts as they peaked and fell away.

They lay side by side, faces down, both of them unable to move. One of his legs was flung over hers, his arm lay limply over her pale back. She shifted and moved out from under his weight, the sheets rustling with her movements. He turned his head and saw her standing by the bed, barely visible in the pale light of the bedroom.

"Jack." She whispered, "I need to go. Your parents are watching Katya this morning and I told your mother I'd be back in an hour."

She sank down onto the bed, as though her first effort to stand had taken everything out of her. Not bothering to argue, he reached over and pulled her towards him. Her body was cold and she shivered as he gathered her in his arms. "Come here." He reached down and pulled the blanket up and over both of them, turning her body with her back against his chest, giving her his warmth.

She sighed low, more vibration than sound. She smelled of lilacs and soap and sex. Her hair was damp and it clung to his bare chest. He drew her closer, one arm instinctively moving to her hips, the other to just beneath her breasts. He moved his hand soothingly, caressing her ribs, her belly, absorbing her chill. They lay together again, not moving.

After a long time, he bent his head down and trailed his lips across her shoulder and back. She shivered as his lips moved back to her neck, and pushed her back further into his chest as though she wanted to disappear into him.

He cursed softly; he was going to be late for work. "I gotta go, sweetheart." He reached down blindly for his jeans, casually adding, "What about moving in together? What do you think?"

She nodded trance-like, staring up at him. "Maybe we could give it a try, for a few weeks, at least until my apartment is livable." He jerked up his pants, invigorated now, thrilled with a battle won. He'd gotten capitulation; the round was his.

## *Twenty-two*

Katya and Sofie had been living with the Rosellis for almost two weeks. It was Friday, December the thirteenth and Katya was at daycare, half days to start. The entire family had joined in the debate about sending her back. In the end, Katya won out, with her innocent smiles.

Sofie dropped Katya off at eleven and met Monica at the bookstore. Today they were taking inventory, dividing books for a fire sale, and everything left stashed in storage until they reopened. Sofie was distracted by replays of this morning's sex with Jack, interspersed with castigating herself for succumbing to him again. She was losing her battle for independence and she hated herself for it.

An hour of dirty work, and Monica threw up her hands. "Let's eat!" She grabbed her coat and ran down the street to Petrova's Deli.

They spread a tarp on the floor, and feasted on Vernor's ginger ale and piroghis. A bar of Godiva chocolate sat between them, pitiable compensation for all the wreckage around them.

"So what are your plans for this weekend?" Monica grinned at her. Sofie's new, improved sex life was a constant source of entertainment for Monica and she couldn't leave it alone.

"I've agreed to move in to Jack's place. We're moving this weekend." The reply fell into the space like a bomb.

"Sofie! You jerk! You never said a word. When did the big decision come and what caused it? It was Jack's unerring sexual prowess, I bet."

Sofie kept chewing her lunch, waited a beat while she took a slug of pop. She nodded her head. "You're probably right. I'm trying hard not to examine it too closely right now. Anyway, I sort of decided this morning. I found myself making a trip to his house at eight in the morning, instead of the thousands of things I needed to be doing. I just got tired of fighting the flow. The justification I give myself is that we have no place to live and we can't stay at the Rosellis' forever. Jack has two bedrooms." She sniffed, trying not to look pleased.

"Yeah, right. So, when are you moving and is it permanent? What do Jack's parents think about it?"

"First, it's sort of temporary-permanent. We haven't gotten beyond the next month or so, but I want to give Katya some stability, so I'm trying to be reasonable about it." She ignored Monica's snort. "And Jack's parents are pleased. I think. They would prefer that we not live together unmarried, of course, but they have four sons and they know arguing about that goes no place. I think they're hoping that once we get into the same house, we'll see the natural conclusion is marriage."

"And is it? The natural conclusion between you and Jack?"

Sofie frowned and looked around at the chaos; it felt like the inside of her head right now. "I don't know, Monica. I really don't. I'm way out of my element with Jack. You must see that." She paused. "There are two issues here. First, I've organized my life to fit in with the way I've been raised. It's what I know." Monica raised an eyebrow. "My family has always done fine without men. We've survived three generations and are on our fourth now. For years, I've struggled with being okay on my own, despite some weird standard in my head that keeps saying I need a man. Now that a man's around, instead of taking what I need and staying independent, I'm throwing it all away, for a little companionship and someone in my bed. It annoys the hell out of me!"

"Sofie. I've known you for six years now and I never could figure out what your problem was, always fighting some weird battle about men and your independence. I never got it." She unwrapped the chocolate. "Give this a try, at least. What have you got to lose?"

Sofie smiled at Monica and grabbed a piece of chocolate. "I say my independence. What if it's all bullshit and in the end it's all just about sex, having really great sex?"

"I'll vote for that. And all those big Italian guys you get to hang with. But why do you work so hard to define whatever you and Jack have? Being with someone and being independent aren't completely incompatible, you know." She raised an eyebrow. "You still believe you can't be a strong woman and need a man." She grabbed the last piece of chocolate. "That idea went out with the sixties. Now you can have them both. But you're going to have to figure that out for yourself."

Sofie grabbed her soda to wash down the chocolate stuck in the back of her throat. She knew she was selling something a little too hard here. Monica always saw right through her. "So, the other thing that's bothering me is that something's wrong with this picture. Jack, the precinct stud and Sofie, the feminist bookstore owner?"

"According to Kim Barber who's now sitting in the psyche ward at Ford Hospital." Monica interrupted.

"From all I've heard, Jack has never shown any interest in settling down or any inclination towards one woman. Suddenly, out of the blue, he's fascinated by my amazing self. He's so taken, either with my sexual acrobatics or my pretty face or whatever, that he's hot in pursuit of me and Katya to move in with him. Monica, it doesn't make sense. In fact, something stinks."

"Why? Every dog has his day, right? Every tree in the forest, etc. etc. He's met his comeuppance and you're it. You and Katya, that is."

"No, I don't think so. I think he's still suffering from the same guilt that afflicted him four years ago, only now he's adopted us as the antidote for it. Even worse, we're substitutes for Dinah he can offer up to his family to lessen his guilt over letting them down. He thinks he wants us, but really he just wants absolution."

She stopped, feeling suddenly small. She'd just run Jack through a pop psychology course in her head and shrunk his feelings down so they were worth about two cents.

"Sofie. Your arguments are impressive, as usual, all very reasonable. But I'm here to remind you that second-guessing people's motives is a no-win situation. I'm living proof—suppositions mixed in with righteous indignation and where did it get me?" Monica had been through a bitter divorce, most of the accusations coming from Monica. It left her with a small income and a teenager to raise alone.

Sofie watched the workmen install new front windows, not really seeing them. "I sound like my mother." She said it without rancor but with some sadness. "I have all the answers, but I'm clueless about relationships." She sighed and smiled impishly at Monica. "Hey, maybe so much sex all of a sudden has fried my brains." She held up her hand. "Nope, I ain't gonna tell you. And I'm putting this therapy session on hold right now. I am moving in with him. And we are considering some sort of future together. I can handle that, at least for now." She gathered up the remnants of her lunch.

~ * ~

It was after five before Sofie said goodbye to Monica, shoved boxes into her Honda and headed to the Rosellis'. She stopped at the only station between the store and their place to get gas. Jack had an early morning court date today and would probably be working late tonight, so Tony was scheduled to pick up Katya from daycare and bring her back to the Rosellis'.

When Sofie stepped into the Rosellis' living room, the air was so heavy with tension, she caught her breath. Tony, Maria and Vincent stood silently next to Jack, who was on his cell phone. He turned and saw her, his face ashen. He put out a hand to her as he spoke, as though to keep her back. She heard his words as though in a dream. "I want to report a missing child. My daughter."

Sofie stumbled forward, her body like lead. She caught hold of him, unaware that she'd cried out as he grabbed her and pressed her face into his shirt, stifling her cries. He continued talking, as he struggled to keep her still. "Yeah, I'm on my way there now. Get someone over to the Little Learning Center on Conant, at the corner of Kirkpatrick, now. I'll meet them there. She was last seen about an hour ago. Someone picked her up. Yeah. Male, around twenty-five or so, dressed in black jacket and some sort of baseball cap. I've got a description of the car. An old VW, maybe twenty-five years old, white, Indiana plates. Put out an Amber Alert."

Sofie struggled to free herself, gulping in air to gain control. She pulled back and turned toward Maria and Tony. "What happened? Where is she?" She looked at Tony. "I thought you were picking her up! What happened?" The words were too loud but she couldn't stop them.

Maria pulled her away from Jack and into her arms, shushing her. "Tony went to pick her up but she was already gone. Someone else turned up, said he was Tony. There was a new person there, an assistant. She let Katya go with him."

She had tears running down her face but held tightly to Sofie. "Shhh!! It's going to be all right. Jack is going to find her. It will be all right." She kept saying the words over and over, as Sofie cried into Maria's shoulder, more quietly now.

Someone reached around and thrust a drink into Sofie's hand. She took a sip automatically and coughed: whiskey. Someone, Maria maybe, eased her down onto the couch, still holding her tightly. Words swirled around her and blended together and she shut her eyes tightly, wanting to wake up from this nightmare.

The room was filling up with more people, talking, arguing. Jack, other male voices, another woman's, then more voices, hushed. Jack was bending over her and she opened her eyes and stared at him. His eyes held hers, willing her to listen to him.

"Sofie. We've got a trace out on the car already. We've put out an Amber Alert. We'll get her back."

Sofie shrank back.

"It's going to be all right!" He said it louder, to make her understand or just to reassure himself. "I'm on my way to the daycare center now. I want you to come with me. The Center got a phone message from the guy. He said for us to wait at my apartment and he'll give us instructions." He grabbed hold of her arms and pulled her up. "I want you to stay at my place and wait for the message! Someone will meet us there and stay with you. Come!"

Jack threw a jacket around her and pulled her towards the door, ignoring the questions thrown at him. He stopped outside, pulled out a handkerchief and wiped her wet face. She wanted to blame someone, the Rosellis, the daycare center, herself. She refused the comfort of his arm around her and silently headed to his car.

It was five-thirty and already dark, the streets busy. Sofie watched cars go by, people living normal lives, nothing interfering with their stupid confidence in the safety of their world. Some insane idea all humans had that they were completely in control of their own lives and nothing could possibly harm them. She clasped her hands, avoiding Jack's that reached for her. He said her name, but nothing else.

He stopped in front of his place. He'd slapped the red light on top of the Jeep and it cast an eerie glow on the front of his apartment. The uniformed cop was standing by the door and followed them in. "This is Mark Cornett, Sofie." Jack threw out the introduction as he picked up his phone to check for messages.

He listened, then shook his head and Sofie turned away, moving automatically to the drawn curtains, tracing the pattern in them with unseeing eyes. Jack moved up behind her and she turned to face him. "Sofie, stay here. It's going to be all right. I promise you." He was holding his automatic, pushing a round into the magazine. His voice was rough with pain that showed in his eyes but she couldn't respond. She could think of no words of reassurance. Nothing. He reached out to touch her face but she didn't feel it; a gray coldness had settled around her and shut down all of her senses.

"Stay here with Mark. When the call comes in, he'll relay it to me." He swallowed. "As soon as I get some word, any word, I'll call you." He turned and headed out the door, shoving his gun under his coat.

The phone rang four times in the next hour and a half. Sofie and the uniformed cop sat across from each other, in Jack's only two chairs, saying nothing. To his credit, he'd tried to reassure her, to make small talk, had explained how the bug on the phone worked, but she ignored him and eventually he gave up.

Sofie picked up the phone each time it rang, her heart pounding, and each time, the voice was familiar, Jack's, his mother's, his second brother's, and one unknown voice, a Bomb Squad detective. She answered them all woodenly, referring most of the calls to Jack's cell. She spoke tersely, ordering each caller to leave the line free and hung up without another word.

The call came three hours after she'd arrived, just after nine. The voice was high-pitched, probably male. She recognized it; it was the same voice from before, the man who'd started this nightmare months ago.

Mark watched her face now, using hand signals urging her to keep the guy talking. He picked up the other phone quietly and listened. She followed the words as though in a trance.

"Go to the warehouse at the foot of Mt. Elliott—on the river. Don't bring anyone except you and Jack. If anyone else shows up, I'll kill the kid."

She tried to absorb the meaning of the words, murmuring okay after each sentence. Desperate now, she demanded, "Let me speak with Katya! Please."

"No!"

She saw the warning in the cop's eyes but she couldn't leave it alone. "Please, how do I know Katya is all right? Please let me speak to her!"

"I said NO! Listen closely. She's alive and she's all right. That's all you need to know. Follow my instructions and she'll stay okay. I don't want to hurt the kid."

"But what do you want, then?" The words burst from her.

"I want you and Jack here! No more questions or you won't see your little girl again!"

Sofie bit down on her lip but felt no pain. Her head throbbed and her stomach rolled. She swallowed repeatedly, trying desperately to keep from vomiting, fighting to follow what he said.

"You've got an hour to get here! Come alone—just the two of you, or you won't see little Katya again! Such a cute little girl, too! The river is cold this time of year. It will be a painless death. Pass that on to Jack. He'd appreciate that."

A moan escaped through her tightly clenched teeth.

"Better get going, Sofie! You don't have much time!" He hung up and she sank back onto a chair, fighting blackness.

She watched Mark place a call to Jack and listened as he relayed word-for-word what the caller had said. He seemed to go on endlessly, saying things she couldn't grasp, her mind still working to make sense of what the man on the phone had said.

Mark hung up and turned back to her, looking apologetic. Then it hit her! She was not going to be allowed to go. Jack had issued the orders and the cop would follow them. They were going to keep her here, and Jack would go himself, and not alone, but with backup.

"No!" She cried out, flinging herself at the cop. "He can't do that! He'll kill Katya if I don't go! Just Jack and me! No one else! Jack can't bring anyone else!" She pounded on him but he handled her easily, pinning her arms, not bothering to answer her.

She sank back again in the chair, her mind furiously working through her options. She felt his eyes on her, wary, assessing, watching to see what she would do next. She shut her eyes and blocked out his face.

He spoke now, trying to reason with her. "It's going to be all right, I promise you. Jack knows what he's doing. He's called in the Hostage Rescue Team. They'll be with him. It's going to be all right." He stopped. "You're in shock. Sit still here and I'll make you some tea."

She opened her eyes and watched him cross the room into Jack's kitchen. She watched as he moved to the stove and reached for the teakettle. She stood up woodenly and walked towards him, trance-like, unsure of anything except her need to get to her daughter. He stood with his back to her, at the stove, adjusting the flame.

Sofie moved up behind him. She hadn't noticed he was on his cell phone. He didn't hear her. She held her breath, reached for an empty pot sitting on the counter and brought it down sharply on his head. *Forgive me, please! But I have to find her!*

He fell to the side and she tried to catch him. He was too heavy and fell to the floor. She reached down and found a pulse. It felt strong. His cell phone lay beside him and she reached down and shut it off quickly.

She needed his gun. The holster was hard to get at from the angle he lay, but time was urging her on. She needed to get out of here, to the warehouse before Jack and the hostage team got there. She worked her hand around and reached under his inert body, unsnapped the holster and grabbed his automatic. It was standard issue, a Glock, like Jack's. She'd seen him pull out a clip and push it back in a dozen times or more, checking to make sure a bullet was in the chamber. She did it now. It was loaded.

Without a backwards glance, she grabbed her purse, stuffed the gun into it and was out the door. As it closed behind her, she stifled a sob.

~ * ~

At one time, the warehouse district was the heart of Detroit's industry, the dropping off point for river goods. Empty factories lay along the river, the Vernor's Ginger Ale plant, Apollo Belts, Diamond Salt—all gone. The warehouse lay off East Jefferson, once belonging to the old Parke-Davis drug company. It backed up on the river, silent and dark, abandoned, like most of the city, for the safety of the suburbs.

Sofie drew her car as far off the street as possible, into the alley. She looked back briefly to see if she was followed—no lights and no sounds. It was Friday night, people out having fun, but no one was around her. Friday the thirteenth, she thought bitterly. She stepped out of the car, and her coat whipped around her, too thin for the wind blowing off the river.

She stumbled down the alley and stepped on a bottle lying beside the curb. The glass hit concrete and echoed around her. She paused, listened, heard nothing, and went on. Her body shook but her terror was overridden by her need to get to Katya. Nothing else mattered but to save her.

She stumbled on, heading for the back of the building and the river. The ice fragments, shifting and moving with the currents, stood out in the dark; the only sounds were waves slapping against the pilings. It grew louder as she came up to it, masking every other noise.

A metal door on the corner of the warehouse stood ajar, and a small light over the door shone down, shielded by the green metal shade over it. She pulled the door towards her, slowly, inching it open, trying to keep the cries of terror in her head from escaping through her lips. She could make out wooden steps, worn down in the center, as though a thousand feet had passed over them for many years.

She had brought no light and was forced to feel her way to the stairs, squeezing her purse under her arm, searching for the first step. She smelled feces and urine, mixed with the musky smell of abandoned building. She held her breath and began climbing. Time stopped, all sound muted now as she climbed.

He said the second floor. As she reached the top step, she saw the faint light, a crack, as though coming from under a door. Her jeans clung to her, wet with sweat, even in the freezing air. She crept to the middle of the room, only yards from the thin pencil of light, stopped and stood, waiting for some signal.

She didn't hear it coming, didn't feel the blow that caught her from behind. It sent her reeling to the rough wooden floor.

Blackness engulfed her, nothing but blackness for a long time. Then, gradually, consciousness began to return. The room spun and she lay panting, swallowing down bile.

Long minutes passed as Sofie struggled to sit up and felt a sharp pain in her side. She felt the familiar wetness soaking through her t-shirt, but the pain from the reopened wound took away her nausea and focused her.

Someone had flung the door open, and light shone out, illuminating air thick with dust. She looked up and saw huge beams that crisscrossed the room. The place was empty but for boxes and crates scattered carelessly, left there decades ago and forgotten.

Katya! Where was she? Sofie eased down onto her hands and knees and began to crawl instinctively towards the dimly lit doorway ahead of her. The floor under her was covered with sawdust and her fingers left claw marks in the white shavings as she moved.

She pulled herself along, inch by inch, towards the door. Within a foot of it, a dark figure appeared, a man, holding something, Katya, under his arm. Sofie sank back on her haunches, limp, fighting the urge to scream out in rage. Then she saw the gun pointed at her.

"Please! Let her go. You can have me. She's only a little girl. Take me!"

He just stood there, not speaking. Then she heard the low moan. "Katya!" Sofie cried out her name.

"Shut up!" The man moved towards her, Katya hanging limp under one arm, his gun pointed directly at Sofie. "Where's Jack, Sofie?" The words seemed to bubble from him, a high-pitched sound, almost as though he were laughing. "Where's Jack? He's going to be so happy when he sees both of you." He laughed again and this time, she knew the voice. "I'm going to make sure he sees that, Sofie. This time he'll know he's to blame. He's going to suffer like me. He's going to watch you die. Then he's going to know I've got Katya. I'm going to take her far away from here. He'll never get her back. I'm going to let him live so he can suffer, like I did, and worry about his little girl, wonder what's happening to her. But he'll never find her!" He stopped and shifted Katya under his arm. "Where is Jack? Why isn't he here yet?"

He moved closer and Sofie squinted up at him. It was Steven Szcepaniak. She saw him every week. He came into the store and talked to her, talked to Katya. She had served him tea, suggested books to him. He'd shared parts of his life with her. He'd been away, working in Indiana. He'd quit his job there and come back to Detroit. He'd said he was unemployed and lonely and she'd felt sorry for him.

Her mind raced over his words now, looking for some way into his mind, some way to make him listen, to make him feel something for them. Her head throbbed now, in time to the throbbing of her side. She edged herself up to a sitting position, gasping for air, searching for words. "Steven! Please! Jack's on his way, but you don't want to hurt me. You know me! You've been to my bookstore lots of times. We always treat you well. Katya likes you, she trusts you!"

He laughed and she knew he was beyond reason. "I know Katya. She's like Dinah. Only Dinah's gone. Jack tried to take her away from me, but now I've got her. He wants to keep her from me, still. I'm going to keep her this time. After Jack gets here, after I kill you. Then I'm going to leave and Jack will never find us!"

Sofie struggled to her feet, slipping on the blood dripping from her shirt. Her purse still hung from her shoulder and she felt the weight of the gun inside. "Please, hand her to me, Steven!" He pulled back the gun and hit her on the shoulder. She cried out and fell back.

She lay prone, holding her shoulder, hiding the purse under her. He stood still now, only a few feet away, Katya under his arm, waiting. Waiting for Jack.

Then she heard the sound. It was more a vibration than a noise, and she looked up at Steven, searching for some sign he'd heard it, as well. But his face was blank, waiting. She moved a hand under her, fingers searching for anything. She found something, a small piece of wood, a broken slat, no more than three inches long. Holding tightly to her purse with one hand, she grabbed hold of the wood, raised up and threw it in one motion towards the steps.

Steven turned quickly, still holding Katya and cried out. Sofie stumbled upright, flung open her purse and reached for the automatic. Without a pause, she flung herself at him, yanking Katya from him as she went down, cushioning her body as she frantically grabbed for the gun.

Steven went down onto his knees, cursing loudly, his feet making contact with Sofie's head, leaving her momentarily stunned. But she had Katya! She pushed her body in front of Katya's as a shield, as Steven reached out, grabbed hold of Sofie's hair and began pulling her up.

"Drop her!" Jack's voice rang out, echoing against the walls and endless ceiling.

Steven yanked back on her hair, forcing her head back, the barrel of his gun aimed between her eyes.

"I said drop it or I shoot!" Jack's words rang out louder.

Steven moved the gun to rest on her forehead and Sofie heard the smile in his voice. "I've been waiting for you, Jack. You're just in time to be part of my little play." He laughed now, and she held her breath. "I'm going to show you how it feels to lose someone you love—I'm going to shoot your Sofie here, Jack. What do you think about that? Then I'm going to take your sweet little daughter and run away. You're never going to find us. We're going away, and this time you won't get her!" Sofie shrank back, trying to put space between the muzzle and her forehead, conscious of Katya, restless now, stirring under her.

A shot rang out and Sofie fell to the ground, stunned. At first she wondered if he'd shot at her and missed. She felt blood splatter on her, smelled it, as he came down hard on top of her, his hand still tangled in her hair. Her upper body caught most of his weight, knocking the breath out of her lungs, before her head hit the floor and darkness closed in.

## *Twenty-three*

Sofie awoke to the bright lights of the emergency room. Again. She moaned once and a warm hand closed over hers. Without opening her eyes, she whispered, "Katya?"

"She's fine, Sofie. She's out in the waiting area with my parents." Jack's voice flowed over her like warm water. "She's okay. She's just a little woozy. The bastard drugged her."

She felt the light touch of his hand brushing hair back from her forehead and struggled to open her eyes. "Lie still, sweetheart. You have a concussion and you tore your stitches. They're going to stitch you up. You're going to be spending the night here while they watch you."

"Steven? Is he dead?"

"Yes." The word was final. He offered her nothing more.

She forced one eye open and worked to focus on him. "Jack, I want to see Katya."

He stood up. "Okay. For a few minutes, only. She's handling things fine. She's more worried about you than what happened to her." He hesitated, deciding how much she could take right now. "She doesn't remember much, except that a man took her in his car and put something over her face." He worked hard to keep his face impassive as he spoke. "We told her you were fine—just getting bandaged up. I'll bring her in for a few minutes, if you promise to not get all worked up."

Sofie squirmed. "I won't. It would only upset Katya." Her head began to throb and she closed her eyes.

He bent down to brush his lips over hers and went to get Katya.

At the sound of Katya's voice, Sofie forced eyes open. The overhead light was blinding and she squinted up her daughter, dangling above her from Jack's arms. Katya reached down to touch Sofie's face.

"Just touch her lightly, sweetheart. Your mommy hurt her head and she has a headache. Bend down and give her a kiss on the cheek, okay?" Jack voice was calm, reassuring to Sofie.

"Mommy! Are you okay?" Sofie reached and caught one small hand and held on.

"I'm just resting, honey. You know how when you hurt your head, you have to close your eyes and rest. I'm fine. I'm going to be okay. They need to fix my side again. Mommy was stupid and hurt it again, but it's going to be better this time. While they fix me up, I have to stay here overnight. Then I'll come home and be with you. You go home with your daddy and Grandma Rosey tonight, okay?" She couldn't stop tears that ran down her cheeks.

"Okay, Mommy. But don't cry. I'll go home with Daddy. Just get better soon, okay?"

Sofie smiled and shut her eyes, grateful when Jack took Katya back to the waiting room. She turned her head away and let the tears fall freely, without making a sound.

She felt Jack beside her again. He reached over and turned her head slowly toward him with two fingers. "I'm staying here with you right now." She stopped and opened her eyes to look at him. She saw the change immediately. Something had loosened in him, freeing up the hard core in the center of him.

His face was softer, more open. "Go ahead and cry. I'm going to, as soon as I get some time alone."

~ * ~

While they worked on Sofie's stitch-up, Jack paced the small cubicle, until she could take it no longer and ordered him to sit down. He spoke intermittent into his cell phone, speaking low, and she only caught a few words, her own name, Katya's, nothing else.

"Jack, if you need to go back to the warehouse, go. I'm okay now."

"Things are getting handled there. I have some time now. Listen, Mama wants to come and see you before she and Katya go home. Can I send her in?"

"Of course, Jack."

He brought Maria back in with him and Sofie opened her eyes again. Maria stood silent, looking down intently at her, Jack standing behind. Two Rosellis in one small cubicle was almost too much.

"Sofie." Maria patted Sofie's hand, straightened the sheet pulled over her, but seemed unable to speak.

"Maria. I'm okay. You should go home. Take Katya with you, please?"

Maria swallowed, answering carefully. "We'll take good care of Katya. We won't let her out of our sight. She's going to sleep with me tonight." Maria patted her hand again. "Just rest and come home." *Home*, Sofie thought. *Home*.

Jack stayed until Sofie was settled into a room for the night. She feigned sleep and sighed with relief when she was alone. Her head throbbed, but the pain meds were beginning to take effect and she fought back her growing lethargy. She needed to think.

She was alive. They were all alive. She felt as though someone had thrown cold water on the war in her mind. Suddenly, all the concerns and the arguments in her head about her future seemed insignificant, almost an indulgence. She'd done what she had to do, she'd gone alone to save Katya, without Jack. If he hadn't come, she probably would have died and Katya would be lost.

She smiled at the folly of thinking there was some place she needed to get to by herself, where she'd learn how to deal with life. Then she'd feel secure and safe. It was all ridiculous. No one was safe and secure, life happened to people, sometimes good then sometimes bad. She'd gone after Katya. That was good. And then she'd needed someone else, Jack, and he'd been there. There was nothing to prove. It had all been a story she'd wanted to believe. She could be strong and she could want Jack. And he hadn't failed them. She closed her eyes and slept.

~ * ~

Monica showed up early the next day, Chrissie in tow, toting newspaper stories about the dramatic rescue and Jack, the hero. "So, sweetie, now what?"

Sofie smiled and eased her head up slightly. "Now Katya and I move in with Jack, like we planned. I guess last night turned out to be my epiphany. Suddenly all the worrying about what I'm doing just disappeared. I'm letting things come as they will. How's that for a transformation via concussion?"

"Good." She stopped and looked over at Chrissie, caught up in a book. "You know, I'm starting to think all that gossip about Jack was a crock. He's outside, waiting for you. He's pacing around out there, like a lovesick teenager."

Sofie's face grew hot. "We'll see."

"No, not we'll see." She narrowed her eyes at Sofie. "That's it, isn't it? All along I thought it was just sex—sex and a father for Katya. But it's way more." Monica threw back her head and laughed, causing Chrissie to look up momentarily. "Ohhh boy, this is going to get interesting, watching you and Jack pretend nothing's happening. You look as lovesick as he does. I can't wait." Monica stood up and grabbed her coat. "Chrissie, honey let's get out of here before Sofie throws something at me."

The hospital released her at one o'clock. Jack rolled in a wheelchair, plopped her in it and wheeled her carefully down and out to his Jeep. "Remind me to buy some stock in Detroit Receiving Hospital." He said, as he pulled her seatbelt around her injured side.

He pulled away from the curb and glanced over at her. "So what have you got to say for yourself? Assaulting an officer of the law? I should get Mark to press charges. This is the third time I've had to use my charm to keep you from getting locked up."

He spoke lightly, without accusation and she blinked at him. This was definitely a new Jack. "I barely hit him, just a tap. And I tried hard to catch him as he went down. But he was too heavy. Is he okay?"

He nodded. "Just a big goose egg. What'd you hit him with?"

"A frying pan—probably one your mother gave you."

"She'll be glad to hear one of her domestic gifts to me was put to good use."

Sofie smiled and didn't answer. Talking made her head throb still.

"How's your head?" Was he reading her mind now?

"Fine—better. Hurts some, but I can stand it. What I'm worried about is, I think I may be hallucinating. I keep thinking I hear you making jokes. Humor, you know?"

"Yeah, I know what humor is." His mouth twitched. "I've been saving it up for a few years, 'til I found someone who'd appreciate my particular style. I think I've found her."

"So, Jack. What is it really?"

He frowned. "What is what, really?"

"You. You're different. What is it?"

He kept his eyes on the road as he maneuvered out into Saturday traffic heading for the mall. "I'm almost afraid to say what it is, afraid it'll leave me." He made a turn onto the freeway. "When I saw Katya lying there, saw that monster grab you by the hair, something snapped, something inside of me." He glanced at her nervously. "I can't explain it, but it felt like a fog lifting. Or darkness, maybe. It was almost like Dinah was standing there with me, watching, telling me it was going to be okay. When I saw him with the gun pointed at you, I knew he wasn't going to win. This time, things would be different."

"Jack, did Steven kill your sister?"

Jack slowed down. He wanted to have this conversation before he got to his parents. "I don't think so. I think her death was what it seemed, an unsolved bombing, either a single bomber or part of a terrorist group. I think Steven knew Dinah, maybe not directly, but I think he may have been obsessed with her.

We've searched his place, found some letters, some pictures and things. Of all three of you, you, Katya, and Dinah. We think he was involved in blowing up your place. We found boxes of C4 in his room. We haven't made the connection yet with the ecoterrorist group. What we think is that he blamed me for Dinah's death and decided he had to get even for that. It became an obsession with him, lasting all these years."

Sofie gazed out the window, trying to grasp how he could be so determined to make Jack suffer, how he managed to weave her into his plans and use Katya for revenge. "So was Steven the person who was stalking Katya all along?"

"I think he was."

"But how did he know about her? That she was your daughter?"

"I can't tell you, Sofie. As we go through his things, I hope we'll get some answers. So far, what we know is he was living in Indiana for the past three years. Then, four months ago, he quit his job down there and moved back to Detroit. He was working for Crane, the Naval munitions facility, as a computer programmer. The plastic explosives we found in his room were from the base. He was tied to the terrorist group in some way, because the stuff we found in his room was out of the same lot, the same box even, as the explosives we pulled in last month on the river. What we don't know right now is how he fit in with that group. We haven't found any affiliations in his past to any terrorist group."

He had pulled up in front of his parent's house and shut off the engine. "Let's leave it for now, okay? I'll need you to come down—Hell! This is the fourth time, or is it the four hundredth time?—to give your statement. Tomorrow will work. Today, you rest."

He came around and opened her door, reached down and swept her up into his arms.

"Hey, buster! What do you think you're doing? Just because you're the big hero right now doesn't mean you can push me around any time you want!"

But she didn't fight it when he kept going, up the steps and into the house with her. Katya met them at the door, jumping up and down. She ran beside him as he headed down the hall to the back bedroom and plopped her down without ceremony.

Rosellis swarmed everywhere, showering her with hugs and food. Maria frowned at the newspaper she held, tisking at the notion of the neighbors finding out about her granddaughter in the papers. She was already planning a party to introduce Katya to the neighbors.

She cringed at a vision of Roselli family and friends everywhere. *I suppose I'll eventually get used to all the noise and commotion.*

~ * ~

It was late afternoon when Jack tucked Katya into his parents bed for her nap. He ushered Sofie to the back bedroom, demanding she sleep as well. When she refused, he began shedding his clothes, threatening to stay in bed with her until she slept.

"That's not going to work!" she shrieked, laughing. "If you get under these covers with nothing on, there's no way I'm going to sleep."

"Is that a warning or an invitation?"

"Jack! Your parents are sitting out in the front room with all the neighbors! Put your clothes back on." He pulled his zipper up and sat down on the edge of her bed, his t-shirt in hand. He reached out, caught her hand and pressed it against his broad chest.

Sofie pulled her hand back as though she'd touched a hot stove. "Now you've done it. My heart's pounding a mile a minute and my head is keeping time. Besides, your mother isn't going to bend her rules again for you. You're either going to have to go home to your own bed tonight or sleep on the rollaway in Vincent and Beth's nursery." He pulled on his t-shirt, bent down to kiss her head gently and left.

~ * ~

Jack sat staring at his computer. It was after midnight and he was back at the Brush Street office, scanning the files he'd had downloaded from Steven Szcepaniak's computer. Steven had kept minute-by-minute, obsessive records of everything. It would take weeks to sift through the shitload of files and emails the guy had saved. Tonight, he waded through anything dating back four years, within a month either side of when Dinah died.

The notes Steven kept were almost stream of consciousness, with lapses into strange speculations on all sorts of events and activities. What caught Jack's eye first was the number of elaborate notes about himself. The jerk had kept references to files and downloads of every piece of digital data he could find on Jack Roselli. Since the guy was some sort of computer geek and a hacker, he had a lot of stuff.

Jack shuddered at the ease with which someone could insert himself into another person's life: insurance papers, deeds, registrations, voting records, hospital and medical bills, phone records, all his employment history since 1996, everything a stalker would need. Jack spotted a reference to Kim Barber and a note beside her name that she was with Vice and too dangerous to use. There was still no clue as to how he'd found Katya.

Jack turned back to a Word file and continued scanning it. It was like a damned diary of every move Jack had made, starting the day after Dinah died. The bastard had even kept tabs on him electronically during the four years the guy lived in Indiana. He scanned down the detailed notes, full of vague references, much of it incomprehensible.

He almost missed it—a note from October tenth. He'd followed Jack to a bar, the Mariner, sat outside bored, fantasizing about revenge. He noted the time when Jack left the bar, and with whom—a woman—Sofie.

Jack scrolled back and read the single-spaced document more slowly. He'd followed them to Jack's place, waited outside for hours, until Sofie had come out again, had decided to follow the woman. He recorded her taxi trip back to her place, recording his patient watch as she unlocked and gone inside her house. His notes continued a detailed tracking of her, waiting for some further sign of Jack showing up in her life. After six weeks and no Jack, at that point apparently frustrated, he'd given up on Sofie.

The next pages—over a hundred of them, were from Indiana, documenting the four years spent at Crane. Jack scanned through the pages, jotting down file names and numbers for later reference. He moved forward, looking for anything dated between September and December of this year. There it was! He'd come back to Detroit in July, hung around Jack again, following him, looking for anything useful.

The first mention of Sofie was from in September. He'd traced her to the bookstore, interested in Sofie again, especially after he wrote, "she's got a kid!"

From that point on, he documented everything relating to Sofie. He'd systematically searched for anything and everything related to her and her bookstore. Jack pulled up referenced files that included hospital records of Katya's birth, insurance papers, immunization records, Katya's daycare application form—including the name "Jack Roselli" listed as emergency contact.

Jack sat back and stared at the screen, stunned at the amount of time this guy had put into his pursuit, It was a four-year odyssey to get even, spawned by hatred and insanity. He apparently came back to Detroit and carefully began again, tracking down Sofie almost as an afterthought. He'd dropped into the bookstore periodically throughout August, watched her movements and spotted Katya.

It was at this point the notes took on an urgency. He'd gone after Sofie, worked carefully, increasing the pressure on her and adding threats until she turned to Jack. If she hadn't turned to him, Jack had no doubt, the bastard would have found another way to bring Katya into Jack's life.

He read over the September files—references to phone calls made to Sofie, detailed descriptions of her bookstore, the daycare center, even the inside of her apartment.

*Goddammit!* Jack rubbed his eyes and expelled his breath; the persistence, the cleverness of the guy, compounded by his insanity, was beyond comprehension. Jack sat for a long time, finally shut down the computer for the night and went home to his empty apartment.

## *Epilogue*

It took three weeks to get the full picture of Steven Szcepaniak's involvement in Jack's life. A loner, both parents unknown, he'd wandered around Detroit, sometimes attending classes at Lawrence Tech in computer science, staying out of trouble, but always marginal in behavior. And brilliant. He'd gotten odd jobs in the late '90s doing computer security with Internet businesses around Detroit.

The collapse of the dot.com world coincided with Szepaniak's exodus to Indiana. It was six months after Dinah's death, and without work, he was forced to take a job at the Naval facility. During his time in Indiana, he'd lived quietly, in the tiny town of Loogootee. He went to work every day, did his job well, all the while amassing enough cash to come back to Detroit and continue his plan for Jack Roselli. While at Crane, he'd systematically amassed a large supply of C4 explosives, det cord, and blasting caps—everything he would need to get Jack's attention. The motive was and always had been Dinah. He'd apparently become obsessed with her sometime in the year before she died, probably at Lawrence Tech, where they'd both taken classes. When Dinah died, he blamed Jack.

The link between the ecoterrorist group and Steven Szepaniak was harder to find. None of the suspects in custody knew the man directly, although they admitted someone had been providing them with explosives and information on bomb manufacturing. From the notes on Steven's computer, it looked as though he hooked up with the group recently, within the past year. The group filled a need, a way for Steven to get to Jack through his work, a diversion away from himself. There was no evidence in his notes that he thought this group had been responsible for Dinah's death.

He'd been looking for a way to get Jack for years. The moment he saw Katya, he realized the opportunity. She was Jack's "blind spot," a child he didn't know existed. He decided to push her into Jack's life, then torment and twist Jack with the threat to her. It was a well-orchestrated dance with Jack Roselli and his life.

~ * ~

Sofie sat at the Rosellis' kitchen table, waiting for Jack to pick her up. He'd gone Christmas shopping with Katya, their heads together all through breakfast, laughing over their plans.

Jack's apartment was too small for the three of them and they were looking for another place. They were even discussing wedding plans, whenever Maria pushed it, willing to look at houses her friends were selling. They were moving slowly, but they were moving—towards being a family. The bookstore would reopen some time in March and wherever they got a house, it had to be close to downtown for Jack but within an easy drive to the bookstore and Katya's daycare.

Jack talked about Dinah a lot these days, all the Rosellis did. They pulled out pictures of her and showed them around. They laughed about stunts she'd pulled, told funny stories about her, shared her with Sofie and Katya. And Katya had drawn a picture of Dinah from a photo. She'd given it to her grandmother proudly and Maria had hugged her and cried a little.

Sofie looked up at the sound of laughter from the hallway. Jack stumbled in with Katya on his shoulders, her small hands covering his eyes.

"Look, Mommy! Daddy knows everything! He doesn't even need his eyes!"

"I know. Daddy's a big know-it-all." She looked up at Jack.

He grabbed hold of Katya and deposited her on the floor. "You're right." He reached out and grabbed Sofie by the shoulders. "And you'd better listen to me, woman! I see all, hear all!"

"Exactly what do you see and hear?" She challenged.

"That you and this little girl here are in my power! That you will belong to me! To my family! I declare there will be a wedding, a huge celebration! And I decree there will be boys— many boys! Brothers for this little girl here! To run after her and torment her for the rest of her days!"

Katya screamed and ran to hide behind a sofa, covering her ears. "No! No! Not boys!"

Sofie leaned back against Jack, laughing. "Katya, right now it sounds awful, but you wait. One of these days, you're gonna want boys around. And what if those little brothers were like your daddy? Would that be so bad?"

Katya pulled herself out and came over to stare up at Jack. "That would be okay, I guess. But only if they're like Daddy." She made a face. "But I like girls!"

Sofie grinned at Jack. "I told you so. It's in our genes. I'm afraid the future you're planning may be around a family of females. I doubt if I could even produce a male!"

He wagged his eyebrows at her. "We'll see about that. You don't know the strength of us Roselli men. It's in our genes to produce lots of strapping Italian boys. My mother survived it pretty well. If you have your heart set on a matriarchy, take your cue from her and you'll do fine."

### Meet Lynn Romaine

Living in Bloomington, Indiana amidst friends and family, and three cats, Lynn has a Master's of Information Science Degree from Indiana University. She is committed to issues
of peace, justice and dialogue that create bridges between people.

***VISIT OUR WEBSITE
FOR THE FULL INVENTORY
OF QUALITY BOOKS***:

*http://www.wings-press.com*

*Quality trade paperbacks and downloads
in multiple formats,
in genres ranging from light romantic
comedy to general fiction and horror.
Wings has something
for every reader's taste.
Visit the website, then bookmark it.
We add new titles each month!*